DELVE INTO THE REALM OF TWILIGHT

ILLUSTRATED BY S&S ANTONSON

ISBN: 978-1-5539-5170-4 (sc)
ISBN: 978-1-4269-8166-1 (e)

Trafford rev. 12/14/2011

 www.trafford.com

North America & International
toll-free: 1 888 232 4444 (USA & Canada)
phone: 250 383 6864 ♦ fax: 812 355 4082

CONTENTS

CONTENTS

CHAPTER 1

THE BECKONING

Encroached upon thickets of wooded trees, where sunlight's rays hardly penetrate, shadows of clouded moisture mist the leaves. A gentle breeze disperses the minuscule drops of dew until, devoid of energy, they settle upon any resting-place. The moisture culminated upon a half buried wooden filigree box partly disintegrated by mold disclosing a delicate emerald gold ring lost through the ages of time. Inscribted on the inner surface, worn so that one could barely read, states:

"Whoever findeth me, will see…(illegible) from where I dwell…will release my soul."

A silver jaguar sped along the winding country road quite carefully, when all of a sudden, a rupture sound of a tire and the tearing of rubber, made the car stop. A tall man emerged to access the damage.

His son, Lucien, woke up from the back seat, asking, "What happened?"

Sebastian, Lucien's father, sighed. "We have a flat. I must have run over something on the road. I will see if I can change it. Everything will be all right. Try not disturbing your sister, Lucien and please see if there is a flashlight in the glove compartment."

Lucien got out of the back seat into the front to find a flashlight.

His sister, Selena, asked. "Why have we stopped?"

"We have a flat and Daddy is trying to fix it." Lucien replied.

"But," Selena put in; "Won't we be late to Uncle Horatio's! "

"There is nothing else we can do." Lucien stated as he searched for a flashlight in the rented car. Lucien looked triumphant. "Father, Father, I found it."

1

"Good," Sebastian replied. "I really need it."

Lucien handed it to his father, while Selena got out of the car to be with them. Sebastian hugged his daughter.

"Can you fix it?" Selena seemed desperate.

"Yes, I have all the equipment. Don't go too far from the car, and don't go into the street. Really, you should stay in the car. Go on."

The area was so beautiful and bewitching as the fog engulfed them that the children were enthralled and remained outside. In the twilight, the intermittent dimension between the day's recession and the night's augmenting influence mingled a duet until the night overwhelmed in strength, dominated. The fog lifted a little from the roadway accenting a fern green pathway adjacent through the trees. A shrill chirp echoed from the tall oak. The blue bird (Tit or Parus caeruleus) sang again, catching the attention of Lucien and Selena. It carried a small acorn in its beak, which it promptly dropped on Lucien's head.

Lucien immediately jerked his head upward in amazement when the bird flew past him, perching itself further in the wood, but on a low enough branch as to dare them to follow.

"Are you all right?" Selena queried.

"I am fine, but why did that bird deliberately drop the acorn on my head? Did you see where the bird flew?"

"Yes, over there, mocking us." Selena pointed.

Lucien followed the bird's direction in an instant the bird altered its course and flew straight for them. Both of them ducked but Lucien's face was caressed ever so carefully by the bird's wing as it tickled his ear upon passing.

"Did you see what that bird did to me!" Lucien became agitated.

"Yes," cried Selena. "She or he seems to like you."

"Oh, that is ridiculous." Lucien retorted.

"If that is so, why is the bird right over your head?"

Lucien eyed above him while the bird stared back in defiance again chirping. Did it wink? Lucien was not sure.

"Very well, you have our attention. What do you have in mind?" Lucien clarified.

The bird nodded its head in acquisition and moved her wings as if to beckon them further into the fog-laden forest. They followed as she soared away.

"Lucien," cried Selena." We have run so far that I am dizzy, please wait for me."

But, Lucien, determined to pursue the bird, echoed back. "Keep up, I barely see the bird if I slow down. Follow my voice."

The bird rested at the foot of a tree. The size alone dwarfed its followers as the bird pointed to the tiny sparkle given off from the imbedded emerald ring. The bird warbled a song not stopping.

Selena puffed, gasping. "What is she trying to tell us?" Selena gazed upon the huge oak tree not believing its enormity.

Lucien scrutinized downward at the bird as she finally stopped singing. Lucien observed the sparkle of the ring as he picked it up also seeing a moldy filigree box.

"What is it?" Selena, being shocked, mesmerized that there was something at the foot of the tree. "Is it buried treasure? Could pirates have been here? What did you find?"

"It is a ring and there is something inscribed inside."

At that very moment, Sebastian had a feeling of doom as he finished tightening the bolts on the tire and removed the jack. Musical tones like the sound of a maiden's voice echoed throughout the sky. A stark coldness filled his heart. Rising suddenly, Sebastian called to his children. "Lucien, Selena, where are you?" But no reply came. Sebastian became more desperate. Still being twilight, he ran into the direction of the maiden's voice as she sang melancholically. The words were sung in French, like prayers, but Sebastian felt he had heard it before, but when? His feet ran faster and faster following the voice as if it were a beacon. He could hear his children's voices. "Lucien! Selena!" Sebastian called again. "Where are you?"

Selena responded. "Daddy, we are here by the oak tree and Lucien with the help of the bird has found a treasure, a ring, see."

Sebastian hugged his daughter and grabbed his son. "I told you not to venture so far out. You don't know the countryside and if anything happens to you, how could I find you. I am very angry with you both. Especially you, Lucien, being older, you should know better."

"But," Lucien stated. "I wouldn't have gone so far if that bird had not dropped an acorn on my head."

"I don't see any bird. I only see you at the foot of this tree." Sebastian interrupted.

"You must have scared her when you rushed here." Selena scanned frantically for the bird but she was unable to located her.

Lucien searched for the bird as well, while the wind rustled the leaves of the trees causing a vortex around them.

"We had better leave. Your Uncle Horatio will be worried. We did promise him that we would help him settle into his new house." Sebastian concluded. "That is odd, I don't hear the singing that brought me here to you. Did you hear anything?"

"Singing, Father, from a bird?" Selena responded.

"No, from a woman's voice."

"We did not hear anything, Father." Lucien replied, still trying but unable to remove the ring from his finger, as if it had shrunk to fit his ring size exactly. It glowed from within ceasing as the twilight ended and the night reigned. "The ring was bigger, but" Lucien's voice trailed off.

Sebastian prodded Lucien and Selena towards the car when he felt deep regret in leaving and heard the sounds of weeping. He glanced hastily all around but nothing but the forest surrounded him. A soft rain enveloped them, which camouflaged the sound.

Both Lucien and Selena entered the car when Selena burst out. "You forgot the box which held the ring. Why did you forget it? It must be a clue to the owner."

Lucien was about to jump out of the car when a hand held him fast. "Put on your seatbelts. We are not going to retrieve it. We are going to your Uncle's."

"But," protested Lucien. "I did not mean to forget it, but when I put the ring on my finger, I couldn't get it off!"

Sebastian, looked at his son's hand stating, "Didn't you say that the ring was bigger than your finger? Well, we will get it off at your Uncle's. Let's go."

Lucien and Selena put on their seatbelts as Sebastian ignited the ignition and drove on. The rain pelted the street harder as Sebastian finally recognized his Uncle's house from the latest E-mail he had received from him a week ago.

Uncle Horatio Simons waited at the door with a huge umbrella and ran out to greet them as they drove into the drive.

CHAPTER 2

THE HAUNTING

Uncle Horatio's house towered to its full three stories. From what Lucien had remembered his father saying, it had been built over a previous foundation. A fire had consumed the original house approximately one hundred years ago. The garage bulged over with boxes that the movers had left covered by a tarp, being too late in its arrival to transport it to the various rooms.

Before they entered the house, Uncle Horatio hovered over the children with an enormous umbrella keeping them dry. The empty rooms echoed as the door shut.

Sebastian warmly greeted his Uncle who abated him about how late it was, as all of them hastened towards the fireplace to instill some warmth.

"The reason why we are late is because we had a flat tire." Sebastian resumed.

"How dreadful. Where were you?" Uncle Horatio directed the children to sit on the blankets he provided them with.

"About a half a mile from here." Sebastian answered.

"Oh, the abandoned grave site!"

"Really, do you think the ring came from a deceased woman who cries at twilight?" Lucien spouted out.

Uncle Horatio, shocked, blurted out. "What did you say?"

Lucien related the story of the discovery of the ring, however, as Lucien completed his narrative. He made several attempts to remove the ring. "I can't get it off my finger!"

Sebastian finally got a good look at it. The ring was eighteen carat gold, yet, a delicate lady's ring. A huge emerald surrounded by diamonds accented the hue of the stone. It was

5

of excellent quality. "The ring has an antique setting. I would have to get it appraised for its age."

Lucien tried to pry it off, alas, to no avail. Uncle Horatio went to get the olive oil to loosen it as Sebastian and Selena stared at it. Sebastian touched the ring and at that instant the ring slipped off Lucien's finger. Sebastian picked it up, awed.

"How did you do that?" Uncle Horatio returned with the oil.

Selena asked, "Can it discern whose finger it is on?"

Sebastian examined it, reading the inscription aloud. "Whoever findeth me, will see, from where I dwell, will release my soul."

A feeling of foreboding encompassed the room.

"What ever does it mean? Can a ring release a soul?" Selena interrupted.

Uncle Horatio gasped. "That is quite prophetic and you found it at the abandoned grave site?"

"Yes, but it is a known fact that grave sites, with a fresh corpse buried in soggy ground can give off methane and diphosphate which when combined, releases itself from the grave site as a fluorescent spark or mist giving the belief of ghosts." Sebastian interjected trying to calm the children.

"Really! I didn't know that, Sebastian!" Uncle Horatio conceded.

Selena inquired, "The abandoned grave site, Why is it called that?"

Uncle Horatio responded. "They call it abandoned, however, that is all I know on the topic. It was mentioned to me by the Realtor."

Selena took the ring from her father's hand and placed it on her finger. "It is very beautiful. I feel like a fair damsel in distress."

Lucien added. "I am hungry."

Uncle Horatio got the hint. "Dinner is waiting. I made hearty chicken soup and sandwiches. It is on the stove, follow me." A hungry band followed him into the kitchen.

Sebastian gathered the plates as Uncle Horatio ladled out the soup.

"Where is the dining room? " Selena wondered. "This house is big just like ours at home and we need more furniture too."

Sebastian added. "How much did you pay for it?"

"I got it for a steal. It seems that the previous owner wanted out very quickly." Uncle Horatio mentioned. "At least the dining room has some furniture, so we don't have to sit on the floor."

Everyone smiled as they seated themselves.

"Sebastian, how is your sister Cassandra?" Uncle Horatio continued.

"Cassandra is doing well, however, I will soon be in some straights, being that she has found the man of her dreams and is soon to be married."

"That will be really a hardship for you, Sebastian." Uncle Horatio spoke rather concerned.

"I know, ever since that dreadful day, when Marisa died in that car accident five years ago, Cassandra has been living with us. She has been taking care of the children as if she was their own mother. Taking them to school, cooking, cleaning, and being there practically every minute. I still don't know how she made the time."

"Now Sebastian, you helped your sister too, making her only work part time so that she could be with the children. You are paying her very well. When did she meet Paul?"

"Two months ago I sensed that they would get married. She will marry him in the fall due to Paul's work as an engineer. But, as I am an architect, my business trips take me here and there. Cassandra is irreplaceable. What baby-sitter could handle my weekend trips?"

"I hate to bring this suggestion to you, but it seems, "Uncle Horatio whispered," that you need a wife."

Sebastian's eyes flashed as he heard the words. Sebastian was a handsome man in his mid- thirties, with blue eyes, a tall slender figure, and sensitive hands.

"Don't look at me like that, you know I am right." Uncle Horatio commented. "I know what you are thinking. Why haven't I married again? One reason is that I don't have young children. My daughter, Ophelia, is married and has two children of her own. She will be visiting very soon from London with her husband. Another suggestion is that you could find a job here and you could live with me and I could take care of these precious children. It seems that your whole family dies of car accidents. My brother, your father, James and your mother, Audrey, died in a car accident by going to your wife's funeral."

Lucien heard a sound from the window. "What is making that tapping sound Uncle?"

Selena turned around and looked at the window. "There is that blue bird again. She is the one who is tapping. She must be magical."

Both Sebastian and Uncle Horatio turned quickly to look at the window.

"Oh her. This bird has been tapping at my window ever since I arrived here. I call her Giselle." Uncle Horatio went to the kitchen and returned quite promptly with some birdseed. "I will feed her at this window. I bought a bird feeder. It would seem that you know my family." Uncle Horatio spoke to the bird as a long lost friend. "This is Lucien, Selena, and my nephew, Sebastian."

Sebastian rose and went to the bird. "Lucien are you sure this is the same bird you saw at that huge oak tree?"

Lucien was absorbed in rubbing the bird's chest feathers. "Yes, Father, this is the one. You see, she has a speck on one of her toes."

"Of course," Sebastian abated. "What could I be thinking."

"Shall we go back to the drawing room?" Uncle Horatio suggested. "It is far warmer than in here. Lucien, persuade Giselle to jump on your finger. She usually keeps me company in the evening."

Sebastian stared at his Uncle amazed. "A wild bird stays with you as a companion? Did you train her? This is so absurd. I can not believe it!"

Selena now also petted the bird as Lucien took the bird to the drawing room.

They all sat near the fireplace. Selena then rose to sit closer to her father as Lucien placed the bird on the perch that Uncle Horatio must have bought for her.

Lucien queried. "Why do you call the bird Giselle?"

"I don't know why I chose that name. It seems that the bird suggested it. Well Selena, stand over there. I want to see how tall you have gotten. Sebastian, she looks so much like Marisa it is astonishing."

Selena sat down on the floor. Her hair was golden not like Sebastian's who had auburn brown hair and vibrant blue eyes. Lucien was the spitting image of his father, when he was younger. Lucien was seven years old. In contrast, Selena's eyes were brown, large with long lashes, which accented her pale smooth skin. Selena was five years old. She smiled at the admiration she was receiving. "Daddy, I am cold. I feel a chill."

Sebastian took off his jacket to cover his daughter with it when all of a sudden the ring made a musical sound or pitch, and from it a vapor emerged from the center of the ring. The vapor engulfed Selena augmenting to twice her size. A presence materialized into a form of a beautiful woman with dark hair that was drawn up in the back, cascading in thick brown black curls down her neck. She had a thick blue silk ribbon on the top of her head that also draped. She had alabaster skin and beautiful large blue eyes with long lashes. She had a very quiet face wearing a blue, satin gown frilled with lace on the bodice. The lace was also around the sleeves and even at the shoulders. The dress cinched at the waist where a velvet ribbon went around and also a velvet bow at the bust line. The skirt puffed out accenting the tiny waist. She was holding a letter in her hand frozen in time. When the apparition completely materialized, the lady seemed to have taken a breath as she gazed around the room until finally focusing on Sebastian. From a seated position like Selena, she stood up away from Selena pondering for a long moment. Her eyes were searching Sebastian's face, trying to read his soul. She spoke pitifully. "Please save me. Save me!" She echoed away and dissipated.

Shock and horror was the only feeling Sebastian had, as he wanted to protect his daughter. Lucien, Uncle Horatio, and Sebastian ran to Selena, as Selena fainted on the floor. Sebastian held Selena in his arms.

"Selena, Selena!" Sebastian called out. "Are you all right? How do you feel? I can't lose you, as well, I just can't!"

Selena responded to her father. "I am afraid, Daddy. Who was she?" She clutched to her father very tightly.

"Did she hurt you?" Lucien blurted out. "What did you feel?"

"I felt her presence, she is very sad, but I didn't feel that she would hurt me. She seems to want to be free. Is she the owner of the ring, Father? Is she the soul that you are suppose to save?"

Uncle Horatio stunned stated. "Well, I am dashed!"

Sebastian held Selena a little less tight. "I am bemused and shocked." Sebastian took his daughter with him and placed her on his lap. "It is all too haunting."

Lucien interrupted, "She seems to know you, Father, from somewhere before. She looks like she knows your soul. She is so beautiful, you must help her."

Uncle Horatio went to Selena patting her hand. "Are you sure you are all right child. You really gave me a scare. Take off that ring, it must be possessed!"

Selena took off the ring and gave it to her father. Sebastian stared at it still not believing what happened. "It 's time to go to bed. We are all tired."

"May I see the ring Father? I can't wait to write Peter about it at school." Lucien inquired.

Sebastian handed it to Lucien. "Only for a little while, I feel that it should be locked up!"

Sebastian put the children to bed. Lucien placed the ring on a tablet of paper, for he was going to write Peter the next morning. Yet, Sebastian became quite nervous about the ring in Lucien's room. So Sebastian decided to check on him. As he opened Lucien's room, a strange light arose from where the ring lay. Sebastian walked up to it quietly and slowly picked it up. As he did, he felt impressions on the page. Sebastian took the tablet and the ring to his own room.

The impressions felt like writing so he took a pencil and etched the graphite up and down to see if there was any lettering. The sonnet begins:

THE SILENT UNRAVELING
Spanning through time for me to behold
Sacrificed endeavors to trade thy soul
So one can live, and the other go, entombed alive forever.
From now to eternity, I vow, I see
A purgatory of mind, never to be free
Don't be fooled by what seems not
For if you do, illusions alter a lot
Discover the key to unlock the spell
For in the Realm of Twilight I must dwell
Shrouded for three hundred years and past
Until you came to me at last
With a whisper of hope, the ring prevails
As a liaison between the ion's trails
Where the witches curse will now be veiled
Find them in their gravely plot
Possess their book, for they are not
To release their spells you will need a key
Buried in a box of filigree.

At the end of the page, the watermarks of tears remained as Sebastian could feel the moisture. Pain and sorrow was the only feeling left. He knew in his heart that he had met her before. Her voice was the same as the one who sang that French song at the abandoned gravesite. It was she, who warned him of the children's plight. What is buried there? Sebastian held the ring, which was the only thing that gave him comfort.

The three witches

HEXE

HAGATHA   BRUJIA

STREGA

THE ROUSING SPELL

Roused from my sleep by a piercing cry
Languishing echoes by a watch-full eye
Stabbed by disbelief, yet, she dares to defy
Purloined ring will transpose through the sky
Mired in my moldy decay
Emerge to vengeance, needs no delay
Embodied with evil and pitted respite
Rising upwards and upwards and on through the night
To finally reach that box with a key
Displaced by that bird, how shall I barb thee?
Closer and closer until I feel a chill
Vortexed as the wind upon the hill
Then will I leave to change my fate?
I shall be waiting forever, don't be late.

CHAPTER 3

RESURECTION

A shrill voice vibrated saying:

THE ROUSING SPELL
Roused from my sleep by a piercing cry
Languishing echoes by a watch-full eye
Stabbed by disbelief, yet, she dares to defy
Purloined ring will transpose through the sky
Mired in my moldy decay
Emerge to vengeance, needs no delay
Embodied with evil and pitted respite
Rising upwards and upwards and on through the night
To finally reach that box with a key
Displaced by that bird, how shall I barb thee?
Closer and closer until I feel a chill
Vortexed as the wind upon the hill
Then will I leave to change my fate?
I shall be waiting forever, don't be late.

Torrents of water soaked the grounds where the filigree box lay. At first, the flow, which loosened it, consequently, cascading it from the oak tree's roots and transporting it down to a ravine had nudged it. Apparently, Giselle pecked at it fervently to aid its removal so when dislodged, it would be harder to locate.

The corresponding plot of earth adjacent to the tree sprang forth with a pair of thorned fingers encompassing sharp rasping movements blandishing an exodus of one of the three witches interred at that site. Shards of wood cracked and splintered by the force.

"Alive again! I told you, if that ring was removed, we would exhume and chastise the culprits. Don't dawdle, remove thyself or shall I seal you in?" Hexe reviled.

Another exited. "You haven't improved your temper much even with all that sleep."

"Well, we would not have ended here in this plight if you actually used the correct ingredients instead of the despoiled ones."

"I forgot they were three hundred years old. Anyone can make a mistake, with time." Brujia contested.

"Enough bickering." Hagatha scorned at both of them. "Help me up, I am too heavy with this wretched water being absorbed in my desiccated gown to flee from this, this, muck."

"You look bloated enough," Hexe added.

Brujia reprimanded. "Don't enrage her. She is bigger than the both of us, oops, sorry Hagatha."

"Cursed sisters, help me this instant." Hagatha remarked.

Brujia yanked at Hagatha's arms while Hexe attempted to push at the rear. Brujia slipped causing all of them to fall back into their former slimy crypt.

"Why, why, why am I stuck with these imbeciles." Hagatha wailed! She scooped up some mud and flung it at her sisters.

"Stop this immediately. I will not endure this for a second longer. We are witches!" Hexe screamed.

"Do you see the filigree box? I sense its departure. How did it get out of our crypt?" Brujia lamented.

Hexe sulked. "Maybe, because it is made of wood, it floated upward?"

"You forgot, dear sisters." Hagatha stated. "It was sealed in with us in the casket."

Brujia pondered. "Perhaps the ring has more power than we had suspected? Arian may have learned some of our spells that she deciphered from the past three hundred years with the help of Giselle. She is quite clever."

"It's all your fault, Brujia. If you had been more careful with your spells, maybe that bird wouldn't have become magical. " Hagatha spouted out.

"Nonsense, that could not make her so enchanted. Nevertheless, I had fabricated the curse for Alexus, oh forgive me, now his name is Sebastian Simons to fall in love with me three hundred years ago. However, that insipid man fell in love with Arian Jovan. He would have been entombed with me forever, never aging, had it not been for Arian sacrificing her life so that he could be free. So for her punishment, I entombed her alone in ageless eternity."

"Gloating again upon your past misfortunes." Hagatha smirked. "Aren't you forgetting something? The ring is missing and if I am not correct, the box has been misplaced. If anyone obtains that key to our book titled, "Anthology of Magical Spells," we are doomed to perish forever. It contains spells that will undo our beings. Not like this temporary reprieve by Brujia, which had been intended to make us younger, but failed using three hundred-year-old lightning bugs for our bioluminescence, instead of fresh ones, which caused our untimely demise. Fortunately, I put a spell on us just in case anyone would interfere with the ring which acts as a liaison between the reality and the twilight dimensions or the key which tinkles like a bell the magical notes for unlocking our Anthology of Magical Spells."

"Must you mention that again." Brujia sighed.

"Let's get the key," Hexe stated while trying to attempt to hold the edge of their slimed wormhole of a crypt, "before the rain inundates us with more cold water." Hexe shouted. "We will drown. The water is rising up to our necks!"

"Swim you fool!" Hagatha yelled.

"It's fine for you two, you can naturally float with your size, but I am thin, so I will sink like a stone!"

Both Brujia and Hagatha flung Hexe out like a javelin, in which she thudded against the tree. Dazed, she fainted.

"Oops, I guess we threw her too hard." Brujia calmly replied.

Lucien awoke from Giselle's persistence in pulling off his blankets. "Oh, It's you. It's four thirty in the morning. Go back to sleep." He automatically retrieved his blankets.

Seeing not much of a response, Giselle chirped at him.

"Giselle, go back to sleep. Father will not approve if I get up at this hour." Lucien closed his eyes again but soon opened them seeing Giselle eyeing him as she rested her head on his. "My you are stubborn. What do you want?"

Giselle flew to the computer and proceeded to press the On-button with her beak.

"What are you doing there?" Lucien queried.

Giselle pecked at the letters, composing a letter on the screen.

"Dear Lucien,

Good morning! My instincts inform me that the three witches have aroused from their gravely plot and will be soon after the key in the filigree box, which I have hidden, to open their Anthology of Magical Spells. If they succeed, all is lost. It is too complicated to explain now because time is running out. Don't just stand there, gaping, please dress now. I will enter the instructions to the map, which you must follow to the letter or the witches will seek you out." Giselle continued to type:

OBJECTIVE: How to get to the Magical Spell Book.

Prerequisite: You must wear the golden emerald-diamond ring. It will flicker if the witches are too close, giving you a warning. Bring a flashlight, a chisel, and a hammer.

Procedure:

1. In the basement of this house lies a series of underground tunnels. It was the labyrinth for the witches approximately three hundred years ago. Their pantry for ingredients is directly under your bedroom.
2. Upon entering your basement from the stairs, turn right to the closet.
3. Open the closet and remove the contents. Inform your Father and Uncle.

4. Take a chisel and a hammer and whack on the left upper corner only once.
5. The stone door on the other side will swing back. Instantly breaking the rest of the wall. Stand back once you strike the chisel. Let your Father do this.
6. When the door opens, all the torches will light themselves throughout the various tunneled corridors. Go to the right side toward the abandoned, gravesite. The reason why it was called that is because that is how the witches harvested body parts from the various deceased and stored them in their pantry. For some odd reason a maddening mob wanted to exhume a former aristocrat to use him in a demonstration. They did not find his body or coffin. It was no longer there. They never buried anyone there ever since.
7. Etc....

As Lucien watched Giselle frantically typing, he still did not believe it. He called to his father. "Father, this is an emergency, please come at once!"

Sebastian hastened to Lucien's room not leaving anything to chance. "What is wrong?" He called, filled with alarm.

Lucien recited while opening his door to his father. "Giselle is typing us a map to obtain the Anthology of Magical Spells and the key in the filigree box."

"Start again, you don't make any sense."

"Why is everyone up?" Selena said, yawning and rubbing her eyes while standing in front of her bedroom doorway.

"What is all this commotion?" Uncle Horatio hyperventilated.

All of them stared in amazement at Giselle typing away at the computer. She flapped with one wing and pressed control print with a foot and beak technique as the computer responded to its commands generating the verbal typed map.

She flew in front of Sebastian's face as if to say," Hurry up!"

Sebastian grasped for the printed sheets reading in disbelief, as he held them, he noticed that the emerald ring was on his finger which caught his attention by surprise.

Uncle Horatio uttered. "It's incredible! "

"It gets worse." Sebastian interrupted "This ring, which is now attached to my finger, had been left on a tablet of paper. When I removed it, I could feel etchings on the sheet below. So I penciled the sheet to visualize the words. It is a riddle!" Sebastian read aloud. "Spanning through time for me to behold ... Does this mean she is immortal?" Sebastian finished the entire poem as everyone pondered in disbelief.

Lucien blurted. "We must retrieve the key in the filigree box at the abandoned grave site!"

Sebastian rushed. "Let's get dressed. Uncle Horatio, you get the chisel and hammer first. I will dress and while I make the hole in your wall, you get dressed. Lucien, help your sister."

Giselle stayed with Sebastian rushing him.

Sebastian inquired, "How soon will the witches get here?"

Giselle just flew to the ring, pondering, she then turned her head demonstrating that they still had time.

Uncle Horatio knocked. "Here are the tools, Sebastian!"

Sebastian grabbed the tools, her sonnet, and the computer print out and read aloud. "Upon entering the basement from the stairs, turn right to the closet." Lucien and Selena were dressed warmly, and at their father's heels wherever he went.

Sebastian continued. "Remove the contents. Lucien, Selena, help me with this!" Everyone, even Uncle Horatio, emptied the contents into a pile on the side.

Sebastian spoke again referring to the printout "Whack, on the left upper corner only once. Stand back, please." Sebastian took the chisel and struck the hammer against it. A stone door swung outward, breaking the rest of the wall into pieces.

Uncle Horatio expounded. "Well, this is a real mess! Yet, who would have thought that I would be owning a witches' labyrinth cave!"

Selena held her father's hand not letting go. Giselle perched herself on Lucien's shoulder. As Giselle predicted, all the torches began to light themselves through the various corridors.

Sebastian took the print out and deciphered. "We must go to the right side toward the abandoned grave site. But, how far do we travel?" Sebastian's eyes implored.

Giselle flew off, down the right corridor as Lucien and the others ran after.

"Can't you wait up for me." Uncle Horatio begged. "I am getting too old for this!"

Sebastian handed Selena to Uncle Horatio. "Lucien, you stay with your Uncle!"

Giselle pointed up toward the ceiling.

Sebastian declared. "You want me to put my hands into that muck and pull the box towards us!"

Giselle nodded.

"But, won't the ceiling collapse?" Sebastian's patience waned.

"It is magical!" Lucien responded.

Sebastian started to probe his hands through the dirt ceiling, when the emerald ring began to flash madly.

Lucien screamed. "The witches must be above us!"

Sebastian plunged his hands upward pulling down upon the box, when something was pulling the box upward. Sebastian, being stronger, pulled it down again so that one could see a pair of witch's hands with thorny fingernails latched onto the box. Selena gasped in horror. Then another pair of hands appeared to help retrieve the box. Voices could be heard from above.

"Sister, did you see that? We are losing. The box is sinking!" Hexe yelled.

Hagatha groaned. "Will one of you think and find out what is causing this?"

Brujia plunged her head downward towards the tunnel emerging out just able to see Sebastian and family.

Sebastian even screamed, as the emerald ring sent a green flashing spark of electricity towards Brujia, singeing her.

Brujia cried. "It stung me, it stung me!" She cried uncontrollably. "I can't see, I can't see!"

Sebastian had the box, and retrieved the key. "Where can we hide, Giselle?" His voice attenuated.

Giselle flew and they all ran after.

"Help me, help me!" Brujia wailed.

It took both Hagatha and Hexe to extract her from the mud.

"Why did you put your head down there, you buffoon? How could you see with all that muck?" Hagatha croaked.

"The ring stung me!" Brujia continued.

"But, where is the ring, the box, and the key, you fool?" Hagatha protested.

"All I could see was a tall man, like Alexus, oh I mean, Sebastian, for that is his name in this lifetime." Brujia groaned.

"What, what did you say, Sebastian?" Hexe screamed. "He is here in England! How can that be? I must have my crystal ball to locate him. I must have him for my own. Oh, how do I look?"

"Stop this nonsense this instant! The important thing is to obtain the ring and the key. After them, we must hurry! " Hagatha exclaimed.

"But," Brujia abated, "the only way to be quick, is to go through the muck!"

"Well, if we must, we will have to go in." Hagatha ordered.

"But, I just rinsed my dress so that I would look good." Hexe complained.

Hagatha and Brujia just took Hexe and threw her down into the muck.

Sebastian picked up Selena and ran with her. The tunnel seemed endless. "Where are we?" Sebastian cried.

There, at the end of the corridor one could see a black wooden door. Giselle seemed to say, use the key. Sebastian inserted the key and turned the lock. Musical notes emanated. It took all his strength to open the door, being so encrusted with mold. The room lit itself. Giselle flew in towards a large table where a huge, padlocked book lay. The book was made of an unusual leather wrapped in chains. The room itself had an enormous fireplace and shelves of ingredients with even a ladder to reach for them. Broomsticks were located on the other side.

Lucien walked towards the table gasping. "This must be The Anthology of Magical Spells."

Giselle pointed with her beak at the keyhole in the book. Sebastian understood and placed the key inside the lock. More musical notes emanated like silver bells. The book began to groan and shake uncontrollably. Light emerged from its edges as sparks protruded from it. Sebastian hesitated, yet, opened the book. Giselle tried to flip the pages to the index. Uncle Horatio ventured.

> ANTHOLOGY OF MAGICAL SPELLS
> INDEX – Expulsion of Spirits
> UNDER E

Cross-reference note} Besides spirits, it is applicable to any form of life, temporarily! (Dispels to a radius of 50 miles)

"This is it!" Sebastian exclaimed. "Giselle where will I obtain these ingredients?" Sebastian procured a flask and recited.

> ***EXPULSION OF SPIRITS***
> Into a flask one must combine
> Successions of ingredients, in specified time.
> A liter of water, which has been blessed

With the use of Black Tara that has been possessed
Petals from one red rose, with a fragrance
Which helps the spell, show some vagrance
One final ingredient comes from the sun
Golden drops counted one by one
Use a candle through the crystal ball
And golden sun drops will silently fall
Into the elixir one should mix very well
To insure the readiness, of the spell
Upon your intended splash with a throng
Repeating the words, Begone, Begone!

"Uncle Horatio, do you see a witch's crystal ball?" Sebastian seemed desperate.

Uncle Horatio scrutinized the entire room. "It's over here." He retrieved it.

"Giselle," Sebastian expounded. "Where is the blessed water, Black Tara, rose petals, and a candle to make sun drops?"

Giselle flew to each ingredient as Lucien and Selena brought them back to the table. Sebastian found a stand for the magic book, as Uncle Horatio lit the candle positioning it near the crystal ball so that the light transversed through it. With another flask he caught the golden drops excising.

"How many drops do you want?" Uncle Horatio called out.

Sebastian answered. "As many drops as possible. The quantity is very vague!"

The candle extinguished and Uncle Horatio brought the golden drops to the table. The potion was complete.

Sebastian stared at the door. "Will they use the door or will they come in by some other ungodly way?" He muttered.

Lucien responded. " The ring isn't flashing so they aren't coming as of yet." But as soon as Lucien spoke, the ring started flashing.

Selena cried," I am afraid Daddy!"

"Lucien, protect your sister! Uncle Horatio and I must coordinate to splash the elixir and open the door at the precise moment."

The doorknob slowly turned as Uncle Horatio held the door fast, so as not to let anything in. All of a sudden the emerald ring transcended Arian's voice, which sings out a prayer of amens reverberating throughout the room.

Hagatha screamed. "Curses, these prayers make me sick! I can not bear them any longer! Arian, I will get thee for this!"

All the witches held their ears crying uncontrollably from the excruciating pain.

"Now!" Sebastian commanded.

Uncle Horatio opens the door as Sebastian splashes the elixir on all of them stating, "Begone, begone!"

In an instant, they completely disappeared, leaving no trace. Selena ran to her father, as did Lucien.

Giselle flew back to the witches' book pointing at one of the words. Lucien followed reading aloud. "According to the cross reference, the radius is fifty miles."

"That will transport them somewhere in London," Uncle Horatio put in. "But, they could take a bus back."

Sebastian held both of his children and stared at the ring. "Why doesn't this girl talk to us? Did you get her name? The witches called her Arian according to their conversation. We also know that your house, Uncle Horatio, is a witch cave built about the same time period of 1690 to 1700 at least. I suggest we should make more elixir to protect ourselves."

"But," Lucien proclaimed, "I am hungry."

"Yes, Lucien, after the elixir, we will feed you. I will need something to quiet my nerves, like a tall drink." Uncle Horatio announced.

"Confounded. Where are we?" Hagatha cursed.

"I don't know, Sister." Hexe complained.

Brujia just stared. "We are in a church. It must be Westminster Abbey, Sister.

Observe. There are one hundred people glaring at us. I am so embarrassed. Oh, I feel a worm on my face from the tunnel squirming." She promptly took it off.

"It's hallowed ground!" All of them shook in fright.

"I'll get them for this. However, how do we get out of here?" Hagatha retorted.

"Walk I guess." Brujia mentioned.

"You know that spell works within fifty mile radius. That's a lot of walking." Hexe recoiled.

"Walk fifty miles, isn't there a spell for expulsion that goes:

TO RID THEE SPELL
To rid thee of an untimely lout
This is where one can spout
Get thee gone by sending them out.

Use in conjunction with a witch's rod." Brujia remembered.

"You fool, that's the wrong spell!" Hagatha ribbed her sister. "Let's remove ourselves. Make haste."

CHAPTER 4

INCANTATIONS

Sebastian glanced around the room filled with jars, bottles, chests, and other paraphernalia that he couldn't comprehend. He locked the Anthology of Magical Spells with the key, just in case, more harms could be released. He replaced the key into the filigree box. He carried both items carefully. "Uncle Horatio, please hold both Selena's and Lucien's hands. Don't touch anything. Giselle, can you guide us back to Uncle Horatio's house so we can have some breakfast and decide what will be our strategy for the next onslaught?"

Giselle acknowledged and flew to a left corridor leading them back to the basement doorway. When they entered Uncle Horatio's kitchen, the children sat at the table while Uncle Horatio busied himself with the preparation of breakfast helped by Sebastian. Giselle flew to Lucien's shoulder.

"What are we going to do?" Lucien implored.

Selena quickly added. "What will the witches do with us, when they return, Father? I am scared."

"Here, have some breakfast so we will have some moments of peace in which I will question Giselle, after she has had her birdseeds, for some answers. Be careful, the tea is hot." Sebastian said soothingly.

"I would never have believed it, if I had not seen it with my own eyes." Uncle Horatio reiterated, shaking his head. "We don't have enough knowledge of spells to outwit those witches who will be upon us with a vengeance."

25

"We will succeed. If you think any witch will hurt any of us, think again. I have my own wrath too." Sebastian countered.

Upon finishing their breakfast and the corresponding clean up, Sebastian supported Giselle on his hand while heading for the computer in Lucien's room. "Please make yourself comfortable since I will ask you a myriad of questions."

Giselle positioned herself in front of the computer keyboard. Lucien, Selena, and Uncle Horatio seated themselves at the computer monitor as close as possible to fathom any nuance of what Giselle would type next.

"Giselle, how can we protect ourselves from the witches permanently, not just temporarily?" Sebastian entreated.

Giselle typed out. "There is a spell in the Anthology of Magical Spells for their undoing, which we should find with no further delay. We also shall seek a spell for a place of sanctuary, just in case the witches find a way to return, which could harm us. Once that is accomplished, perhaps there is a way to release Arian from the Realm of Twilight."

"The Realm of Twilight, what is that?" Sebastian beseeched Giselle.

She typed. "The Realm of Twilight is another dimension where Arian Jovan has been banished to live for eternity by the witches."

Lucien's interest peaked. "That must have been the lady that possessed Selena when she wore that ring!"

"You must be correct." Sebastian stated," but I believe the sanctuary spell would be the wisest thing to do considering the time involved in any of the spells in which case we all will have to return to the witches' labyrinth to complete the task." Sebastian indicated to Giselle.

Giselle nodded and flew toward the basement followed by Lucien, Selena, Uncle Horatio, and Sebastian who carried the book along with the filigree box.

Selena appealed to her father. "What did Arian do to be banished for eternity?"

Sebastian answered while walking through the labyrinth corridors. "We have no way of knowing without asking Giselle to type it into the computer. We don't have any outlet here to bring the computer with us."

"She sounds very mysterious and beautiful." Uncle Horatio verified.

"On you too," Sebastian interrupted. "She seems to have that affect on everyone."

"Oh, here we are again." Lucien wondered while investigating the room.

"As I have repeated before, no one touches anything. Stay with Uncle Horatio or myself. Understand!"

"We understand Father." Lucien and Selena stated in unison.

"Good." Sebastian took the key from the filigree box and inserted it into the lock. Musical notes emanated like before while Giselle fathomed for the word sanctuary under S.

SANCTUARY SPELL

Into the circle of the one to defend
A mixture of Holy water one needs to depend
A protective shield without an end
Rimmed with strength that shall not bend
A lightening spark will once inspire
A circle of indistinguishable fire
Add molten lead into the cauldron's pot

Watching the patterns that will begot
Add salt for the crystals will devour
The ionization of Satan's power.

"These spells are becoming more frightening than before. What are we dealing with?" Uncle Horatio spoke confounded.

Sebastian shook his head. "I agree. It is a nightmare that I believe will become worse before it will be better. Imagine, this is how I am spending my vacation."

Giselle dispatched to her task for finding the ingredients, though where to find a jar of lightning sparks seemed to be illuminating, luckily, it was in a dark container.

Sebastian and Uncle Horatio lit the wood timbers beneath the huge black cauldron. Lucien was designated to stir the mixture while Selena helped Giselle locate and pointing to the ingredients, which Sebastian needed. Sebastian didn't want anything unnecessarily to fall from the shelves and cause more havoc. They all perspired from the heat generated from the spell and the cauldron.

Lucien stared at the mixture, spellbound. "How do they stock their ingredients? I wouldn't know how to make a lightning spark keep in such a small bottle."

"It's a mystery." Sebastian retorted." I can't explain it myself."

"How will we know it's done?" Selena leaned on her father's legs exhausted.

"Well, what do you think, Giselle?" Sebastian hinted." Do you think it's done?"

Giselle nodded and fetched a ladle to spoon it into another flask on the table. Sebastian understood and ladled the glowing mixture into the vessel.

"How are we to dispense this potion Giselle?" Sebastian inquired

Giselle pointed to the book. In a circle, but she took a quill pen and dipped it into the ink. "Don't forget, and under, or the witches will bury their way to you."

"Oh my, Daddy, I am scared. I will sleep with you tonight." Selena wailed, being overtired.

"Do you think this is enough to protect the house and the and under?" Sebastian wanted some kind of guarantee. How long will this spell last?"

Giselle searched through the cross-reference and pointed again.

Lucien read out loud. "Approximately one month, if there is no full moon."

"Does that mean a full moon will negate the spell?" Sebastian gasped.

Giselle nodded.

"That means we have to make more potion and find out when exactly a full moon will occur or this will fail!" Sebastian concluded. "Uncle Horatio have you subscribed to the newspaper yet?"

"No, I just moved in, but we could retrieve the information from the Internet!" Uncle Horatio added.

"Good, let's make another batch of the sanctuary spell."

They all sighed, when Selena said, "again, I am so tired Father."

"Here, sit quietly in this chair. You can watch us." Sebastian smiled.

Completion of the spell took concentration and determination which, Sebastian had in abundance for the fear of tangling with those witches was not an option to be ignored. "Let's dispense this potion." Sebastian poured a little on the floor, for the "and under."

"Will it leave a stain, or will it burn if you pour it in the house?" Lucien inquired. "It contains lightning sparks!"

In the mean time, Hagatha, Hexe, and Brujia were walking, trying very hard not to be noticed.

"My feet, oh my feet!" Hagatha wailed. "They will pay for this! This is such a disgrace. We are witches and we are walking. I never thought I could have so many blisters. My bunions hurt as well."

Brujia retorted. "My feet are fine!"

"Be silent! You always could wear any pair shoes in the house, large or small and your feet never hurt." Hexe complained.

"They must have the book, the ring and the key. They must have had help from Giselle to make the sanctuary spell! Lucky my bunions always hurt with a full moon." Hagatha bemoaned.

"Maybe, we could hitch a ride? I am so tired and we had nothing to eat for one hundred years." Hexe grunted.

"Behold, Sisters, someone is coming out of that small carriage without a horse. Maybe we could try to use it to get home? How hard could it be?" Hagatha suggested.

They all entered the car. Hagatha sat at the steering wheel. "I saw people move this wheel to steer, but, how do we start this thing?"

Brujia sat in the back seat, but she sat up to examine the control panel. "It confounds me!" She retaliated.

Hexe took her finger, being in the front passenger side, and gave an electric spark to the ignition. The car's engine started.

Hagatha bemused replied." Splendid, splendid, now what should I do, Sister?"

Brujia stared again asking. "What do the petals do on the floor?"

Hagatha pressed them. "One revs the motor and the other, I have no idea."

"What do the levers do?" Hexe pressed the button and moved the lever back in reverse.

"Let me see. If I put my foot on this petal." Hagatha replied. The car went quickly backwards and with Hagatha steering it, it crashed into the street lamp.

Brujia started to cry out of fear.

"Stop that, we are evil. We can not cry. Pull yourself together." Hagatha screamed.

Hexe pointed. "There is a man dressed in some kind of uniform approaching us, Sisters."

An officer came up to the window saying. "May I see your driver's permit please?"

Hagatha attested. "A driver's permit, oh, a driver's permit." Hagatha stared for help from her sisters, but sees no response." I guess I need one." Hagatha still looks at her sisters but does not know what to answer, continued. "I must have left it at home."

"May I see your insurance or liability card please?" The officer continued.

"Oh, my insurance or liability card? Oh, that's at home as well." Hagatha kindly replied.

"Where do you live?" The officer remarked with out a smile.

"Oh, my house burned down. I would like to help you. We are lonely ladies without funds, a home, or basic comforts of life. Couldn't you refrain and be merciful?" Hagatha begged.

"Sorry ladies, but, I have to take you in. Please step out of the car." The officer motioned with his hands to get them out.

"Oh, is this a car? Well, of course it is!" Hagatha exclaimed." Oh, Hexe, do you have some toad spit? I think we will need some."

Brujia replied. "I do, Sister."

Hagatha commented. "That's marvelous. Why don't we go with the officer?"

"Oh right," said the officer." My car is over here. Please come this way."

Brujia dove into her pocket and grabbed a large toad. "OK, give me some toad spit. " She whispered.

Hagatha demurely stated. "Oh, this must be your car. Well, have you ever heard the spell, The Cloak of Invisibility?"

THE CLOAK OF INVISIBILITY
Auspicious signs that must be quenched
No trace, no imprint left but drenched
From head to foot anoint thee must
With a bit of toad spit yee must thrust
Once upon thee, a cloak of dark.
Will cover thee effervescently with a spark
Clandestine now so don't delay
It's time for thee, to get away.

They anointed themselves saying, "BYE, BYE!" Which was all one could hear as they disappeared. Actually they were still there, yet, invisible. Now, they tried to walk quietly away.

The officer remained in a state of shock, staring in thin air, trying to locate them.

Sebastian and family decided to return upstairs from the labyrinth to Uncle Horatio's, as the time was nine P.M.

Uncle Horatio mused. "Now, I have to go to my computer and find all the information about the moon phases. What if there is a full moon tonight?"

"We made another batch." Sebastian carried Selena to bed." I still have to dispense this potion. You don't happen to have, by chance, a fire extinguisher handy?" Sebastian tried to be jovial.

"Sorry, I have one, but, I still haven't unpacked it yet."

"You stay with the children and find out about the moon phases." Sebastian replied.

"But, maybe I should be with you. This potion looks dangerous." Uncle Horatio warned.

"If I need you, believe me, I will scream very loud!" Sebastian added.

Sebastian took the flask outside noting the clouds that blocked the moon entirely. He opened the flask ever so carefully. The substance glowed dropping sparks as it was poured out slowly, drop by drop. He walked all around the house. The substance united into a circle like glitter. Slowly it was absorbed into the ground leaving no trace. The fog rolled in, giving a feeling of mystery. Sebastian pondered concentrating on the beautiful Arian Jovan. Her eyes were so intriguing. He wanted to ask Giselle more about her, but Giselle looked exhausted when he left the house. His feelings were foreboding "What happens next?" He locked the front door and went to Lucien's room, alias Uncle Horatio's computer room. The two children were asleep in one bed exhausted while Uncle Horatio typed away.

"Oh, Sebastian, in about one week there will be a full moon. I have the date written here. That makes me feel a little better. We all can't sleep in this bed. I will go to my own room. Where are you going?"

"I will camp out on the floor here tonight. Maybe I will take the mattress off my bed and drag it here. Good night Uncle."

"This evening has been the strangest day I have ever spent! Even if I went to the police, they would lock me up. Giselle, is also the key." Uncle Horatio revealed his worry.

"Maybe the ring can give us a clue. The inscription is worn but, if I enhanced it or enlarged it, we might be able to read it and if that doesn't work we will ask Giselle tomorrow. Here, the computer is still on, let's place the ring on the scanner." Sebastian scanned the ring as Uncle Horatio kept him company. The scanner picture enlarged the ring but the printout was completely different. The picture showed a chateau with Arian Jovan standing in an enormous archway leaning against a column with balustrades enclosing a terrace wearing a 17th century dress and hanging from her neck, a necklace draped through a man's emerald ring looking much like Sebastian 's ring from the filigree box. Sebastian stared at the print out that he held in his hand.

Uncle Horatio spoke softly. "Bewitching, isn't she! Why don't you enlarge it? The more I see of her, the better! Who could not fall in love with her." The picture was enlarged. "She looks quite forlorn. What makes her so?"

Sebastian couldn't take his eyes off her. "We must get the words off that ring. I will scan the ring again." Sebastian pressed the buttons again but the print out came with even more pictures of different parts of the chateau with Arian in every one of them.

Uncle Horatio smiled. "I could put all these printouts all over the house. They are so lovely."

"Where is Giselle?" Sebastian pondered out loud.

"She is on her perch as usual, asleep. Of which I am going to join her right now. Do you mind if I take one of those pictures with me? One can still dream you know."

"Which one do you want? They are all beautiful." Sebastian expressed.

"That one."

"It seems we like the same one." Sebastian replied.

"Well, how about this one." Uncle Horatio hoped.

Sebastian hesitated. "All right."

"Good night."

"Good night." Sebastian did not let go of the pictures. He gazed at them. He had to get some sleep, so he retrieved the ring and placed it on his finger again. He went into his own room and took the mattress off and dragged it to Lucien's room and made his bed on the floor. As he climbed into bed, he still held the pictures. He knew somehow that he had met her before, but how? He places the pictures close to his bedside and went to sleep after an exhausting day.

CHAPTER 5

THE GLIMPSE OF THE PAST

Deep, deep asleep, Sebastian relived the days past events. He focused on Arian's computer generated pictures as she gazed upon the garden's grounds. The parterres separated with fountains spouting water jets in full force as the diamond droplets, caught by the sun's glow, glittered radiantly, showering its beauty into cascades, as if fell from one of three tiered sections, until recycled back up to the top.

He, mesmerized by the water, noted a change in scenery. Now he, was the one riding a horse along side his Uncle's horse in a country back through time for he had not seen any cars, paved roads, or houses, just endless beautiful countryside etched with forest as he heard the singing of the birds. The sheer numbers astounded him.

"Sir Cecil Simon, (alias Uncle Horatio), are you sure you have the correct instructions? I believe we are lost. We were supposed to be at St. Denis, then to Paris, and on to Versailles. However, I don't see any of the roadways on your map that correspond to anything I see here." Alexus (alias Sebastian) related.

"Don't worry. Something will turn up. It always does." Sir Cecil reassured.

"That is what you said the last time and we ended up in Flanders." Alexus retorted.

"Don't start that again. Just concentrate on finding where we are!"

Alexus rolled his eyes toward the sky and pursued his Uncle's direction. "I think it would have been wiser if we traveled by coach next time. Uncle, stop, I see a farmer. Maybe he can direct us?"

"Oh, very well. How is your French? Nobody ever understands mine."

"Yes, I know. I have heard it before." Alexus conversed with the farmer for quiet a long time.

Uncle Cecil interrupted them in English, "Well, where are we or does he know?"

"Be patient, Uncle. He is trying to give me directions on our map. Do you know that this map is at least sixty years old? No wonder it doesn't have all the information."

"Yes I know. The gentleman from whom I purchased it, said, it was about the same as the new one, for less. What could happen in sixty years?"

Alexus, shocked, blurted out. "Yes, of course, whatever was I thinking?" Alexus returned to the farmer. Both of them were engrossed in the map. He shook the farmer's hand saying, "Merci. " He returned to his Uncle. "All we have to do, is go approximately fifteen miles West. There is an inn that we can take a coach that will take us where we want to go. We will just tie up our horses to the rear. I just wish we hadn't lost our luggage."

"Splendid about the inn, but about the luggage, they always lose it especially with the help you get these days."

Thunder cracked in the distance as it began to rain. In the meantime, Alexus and Uncle Cecil scrutinized for any traces of an inn.

"There it is!" Alexus announced.

"That little hovel, you can't be serious. We can't stay in that!" Uncle Cecil protested.

"We are drenched with no other place to go. So we don't have much of a choice."

"You do have a very good argument." Uncle Cecil concluded. "What will they be serving us for dinner?"

"I cannot say."

After a little more than a week traveling, they finally reached Versailles. The grandeur shined through to every detail: the grand chateau, the gardens, and the fountains. Everything in the garden was minutely clipped to perfection.

Alexus and his Uncle strolled through the gardens viewing the water parterres when Alexus beheld, (leaving his Uncle to wander), a beautiful lady dressed in a lavender silk brocade siting at the edge of the parterre apparently writing a letter, gazing back at him, smiling.

A gust of wind blew forcefully causing the beautiful lady's letter to land in the middle of the water. She, being unable to reach her letter, sighed.

Alexus gallantly walked into the water parterre to retrieve her letter, when he read what she had written. It described a gentleman, himself, exactly, and that she was falling in love with him. He glimpsed her reaction. She seemed distressed with an unsettling nervousness about her. (She bit her lip.) Since she now knows that he discovered her secrets indelibly written on the page.

Arian thought. "Oh God, he has read my letter!" She fidgeted with her quill pen. He is coming closer. Her heart pounded. He has recognized himself. What does he think of me? Why did this have to happen?" She could feel the blush emerging into her cheeks.

Alexus now standing in front of her, bowed. "I believe this is yours." He beamed. "Forgive me. I have not introduced myself. My name is Alexus Simons, Earl of Sussex."

Arian let her eyes rise to his face slowly trying to control her emotions of complete embarrassment. She calmly, or so she attempted, to speak. "Thank you Monsieur," was all that she could whisper.

He held out the soggy sheets of parchment for her.

She glanced at him and smiled, saying. "You have me at a disadvantage, Monsieur, I hardly know what to say."

"I quiet agree. You have written it most charmingly in your letter. Is Marianne your cousin?"

"Yes, she is, Monsieur."

"Please call me Alexus. May I ask you your name?"

"Arian Jovan. My father is the French ambassador to England."

"Would you like to acquaint me with the gardens? This is my first day here. I am traveling with my Uncle, Sir Cecil Simons. Unfortunately, our luggage has strayed, so I must keep to the sun to dry off."

Both of them laughed.

"You honor me. You are quite the gentleman not to tease me after reading my letter with such respect."

"Shall we?" He gave her his arm.

"Yes, I would be glad to, but, I must signal to my chaperone, Louise."

"Of course. Please tell me everything about yourself. Don't leave out anything."

Louise kept her three pace distance, while Alexus and Arian promenaded through the gardens to the fountain of Apollo clenching the reins of four horses and four dolphins spouting torrents of water.

"There will be a fete tonight in the hall of mirrors for the King. I am sure you and your Uncle have been invited. My father and I will be there." Arian fluttered her eyelashes and demurely looked away from him into the distance.

"Really. I hope that my Uncle and I are invited. Do you live far away from Versailles?" Alexus stared into her eyes but noted in the corner of his eye how Louise came closer and refrained.

"My home, besides a temporary residence here, is in the Loire valley."

"I am told that it has a lot of charming castles, chateaux, and rolling green hills along the river."

She smiled. It transcended through his soul. "Maybe you could borrow some clothes? At these functions one must dress well. I dare say my father may know someone that could fit your size. Come with me." Arian teased him.

At the fete, Uncle Cecil spoke to Alexus. "These borrowed clothes are too tight. I will have to stand through the whole party sucking my stomach in. Oh, by the way, I have heard all about Arian Jovan. She is related to the Duke of Anjou. She is fluent in several languages: German, Italian, English, Spanish, old Greek, and Latin. She plays the violin, the harp, the lute and the harpsichord. She sings like an angel. She is interested in the sciences, for example, astronomy. So I believe she would be a perfect wife."

"Your wife. You must be mistaken. Think of the difference of your ages, for one reason. Besides, I happen to know exactly what she thinks of me."

"What is this? You think I am not suited!"

"You misconstrue. It is just that when I met her, she had written a letter to her cousin, Marianne, of how, even though she had just glimpsed me in the garden, she loves me."

"That is absurd. Once she sees how stable I am with my finances. She will prefer me, money talks."

"We shall see. My father is just as amply endowed."

"Is this a challenge like placing the gauntlet before me?"

"Indeed, yes, and may the best man win."

"So be it." Uncle Cecil affirmed.

While Uncle Cecil had discussed Arian Jovan, Alexus had tightened Uncle Cecil's belt by placing his gloves in Uncle Cecil's waistband ever so carefully. Alexus thought to himself. Next will be dinner. With his knowledge of how much Uncle Cecil could eat, he knew it would make him feel ill, so that he will have more of a chance with Arian. He grinned at the prospect.

At that instant, Arian and her father entered the room.

Alexus and Uncle Cecil bowed correspondingly. Arian curtseyed, as her father bowed. Alexus stated. "You look radiant tonight Arian."

She smiled.

"By the way, you had dropped your handkerchief in the gardens. Here it is." He had purloined it promenading that afternoon. "I should have returned it earlier, but, I enjoyed its' fragrance so much. Forgive me."

"Why thank you, Monsieur."

Alexus purposefully released it from his hand.

Uncle Cecil's immediate response was to say. "Oh, allow me," as he bent to pick it up, a tearing noise could be heard. He rose quickly returning the handkerchief to Arian.

"Thank you again, Monsieur. My father has some pressing business that he must attend to."

Monsieur Nicolas Jovan stated. "Alas, that is the affairs one must adhere to. Please excuse me." He bowed again.

"What a coincidence." Uncle Cecil concurred. "I must attend to some business as well. Though I would have liked to stay. I cannot delay." Smiling with the smallest bow he could muster without tearing anything more, he departed holding his cloak wrapped tightly around him.

"Good night Uncle." Alexus bemused. He pivoted to Arian. "May I have the first dance?"

"You may. It is hard to refuse you, when you know my heart already. I don't know how to rectify it, unless, I shall undo it with a spell. But I love you too much to be so foolish as that. Forgive me for being so blunt. Words should be hidden in mystery but with you I cannot. Oh dear, I have said too much. She slipped away into the gardens.

Alexus hastened to follow. "I shall never let you escape. You have bewitched me the moment I saw you. Since both of us have declared our love, there is only one solution."

Arian placed her finger over Alexus' lips. "Shh! You go too fast. Let us dance here in the moonlight and enjoy the firmament as well as the music."

Louise finally found them. "Here I am. Thought you could deceive me, not so. I am experienced." She shook her finger in disapproval.

Alexus smiled quietly while taking Arian onto the dance floor, shadowed by Louise.

Once the dance commenced, Alexus whispered, in Arian's ear upon passing. "Will you marry me?" He placed a ring in her hand once they pirouetted.

Locked in each other's embrace as they came together for the dance and separated by the music's dictation she shyly answered, "Yes."

"That acquiescence you have just given me, has transcended my whole world into rapturous joys, that I have never known, except for you."

A flurry of images flooded Alexus' (alias Sebastian) mind: Their marriage, how they lived in England, how Uncle Cecil forgave Alexus, (what else could he do since Arian pleaded with him), their first born son, Dorian, and the knowledge of the second child to come.

The images slowed again and recommenced with Arian being worried about the delivery of her second child.

"Don't worry, you will make yourself ill and that is not good for you." Alexus tried to soothe Arian.

"Maybe one of those fortune tellers could have more advise of how this pregnancy will be after such a bad experience with our first born. Some of them know a little more, being midwives."

"Would that make you feel better?"

"I am not sure, I just have so much foreboding."

"I will ask the housekeeper, Anne, if she knows of any good soothsayers in town. "He rang for the housekeeper who promptly answered the bell.

"Yes, sir." Anne waited for her orders.

"Anne, do you know of any fortune tellers? Madame would like to consult with one." Alexus continued.

"I think there are three gypsies in town. They have just arrived. Many say their predictions, seem to be accurate. If you want, I could set up an appointment with them, Sir." Anne responded.

"Very good. Please set up an appointment here in the house. I want the butlers present in case something is missed." Alexus concluded.

"Yes sir. Most likely they could be here tomorrow."

"Thank you."

"You are welcome, Sir." Anne curtsied and left the room.

Alexus stayed with Arian when the gypsies arrived. He was also curious of the outcome. There were three of them, Hexe, Hagatha and Brujia. Their last name was Strega. They were wearing their best. James, the butler, seated them at an oval table in the library.

"How do you do." Alexus announced. "How much is your fee?"

"Our fee, Sir, is one sovereign." Hexe eyed him.

"First the fortune," Alexus reminded.

The witches placed their paraphernalia on the table: one crystal ball, a set of dice, a set of cards, one skull, etc.

"What is your name, my dear?" Hagatha inquired.

"My name is Arian Simons and I am two months with child."

"Oh, you are going to be a mother! How exciting! "Brujia added.

"Let us begin, Sisters." All three recited:

THE SOOTHESAYERS' PROPHESY
Who will tempt fate and have their fortune read.
We can make a believer out of you, for we call upon the dead.
Spirits rise and encircle us,
Whisper truths, unbeknownst and feared.
Love potions, spells and amulets we give out.
To protect you and entice you, and throughout.

Despondent cries pierce the night.
Goblins, ghollies scream in fright.
Demons, witches, and apparitions enthrall
For Strega, the gypsies will now tell all.
Be patient as we consult our crystal ball
It's fogging up!
Please place your hands on Sir Andrew's skull.
For he is our liaison from the world above.
Now, shuffle the cards, for your vibrations ensure,
The card of your future shall then endure.
Place the card face up and await, for we, the Stregas, will tell your fate!
Keep your eyes shut, and make no moves,
So to concentrate our thoughts, for we can amuse.

Arian picked a card of which Hexe laid out upon the table for everyone to see.

"This card implies danger, but, not exactly for your child. Stay at home for your pregnancy, so you won't lose it. Also stay off your feet. Another important matter is to see if everything is in order. Let me see your palm. Yes, you have a exceedingly long lifeline. How old is your son, Dorian?" Hexe commented.

Arian looked shocked. "He is but three years old." Arian grabbed for her husband's hand.

Alexus commanded. "Please, let's end this, you are upsetting my wife. I thought you could ease her mind, however, she needs calm. I will pay the sovereign. Now, please go."

"If you insist, Sir." Hagatha recoiled. "Would you like your fortune read?"

"I am sorry, but no, no thank you! " He took Arian out of the room with him.

"James, the butler, remained to make sure everything was in order and that the three gypsies left the house.

"What a beautiful house, Sister." Hexe indulged. "And did you see that man, Sir Alexus Simons? I must have him for my own. We will come back tonight."

"But," Brujia queried, "What are you going to do with him?"

"Idiot!" Hexe brooded. "I want him to be my lover. Never, in my lifetime, have I seen such a handsome man. He will be mine."

Hagatha added. "Is this your true love? I have given up on those! For one thing, they, being mortals, never live long. Then they get bald and sometimes fat. If you want a lover forever, you must extend their lives like ours. There is a spell, but then you also need a place to keep him. A place with a certain vibrations and magnetism. For example: the place where The Holy Grail is kept, or Camelot. There is another called *Quintessence*. The name refers to the Realm of Twilight. "

"We must prepare!" Hexe rejoiced.

Arian didn't let go of Alexus's hand. "Don't leave me. I even feel worse, as if I will lose you and the child. I can't bear that. It was bad enough that I lost my mother."

"Don't let them hurt you." Alexus soothed her. "Uncle Cecil is coming for dinner. He will cheer you up."

"Is your family coming?" Arian wondered.

"No, they will be here tomorrow. Look, there is Dorian. Why don't you play with him? I really have some business to attend to. I will be back momentarily."

Arian's eyes looked spooked for what was yet to come.

At that moment, Uncle Cecil arrived. "My dear. Why are you so forlorn? I will cheer you up. I have all the news and some letters from your father. Come with me."

Arian dragged Dorian.

That night Arian had Dorian in their bedroom and held Alexus as if it would be the last time.

Alexus complained. "If you hold me any tighter, I won't be able to breathe. Please, calm down. Dorian just fell asleep and I would like to sleep as well."

"Oh, I am sorry." She loosened her grip, just a little. "Is that better?"

"Couldn't you just hold my hand. I promise I won't disappear."

"How can you joke?" Arian replied." They weren't gypsies. They were witches. I could sense their evil. The pretty one Hexe, wants you, can't you see?"

"Believe me, no one in the world could ever make me give you up. I am so happy with you. I love you very much. Please, try to get some rest."

"What was that sound?" Arian cried. A candle lit itself and floated around the room.

Alexus held Arian closer not believing what was happening. The whole room became lit and so brightly that one could hardly see. The three witches surrounded them.

"Well, well, well, cat has got your tongue? What a pretty picture." Hagatha cried.

Alexus brought Arian closer as they rose from the bed." How dare you. Begone!" Alexus rang for the servants.

"I wouldn't bother. All your servants are asleep, at least until the next day. My sleeping spell usually works!" Hexe ordered.

Alexus put Arian behind him. "What do you want?"

Hexe forwarded herself. "I want you for my lover and I won't take no for an answer, so if you don't want any trouble, come peaceably and we won't hurt your wife or your son. Handsome, little boy, Dorian, what a nice name. Sleep child, sleep." Dorian, who was about to cry, went instantly to sleep.

Alexus replied. "Please let me take my son to my wife."

"No," Hagatha laughed. The child became suspended in space floating towards a caldron that just appeared from nowhere which was boiling. "Come here and maybe the child will live!"

Alexus crazed, jumped toward his son grabbing Dorian before he would fall into the cauldron.

"My your are quick." Hexe said admiringly.

Arian held her son and her husband closer.

"You see what we can do, so come." Hexe commanded.

Hagatha retorted. "Look, we won't kill your son. He is so handsome, we will come back for him later."

"Never," Arian called out. "You will have to kill me first."

"Well, all right," Brujia retorted. " If that's what you want?" She sent a lightning bolt towards Arian.

Arian collapsed as Alexus knelt and held her to see if she was still alive. Arian started to move slightly. Dorian didn't cry, but stayed asleep. Dorian was still cradled and protected in Arian's arms.

The room started to quake as vibrations reverberated. From the cauldron a green potion boiled causing vapors to emit. Hagatha grabbed a ladle, filled it with the substance, and tossed it in the air. The green potion completely vaporized into a green circle of mist, which created sparks to levitate around the room.

Alexus picked Arian up, as she finally got back on her feet. She held Dorian again.

"Come Alexus, come to me, my love," Hexe repeated demurely.

"Never, I would rather all of us die then go with you."

"Now, that's not true. Can you really see your wife die, because of you?"

The three witches recited the transferring spell to the Realm of Twilight:

TRANSFERRING SPELL
Vanquishing from time and space
Where gravity and magnetism are displaced.
Where purgatory dwells, no time can escape.
Trapped between the ether.
Vibrations compound the ion's trails.
As the Pillars of Hercules communicate quails
Energetic bursts like x-rays wails
Vacuuming through an endless void
Transformed as a vapor being employed
This is the Realm of Twilight.

Hexe then sent another lightning bolt towards Alexus hitting him, but Alexus stood his ground. He was enraged. Arian now started to sing French prayers.

"Stop it," Hagatha ordered. "Not prayers! Stop it, I say." She hit Alexus with another bolt.

Alexus protected his family by staying in front of them, anguishing from the pain.

Hexe screamed. "This will do it. " She threw the largest lightning bolt ever.

Arian placed Dorian behind Alexus, as she jumped in front of her husband saying. "Take me! Take me! Take me!"

The lightning bolt struck Arian in the chest. She started to bleed. The green vapor surrounded her as she disappeared.

Alexus barely could move from the pain of the last lightning bolt, screaming "Arian! Arian! Arian! "He still protected his son.

"Curses! That bolt was meant for you for the spell to work! Now, Arian is in the Realm of Twilight, never aging and immortal. That is where you, Alexus, are supposed to be." Hexe cried. "We don't have enough potion! The ingredient takes three hundred years to ferment to work! " She started to tear her hair. "I will never have you now." She lamented.

Brujia yelled. "I am sorry Hexe, I guess we will have to go home."

"Where is my wife? Bring her back to me, please!" Alexus implored. "Please!"

"Arian will pay for this!" Hexe vowed. "The electric shock has killed your daughter. Yes, she was going to give birth to a girl. I think you would have named her Selena. Oh, now

Arian will live forever, seeing you, for as many lifetimes, being married and having children without her, but with everyone else in your next lives."

The three witches disappeared in a puff of black smoke. The room reverberated as the light escaped.

At that moment, Dorian woke up crying. "Mommy! Mommy! Mommy!"

Sebastian woke up screaming. *"Noooooooooo!"* His eyes were moist from the tears.

Lucien and Selena ran to their father.

"What is wrong, Daddy?" Selena cried. "Why are you crying?"

Sebastian held both his children closer.

"Did you have a bad dream?" Selena continued.

"Oh," said Lucien holding the pictures of Arian. "Where did these pictures come from?"

Uncle Horatio knocked at the door. "Are you all right? Why did you scream no?"

"Come in," Sebastian answered.

Uncle Horatio entered. He had Giselle perched on his finger.

"Tell us, Daddy!" Selena began.

Sebastian related his nightmare.

Uncle Horatio gasped! "That is a horror and it seems that we are all back with you. Lucien as Dorian, Selena, yet never born, but her soul was there, and I am Uncle Cecil. Did I change Alexus or Sebastian? Remember it is three hundred years. That potion is ready for you, again Sebastian."

Selena started to cry.

CHAPTER 6

WHAT IS YET TO COME?

Giselle flew to the computer and started to type. Sebastian and family followed to see. Giselle's printout read: "The witches are very close, now. Did you pour enough of the potion under the building or they will bury themselves through?"

Sebastian, distressed, went to collect the potion to pour it onto the basement floor. Uncle Horatio made breakfast for the family. All Sebastian thought of was his wife Arian, waiting for three hundred years and that those three witches killed his child.

The morning was clear and warm with no fog as the three witches trekked along the roadside.

"It's too sunny. Why couldn't it rain? I love the gloom. "Hagatha complained.

"I don't know." Brujia reprimanded. "I like sunny days too."

"What is wrong with you!" Hexe screamed. "We are witches! Witches like gloom. Where can your mind be?"

"We have spent one awful night, camping out with no comfort. My back is killing me and Brujia kept tossing and turning, making all, that racket! Then, you kept squashing that toad. You made all that fuss." Hagatha moaned.

Brujia retorted. "I had to feed the toad. You didn't have to catch all those bugs. What are you complaining about?"

"Quiet! Sisters." Hexe cried. "I have a headache."

A homeless man approached them holding a gun screaming. "Don't move and give me all your valuables!"

43

"Sisters," Hagatha exclaimed. "What is that, and what does he possess?"

Hexe grunted. "I don't know? Do you think it is dangerous?"

Brujia wailed. "What does your weapon do?"

"Don't you know!" The man yelled. "It puts bullets into you."

"Bullets!" Hagatha continued. "What are bullets?" All the witches stared at each other. Does he mean that the weapon is a musket?"

"Pieces of lead, bullets. Do you want a demonstration? I will kill you! "

"Oh, I think not." Hexe sent a lightning bolt searing towards the man, making him unconscious.

"Well, we should tie him up and write a sign that he is a thief! Lets' tie him to that tree." Hagatha grinned.

"I know," cried Brujia." Let's write the word thief on his forehead with indelible ink and add a sign stating, Thou shall not steal!"

"Sounds fair, Sisters," Hagatha asserted.

"Well, he looks better now. Let's take his money and hitch a ride. How much do you think it will cost?" Hexe concluded.

"Hush! Someone cometh." Brujia added." Let's take his weapon and dump it!"

With only a few hours sleep beset by his nightmare, Sebastian hastened his family, Uncle Horatio, and Giselle back to the Anthology of Magical Spells to find some clue that would help them from their predicament. His mind had been wracked with the emotions that he had to get a hold of so he could act accordingly. The sky changed to a steel gray gloom. The fog rolled in and it drizzled slightly with a constant rhythm, accenting his confinement. He stared at the emerald ring and the key in the filigree box. Maybe in the Anthology there could be a reference about emeralds to unravel the spell of the Realm of Twilight? He set the book down. Giselle perched herself on his shoulder in order to overlook the procedures. Sebastian turned the old pieces of parchment carefully with respect, for he had seen the power saturating in its content. Sebastian read aloud:

"Definition: Emeralds- a bright green transparent precious stone/ green variety of beryl or corundum. Cross-reference: Pillars of Hercules- two headlands on either side of the straits of Gibraltar, one pillar on Gibraltar (ancient Calpe) and the other pillar at Ceuta (ancient Abyla) on the African coast. It was considered "Sun Pillars"/ "Stone of Gods". As per Herodotus, the two connected stones, one made of metal (gold) and the other of precious stone (emerald) was used for communications giving off eerie radiance's as it emits high-powered beams.

Sebastian marveled at the information. "Let me see the computer generated printouts again."

Lucien had the sheets with him. "Which one father," He displayed them all.

"This one. See! She wears an emerald ring on her necklace about her neck. It matches the one we have here. Maybe, we can use it for communications. Giselle, do you know its meaning?"

Giselle flew to an ink pen and sheets of paper provided to her by Selena who held it for her on the table. Giselle wrote out. The ring had been designed for the witches. One, that would have been worn in the Realm of Twilight, with the other, worn outside in the Realm of Reality. It should have been Sebastian who would have been trapped for eternity, but Arian sacrificed herself instead. Arian had been keeping up with the magical books kept at "Quintessence" the fifth essence or the Realm of Twilight. She had discovered that when she etched the emerald ring

44

in her possession that it, being linked to the other, would be in the same image. Though, to do so she had to endure the electrical charges that had come from the endeavor. As you can see for yourself, it has been worn in places of the text due to the counter electrical charges dispensed by the magical key, obliterating some of the inscriptions. The electric currents burned through the coffin's lid and eventually separated the filigree box during the process from the witches' casket.

Uncle Horatio interrupted Giselle. "May I ask, how can you do all these feats of magic? Are you enchanted?"

Giselle wrote with a steady foot as she controlled her letters with skill. "I was just a fledgling being taught by my mother of what selections of food were edible or not. When I detected from my perch high up in a tree, multicolored smoke, rising from the forest. I flew to discern its origin. Fortunately, I discovered a bunch of lovely ripe grapes, gleaming with its juices in the perfection of its age. So I ate some. I didn't realize that it was enchanted. Apparently one of the witches had concocted a spell to improve her wit. I had already consumed all of them, which infuriated the witches. The magic gave me longevity as well as wit. I am as old as Arian, being magical, I can traverse to the Realm of Twilight for snatches of time. I have been her only companion. I am determined to help her. It was I, who put the nail on the roadway so you would have a flat. It was I, after all these years, who made small canals around the witches gravely plot, so that their casket would erode eventually exposing the filigree box of wood allowing for the magical properties to slowly rise so that it could be accessed. I have worked for centuries. Note, there are other problems that you should be aware of."

Sebastian filled with alarm, "What else should there be?"

Giselle hastened to write on the page. "There will be a full moon in six days. Within this time period you will have to discover how to dispose of the witches because even though you are protected, they can still haunt you. You will need to access outside of your sanctuary, to solve the spell to release Arian from her imprisonment, a task that seems difficult at best."

"What type of haunting?" Sebastian attenuated his voice.

Giselle concluded on the page. "They, being witches, are capable of most anything."

Uncle Horatio uttered. "Oh my God!"

Selena started to sniffle while Lucien swallowed. "Can't we go home?"

Sebastian confounded stated, "Where is safety after what we have been through?"

The sun peeked out from the clouds again shining as the witches rested for a while.

"Are we in the vicinity of our house, yet? I cannot bear to take another step. Imagine! They didn't have any brooms! They suggested a vacuum cleaner. What is that anyway?" Hexe panted holding her foot in the air but being so tired she toppled over.

I don't recognize anything. Not even the direction we are heading." Brujia flounced down to join Hexe on the ground.

"Will you be quiet, I can't concentrate!" Hagatha warned. "I can't get any vibrational rhythms from our abode with you two squabbling making it practically impossible."

" Everywhere we go, we are stared at, you think they never saw witches before." Hexe lamented.

"Hush, I am trying to get a reading but nothing is resonating." Hagatha's fury rose.

"Well, just rest. Being a sourpuss won't make the situation any better." Brujia retorted.

"My patience is waning." Hagatha stomped.

Brujia pulled at Hagatha's dress so that she joined the others. "These paved roads with the mechanical things whizzing by make it more difficult to cross. Why can't they fly? It would be less noisy."

Hexe held up both her feet. "I have worn out my shoes. See the holes."

Hagatha assured her. "Well, now it matches your clothes, dear."

Brujia scanned through the trees. "Do you think we could make brooms? All we need is a bit of stiff straw tied to a stick. How hard could that be?"

"Yes, now that is a productive thought, a broom. They would most likely keep bundles of straw in a stable. Has anyone seen any stables lately?" Hagatha beamed.

"No," Hexe answered." But I do see this stiff ragweed, would this do?"

"Why not? I am not fussy. What do you think? Brujia?" Hagatha confirmed.

"They make me sneeze."

"Oh, who cares as long as we can fly. Now, all I have to do is climb this tree to harvest some suitable branches. You two, give me a boost. This tree is taller than I thought."

Both Hexe and Brujia managed to push Hagatha up to their shoulders.

"I can't reach. Put your backs into it, my dears." Hagatha strained.

"We did." They both groaned.

"Why don't you climb up?" Brujia insisted.

"With this wide trunk? You have got to be kidding. No just put me down, "Hagatha hyperventilated.

"That is easy." Both Hexe and Brujia stepped aside and let her fall.

"Don't get angry," Brujia hesitated," you have to admit you are very heavy."

"Forget that. We will have Hexe obtain the branches. We can throw her."

"Oh no! The last time you did that, I crashed into the tree. I still have a headache." Hexe scolded.

"What do you think?" Brujia and Hagatha eyed her. Both of them tossed Hexe into the air.

"No!" Hexe wailed.

Hexe landed hanging on a branch.

"Use your legs to get a hold of the branch." Hagatha coached.

"I am trying." Hexe responded. She swung herself upright but then slipped off underneath the branch.

"Don't worry, you are doing fine." Hagatha put in.

"I don't know. I seem to hear some crackling sounds." But, too late, Hexe along with the branch collapsed earthbound.

"We have the branches." Hagatha announced enthusiastically.

In the witch's liar surrounded with chemicals of who knows what, Sebastian, Uncle Horatio, and Giselle tried to coax the secrets out of the Anthology of Magical Spells while Lucien and Selena sat next to the table observing everything.

"Father," Lucien interrupted.

"Yes, what is it?"

"If you would turn to page forty two, the pages seem to flicker as if it can't decide whether it is glowing or staying in the darkness."

"That is odd, but, for this book it may be normal." Sebastian turned to page, forty-two. On the top of the page was titled: The Exodus from of the Realm of Twilight:

EXODUS FROM THE REALM OF TWILIGHT
Upon a blue moon where moonbeams derive
Will transverse through the stone, becoming alive
Once the center of the stone's vibrations accelerates
An ionizing vapor exudes and disseminates
A corresponding wave will sinuate through the past
But hurry, follow it expediently, for it will not last
Through the ethereal and to the beyond
Vessels across the threshold of an eau of a pond
Vacillated through a medium to dispense
The pedestals of time will recompense.

Sebastian contested. "This is utter nonsense. How will we solve this?"

Giselle shook her head while Uncle Horatio clasped his face in non-comprehension.

"Maybe," Lucien stated," we should keep looking for the witches undoing spell. Could it be worse than this?"

Giselle flapped her wings to attract attention. She promptly wrote that if the emerald ring that Sebastian wore, was laid on a tablet of paper, Arian could communicate with us in concurrence with her emerald ring, using it like a pencil as she writes upon her tablet. The emerald ring can also transcend Arian's prayers as a positive thought but it can not be used as communications. It is only one sided in that respect. The use of both rings must be used in conjunction for a written communication.

Sebastian immediately took off the ring and placed it on a sheet of paper. Small etching sounds could be heard writing the following: as Sebastian sketched it in pencil as it was transcribed.

Dear Monsieur, I address you in this manner, for after three hundred years, I would not presume to solicit you as my beloved husband, Alexus. Please forgive me. Your name is now Sebastian. I only ask for pity's sake, to be released. I have been sequestered here for so long, but, to be expedient, for there is hardly any time to express my thoughts. I should inform you. When the full moon does appear in six days, it will dispense the Sanctuary spell. It will also be a blue moon. Blue moons are full moons that occur twice within the same month. This blue moon is essential in my release. But to the immediate problems, the witches are two miles away from you, since they have discovered how to make brooms from branches and ragweed. If you would use the witch's crystal ball, you could see it for yourself. I have a crystal ball on this side of the parallel dimension yet it isn't activated. We could communicate together in this way if you can activate both of them. Another thing I should mention, if you dream, the witches can also enter in your dreams, as well as I did. I am sorry that I did, but I thought you should know the truth. I wish I could find some way to give you some comfort, but I can not. To activate the crystal ball, one has to take the witch's rod which is only on your side and wave it over the crystal ball saying this spell:

TO ACTIVATE THE CRYSTAL BALL
An amorphous orb that one conjectures through
Delphic in nature, which procures omens too.
Where illusions or images profess and beguile

Foreshadowing events including denial.
A wave of my rod will now instill
The power prophesied, shall be thy will.

By using your crystal ball you can spy on the witches until they will realize it and become more discrete. The ring you wear emanates a lot of power and it is the crux of most of their spells.

Sebastian, touched by the words that was etched on the page, asked. "Giselle, where is the witch's rod?"

Giselle flew to the closet, and pointed.

Sebastian ran to retrieve it. As he opened the closet, there were three gnarled, black, and encrusted rods that were very lightweight. Sebastian took the largest one. Uncle Horatio placed the crystal ball on the table as Sebastian read the spell out loud. As he waved the rod, the crystal ball, which looked opaque even when the sun drops were excised, became totally lucid and bright. Sebastian then asked the crystal ball to focus upon Arian Simons.

Arian promptly appeared smiling and then said. "Good morning, Messieurs and Mademoiselle. This is my first image that I can actually converse with live, in three hundred years. I am quite honored to make your acquaintance. May I introduce myself formally? How do you do?" She curtsied as if she addressed a King. "This, must be Lucien and Selena, they are so precious. Monsieur Sebastian Simons and this must be Uncle Horatio Simons. I am afraid to say that you, Monsieur Horatio Simons, look the same as Uncle Cecil except a little taller."

"How do you do?" Sebastian stated impressed by her. "It is a pleasure to meet you at last."

Arian proceeded. "No, the pleasure is all mine."

Uncle Horatio's mouth opened like a codfish professing. "Oh, excuse me, How do you do?"

Arian continued. "How can I be of service? My accent might be a little awkward, since I have not spoken English for a long time. Also, I speak from the 17th century, not knowing your jargons. Oh, excuse me, I must thank you Giselle, how can I ever repay you. You have been so faithful."

Sebastian was captivated and enraptured by her manners, her charm, and her beauty.

Lucien inquired. "Where did you find any clothes? Weren't you in your nightgown when you were taken?"

"Oh," Arian replied." Yes, the clothes that I was wearing were singed and bloody. I stayed on the ground for three days being unconscious due to the lightning bolt, steeped in my own blood, but eventually I regained my ability to move and found the witches' chateau, where I found some dresses to wear."

"But, what about the baby girl?" Selena added.

Sebastian just shook his head in disbelief.

"Yes, I lost the child." Arian looked down but then her eyes rose to them, and added, "but time does heal the soul. However, I think your father would like to elucidate on the problem at hand."

Sebastian hastily apologized. "Forgive them, I know that in your time, topics like this were kept quiet. I am sorry if they have embarrassed you. According to this spell book, your

Exodus of the Realm of Twilight, runs like this or maybe you can read it through the crystal ball?" Sebastian placed the book in front of the crystal ball for Arian to read it.

Arian asserted. "Monsieur Simons, may I copy this spell and reflect more to you later? This chateau, has a library of spells as well, if I could cross-reference, I could expound more on the topic. I must also mention that the witches have just landed and are ten feet away from your house."

Sebastian shocked replied. "Oh my God! But, may I call you by your first name, Arian and you call me, Sebastian?"

Arian looked surprised. "Well, yes, in a strange way we are not complete strangers, Monsieur, oh forgive me, Monsieur Sebastian. I must study this, adieu." Arian disappeared.

Uncle Horatio mesmerized and spellbound, teased. "My she is gorgeous and her English doesn't have a French accent, but according to your dream, she is a linguist. She is not like Marisa at all."

Sebastian vexed replied. " How can you even think of that at time like this. Let's not discuss this any further."

Uncle Horatio apologized, saying. "I am sorry, but you did love both of them depending on time."

Sebastian asked the crystal ball to focus on the witches.

"Well, Sisters, we are finally home! Home at last." Hagatha rejoiced.

Brujia sneezed. "My eyes are swollen and red. My sinuses are congested, I have a splitting headache, and I can't stop sneezing!" She sneezed.

"Stop that! We needed to fly, for that was the only way that we could save time and our feet. So stop complaining." Hexe groaned.

"That's easy for you to say, you don't have this sinus problem." Brujia moaned.

"Sisters, Sisters, we are home! Let's go inside." Hagatha bubbled. Hagatha walked towards the cave area, which was near Uncle Horatio's garage, when thud! She was repelled "Curses!" She screamed holding her head. "You could say that we are locked out!"

Brujia cried, "But, I am hungry, we traveled so far for this! " She sneezed again.

Hexe swore. "I should have known that Giselle would have discovered the sanctuary spell, but, I was hoping that she wouldn't have remembered every room. Now, they have the laboratory with the pantry with all our ingredients. What are we suppose to do?"

Hagatha raved. "She couldn't have remembered everything. We will rouse the dead for this!"

"Do you remember the spell?" Hexe reeked with revenge.

"No," Hagatha wailed. "They have the crystal ball, the spell book, and all our magical substances, not to mention our cauldron. Also, I wanted to sleep in my own bed."

Brujia began to cry.

"Stop that, Brujia!" Hexe demanded." Hagatha, don't you remember any spell?"

"I am so famished and we have been dead for one hundred years. It is hard for me to concentrate."

Brujia related. "But I have a spell book! It helps me remember the small and more useful spells. I write the most common ones down."

"Perfect, let me see it." Hagatha commanded.

"Here." Brujia handed the book.

Now, let me see. What do we have here? Boils, pimples, warts, lameness, memory loss, a silence spell, invisibility, a sleeping spell, baldness, changing people to animals, oh, here 's one, spider soufflé! Oh, this one is perfect. We will have to collect some spiders but we still need to buy a cauldron and cooking utensils."

"Well, we could use our invisibility spell and steal the items. There is a store down the road from here. " Hexe suggested.

"Let's go. We fly Sisters!" Hagatha insisted.

Brujia demanded. "I am staying here. My sinuses are killing me! I want to get away from this ragweed broom as much as possible. " She tossed it as far as she could.

Hexe conceded. "Very well, we will be back in no time, but hand over the toad."

Brujia scolded. "Don't eat him, he was difficult to find in the first place." She promptly lay in the grass.

Hexe and Hagatha recited the cloak of invisibility and anointed themselves with the toad spit as they disappeared. When they jumped on their brooms, the brooms flew away witchless towards the direction of the store. They left their brooms outside of the store so that it would not attract any attention.

"Is this the right store? All I see is food, human food. It might be worth trying." Hagatha seemed desperate.

"Sister, How can you say that?" Hexe seemed shocked.

"I know it tastes awful, but I am that hungry. Maybe, at this time, their food could improve. Hexe, don't touch the candy, I can't bear that, but this chicken looks good and look over there, a tiny pot. Well, it is better than nothing. I will take the cooked meat, and some raw, and you, Sister obtain some spices and ingredients over there. They might be the same as ours. No, on second thought, take them all. We will discover what they are like at home."

Hexe reminded. "The items that we steal will float in the air. I can't disguise them."

"Well, so will the meat that I have." Hagatha cried." Don't worry, when we are on our brooms, no one can follow us? We will fly very fast."

"See, you." Hexe retorted.

"Bye, bye, but be quick." Hagatha screeched.

"Wait, Hagatha wait. The brooms are not invisible anyone can follow their direction."

"Who cares." Hagatha grunted as the food floated in the air heeding the broom, stopped for a moment for Hagatha to jump onto her broom, and continued displaying a trail of food flying off too. This also happened with the spices and the paraphernalia, which accompanied Hexe, as throngs of people screamed and ran away from the store.

Sebastian and family were still in the spell room, trying to find the demise of a witch spell, but the Anthology didn't have that in the index.

"What are we going to do? "Uncle Horatio sounded worried." It is not noted in the table of contents either."

"Maybe we should ask Giselle?" Sebastian suggested." Do you happen to know where we should be looking?"

Giselle shook her head motioning that she didn't know.

Lucien hinted. "How about the words to undo a witch?"

"Sorry, Lucien, Sebastian replied. It is not in the index or table of contents."

Uncle Horatio sighed "I feel so useless. Here we are wasting our time. How about coup de grace, forgive my French, I could never pronounce it."

"Sorry, " Sebastian became discouraged.

"What about a skull and cross bones?" Uncle Horatio blurted.

Sebastian smiled, as he quickly looked it up." Sorry, that means poison. Maybe we could poison them, but would they eat it?"

"Let's ask Arian?" Selena added.

Sebastian asked the crystal ball to focus on Arian Simons.

The image emerged. Arian was in the library having the crystal ball near her and books and scrolls all over the table. Focusing around the room, there was a harpsichord with music upon it composed by Arian Simons. Sebastian didn't want to disturb her, as he just stared at her admiringly. Arian was singing a French tune as she perused through the magic books. The song was quite enchanting.

" Please, excuse me." Sebastian spoke quietly." May we disturb you for a moment?"

Arian expressed surprise. "Oh, I forgot Monsieur, what is it that you desire? Forgive me, it is strange to talk to someone. And you want to be called, Monsieur Sebastian."

"We would like to know, where in the Anthology would a demise of a witch be indexed?" Sebastian was so taken by her.

"Maybe, it would be under *Debitum Naturae*. It is a Latin word or phrase. Debitum meaning debt or liability but in the theological term meaning sin. When you link them together the meaning changes to death."

"I forgot, you know Latin as well. I am quite impressed with you."

"Thank you Monsieur, I mean Monsieur Sebastian. Please correct me, if I lapse into French. It is just a habit. I have been studying this spell of the Realm of Twilight. I am assuming since the pedestal could imply pillars, that the stone, which is implicated in the verse, could be the emerald that adorns these rings. But how you could follow a vapor unless you use one of the witch's brooms to fly, could remain a mystery. Then again, I may be wrong. What do you think? Oh, I see your engaged in deciphering where to look to rid yourself of the witches. Please, do not let me interrupt your study. You will be in more danger than I." Arian related.

"That is not so comforting," Sebastian eluded." May I add that after so long a time in solitude, your mental health seems quiet unalterable. I don't know if I could be so. My hate would be my undoing."

"You forget that no matter what pain you endure in this dimension, eternity, as time, does heal. Please find that spell. I fear for you, your children, and your Uncle. The witches are merciless."

"Yes, of course. Please wait while I consult the Anthology of Magical Spells." Sebastian checked under D, Debitum Naturae see page 666.

Uncle Horatio sighed, "Is this symbolic?"

Sebastian shrugged. "Let's see."

Lucien asked, "Do you think something will hop out and get us?"

Sebastian assured, "Maybe, both of you should stand back, just in case." Sebastian turned to the page 666.

Uncle Horatio distanced himself a little from the book, but his curiosity kept him close.

As the page turned, the print of Debitum Naturae lit up in blood red letters reflecting onto the ceiling but the spell did not appear. It was a blank page.

"I don't believe this. The spell is not listed." Sebastian whispered lest something else would happen.

Uncle Horatio confirmed, "I don't see anything either."

Arian interrupted "Maybe, it was written in invisible ink, because the witches never would want anyone else to use the spell, or it could be safeguarded by another spell."

Sebastian reiterated. "Do you mean a spell of the spell?"

"Yes, Monsieur Sebastian, "Arian stated. "Please cross-reference it with a security spell combined with invisible ink or you could try placing the witch's crystal ball over the supposed lettering. It, being an orb, looks into the future which may help."

Sebastian held the witch's crystal ball over but not on the page. Sparks of seared blood red letters impressed deeply upon the page as Sebastian held the crystal ball over each successive line. "It seems to skip every other line."

"Oh, Oh, "Uncle Horatio's surprise escaped his lips. "This is only a partial spell."

Giselle flew in circles; Lucien noted it and inquired.

"What is wrong, Giselle?"

Everyone watched her. She took a pen and began to write. There must be a combination of two spells to obtain the death spell of eternity.

Sebastian complained, "Nothing is straightforward, not even in a spell book!"

Arian replied, "Alas, all spells are written in riddles. It is just the way it is done. Your children appear that they should have some nourishment and a good night's rest. Since the witches are still preparing for their next strategy, maybe, they should get whatever rest they can."

"How attentive you are," Sebastian thanked her. "Yes, I am a bit single minded at the moment. Uncle Horatio could you make some sandwiches as fast as you can. Take Giselle with you and the elixir for expulsion, just in case, while the children sleep on the table on my jacket."

"Right you are." Uncle Horatio with Giselle and the elixir exited the room.

"Lucien, Selena come and lie down on the table. You can use my jacket for a pillow while I and Arian will try to sort this out."

"All right, Father." They both responded.

When Hexe and Hagatha returned with a file of ingredients which dripped not being totally contained, they found Brujia snoring and snorting with her blocked sinuses and her mouth fully opened.

"Wake up, Brujia, before you attract the flies." Hagatha yelled.

"Ugh," Brujia responded.

"Never mind. Help us with these items." Hagatha badgered Brujia. "What do you have here Hexe?"

"Oh, those. When I swished by with my collection spell, these items also followed."

"But, what are they?" Hagatha curiously scrutinized them.

"Ugh, let me see," Hexe exclaimed. "Decongestant, my, what is that?"

"Well, what else does it say?" Hagatha cajoled." Just read that funny label."

Hexe said, "These words can tie your tongue in a knot, but, I will attempt it." Hexe held the box closely to her eyes, "According to the label which has the smallest writing I have ever seen, it states antihistamines. Doesn't that clarify things?"

"No, but do they taste good?" Brujia wondered. "How many does one take?"

"It states," Hexe wrinkled her nose. "According to the text, to get rid of a runny nose. Does that mean people's noses run off?"

"Fiddle sticks, that is impossible. Read on." Hagatha commented.

Hexe continued. "Good for the symptoms of colds. Dosage: two tablets per every four hours."

"Really?" Brujia sneezed again." I should take some."

"If you want to risk it. It could have side effects." Hexe reminded.

"Could I look worse than this? Brujia admitted.

"Is this a trick question?" Hexe asked.

"Oh, stop it you two. These ingredients are just spices and sustenances. A lot of these labels have the words low fat and diet. Is diet the past tense of die? We better not use them." Hagatha concluded.

Brujia examined the items. "For our spells, we will need something more exotic like termite egg juice. I can't find that!"

"Hagatha! It seems they don't stock stores with anything worthwhile. What shall we do? If we use the wrong ingredients on our spells, our spells will go awry."

Hexe thought. "We need our laboratory back. Why don't we scare them out? We could rouse the spirits to help us. Then I could have Sebastian. How does that spell go?"

AWAKEN THE SPIRITS
Strangled through the inside out
Muffled cries, attempt to shout
Awakened from untimely sleep
Scathed by burdens, that must weep
Stirred up jealously and doubt
Now from a stupor, will all come out.

The earth beneath the witches quaked as the spirits exited from the quagmires awaiting their instructions as they loomed out from hell.

CHAPTER 7

DON'T BE FOOLED
BY WHAT IS NOT

Arian played the harpsichord to hasten the children's sleep on the table. Uncle Horatio brought blankets, pillows, etc. in addition to hot assortments of sandwiches. Lucien immediately smelled the aroma of the steaming food and rose while Selena slept serenaded by the music. Even Sebastian calmed down with the piece, listening instead of making sense of the spells. Giselle's wary eye missed nothing. She signaled by chirping the alarm. All ceased and focused on Giselle. She forewarned them by writing that the witches have aroused the spirits of the dead to harass all.

Arian sang a religious song as the pounding of fists assaulted their room. Screams of fright echoed in a crescendo to overwhelm Arian's singing. Sebastian and Uncle Horatio hovered over the children. The positive energy from Arian's singing caused an incandescent light to emanate from the witch's crystal ball. It reflected the one thousand spirits circulating about them augmenting in numbers and fury, bending, contorting and banging their fists on the walls. Their white translucent shapes of evilness filled the crystal, as the crystal enlarged in size. Selena screamed. Hagatha's face and then figure emerged as a hologram as the spirits flew through her form.

"Impressive is it not! To think this is the very beginning. Are you sure your children will endure? You see! Children are more impressionable than adults, who reason. "Hagatha laughed.

"Make them go away, Daddy!" Selena wailed.

Sebastian repeated the spell of expulsion while pouring the elixir onto the witch's rod and waving it over the crystal ball saying. "Begone, begone."

The ghosts dissipated taking Hagatha along. But her echo could be heard saying, "Blast you, not again!"

Selena held tightly to her father, sobbing. Uncle Horatio, Sebastian, and Lucien stared in disbelief.

Arian stated imploringly. "Are you all right?"

"We seem to be." Sebastian supplicated breathing more easily. "Obviously, we will have to make more of the elixir for expulsion spell, but the witches will be more malicious with each attempt."

Giselle started eating her birdseeds provided by Uncle Horatio.

"Thank God that is all over." Uncle Horatio beseeched.

"Lucien and Selena, you can look now. They are all gone. Let's put you to bed." Sebastian insisted.

"Who can sleep at a time like this?" Selena complained.

"You are." Sebastian hinted." Come on. Here, I will make your beds on the table away from the floor so I can keep an eye on you."

Lucien and Selena obeyed their father's wishes with no further delay taking their sandwiches and eating them.

Arian softly spoke. "Why don't you cross reference the index of Debitum Naturae with annihilation. They seem to go together."

Sebastian thumbed through the index for annihilation page 333, which was exactly half of 666. "Maybe, you might have something there?"

Uncle Horatio, munching on a sandwich, suggested. "It is worth a try from what I have seen." He then started to copy one of the spells down on a separate page and then the other.

Sebastian, with the help of Giselle, concocted another expulsion spell for the next onslaught.

Arian sang a lullaby for Selena and Lucien to expedite their sleep. Arian noticed that the children were asleep, as she whispered. "Monsieur Sebastian, I wish I could help you more from this side."

Sebastian smiled. "You are an immense help as you are. You certainly know how to calm the children down. Your songs have a very soothing effect even to me. I should have bought some 17th century music CD's. They are quite beautiful."

Arian inquired. "CD's? I am afraid I do not understand what you are talking about. However, the witches should be exhausted and might leave you in peace tonight."

"Sebastian?" Uncle Horatio interrupted. "Have you heard this spell? It could coagulate the stomach."

"Well!" Sebastian stared up as he was mixing the ingredients. "Recite the spell."

"It starts out with Cerberus the dog. What does that mean?"

Arian answered. "Cerberus the dog had three heads, gnashing teeth, and a spiked tail. Once entering Hades, the souls could never return again. But, first the souls were brought down to Hades by the god Hermes and left at the river Styx. Styx was or is a murky, stagnant, river that flowed around the underworld. Hermes left the souls in charge of the ferryman, Charon. He is supposed to look like a cloaked skeleton, but the literature that I know of, is vague. One had to pay to be ferried across the river. If one could pay the fare, Charon would take you across. Those who could not pay had to wander about till they found the pauper's entrance to Hades. That is why, when anyone dies, his kin places a coin under the tongue to pay the ferryman."

"That's charming." Uncle Horatio contented." I never knew that."

Sebastian added. "Isn't this from Greek Mythology?"

"Yes." Arian commented." I haven't thought of it in three hundred years."

"Well," Uncle Horatio continued." The spell gets worse. I will start again."

DEBITUM NATURAE/ANNIHILATION

Cerberus, the dog, cries at the gates of hell
Mutilates the intended from where they must dwell
Massacred in devastation with mutable disarray
Mottled, misshapen, flailed and betrayed
Desecrated bones added to the acrimonious brew
Created by sulfuric acid to improve the stew
Titrated with potassium hydroxide for the crux
Defaming sounds waves added with a thrust
Add some ferric ions to make a magnetic flux
Consecrated curses, contused is a must
Now add some fresh hemlock aged with time.
Electrophoresised to separate distinguishable brine
Placed into a Infernal Abyss that animates the dust
Shriveled rapaciously becoming musk
Governed by the Alter of Twelve.

Sebastian became appalled. "Where is this place? The Infernal Abyss?"

Arian asserted, "That would mean the Pit of Tartarus, where Zeus locked the Titans that were guarded by a hundred armed monster, also in Greek Mythology. Maybe their souls will remain there?"

Sebastian exclaimed. "How can we find that pit?"

"Maybe, the spell will send the witches there?" Arian concluded." But, that is only conjecture."

"This is a horror. This is worse than a nightmare!" Uncle Horatio sighed.

Giselle's exhaustion showed as she finally, after a previous attempt, maintained to sit on her perch.

Sebastian concluded." I have finished the elixir. How late is it?"

Uncle Horatio scrutinized his watch. "It is eleven P.M. I say we get some sleep, but where? I could drag the mattresses down here. Though, I would have liked to sleep in my own bed, but, that may be risky."

Sebastian replied. "I will help you Uncle. Arian, would you be so kind and watch my children?"

"With pleasure, seeing yours. I really miss mine. Oh forgive me." Arian sighed.

Sebastian gazed at her with such compassion. "I really understand." He went off to follow his Uncle.

Sebastian and Uncle Horatio returned with all the paraphernalia.

As they were setting the mattresses up Sebastian inquired. "Arian, what are you going to do?"

"I will keep watch over your family so that you will be safe. I will use the crystal ball to survey the grounds and the witches. Please, you need your sleep."

"But," Sebastian contended. "You need your sleep as well."

"Monsieur Sebastian, I realize that what you are inferring is true, however, you are the only ones that can concoct the spells. I have spell books here, where I reside; yet, the witches left no ingredients, for I would have tried to escape a long time ago, if they had. For a future of hope for me, you must be rested and ready. If I lose my sleep for one night or a week, I will be tired, but to escape from this place. Please try to understand." Arian pleaded.

Sebastian asserted. "I guess you are right. I am sorry to doubt your wisdom. Forgive me and good night."

Uncle Horatio moved the children to the newly, made beds.

Arian spoke softly. "Good night." She then left with the crystal ball to the chateau's kitchen to make a pot of tea for the long vigil.

In the meantime, Hagatha found herself in a very familiar place. "Curses! I am back at Westminster abbey!" Hagatha wailed. The spirits fly screeching away back to oblivion.

Brujia and Hexe stared at each other.

Hexe complained. "I bet Hagatha is back at Westminster Abbey again!"

"Really?" Brujia answered." Well, I am not getting on that broom of ragweed. These cold pills are finally working so you will have to go all by yourself. Besides these pills make me lightheaded."

"Oh, very well. I will see you in an hour." Hexe flew off.

"Hi, Hagatha. Had a nice trip?" Hexe confronted her.

"Shut up and get me out of here. I hate Sebastian for this! I have been humiliated. They will pay for this. Besides, what took you so long?" Hagatha yelled.

"Bad cross winds. Let's go home." Hexe concluded.

"You would think that you would have brought my own broom?" Hagatha grunted.

"Picky, picky, I didn't have to pick you up. I could have made you walk, so be quite. So, they won the first round. It is the last battle, which is important in any strategy." Hexe reassured Hagatha.

"Well, as we are going home, let me see Brujia's spell book. Her spells that she had copied aren't very good. Oh, here's one, memory-loss. If Sebastian were bombarded with that one, he wouldn't be so inventive. We would have to make it with that tiny pot, but we could enlarge it. Let's see the ingredients." Hagatha read out loud.

MEMORYLOSS SPELL
To simulate a bump on the head
Where facts are lax, from what you've read
The attention span of the intended will fall
Very oblivious of it all
An hallucinating power with a libation

58

Will be the only inspiration
In a mixing bowl combine
Some brandy and a lot of wine
A quantum of lightning to disrupt
So your spinal cord will be cut
In a powdered form of dust
One inhales it with a gust
Resulting in an ignominious oaf.

Arian listened and wrote down the spell, verbatim, so that Sebastian could make it and maybe could dispose of the witches.

Hagatha looked at the spell. "How can we get the ingredients? This stuff that we have obtained is no good. Curses! We will sleep tonight and in the morning, I will make a hornet's nest attack the house to drive them away. Sleep, sisters."

Hexe sighed, "Good night."

Brujia never noticed Hexe or Hagatha come home, all she did was sleep.

The next morning quite early, Arian spoke softly into the crystal ball to awaken Sebastian. "Monsieur Sebastian," she tried again," Monsieur Sebastian. Please awaken, there isn't that much time, please, Monsieur Sebastian."

Sebastian heard her voice and stirred and looked at the time. He rose and walked towards the crystal ball, as he felt his face noticing that Arian will see him unshaved. He was dressed. He didn't change because he had to be ready, if needed in an emergency. Sebastian picked up the crystal ball and walked to another room so not to disturb the rest of the family.

"Good morning," Arian said smilingly." Did you sleep well?"

"Good morning," Sebastian replied." I did sleep, yet, how was your night?"

"I am all right, but, "Arian pressed. "The witches are about to send you a few hornet nests. You must block every entrance that the insects could possible enter, for instance: the chimney, door edges, windows, vents, and the like. Giselle told me that there is plywood in the witches' cave, so everyone must get involved. The hornets can't sting you due to the sanctuary spell, but they will frighten you as they will attack you."

Sebastian cringed. "Selena is so susceptible to insect bites. She is allergic to bee stings if they can sting."

"The witches were also going to inflict a memory-loss spell on you, but unfortunately, they don't have the ingredients. However, the spell duration is two days. This would alleviate us, if you could dispense it on them when the blue moon appears. At least it could give us more time to decipher the riddle for my release." Arian continued.

"Thank you," Sebastian reaffirmed. "Are you going to rest now?"

"No, I will tell you when the witches awake. Please hurry and rouse your family. Don't worry about the witches' cave, it is sealed by a magical stone."

Sebastian rushed to his Uncle, calling his name. "Uncle Horatio, Uncle Horatio!"

Uncle Horatio woke up saying, "Huh, Huh, oh. What is it? Do we have to rise now?"

"Yes," Sebastian urged. "The witches are sending us hornets. We must stop their infiltration. There isn't a moment to lose. Do you have duct tape and a saw? We have wood in the witches' cave. Lucien, Selena, It' time to get up!"

Uncle Horatio ushered the children towards the house. Lucien helped his Uncle Horatio tape the windows and doors while Sebastian, with Selena holding the wood steady, sawed the plywood to cover the fireplace. They then pushed the dining room's table against it and then added more heavy furniture. They taped all the vents in the house and round all the doors.

"Do, you think we have covered everything?" Uncle Horatio said dismayed. "Look what this tape is doing to my painted walls and window ledges!"

"I am very sorry, Uncle." Sebastian apologized. "But, which is worse? I promise, if I ever get a vacation, a real vacation, not like this, I will help you paint."

Arian appeared in the crystal ball. " Monsieur Sebastian." She called out gently. "The witches are having their breakfast. May I suggest that you should as well?"

"Yes, we shall. " Sebastian replied.

Selena held her father's hand. "I am so afraid, Daddy."

Sebastian held his daughter. "Let's try and have some breakfast." He took Selena and the crystal ball towards the kitchen.

Uncle Horatio suggested. " Let's have sandwiches. It's quicker."

Sebastian made the coffee and poured the milk, while Uncle Horatio made the sandwiches.

Sebastian talked to Arian as he poured the coffee into the mugs. "What are you going to eat on your side?"

Arian mused. "You probably wouldn't know, but everything here, I have to make myself. The bread, from planting the wheat. There is no butter, no milk, no sugar, no salt, and no meat. I have yeast, to rise the bread, but even that, has to be maintained. I plant vegetables. There are apple and pear trees, wild raspberry bushes, orange trees, and olive trees. I have to cook it to preserve all that I can for the winter. If I run out of food, I starve, but I never die. I only have the pangs of starvation."

"Oh my God!" Sebastian said in disbelief." Do any of your plants propagate to prevent this?

"I have become quite a good gardener for my own preservation. If I cut myself, or when I broke my arm or when I had that lightning bolt sear me, I never die. I have the pain and heal. Oh, excuse me, the witches are now rousing the hornets from their nests! Prepare!"

Sebastian ran to the window witnessing a horror. A few hundred swarms of hornets approached them. "Oh my God!"

Uncle Horatio ran to the window. "Did all hell break lose?"

Sebastian went to the children taking a tablecloth to cover them. "Don't look. Maybe you won't be so frightened!"

The hornets bombarded the house's windows and walls. But, then they turned their attention toward the windows only. They tried to push against the glass in waves, again and again. One could hear the thudding sounds now banging against the fireplace. The walls echoed the vibrations.

Selena cried. "They are cracking the walls. They will come in. " She kept on crying.

Sebastian suggested. "Let's lock ourselves in the bathroom. It is the most secure or has the strongest walls in the house."

They all ran with the crystal ball and the expulsion elixir to the guest bathroom. Closing the door, one could still see the massive hornet swarm hitting the windows as Uncle Horatio covered the window with the curtain while they waited. The thudding continued for a half an hour, and then all was quite.

Arian rejoiced saying. "It's all over. The hornets are leaving!"

Sebastian released Selena and Lucien as everyone exited the bathroom in relief.

The witches sat on a log brooding with their hands towards their faces and their elbows on their knees.

"Sisters, I feel like such a failure. Everything that we have done turns out wrong. Even the hornets didn't work! It is like they know our plans!" Hexe cried.

"Sister, you maybe right. That means that Arian has been spying on us using the crystal ball. Curses!" Hagatha lamented. "We can't even retrieve it."

"Does that mean Arian knows also about the memory-loss spell?" Hexe spouted.

"Good heavens! What if they are making a brew now? We must be more vigil. We must take watches to protect ourselves." Hagatha groaned.

"Brujia, what is going to happen to us if we forget?" Hexe inquired

"I don't know." Brujia responded.

"But, don't you know? You wrote the spell in your spell book." Hagatha complained.

"I think it lasts two days which could be very dangerous." Brujia retorted.

"We are going about this the wrong way. First, we must speak in our native tongue, so Arian can't understand what is being said." Hagatha replied.

"What is our native tongue?" Brujia asked.

"Latin, you buffoon!" Hexe lamented. "We must find a way to bother them psychologically!"

Sebastian assembled his family members along with Giselle and the crystal ball to make the memory loss spell that he had diligently copied. Then he could equip his whole family with the powder, just in case. So they all entered the witches' laboratory for more conjuring.

Uncle Horatio commented, "We will be experts in spells after this."

Sebastian ordered. "Lucien, have Giselle locate the following: hallucination powder, brandy, wine, and the lightning bolts."

Lucien answered, "Oh, I know where the lightning bolts are. We used it in the sanctuary spell. How much is a quantum?"

Sebastian noted. "A quantum is one unit of lightning bolts. I assume, but if we use more, maybe the spell will last longer?"

Selena pondered. "I like spells when they glow."

Sebastian smiled. "Oh by the way, Arian, thank you for your help. Please, rest now. You have had no sleep for some time." When Sebastian gazed into the crystal ball, he could see Arian smiling back at him, as she carried her crystal ball to her bedchamber. It was a canopy bed with a silken brocade bed spread. Tassels held back the velvet panels.

"If you would excuse me, Monsieur, but a lady needs her privacy." She placed a lace handkerchief over the ball." Good night, I shall sleep for a few hours." As Arian spoke, they could hear the silken gown being taken off and placed onto a chair.

Sebastian whispered. "Stop smiling Uncle."

Uncle Horatio looked at Sebastian saying, "Oh, yes of course, but what about you?"

Arian whispered back. "Shh! This communication goes both ways."

Selena asked. "Why are you smiling?"

Sebastian promptly answered in a whisper, "Never mind. You are too young. Here, put the emerald ring on. I don't want it to be next to the ingredients."

Giselle and Lucien gathered all the ingredients and arranged them on the table, "We are ready, Father."

"Very good. Let's begin." Sebastian patted Lucien on the head.

Upon stirring the last ingredient, the spell condensed into a purple, speckled, blue residue, which then converted into the powder.

"How do you suggest to collect this powder? Remember, if inhaled, you forget." Sebastian asked anyone for an opinion.

Giselle flew to a magical syringe.

"That is an idea." Sebastian concluded." We could very carefully aspirate it up." Sebastian expressed the air from the syringe by pressing the plunger down and then aspirating the powder by vacuuming it, and expressing it into a bottle with a ground glass cap to make sure it would be tight.

Lucien contemplated. "I remember your dream when the witches transported Arian to the Realm of Twilight, you mentioned a green vapor that dispersed through the room with a lightning bolt. Do we need that for Arian to come back with the blue moon spell?"

Sebastian recollected. "That is a very good question. Maybe, it is needed upon entering, not exiting, but really you have me in a quandary in which I simply cannot answer, Lucien. Besides we better make the Debitum Naturae. I want those witches to leave us alone. Let's gather the ingredients: desiccated bones, sulfuric acid, and potassium hydroxide. Note: only Uncle Horatio or myself will handle the latter two ingredients. Ah, yes, consecrated curses, defaming sound waves, fresh hemlock, aged with time. What ever are these? How do we set up the electrophoresis, unless we have a machine?"

Giselle flew to the lists of contents in the witches' pantry and pointed.

Sebastian followed. "The electrophoresis is on shelf thirty five."

"Astonishing!" Uncle Horatio emphasized." It is baffling. How did they electrophoresis three hundred years ago?"

"Don't question, as long as we have it." Sebastian affirmed. "This will probably take the rest of the day. So we had better do it as fast as we can."

Uncle Horatio and Sebastian set up the paraphernalia from the list given. They labored on it for hours. Selena, being tired, rested her head on the table and fell asleep.

In the meantime, the witches, still furious at their lack of progress, paced for ideas of what type of mischief they could do.

"Ah ha," Hexe exclaimed." The little girl, Selena, is asleep at last. I will place a suggestion in her mind to go out of the room for something to drink."

"Excellent, Sister," Hagatha gloated," and then?"

"And when she does, the hallway has a small fault line underground. There the sanctuary spell will be weaker, since the fault line declines back toward the room of the laboratory. So if she stands on the wrong side of it, I will grab her from the other side!"

"Finally," Hagatha laughed." We could kill her and bargain for Sebastian at the same time."

Hexe whispered giving Selena the suggestion. "Rise and get a drink in the other room. You are very thirsty."

Selena, still asleep, but now in a trance rose from the table and quietly walked into the direction of the exit. The others, engaged in working out the details, didn't notice her except Lucien, who noted that Selena still had her eyes shut.

"That is odd, Father?" Lucien questioned.

"What?" Sebastian's mind was not paying any attention but concentrated on the set up of the electrophoresis.

"Selena seems to be sleep walking." Lucien added.

"Are you sure?" Sebastian looked for Selena but didn't see her." Maybe, she is helping Giselle find another ingredient?" But Sebastian noted that Giselle just had flown back with no Selena." Uncle Horatio, is Selena on your side of the cauldron?"

"No, she is not." Uncle Horatio stated.

Selena walked partially on the correct side and partially on the wrong side of the hall. In the pathway two thorny fingered hands, just waited for the right moment to snatch her away, were poised and ready. Hexe was accompanied with Hagatha for a back up.

Arian had an awful foreboding when asleep in her bedchamber. She had her under garments on so she could dress quickly, if needed. She hurried and unveiled the crystal ball. She noticed the danger Selena was walking into. Arian noted that Selena wore the emerald ring. Arian, like she had done before when Selena had worn the ring, exerted her energy to enter her psyche into Selena's body because there was no time for Sebastian to be warned.

Arian completed her materialization into Selena's body as Selena still slowly approached Hexe's arms. Hexe couldn't push her arms entirely through because the sanctuary spell held half of the hallway. Arian screamed " Sebastian," finally making the transition into Selena's body.

Upon hearing Arian's scream, Sebastian, Lucien, Uncle Horatio and Giselle accessed the hallway to see part of Hexe's arms holding more of Arian instead of Selena's body, who was now crying. Hexe and Arian were pulling and pushing each other trying to either yank Selena out of the sanctuary or back into it.

Hexe screamed. "I will kill you, Arian, for interfering with me."

Arian defiantly stated, "Just try, I will never let you have Selena."

Sebastian furiously held onto both Arian's waist and Selena's while Uncle Horatio and Lucien held Sebastian's waist.

Arian pulled at Hexe's nose twisting it hard while Hexe clawed Arian for a better grip. Hagatha tried strangling Arian but Sebastian manipulated Hagatha's arms off, with such strength so that Arian could breathe.

Arian gasped. "Don't let them get a hold of you. It is you, that they want."

Hexe let go of Selena/Arian and hurled a lightning bolt at them both. Arian pushed Selena down and out of the way back into the sanctuary and took it in the chest.

Sebastian stunned, catching Selena, watched Arian on the floor in a pool of blood. He gave Selena to Uncle Horatio as he tried to pick Arian up but she dissipated back into the Realm of Twilight. Selena screamed uncontrollably. Uncle Horatio held Selena and Lucien with an iron grip.

Sebastian frantically called, "Arian!" He took his family back into the witches' laboratory where he consulted the crystal ball. It focused on Arian still lying on the floor of her bedchamber, not moving, blanched white from the scorching lightning bolt and bleeding. Sebastian still held onto his children calling. "Arian, are you all right?"

There was no response. She slightly moved as her eyes teared from the pain. She barely heard some voices calling her. Sebastian attempted again to call her, as did Uncle Horatio, Lucien and Selena, while Giselle chirped very loudly. Arian tried to rise but collapsed screaming in utter agony.

Sebastian said, "If only I could help you. How did you manage to protect Selena? If it was not for you, they would have killed her."

Arian spoke spastically from the floor. "Don't worry. I am still stunned by the incident. Hexe must have been angry or she would have aimed better. She missed my heart. There must be a fault line in the hall causing the sanctuary spell to be weakened. Only traverse on the left side while exiting and only the right side while entering." She gasped as the tears fell from her face." I am too weak to rise. Apparently, Hexe entered Selena's dreams suggesting her to walk away."

"I should have been more vigilant. Lucien noticed Selena's departure, rather than myself. Lucky, for me, I have you to thank, which I can't express enough of my gratitude as I do now. How are you?" Pleaded Sebastian.

"I am in pain." Arian attempted a small smile but never could. "Please check your spell. It may be boiling over."

"Oh my God, and that is the death spell. Please excuse us." Sebastian became frantic. "Help, Uncle Horatio, put the cauldron higher from the heat." Uncle Horatio complied.

Giselle chirped intermittently.

"What is wrong, Giselle?" Lucien asked.

Giselle pointed to the Anthology of Magical. Spells, under L page 1222.

Lucien turned to the page and read." If struck by a lightning bolt, use lightning bolt mending ointment. Apply, with a magic wand, or witch's rod. Father, Father, read the spell. It is a cure for lightning bolts." Lucien jubilantly stated.

Sebastian had Uncle Horatio mix the cauldrons' potion while he ran immediately to Lucien reading it instantly. "It's not a spell, it's an ointment? Where is it located, Giselle? What a help, you are."

Giselle flew to the corresponding shelf and pointed at the jar. Sebastian took it off the shelf carefully and obtained the witch's rod. He rubbed it onto the witch's rod and waved it over the crystal ball. All of them watched it enter Arian's room. Tiny bursts of minuscule lightning flashes progressed toward Arian's bedchamber as it swirled over Arian. All one could see was the vortex of sparks. It cleared and Arian slowly raised herself on one elbow. Where the lightning bolt had struck her chest, changed from being scorched, blackened and bloody, was healed. Sebastian could see the scratches heal on her arms and back. Only the bloodstains remained over her corset still moist and crimson silhouetting her shape and small cinched waist. Her slip had been torn from the fight. She breathed very laboriously.

"Thank you, for sending the ointment and finding it, Giselle and Monsieur Sebastian. I am better. Please forgive my appearance." She gazed at all the faces in the crystal ball. "My, I am not used to having an audience. "She sat up and unsteadily rose while trying to ease herself into the bed. "I just need a little rest."

Sebastian relaxed upon seeing her improvement. "Please, take care of yourself. For you are very dear to me. I am indebted to you, Arian."

Arian smiled, too exhausted to speak any longer.

Sebastian stated, "Sleep well."

Selena added. "Thank you for saving me, Please, get well "

Uncle Horatio and Lucien echoed. "Yes, please get well soon."

Giselle chirped.

Arian slightly waved her hand to say she had heard what they had stated. Sebastian ushered them away from the crystal ball but he noticed Arian's perfume upon his clothing from the previous embrace.

Uncle Horatio detected the fragrance on Sebastian as well. "How enchanting! How was it like, holding her?"

Sebastian's eyes stared at Uncle Horatio. "Unbelievable, as if she was really there, as well as Selena, yet not at times. I can't describe it exactly. Let's not forget the potion again."

Hexe held onto to her nose, which ached from being tweaked by Arian. "You know I missed killing her, when I had thrusted the lightning bolt. Oh, how I wanted to finally end her interference. But, without my ingredients or spells, I can't even enter the Realm of Twilight to finish her off."

Hagatha commented, "Sebastian had quiet a grip on my hand. I flinch from the pain. Brujia, haven't you jotted down a how to dispense a anti-pain spell?"

Brujia, still sleepy from the decongestant mumbled. "Oh, am I supposed to have remembered that? I forgot. I still have ointment. Now, let me see. Where did I put it?"

Hagatha waited. "Well!"

Brujia's face lit up. "Here it is!" She pulled it out from one of her pockets. "Oh, oh."

"What is it?" Hexe demanded.

"It's all dried up after one hundred years, sorry. " Brujia apologized.

"Well, that's just perfect. What are we going to do?" Hagatha kicked a stone in the path but accidentally missed and kicked the log instead, then hopping to the other foot she grimaced.

"That was stupid." Brujia stated.

"Oh, be quiet and think." Hagatha screamed.

Hexe beamed, as the evilness exuded through her eyes. "Why don't we lure them out by transforming ourselves as one of them, so that, if seen, they would leave their sanctuary to save the other."

"Perfect." Hagatha commended Hexe by slapping her back.

Hexe complained. "Hagatha, you didn't have to hit me so hard. My nose still hurts!"

"Oh, that was just a little tap." Hagatha admitted.

Hexe shook her head, but that hurt too.

Brujia inquired. "Who will transform to whom?"

"Well," Hexe continued. "I will change into Selena, for she, being the smallest, would rouse more protection."

"Good." Hagatha came close to hear. The more evil that could be inflicted brighten her interest." Whoever, sees Selena, will come to her rescue, so that we will get one or more out from the sanctuary." Hagatha commended.

"Marvelous, I must say, I like our thinking, Hagatha." Praised Hexe.

Brujia stated. "It still leaves a lot to chance. I better check my transforming spell, especially since you will have to turn so young, that adds to its difficulty."

TRANSFORMING SPELL
To alchemize from one configuration
Barter thyself an altered fabrication
Metamorphosed and rearranged
Until what is left, is utterly changed.

"Maybe, we should say the spell twice? You will need it! "Brujia insisted.

Hagatha persisted. "We must do it immediately, Sister. Arian is quite incapacitated."

"What is Sebastian's family doing now? It is impossible to be precise when I can't use my crystal ball." Hexe raved.

"Sister, it is tea time, Uncle Horatio will be brewing some. Maybe, Sebastian will be all alone in the laboratory. Brujia, change Hexe! Then, we will be ready for him! "Hagatha cackled. "We also need an illusion for Giselle being scorched. The child will cry, that will be you, Hexe, and cover your face a lot."

Hexe transformed, yet, she didn't look perfect. "How'd I look?"

"Terrible! "Brujia said, shocked, "I better zap you again. Oh, it seems that it is the best that I can do, considering!"

"Stop that. Don't I look like a child?" Hexe expounded.

"No, you look like an ugly short dwarf." Brujia joked.

"Hagatha, I can't work with her." Hexe fumed.

"I can't make you look any prettier than you are." Brujia insisted. "It's past the power of magic."

"Stop it, the both of you! We are witches. This is not a beauty contest. Hexe, how is your voice? Can you cry like Selena?"

Hexe cried exactly the same.

"Yes, that is perfect. Now, let's send the image to Sebastian through our crystal ball in the spell room protected by the sanctuary spell. Make sure that no sounds will alert Uncle Horatio. Make the illusion that Lucien and Uncle Horatio are trying to help and console Selena. Brujia, you will position yourself on top of the roof, ready to grab Sebastian the moment he steps out of the sanctuary border. I will be near Hexe, hidden behind the tree. Hexe, will be a distance off the tree, in the front yard. Sisters prepare! We shall win this time." Hagatha gloated.

It was teatime, as the family seemed hungry. Uncle Horatio suggested. "I'll go and make a snack for all of you. Selena, would you like to help me? And Lucien, you can carry the tea down to your father. Will you be all right alone, Sebastian?"

"Maybe." Sebastian inferred. "You should take the expulsion spell and Giselle with you, just in case. She can warn you against the witches."

"How long does that death spell stuff have to boil?" Uncle Horatio wondered.

Giselle looked it up in the Anthology and pointed.

Lucien rushed to read it, announcing. "Another hour!"

"Why don't you come up with us? You don't think it will boil over again."

"No, I would love to, but, this potion is the worst. I think I should watch it. "Sebastian said dismayed.

Uncle Horatio, Lucien, Selena, and Giselle left, but Giselle felt misgivings.

Sebastian stirred the brew carefully so that it wouldn't boil over. Suddenly, he heard crying from the crystal ball. "Arian?" He whispered, but as he heard the sound again, he knew that it was Selena. He ordered the crystal ball to focus on his daughter.

The crystal ball focused on the illusion of Selena, crying with her hands covering her face. He saw Giselle scorched, with Lucien and Uncle Horatio trying to talk to her.

"Selena!" Sebastian called as he ran for the witch's rod and the elixir of expulsion. He hurried upstairs.

Arian heard Sebastian call to her and Selena with such urgency that Arian turned to see the crystal ball 's image of Selena. Selena was stirring the tea. Arian then asked the crystal ball, what image was on Sebastian's crystal ball. It focused on the illusion of Selena, with a dead Giselle. Arian screamed. " It is an illusion! Sebastian!"

She had no time to lose. She had to materialize to whoever was wearing the ring. It was Sebastian. Sebastian was running faster, as he felt a sensation of an entity entering into his body. But, his mind was preoccupied on helping Selena. Sebastian got to the front door, where Selena/Hexe was knelling over Giselle, by the tree in the front yard. Uncle Horatio and Lucien were consoling her.

"Selena!" He shouted, but hearing Selena cry more, made him rush faster. Arian appeared, turned, and pushed against him.

"Sebastian! " Arian gasped.

"I must help Selena, out of my way!" Yet, Arian didn't budge. He was shocked how strong she was.

Selena/Hexe cried even louder, but only in Sebastian's ears so that Uncle Horatio couldn't interfere.

Arian screamed." Stop Sebastian! This, is not real, this is an illusion. This is not Selena, listen to me. Please! This Selena is out of the sanctuary border. She is an illusion!" She held Sebastian back by his shoulders.

"I must save her!" Sebastian combated." Get out of my way!" He was angry.

"No, Sebastian. Why don't you call her? Uncle Horatio, Lucien, Selena come to your father, he needs help. We are at the front door. Giselle!" Arian cried.

"This is my child! My baby!" He pushed her again and he was winning.

"Don't be fooled by what is not! Sebastian! I am determined to help you. If this were your child, she would run to you. She loves you."

Sebastian pushed a little less.

Arian urged. "Call her! Selena would come to you! " Arian still held Sebastian by his shoulders.

Sebastian called out. "Selena, please come to me!" But Selena/Hexe didn't move.

"Would I lie to you?" Arian stared into Sebastian's eyes.

Sebastian finally stopped, but too late. Both, Arian and Sebastian were out of the sanctuary border. Brujia grabbed Arian's arms. Arian screamed. Sebastian had to do something so he grabbed Arian's waist and pulled her back. However, Brujia used her broom and flew straight up taking Arian and Sebastian, like feathers, at least two stories high and still climbed.

Arian called. "Let go Sebastian! It is you that they want! Use the witch's rod. "

Sebastian yelled." I can't leave you nor can I stand seeing you hurt." Brujia flew even higher.

Giselle flew to the laboratory to obtain the memory loss spell as she quickly returned.

Uncle Horatio called to Sebastian. "Oh, my God, Sebastian!"

Lucien and Selena called to their father. "Daddy, Daddy!"

Arian remembered, when she watched Sebastian pull the filigree box from the witches. The emerald ring sent a lightning bolt at Brujia. So, now Arian took her emerald ring and sent a lightning bolt towards Brujia. Brujia screamed in pain and let go of Arian's arms. They were both falling down. Sebastian was still holding onto Arian's waist. Hagatha and Hexe flew toward them. Arian used her ring again, and sent one at Hagatha, To avoid being hit, Hagatha dodged it. But, unfortunately, she hit a tree and collapsed instead.

"Sebastian!" Arian called. "Use the witch's rod to soften our fall!"

Hexe came flying toward them avoiding Arian's lightning bolts, but Arian sent so many of them, Hexe didn't have the time to fire back without hitting Sebastian.

Sebastian held onto Arian and pointed the witches' rod toward the ground to buffer the contact, which would be eminent. They were slowing. Sebastian made contact with the ground first. Arian fell on top of him.

Brujia wailed from the pain of the lightning bolt, as Giselle dropped a vial of memory loss spell on her head. The vial broke and the powder dispersed all over Brujia's head as a purple speckled cloud hovering as it was inhaled and was excised through her ears as a white smoke. Being at a loss, Brujia, just sat dazed. The speckled powder left a ring formed cloud around her head.

Hexe flew close to Sebastian, but not too close for Arian could send another lightning bolt at her. However, Uncle Horatio picked up the expulsion vial that Sebastian dropped to hold Arian, and poured it over Hexe.

Uncle Horatio quoted." Begone, begone!"

Hexe disappeared suddenly as one could hear her scream. " No!"

Selena and Lucien ran to their father and Arian. "Father, are you all right?"

Both Arian and Sebastian were in pain. Sebastian got the brunt of it.

Arian feebly tried to get off Sebastian, but she wasn't strong enough. Arian called gently " Are you all right? Did I hurt you? How is your back? Please speak to me. Say something?"

Sebastian looked in pain but he was holding Arian so close. His mind focus on her, but the pain won out. "My back!"

The children were trying to help them up. Uncle Horatio immediately helped Arian up. She stood weakly.

"Thank you Monsieur." Arian responded.

"My pleasure Madame." Uncle Horatio said enthusiastically.

"Sebastian, let me help you up." Arian urged.

"Please, don't touch me! Leave me be." Sebastian moaned.

Both Uncle Horatio and Arian slowly helped Sebastian onto his feet. His children were all around him.

Selena only cried. "Daddy!"

Out in flash, Hagatha arose and flew at Arian. Arian called to Giselle, to help but there was not much she could do. Arian faced her opponent, as Uncle Horatio tried to get Sebastian to the sanctuary border telling the children to do the same but it was too late. A lightning bolt came hurtling towards them. Arian then sent her lightning bolt at Hagatha's. The bolts crashed together canceling them out in a total annihilation. Sebastian grabbed his children out of the way of the sparks. Arian reached the sanctuary border and Hagatha cursed, flying off to pick up Brujia.

Sebastian turned to talk to Arian as she faded away. "Arian," he called. "He then turned to Lucien. Get the crystal ball, I need to talk Arian."

Lucien retrieved the crystal ball as Uncle Horatio slowly seated Sebastian on the sofa. Lucien gave it to his father. Sebastian and family called to Arian.

Arian was lying in bed. She turned to talk. "I am sorry, I had to leave you, for, I am too exhausted to have stayed. I have harnessed too much energy to materialize. I will be fine with rest. I have some bruises but how are you, Monsieur Sebastian?"

"It's my back. I am sorry that I doubted you. If I had listened, maybe we could have avoided this." Sebastian replied regrettably.

"I would have done the same for my child. I am sorry. I must rest. Oh, is the debitum naturae still boiling?" Slowly she faded from the crystal ball's view.

"Oh my God!" Sebastian burst out." Not again! "

Uncle Horatio exclaimed! "I'll get it," he turned to go. He quenched the fire under the cauldron. Then he returned." Now, I am going to run you a hot bath. The tea is ready. I will give you something for the pain. Selena will watch over you."

CHAPTER 8

THE UNRELENTLESS SIEGE

Hagatha seethed with rage, as she talked to Brujia. "How I hate to lose. I am so angry I could kill some one! Brujia, do you know me?"

"Who are you and can you help me? I am scorched. I can't stand the pain. This broom makes me sneeze. Why do I have a broom? Do I have to clean a house?"

"Oh God, I am stuck with you all evening till Hexe gets back. Come here and I will see what we can do for you. Here, try this ointment." Hagatha recommended.

"It doesn't help much, besides who are you?" Brujia still looked dazed.

"I am your Sister! Brujia, now be a good girl and lie over here. I will feed you."

Hexe flew by at that moment looking quite bedraggled and out of breath. As she puffed in and sat down throwing her broom to one side, she collapsed on the grass with her legs stretched out.

"There you are Hexe, I thought you would never get here! What took you so long?" Hagatha questioned.

"Didn't you see, Sister. My broom fell apart. I was loosing the ragweed shoots all over the place. It's like a rudder. I could hardly steer. And trying to retrieve it going past the freeway was murderous. I still can't understand that we failed. I am so angry! How is Brujia?"

"She qualifies as an ignominious oaf! She is useless!"

"Who am I?" Brujia repeated.

"Stop that! We don't care who you are. Take a nap!" Hexe complained.

71

"This is the last straw!" Hagatha fulminated." We will haunt and burn them out! It will be an illusion of a fire but the smoke will be real. I will smoke them out of the house. No man or Arian is going to win over me! Sister! Oh God, the cold pills I gave Brujia put her out again. Let's start!"

"What illusion do you want? " Hexe grinned.

"Our selection will be, ghosts, devils, dead corpses, and me. They will glow in every window, wall, mirror, and glass. The devil's shadows will dance on the every wall as large as life. The ghosts will screech and fly around the house like they did before. The ugly corpses will pound the windows till they break. Of course, my face will be on every mirror, and glass. This is psychological warfare." Hagatha glowed with evil.

Sebastian was taking his bath when he gasped. On his walls and ceiling were human size devils dancing and moaning some horrible sounds. Sebastian got out of the tub to dress quickly.

Hagatha screamed. "How do you like this Sebastian?" She kept on laughing and laughing.

Hexe appeared next to Hagatha both staring at Sebastian without his clothes. Furiously Sebastian rushed for a towel.

"My your body is handsome." Hexe gloated." I adore you. I will have you, my love for my very own. You will succumb to me. Every wish and every command, you will obey me. I will make you mine. Why don't you come to us now? I await you!"

"You are sick!" Sebastian was appalled." Stay away from me! You disgust me thoroughly!" Complete revulsion was in Sebastian 's mind as he got dressed.

He heard the children scream first and then Uncle Horatio. Sebastian finally looked at his reflection in the mirror. It changed into a larger one of Hagatha as she eyed him. Sebastian left the bathroom to help his family.

Uncle Horatio ran towards Sebastian, yelling. "Have you seen this? There are ghosts flying outside, moaning corpses banging, as if the windows will break, trying to get in and Hagatha's face is on every glass and mirror in the house. The house is vibrating so much the walls seem to be cracking. The worst is why did they pick Hagatha? She is one of the ugliest of all the witches."

"I heard that!" Hagatha thundered back. "I'll get you for this!"

Selena kept on crying as Sebastian tried to comfort her. Lucien's eyes were wide with fright. Sebastian repeated. "They can't harm us. They are illusions." He now held both of them.

"Well, they are scaring me out of my mind." Uncle Horatio added." Look at that! Now the walls are bleeding."

Selena screeched.

Sebastian held her, so she couldn't see as she buried her head into his chest.

" Where is the crystal ball? We must call Arian."

Uncle Horatio rushed for the crystal ball and gave it to Sebastian as Uncle Horatio petted Giselle for comfort.

Sebastian called. "Arian, Arian!"

Hagatha's face showed up in the crystal ball instead. "We are jamming you. It takes all our minds to do it but you won't get any help from Arian, if I can help it!" She kept on laughing.

Sebastian took his family to the center of the room as he protected the children. "Let's try to ignore this."

"How long do you think this will last?" Uncle Horatio yelled still supporting Giselle.

"I don't know! Why doesn't Arian do something?"

"She is exhausted. She didn't sleep for at least three whole days. She wrote that sonnet. She made you dream that nightmare, and then she kept a vigil on us last night. Not to mention she saved Selena and you. She materialized twice. She is dead tired." Uncle Horatio replied." What more can she do?"

Selena just kept on crying as Sebastian rocked her back and forth. Five hours had past. Selena was exhausted and stop crying long ago.

Sebastian declared. "This is psychological warfare!"

Lucien cried." Look, what's on the floor? It looks like an army of bugs crawling towards us!"

"Good God! This is it." Uncle Horatio screamed." I hate bugs. I could try to step on them, but, I would be infested and go mad."

"What are we going to do? Eventually they will get us!" Lucien cried.

Sebastian replied. "Let's try the expulsion spell." Uncle Horatio took Selena as Sebastian rushed and poured the expulsion spell on the insects. Nothing happened!

Uncle Horatio called out. "Why isn't it working?"

Sebastian responded alarmed. "The bugs are illusions. Illusion don't exist, therefore, they can't disappear with this spell."

"Good God! What do we do?" Uncle Horatio screamed terrified. "How long can we run from them before." Uncle Horatio didn't finish the sentence, watching the insect's steady advance.

Arian woke up, still very tired but, she felt foreboding so she called." Monsieur Sebastian." But when she saw the reflection, Arian screamed in horror. She sang prayers as loudly as she could. Arian's voice vibrated, as the prayers were so beautiful that all the illusions ceased.

Arian called. "Monsieur Sebastian? How are you and your family?"

Sebastian ran to the crystal ball." What happened to you?"

Arian looked very upset and hurt from Sebastian's remark. "I fell asleep. I am sorry." Her eyes brimmed with her tears.

"I am sorry. "Sebastian spoke apologetically. "It's that we have been bombarded for five hours with everything that could come from Hell!"

Arian repeated. "I am sorry. I will sing all night to protect you from them. Why don't you take the children to bed including yourselves? You don't know how terrible I feel that I couldn't protect you. I just want to say that I am sorry."

"Now I feel sorry that I yelled at you. Forgive us. We have been under a lot of stress. Forgive me."

"I forgive you and I understand. I am a bit overtired. Please get some rest." Arian sang all the prayers she could remember.

Sebastian holding Selena and dragging Lucien went to Uncle Horatio's room. Since it contained the largest bed, everyone tumbled in. Uncle Horatio was on the outside, while the children were protected in the inside as Sebastian lay on the opposite side. Giselle went to her perch. The prayers allowed one to dream of security, as all of them being so exhausted fell asleep instantly.

The witches were siting on the same log brooding.

"Curses! Those blasted prayers! They might dispel illusions but not entities. Yet, Sister, I can not endure it much longer." Hagatha lamented while holding her ears.

Hexe assured her Sister. "Don't worry, we will start the fire soon and Sebastian will be mine the moment Arian rests from singing."

"How long could that be? "Hagatha groaned.

Arian stopped singing for her throat was dry as she changed to a different corset and slip. She washed the blood from her chest. She then drank some water as she stared at the crystal ball. Horror, the house was on fire! Arian knew that the fire was an illusion, however, the smoke was real. The witches were going to smoke them out. Arian called louder and louder to arouse Sebastian, but the whole family didn't respond. Were they asphyxiated? Arian's impulses of imminent danger terrorized her. Her only course of action was to materialize into the one who wore the ring to rouse them. She scrutinized the crystal ball and discovered it was Sebastian. She doused herself with a glass of water transforming into Sebastian. He too, would become wet. She angled herself towards the edge of the bed, so when she would fully materialize, she would be off balanced inducing him to fall off the bed with her.

Soaked, she felt herself entering Sebastian's body. She could feel his exhaustion and his shallow breathing. She leaned at the edge of the bed and because of the added weight and pressure applied on his body he fell off the bed landing on top of Arian.

Sebastian shocked by the onslaught of water and falling off the bed uttered "Damnation!" He fell on Arian smashing Arian's lower body as she faced him, while he tried to prop himself up by his arms to protect his head. He suddenly realized Arian was underneath him. "Why are you here?"

Arian answered hastily. "The room is filling with smoke. The witches plan to murder all of you and then afterwards, resurrect you back so Hexe can be your lover. So, if we don't hurry and bring the rest of your family and Giselle down here where the air is better, they will perish. We must get to the spell room and transport everything including us into the Realm of Twilight or the witches will win. We better hurry." Arian stared upon Sebastian. "I can't move unless you get up!"

"Oh, excuse me." Sebastian immediately got up on one knee so Arian could move at the same time, dragging Selena off the bed, with his long arms. He gave her to Arian. He then got a hold of Lucien and manipulated him off the bed as he did Selena. "I think I will need help with Uncle Horatio."

Arian rose coughing from the acrid smoke that stung her eyes. She grabbed Giselle and gave her to Lucien, who woke due to the better oxygen. Between Sebastian and Arian they both yanked Uncle Horatio from the bed to the floor. Arian crawled with Selena and Lucien, while Sebastian dragged Uncle Horatio. Lucien crawled very carefully with Giselle trying not to crush her, as she seemed to resuscitate.

"What is wrong? Why am I being dragged on the floor?" Uncle Horatio inquired.

"The house is filled with smoke. We are down here because the air is better."
Sebastian expounded.

"Good God!" Uncle Horatio blurted out.

They managed to enter the witches' laboratory and spell room. The air was clear so they could breathe. Arian immediately shut the door so the smoke stayed out. She hastened to the Anthology of Magical Spells, while the rest of them had some time to catch their breaths.

Lucien smiled. "It is nice to see you again. In fact we can talk to you this time." He still held Giselle petting her gently.

Arian smiled. "Thank you Monsieur Lucien. Forgive my informal attire. I didn't have time to fully dress." She searched for the spell of the Realm of Twilight, entrance not exodus. "Here is the spell. Let me check the cross- reference. Just as I thought." Arian spoke aloud." Only if you want the intended to be immortal and ageless will one need the immortality substance which ferments after three hundred years with the aid of a lightning bolt, but the spell will work to transfer things or persons. To reverse it: if your are immortal being trapped in the Realm of Twilight, use the exodus spell. To implement this use the witch's rod to include what paraphernalia will be taken as you recite the spell. Stipulate, where the items will be transported, by thinking of a location. Please prepare yourselves. I will send you first. I will follow later." Arian announced.

Smoke entered into the edges of the doorway.

Selena grabbed her father. "Daddy. I am scared."

Sebastian reassured her. "We all will go together."

Arian recited the spell and waved the witch's rod while thinking that she will send them in front of the garden entrance of the chateau. Sebastian focused on Arian until she faded and then his vision blurred. He woke up dizzy. He still held Lucien and Selena. He steadied his senses, which still revolved in circles. In the distance he could see thick forests, grass parterres arranged with flowers separated by gravel walkways. He glanced behind him to see Quintessence. It had white stone walls with a blue glazed roof. Its beauty just struck awe.

Selena peeked out. "It's beautiful here. I can't wait to explore it!"

Lucien exclaimed. "It's like a dream!"

Uncle Horatio commented. "It's quite a romantic setting after all this is the second time Arian materialized into you."

Sebastian retorted. "What am I going to do with you? You are an incurable romantic."

The double doors unlocked and separated revealing Arian in her blue silk gown trimmed with lace and velvet. She curtsied. "Welcome to the Realm of Twilight, please enter Quintessence chateau. You can leave the witches' paraphernalia where it is until I find a place to safely store it. I have checked the crystal ball. It shows dense black smoke, so I cannot tell what is the status of your house, Monsieur Horatio Simons."

"They were going to murder us!" Uncle Horatio's fury rose.

"I believe that was their intention, but I don't think they would have wanted to arouse the neighbors. So the fire was your illusion but the smoke was real." Arian elucidated.

Uncle Horatio shouted. "Contemptible! "

But Sebastian interrupted quickly. "Uncle, don't say that in front of the children."

"Please, may I make this stay here pleasurable. Remember that this is three hundred years ago. There is no modernization. I will give you a short tour of the chateau while I show you to your chambers. I never had guests before. You are the first."

Lucien ran to Arian. "Let's go!"

Sebastian asked. "Where did you get all this energy, Lucien?"

Selena's curiosity augmented. "I am excited too!"

Arian held out her hand to Lucien and to Selena. "Shall we, Messieurs and Mademoiselle? This is the foyer connected to the great hall. This is a facsimile of my home before I became trapped into the Realm of Twilight. Apparently the witches wanted to have Alexus Simons feel

at home. This portrait above the fireplace is of Alexus and my son, Dorian. He was about three years old when the portrait was commissioned."

Selena stared. "It looks like both of you, Daddy and Lucien, in old clothes. How did you do that?"

Arian smiled. "I assure you the portrait was painted in 1699, March 16th."

Uncle Horatio marveled at the brushwork. "A spitting image except the hair. How old was your husband when this portrait was done?"

Arian glanced at Uncle Horatio. "He was thirty years of age. Let us continue. It is well past our bedtime. The rest rooms have water closets. Running water is located in the kitchen. I will fill your water ewers and pass out the candles and wicks for our journey upstairs." She took them to the kitchen and activated the pump by thrashing the handle back and forth as the water sloshed into the copper buckets.

Selena stared in awe. "Don't you turn the lever?"

Arian shook her head and continued. "This was already considered a convenience instead of going outside to a well or river."

"Oh," Lucien stated.

"Here," Sebastian released Selena, "Let me help you. This is far too heavy for you to handle."

"Thank you," Arian smiled." But I am quite used to it." She handed the bucket to Sebastian and lit the candelabra." Please, if you would follow me to your rooms. "

They accessed the huge stairway. It connected to a landing, which connected to two stairways going into opposite directions." This will be your room Lucien, and across the hall is Selena's room." As she showed each chamber, she lit the candle, which was located just inside the doorway. "This will be yours, Monsieur Sebastian and adjacent will be yours, Monsieur Horatio Simons. Each room has clean wash clothes." She filled the ewers with water. "The master bedchamber is here." She opened a double doorway." Please, do not hesitate, if you need anything. Just knock at my door. Would you like to eat or drink anything before you retire?"

Lucien commented. " I have never seen such a large bed. It is so high that Selena would never reach it."

Giselle flew to her perch in Arian's chamber. Lucien followed her to catch a glimpse of the view.

Sebastian added. "Thank you for all your hospitality, but, I believe the children will sleep with me. We had quite an eventful day. We will not need anything. Thank you, again."

"You are quite welcome, Monsieur Sebastian. I will only light the fireplaces in yours and your Uncle's room." Arian curtsied. "And you, Monsieur Horatio Simons?"

"Well, I would like a drink." Uncle Horatio hinted.

"Cognac or wine, Monsieur."

"Cognac."

"If you would excuse me, I will return momentarily." Arian took the candelabra as her shadow descended the stairway.

"Please, stay with us Uncle Horatio, until Arian brings you the cognac and lights the fireplaces." Sebastian offered. The entire family entered Sebastian 's room.

"The ceilings are so high, the rooms echo. " Lucien inspected his new surroundings.

Selena stated. "I cannot reach the bed and what is a water closet?"

"I am astounded. That picture in the hallway really looks like you." Uncle Horatio remembered.

"Uncle, not again." Sebastian held onto Selena. "The water closet is the bathroom."

Arian's candelabra's light shown at the doorway. Arian balanced a silver platter with two crystal goblets filled with cognac." For you Monsieur," as she placed it upon the table." and for you Monsieur Sebastian. Let me light the fire place."

"May I ask the vintage?" Uncle Horatio presented a goblet to Sebastian.

"1628," Arian recollected." I don't know, if that is a good year or not. It was, believe it or not, before my time."

"Oh, of course." Uncle Horatio smiled." This is the highlight of my evening."

Sebastian walked to the fireplace where Arian knelt to light the fire. The flames ignited immediately. "Arian," Sebastian sounded serious.

"Yes." She rose from the fireplace almost reaching his height and stared right into his eyes.

"You have saved us all. We are all indebted to you again. How can we ever thank you?" Sebastian entreated.

"You are all so charming, how could I refuse." Arian smiled." It is getting late. I have already lit all your bedchambers. If you would excuse me, I will retire. Good night Lucien, Selena, and Messieurs, sleep well."

Lucien echoed. "Good night, Arian."

Selena being exhausted waved.

"I will retire as well. Good night, my dears, Sebastian, and Arian." Uncle Horatio went to his room.

Arian entered her bedchamber. She reeked from the smoke. It was in her hair and clothing. She went to the kitchen to boil some water. She carried two large basins filled with hot water carefully. They had lids to prevent the heat from escaping and also from spilling. She filled the bath. Upon entering the water with her foot, she heard a knock at her door. "Yes," she answered, as she hastened with her silk robe to the door. "Who is it?"

"It is I, Sebastian. Forgive me, it being so late, but." Sebastian stared at Arian who had partially opened the door. She had her hair down in loose ringlets that fell well past her waist. Sebastian stopped talking absorbed in her presence.

"You were saying?"

"Oh, yes, the children need a bath and night garments if you happen to have any? I would also like a bath. The smoke is on everything."

"I quite agree. That is what I planned to do. Since my bath water is ready, why don't you wash your child in my room while I go back to the kitchen to boil more water for your room? Please hurry, before the water, cools down." She opened her door to show him where the bath was located.

Sebastian entered the master bedchamber. On the white wood paneling inlaid with gold trim designs, above the fireplace, was a large portrait of Arian, in a beautiful lavender brocade gown. He stood spellbound.

"Monsieur Sebastian, here is the bathroom with it's own, fireplace, and screen. Monsieur Sebastian?" On seeing what preoccupied his mind Arian continued." My husband, Alexus commissioned this painting. It was the dress that he first laid eyes on me, next to the water parterre in Versailles." Arian replied.

"Oh!" He realized that he stared a bit too long at the painting and resumed. "That is right. I think I will have Selena in first. She detests the smell of smoke."

"While you get her," she opened her wardrobe," let me see what she could wear. Oh, this is Dorian's. He was very tall for his age. I am sure this nightshirt will fit. For you, you can wear Alexus' clothes as well as for Lucien, since I don't have anything in-between. I apologize. I don't have anything for Monsieur Horatio Simons. Maybe a sheet will do?"

Sebastian smiled broadly.

"The towels are behind the screen by the fireplace in the bathroom to keep warm."

"Forgive me again for intruding upon your bath, but I better get the children. Lucien, Selena, please come to Arian's room so that one of you can take a bath."

Arian had to brush past Sebastian from the screen to access the doorway. "I shall return shortly with more water."

Sebastian heard the silk robe rustling "Yes, of course", seeing Arian's bare legs since she had to make a large step around him. She ran down the corridor with the candelabra.

Lucien with Selena appeared in the doorway.

"There you are, all right, Selena. The bath water is ready, undress behind the screen and take a bath. The soap and towels are next to the fireplace. Do you think that bath tub is too steep? Do you think you need help?"

Both Selena and Lucien ran into the bathroom and behind the screen to observe the bath. Selena replied, "I think I will need help, Daddy."

Lucien stated. "I will be fine."

"All right, Lucien you will wait over there in the leather chair until Arian supplies our room with hot water, while I help Selena in and out of the bath."

They heard a knock at the door. "I have the hot water in your room. I brought extra for your bath, Monsieur Sebastian. These hot water basins are for my bath." Arian held two large basins, which were covered to maintain the heat.

"Here, let me help you with that." Sebastian transferred the basins next to the screen. "Thank you. This will hasten them to sleep."

"I will place these clothes and robes in your room." Arian left the room again.

Lucien explored Arian's room while Selena could be heard splashing in the water in the bathroom.

Sebastian warned. "When you are ready, call me so I can take you out."

"I will Daddy. " Selena responded.

"Look at that. A sword is on the wall over there. It's wonderful." Lucien contemplated.

Another knock at the door was heard. "It is I, Arian. Your room is ready."

Sebastian said. "Thank you. Come Lucien. Let's take a bath in our room. "

"Here, I will help Selena and when she is dressed, I will knock at your door. I left extra towels. I don't want anyone ill."

"Thank you. How do you lift these basins?" questioned Sebastian.

"Practice." Arian stated." Please, close the door when you leave. I don't want Selena to get a draft. Good night, I will see you shortly when Selena has finished her bath."

Sebastian nodded.

Selena addressed Arian. "I am ready now."

`Arian grabbed the towels and draped them over Selena as she picked her up. "My you are as light as a feather."

"Really!" Selena glanced up. "That is such a lovely dress. I wish I had a dress like that."

Selena stared at Arian's portrait.

"I can make one for you if you like." Arian bemused.

"Would you?"

"Yes, but, let's put you on the bed." Arian tickled Selena.

Peels of laughter echoed down the hall. Even Sebastian heard it.

Lucien asked. "They seem to be having fun."

The laughter seemed so infectious that it roused Sebastian 's curiosity to investigate. He peeked into Arian's room to see Selena in a laced nightshirt and a towel about her head as Arian was tickling her tummy in little bursts. Selena tried to avoid Arian by rolling over in the bed while Arian ran from each side to catch her.

"I think I better put you to bed. Your father is waiting for you. Come along." Arian picked up Selena and turned in the direction of Sebastian's room.

Sebastian, not wanting to be discovered dashed across the hall to where Lucien was.

Lucien exclaimed. "What are they doing over there? "He was still tucking at the nightshirt.

I thought this nightshirt was too long for you, Lucien. I guess Arian either found one for you or she altered it." Sebastian seemed amazed as he heard a knock at his door. "Yes," as he opened the door, trying not to look guilty.

"I am depositing this precious cargo back to the original owner. Do you want to take her or should I place her on the bed, Monsieur? "Arian replied.

"I'll take her." Sebastian held out his arms to hold her.

"Monsieur, have you ever run the marathon? Both Selena and I noticed you spying on us. You should be commended in your speed. "

Selena giggled. "We saw you Daddy!"

"Shh! You are supposed to be on my side. I was volunteered to investigate the sound of laughter. I thank you, Arian, for all the joviality you are giving Selena. We have been so stressed and I really appreciate all you have done but, you must excuse us, my bath water is getting cold. Thank you and good night."

Arian had some tears of happiness by the words that Sebastian had expressed. "Good night. " Arian closed their bedroom door and left for her own room, but at the moment she closed the door, she saw Sebastian's eyes upon her. She remembered that look of long ago and what feelings it had always inspired. She was as much in love with him as when she first laid eyes on him in the garden at Versailles.

The witches were waiting outside, as the dark of night and the fog rolled in reflecting and accenting the half moon waxing.

Why haven't they run out of the house?" Hexe complained.

"I think I know. It is my fault. Don't be angry with me, Sister. I should have put more thought into it." Hagatha mumbled.

"What is it?" Hexe screamed.

"I guess, I put in too much smoke. So I must have asphyxiated them. So they must be dead. But, I know off the top of my head, the resurrection spell." Hagatha befriended her gingerly.

"What? You killed my Sebastian! Sebastian! I am stunned, shocked and appalled! How could you do that? My love, My love!" She burst into tears. "I will never forgive you for this! How could you?"

Brujia responded "Who are you?"

"Oh go to sleep." Hexe pushed Brujia's face into the grass. "How could you be so stupid?"

"Now Hexe, don't be so upset. I told you. I can fix him and put him back together again. Now just try to relax." Hagatha tried to be nice.

"Relax?" Hexe screamed. "You know as well as I do to resurrect you need a soul. My lover is dead. His soul is probable hovering over his body right now. But you also need a live soul for the exchange. What do you say about that?"

"Sister, I already know that and I have a volunteer, a perfect one, Arian."

"Well, I feel better. That's all right, we have Arian's soul and body trapped in the Realm of Twilight. But, we can't get to our spell book or our crystal ball or witch's rod. I can't wait that long!" Hexe wailed.

"Hexe," Hagatha reassured her. "The time will pass quickly. So let us sleep, Sister."

Brujia asked. "Who are you going to torture?"

"Oh go to sleep!" Hexe and Hagatha yelled in unison.

Arian day dreamed, thinking of Sebastian, as she tried to sleep, but could not. The chateau felt like a home at last with the children and their laughter. She collapsed.

The morning came in with a burst of sunlight filling the entire room as the sunbeams struck the chandelier in the center and sent off rainbow patterns on the walls waking Arian. She looked at the time as she heard a pitter-patter of feet and a knock at the door. "Who is it?" Arian inquired.

"It is us." Lucien replied." I know we should stay put and wait but Daddy is so sleepy and the chateau is so pretty. We want to explore it. May we come in and join you?"

"By all means." Arian opened the door as they bounced into the room and towards the bed.

Arian asked. "Did you sleep well? You look better. My, my, may I ask? Do you usually get ready first or should I feed you right now?"

"Let's eat." Lucien nodded.

"All right, but first, let's get something on those feet. I don't want you to catch a cold. Selena and Lucien let me see, I think these socks are a bit big, but it is the best that we can do. But, first, why don't you look around the room, while I make my bed, and if you aren't out of that bed, Lucien, when I get there, I will have to make you into it."

"You wouldn't." Lucien looked surprised.

"Yes, I will!" Arian ran towards them.

"I'll help!" Selena said trying to get into the bed while Lucien hid in the covers.

"I'll help you up." Arian lifted Selena and put her in the bed. "Now, we must capture him." Lucien went deeper.

Lucien shouted. "Oh, oh."

Arian played with them and finally made her bed. She dragged her little band down the stairs toward the kitchen. "This is the kitchen. You can explore a little by looking out of the window. You can see the garden right off the side where I will take you the moment I have fed you and made us presentable. Lets' see, breakfast. I have sliced apples, raspberries, toast, and oatmeal with cinnamon with tea. She took a cart to transport the food. Now, let me take you to the dinning room."

Arian went through the long corridor to the dinning room. It had six chandeliers and a very large center table. If necessary other tables could be brought in as well, depending on the number of guests. The epergne had small cream rose buds within it and the beautiful tablecloth and candelabra in gold, focused the sunlight which radiated through the crystal, reflecting rainbow patterns sparkling across the room, accenting the brocade wall paper.

"My," Selena replied." This room is beautiful."

Arian set the plates and arranged the breakfast. "Now, Monsieur and Mademoiselle. It is time we got ready." She took the dishes to soak and bundled the children to her bathroom.

"What do we wear?" Selena wondered.

"You will wear 17th century apparel. "

Sebastian awoke to find that he was alone in his room. "Where could they be?" Sebastian mumbled. He heard beautiful music being played outside his window. He accessed it's location to behold a beautiful park or garden where his two children danced a minuet dressed in 17th apparel as Arian played a small harpsichord. Arian saw the curtains open as she rose and curtsied to acknowledge his presence and then continued playing. He couldn't believe his eyes. He felt he knew the piece, as though he was going back into time. Then he noticed a note on the table with a glass of wine and sandwiches. The note read: Monsieur, I am sorry you were not awake. Your children were so excited to see the chateau and I didn't want to disturb your sleep, so they are with me. I have taken your clothes for they are being washed and are drying at this moment. Please, you must wear the apparel I have left you. I have left your shaving blade in your bathroom, as well as your other accessories. We would be honored and are looking forward to your company whenever possible, Arian.

Sebastian quickly got ready but as he was dressing he heard a knock at his door.

"Sebastian?" Uncle Horatio called." Are you awake?"

Sebastian responded. "Uncle?" He opened the door.

Uncle Horatio looked embarrassed. "Did you see this? I look like a Roman emperor in this toga. I can't wear this. Arian took my clothes, they are washed and drying and I slept through it."

Sebastian started laughing.

"Stop that. That's not polite!"

"I can't help it." Sebastian smiled.

"Try!" Uncle Horatio spoke with his teeth clenched." I forgot that there is nothing to eat in this place except berry sandwiches. I guess I will have to become a vegetarian."

Sebastian stopped laughing. "Well, Uncle, I must admit, you do look good in a toga. Arian did tell me that she didn't have anything that would fit you last night."

"Last night? You talked to her after I left? I thought you went to bed. What did you discuss?"

"The children told me that they couldn't stand the smell of the smoke and that it was making Selena sick so I disturbed Arian to give us all bath water."

"You had a bath! I didn't! I went to bed smelly. "Uncle Horatio became indignant.

"Well, after we put the children to bed."

"So, there is an afterwards! So you discussed that, did you?"

"Uncle, what is wrong? I went to bed after the bath with the children."

"You know there is no running water, except at the kitchen and the water closets. You had that thin girl carry all that water!"

"Well, I did help a little." Sebastian put in.

"Well, I feel that I missed everything, but why are you so well dressed? Oh, that's right, you are Alexus! What am I doing in this?" Uncle Horatio muttered.

"Come! Look at my window." Sebastian gently urged his Uncle.

"How did Arian train them to dance that? That is pretty. I guess I have to come down, but I will be the laughingstock of the entire family."

"Arian will be so disappointed, if you don't come down. "Sebastian replied.

"Looking like this? I guess, she will be disappointed." Uncle Horatio seemed stubborn.

"Uncle," Sebastian urged." Let's go down."

"Which way?" Uncle Horatio was giving in.

"If, I recall, this way should be to the garden."

"How would you know that? Arian didn't show us or do you remember from your past life?"

Sebastian stopped amazed." I guess, I am remembering, " Sebastian opened the door to the terrace.

Arian saw them approach. She rose from the harpsichord and curtsied as the gentlemen entered. Selena and Lucien mimicked Arian, as they also curtsied and bowed. Both ran to their father wanting to be hugged. Sebastian kissed Selena's cheek and hugged his son.

Arian spoke softly. "Good afternoon, or should I say, good evening, Messieurs."

Selena smiled at her Uncle wanting a hug and inquired. "Why are you wearing a toga?"

Uncle Horatio blushed clearing his throat. "That did it. I am going back up."

Sebastian held his Uncle's arm so he couldn't escape saying very pleasantly. "Good evening."

Arian then replied. "Would you care for some tea?"

"Yes." Sebastian said staring at her. "The piece that you have played is so charming and I am impressed that my children dance so well."

Arian smiled and walked to Uncle Horatio. "I am so sorry about your attire. Actually you wore that costume at our fete on June 16th on Dorian's second birthday in 1698. I recall your left it here because you were embarrassed to wear it then. Please forgive me. Your clothes are still drying. I washed them first."

"I am so thrilled!" Uncle Horatio groaned.

"Being such a cavalier you will forgive me, Monsieur. Won't you?" Arian's eyes were very imploring as she gave such a look that could melt your soul. Sebastian could hardly keep himself back. "But, I guess we must return to the problem at hand .We should look at the crystal ball."

Sebastian asked still staring at her. "Where is it?"

"In the study, maybe I should make dinner so we all can concentrate. Food helps the mind. Come Lucien and Selena, I need helpers." Arian passed Sebastian and Uncle Horatio opening the terrace door for the children as she curtsied to be excused.

"It is a lot of fun living with Arian, "Uncle Horatio paused, "than just staring at her through the crystal ball. But let's see what those witches did to my home?"

Sebastian went to the study as Uncle Horatio followed.

"Sebastian, how do you know where the study is?" Uncle Horatio added.

"I don't know. I feel that it is in this direction." Sebastian opened the door. There, on the desk was the crystal ball.

"Oh, of course!" Uncle Horatio commented.

Sebastian asked the crystal ball to focus on Uncle Horatio's house. Dark luminous clouds of black covered the room caught in the matrix due to the added protection against the hornets.

"Look at this!" Uncle Horatio cried. "That acrid smoke will ruin everything." At that moment one could hear the telephone ring with a message being recorded." Uncle Horatio, Sebastian! This is Cassandra, where are you? Why don't you call me back? I am so worried about you. Please!"

One could hear a silver bell beckoning them to dinner.

"That's dinner and how are we going to call Cassandra?" Uncle Horatio spoke concerned.

"We can't go into the house without a spell, and who can survive that smoke. When we return we will have to dispense the smoke, maybe with the expulsion spell." Sebastian related. "We must go to the dining room."

The dining room was exquisitely set as the soup tureens and the platters were laid out with the epergne displaying the red and white roses accenting the crystal glasses and the fine china. The meal consisted of tomato soup, salads, sauces, and noodles. French bread was neatly cut into different designs surrounded by beautiful fruit. White wine was served.

"Arian, the table is superb. It is gorgeous." Sebastian expounded.

"I am sorry it is a vegetarian dinner, but if someone wants to go hunting, and cleans it, I will cook it." Arian suggested.

"Why is everyone looking at me?" Uncle Horatio protested.

Sebastian responded. "Oh, nothing!"

Lucien spoke. "Father, do you know what we did today? Arian showed the entire chateau, not to mention the gardens, and the lake. We rowed a little. Then there are the woods where most of the hunting took place, and there are vegetable and spice gardens. Also fruit trees, orange groves, and olives trees which consists of fifteen acres."

Arian served the dishes smiling at her guests and helped Selena.

Selena became bold stating. "Arian also told us lots of stories about her relatives. Did you know one of them was a pirate? And then there was her cousin who she was supposed to marry at seventeen years of age but he was lost at sea. She would have had to live in Mexico. His name was Alain De La Vega."

"Really?" Uncle Horatio added with curiosity. "Did you love him Arian?"

"I never meet him. It was arranged when I was three years old. Monsieur Alain De La Vega had an arranged marriage at the age of 17 to his first wife, Maria Alicia Alacron. She bore him three sons. She died giving birth to his last son, Miguel. So he was going to wait for me unless he found someone else in the meantime, of which I would be given to his first son, Diego. However, I did meet him when I was twenty. Monsieur Alain De La Vega was forty at the time; I would have been his second wife. He was one of the finest swordsmen in Spain. He owned one of the finest estates in Mexico. He was still angry with my father for not making me wait for him since he was found at sea a few months later, but the mail was quite late, and that

I married Alexus. He even tried to ask Alexus if he would give me up when he came to France to my father's home and saw my portrait as he then traveled to England. I guess he must have liked me. Alexus fought a duel against him for even suggesting that. Alexus considered it an insult and won the duel. It was fought here. I couldn't talk Alexus out of it. I was very lucky. In my time only rarely was love ever considered in marriage, money or finance was important."

"The nerve of that man! "Sebastian vented.

"Did he die?" Uncle Horatio inquired.

"No, fortunately." Arian cleared the dishes from the table onto a serving cart. She rolled the cart through the doors of the formal dining room and headed into the direction of the kitchen. She returned with brandy in crystal goblets and a crystal decanter. Giselle perched herself on Arian's shoulder's, while she poured the glasses for Monsieur Sebastian and Monsieur Horatio.

"Forgive the delay," Arian apologized," but Giselle has written a lengthy discussion about the day's events while spying upon the crystal ball in the Realm of Reality. Giselle has very exceptional writing. Lucien would you care to read it to us? I am sure everyone will be interested."

Lucien felt honored that he was chosen to read. "Yes, I will." He held up Giselle's written parchment. "The witches have realized that anyone living in the house must have been asphyxiated by now. So the only alternative is to resurrect Sebastian so that Hexe will have her will of him. Unfortunately, to be resurrected, one trades a living soul from any person, causing the victim to die. The abducted soul will then re-lyophilize the dead one's corpse as it retrieves the dead one's soul back, resurrecting the dead back to life! Hagatha is distressed that she has killed Hexe's favorite but she claims to know the spell by memory. However, she cannot enact the spell because she lacks her witch's rod to deliver the spell, which is kept inside the witches' lair protected by the sanctuary spell. But that will change when the moon is full. Hagatha made certain that Arian would be used in the exchange because of her meddling behavior. So at present they will have to wait until the sanctuary spell is broken. Hagatha recited the spell verbatim to prove to Hexe that she knew it. It is as follows:

THE RESURRECTION SPELL
Squashed from sod six feet and under
Hackneyed and decomposed in slumber
Languid from sleep in years gone by
Lachrymations, in acrimonious cries
To resurrect, one has to die
Then trade thy soul, for the other to lie.
Interchanged and disconnected
Excised first, and reconnected
Writhing, squirming, before affected
Emboldened upward, towards the sky
Passing each other, being awry
Now your stir, while the others putrefy.

As Lucien ended the refrain, the others displayed abhorrence.

Sebastian stated. "This gets uglier. They condone murder to get whatever ends needed to satisfy their warped mentality."

Uncle Horatio stated. "We better start delving back to alternate strategies to combat these villains. I must admit, Giselle has kept quite a vigil. I do commend you."

Giselle blinked her eyes in thanks to all of them.

Arian commented. "Come Giselle, I have your favorite, raisins. "

Selena asked. "Could we have some?"

"Of course, I will bring them to you so you can feast upon them." Arian smiled wryly.

Lucien bragged. "Arian said she would teach me how to fence with Dorian's sword. May I, Father, for tomorrow?"

Sebastian astounded confronted Arian with a non-believing stare. "You? It wouldn't be ladylike."

"You forget." Arian reminded him." I was the only child until my father remarried and had a son. It was after my marriage to Alexus. So I had been taught at the early age of four in the art of fencing."

"Imagine that." Uncle Horatio's curiosity grew. "How good were you?"

"I only practiced with my father, my cousins, my husband, and with my son, Dorian. He had beginning lessons. But, I have perfected it after three hundred years for my protection since I never knew when the witches were going to finish me off. If one has so much time in front of you, one should set goals. However, in your century it is a lost art."

Sebastian smiled amused. "Lucien, if you want to that much, indeed, I will say yes."

"Me too." Selena pleaded gazing empathetically into her father's eyes.

"Why not. How can I refuse since I am out numbered." Sebastian consented.

Uncle Horatio hinted. "Maybe, we should learn?"

"Uncle, I need someone to help me with the witches."

"Oh yes, of course. Though, I think fencing would be more fun." Uncle Horatio sighed.

"Now back to the problem at hand. We haven't discovered how to deliver the debitum naturae. Arian, where did you store all the witches' paraphernalia?" Sebastian queried.

"In the cellar. I assumed since it was kept underground, it follows that the substances are unstable and need to be stored somewhere cool." Arian replied.

"That does seems safer, if they are unstable." Uncle Horatio professed.

Sebastian countered. "We only have three days to come up with a strategy, which doesn't leave us with much time. We have to find out how long will the full moon be? Let's go to the cellar. Arian, please show us the way."

Arian took the lighted candelabra to the trap door located on the wood paneling from the dining room as it led to a stairway. It held sconces at evenly spaced intervals. Arian lit the candles on their descent to the cellar. At the foot of the stairway, bottles of aged liquors could be seen, racks and racks of them. She directed her followers and Giselle, who flew down the cellar, passed the bottles to a spacious area with shelves. She aligned the witches' paraphernalia as they were previously grouped.

Lucien commented, "How many secret passages does this chateau have?"

Arian answered. "Maybe twenty or more. This house is just too large for one person to handle, so there are sections of this house that I haven't been in for years."

The cauldron was set in the middle of the section with firewood placed underneath it. There was furniture to accommodate all of them if they had to spend an extended time there. On the podium, the Anthology of Magical Spells lay open to the page debitum naturae. The cross-references were listed on every other line, which had to be combined with the Annihilation spell cross-reference stated. Once properly made, place it into vials. The liquid will be ruby red in color. It must be splashed at least three drops onto the victims' skin for the desired effect: death. PS.: No antidote. It is lethal to anyone who accidentally touches it.

"When did you have time to set all this up? "Sebastian contemplated.

"In the early morning, on your first full day here. "Arian responded.

Uncle Horatio stated. "You are amazing to put all this away so quickly."

"I had no alternative, since we still don't know what we are dealing with." Arian acknowledged. "I used the transport spell for the heavier items."

"In order to kill the witches, one has to place the liquid in direct contact or set up a splashing mechanism that can be aimed, dropped and or fired so that three drops or more will touch their skin." Sebastian affirmed." We are planning self-defense resulting in death. Something I thought I was incapable of. But, I don't know how to circumvent it."

Arian held Sebastian's hand. "What else can we do? I have watched them for two hundred years. At that time they wanted to make themselves younger. They used unstable components. Let me see. It was spoiled lightning bugs. However, before they do a spell, they countered it with another spell to ensure that, if the spell goes awry, that they will be able to undo it. They have been dead these past hundred years. Only when the ring was taken, did they have a rousing spell, so from the dead you see them alive. (She noticed Sebastian did not release her hand).

"They don't die? Can't we suspend them?" Uncle Horatio suggested.

Arian related. "Suspension is only temporary. So at some time or another they will return and terrorize more people."

At this point Sebastian pulled Arian closer to him and placed his arm around her shoulder. "You have suffered so long in silence, you astound me. How do you endure this solitude?" Sebastian looked deeply into her eyes with such sympathy.

Arian met his eyes and stared at the floor." That is why I sing so much or play my instruments. Your mind escapes because it is so occupied that those thoughts cannot surface, you have to concentrate."

Sebastian hugged her while Lucien, Selena and Uncle Horatio hugged her as well. Giselle chirped.

Arian blushed as tears came into her eyes while Sebastian held her closer to comfort her. He had a very strong hold. Arian had forgotten until she was in his arms again.

"I am a bit over emotional." Arian stated, trying to compose herself.

"That is all right. I will hold you until you feel better." Sebastian said soothingly.

Lucien and Selena both emulated. "We will all make you feel better."

"Oh my." Arian smiled.

Selena stated. "I cannot reach. I am not that tall."

"Here, I will hold you." Arian bend to pick her up, while the others never let go.

"Very tricky business." Uncle Horatio conceded trying to make Arian more jovial.

"It is time the witches were fooled instead of us. What we need is the illusion of ourselves to lure the witches in while someone will have to learn how to fly a witch's broom to drop the vials on them and be able to get away." Sebastian affirmed.

"Oh!" Selena glowed with excitement." I would love to fly."

"Oh no, not you. It is too dangerous." Sebastian announced.

"Here are the brooms." Arian pointed to the corner. "Why don't we check the index for the spell to fly one? It would be under f."

Sebastian never released Arian from his side, as Sebastian recited.

TO ACTIVATE THE WITCH'S BROOM
Blithe in spirits, so one transcends
To flit and flee to no ends
Soaring like wind in levitation
Rising upward with anticipation
In a whirl, one alights
Hovering, gliding, in delights
On thy broom one tends to sweep
Until lifted, from thy feet
Absconded through, one darts and weaves
Bursts of energy, like fluttering in the breeze.

Lucien and Selena 's faces were in awe upon the thought of flying on a broom.

"I think one should take lessons tomorrow." Lucien stared at his father for approval.

Sebastian stated, "I believe if one starts, one should see if the spell actually makes the broom move. That would be the safest thing to do. Once that is established, then one could practice. However, I don't think I will risk anyone except myself."

Lucien and Selena sighed.

"Now, let us see what the Anthology states for illusions, Under I. Sebastian pursued the index.

THE ILLUSION SPELL
Altered visions to demonstrate what is not
Misconceptions, to deceive one from the untimely plot
Tossed in fallacies, delusions, or dreams
Misapprehensions, to hallucinate from what seems
A mockery or sham to fleece one's ghost
Betrayed to divert it from the real host.

Cross-reference: To make the illusion one has to create the image. A facsimile or replica is needed. Have the person or object set as a virtual image produced by a convex mirror. Place the witch's rod on the virtual image in order to transcend the specter. Recite the spell and place the phantom where one chooses by thoughts.

Sebastian, while contemplating the spell, embraced Arian who still held Selena, with such familiarity as though he never wanted to be parted. He smiled at her as he placed his cheek on hers caressing her forehead. "This could work."

"Well, Giselle." Uncle Horatio interrupted. "Where is that convex mirror?"

Giselle checked the list of ingredients and locations and pointed to the reference.

Uncle Horatio confirmed. "Hadn't we better get back to work? It is late for the children, so maybe they should retire?"

Sebastian was too absorbed in holding Arian with his children. He half understood what Uncle Horatio said and stated. "What was that you said?" He glanced at Uncle Horatio for confirmation.

"Oh, never mind. Let's retire and start afresh for tomorrow morning." Uncle Horatio confessed.

Sebastian holding onto Lucien, Arian, and indirectly, Selena complied. "I agree, shall we?" He peered into Arian's eyes.

Arian was about to put Selena down to take the candelabra from the table, when Selena wrapped her arms around Arian's neck.

"I like it up here."

"Do you? I am sure your father can hold you higher than I can. Can't you?" She delivered Selena to Sebastian who had to relinquish his hold on her." I will have to extinguish the candles as we ascend the stairs."

Lucien volunteered. "I will do that for you."

"Thank you, Lucien. You are very helpful." Arian commented.

Uncle Horatio held Giselle. "Well," whispering to Sebastian." It is amazing Arian had enough room to breathe with you holding on to her so close."

"Uncle!" Sebastian's eyes flashed.

Uncle Horatio continued. "I am not blind."

Arian reached the top of the stairs and waited for the rest to come up. After they passed her, she then pressed the secret release and closure button. Lucien was enthralled with the passage. "I promised Uncle Horatio to bring him his hot water for his bath. I also will fill your water ewers so if you will retire," she handed the candelabra to Sebastian," I will bid you good night when I come up again." Arian reassured them as she patted Lucien and Selena's heads.

"Don't forget." Selena insisted.

"I won't." Arian hastened to the kitchen.

Sebastian took his children up to his room wishing Uncle Horatio, "Good night."

"Good night." Uncle Horatio echoed as he shut his door.

Sebastian heard a knock at his Uncle's door as he heard Arian giving him the hot water. After a few minutes, Arian bid Uncle Horatio good night and knocked at Sebastian's door. Sebastian sprang up quickly opening the door. "Good evening Arian, Here let me help you."

Arian smiled. "Good evening, Monsieur Sebastian. I brought your water and I wish to tuck the little ones in tonight." She glanced at him for approval.

Sebastian murmured. "You are always welcome. As you can see the children are in bed."

"Are they asleep? Perhaps I should not wake them."

"We were waiting for you." Lucien and Selena both sat up in bed.

Arian slipped past Sebastian. "I am sure your father has already tucked you in, I will bid you good night." She kissed both of them and replaced the blankets snugly about them.

She walked quietly toward Sebastian. "Good night, I shall not keep you from your bed." Arian turned to go.

"Allow me to escort you to your room." Sebastian added as he followed her out of the bedroom.

"That is very kind of you, but you need not trouble yourself." Arian whispered.

"It's no trouble at all." Sebastian insisted.

"Very well, Monsieur."

Sebastian closed the door softly, while two sets of eyes pondered from their beds. Sebastian walked Arian to her room. Arian turned to face Sebastian.

"Good night, Monsieur Sebastian."

"Please call me Sebastian. You need not make it so formal by adding the Monsieur." His eyes stared at her.

"If that would please you."

"Yes, it would. Thank you for taking care of my children, my Uncle, and myself especially. I am a widower. Marisa died in a car accident five years ago. Ever since I have heard you singing in the area adjacent to the abandoned gravesite, you have preoccupied my thoughts. When I first beheld you, as you materialized into Selena, I have been struck by your beauty, intelligence, and you loving, forgiving character."

"I didn't know that your wife died. I am so sorry, but I thank you for your complements." Arian blushed crimson.

"Would you bestow the honor upon me? I would like to kiss you." Sebastian inched closer caressing Arian's chin.

"If you please." Arian closed her eyes waiting patiently.

At that moment two heads peered out from the doorway, Lucien's and Selena's.

Arian heard the door, opened her eyes and indicated to Sebastian, "I think we have an audience," seeing the children.

But Sebastian was oblivious of anything except Arian. He kissed her softly.

"Are we going to be kissed again too?" Selena asked with Lucien.

"What are you doing out of bed?" Sebastian turned to see guilty faces smiling at him.

Uncle Horatio then stated. "And what are you doing, Sebastian, out here in the hall?"

"Uncle, isn't your bath water getting cold?" Sebastian said exasperated.

"I have time." Uncle Horatio observed his watch.

"I think I will put the children back to bed. Come along." Arian shook her head.

"Can you read us a story?" Lucien implored.

"No, but I can sing you a lullaby." Arian promised, as she entered Sebastian's bedroom.

"Good timing, Uncle, as always. It could not have been in a more inopportune moment."

"Yes, I know." Uncle Horatio smiled." Age has some fun you know. Good night."

Sebastian entered his bedchamber as he heard Arian singing to the children. When she finished, she smiled at Sebastian as her eyes beckoned him closer. He kissed her again in front of the children very softly.

She could feel herself feeling weak. She glanced at the children again. "I dare not stay any longer. Not only do we still have eyes in here; we have ears out there. Good night, Sebastian."

"Good night Arian." Sebastian released her regretfully." Until tomorrow."

CHAPTER 9

THE SPIRITS OF THE DEAD

The night's chill winds hastened through the trees as the waxing moon glowed. Its moonbeams revealed three shadowy figures huddled next to a small fire, sitting on a log.

Hexe stood up from the log that she had sat on. "I will get splinters from this. I am so bony it hurts to sit on something with bark. I want to sleep on a real bed."

"Oh, stop your complaining. It is bad enough to consistently hear, "Who am I?" and now you. You two are making me sick!" Hagatha wailed.

"I was not the one who killed my love." Hexe complained.

"Not that again. You are worse than a snarling dog. At least you fed it, it stops barking, not like you." Hagatha recoiled.

"Liken me to that of a dog, when I am the pretty one. You are still fat." Hexe spat out.

"Who am I?" Brujia blurted out.

Hagatha screamed. "Quiet, before I choke you!"

"That is not very nice. Who are you?" Brujia sneezed again.

"I will help you, Hagatha. I can't even take this. Don't we have a improve a wit spell?"

"Yes, of course, but they have my book!" Hagatha cried.

"If only we could ask our crystal ball." Hexe cursed.

"Wait a minute. We could call upon the Evil One. He can foretell futures as well. Why haven't I thought of it before?" Hagatha pondered. "I guess I am a dunce."

"It's probably due to a lack of food and lodging, for one." Hexe reminded her.

"We must prepare. The fire is much too small. Um, what could we burn?" Hagatha wrinkled her forehead even more as she thought.

"We could cut off some of Brujia's hair. In her state, she wouldn't notice the difference." Hexe retorted.

"That won't do. It is not enough. All it would do is a slight flair of a sizzle. Come, we must think." Hagatha urged.

"But, I had to scrounge just to find the wood we are using now." Hexe brooded.

"Maybe we should be in a more secluded area for this. We don't want to attract attention. Do we?" Hagatha commented.

"We could use the cave ten miles away." Hexe contemplated.

"It's too close to the water. It drips, which will quench our fire." Hagatha stated.

"There is a clearing next to the lake." Brujia tried to concentrate.

"You are talking logically? Can it really be you?" Hexe asked.

"What do you mean? My head is pounding. It is like everything is not there." Brujia closed her eyes tightly trying to clear her mind, which didn't work.

"Well, Brujia. That is an excellent idea. We shall go there immediately. You can dance." Hagatha seemed to be polite.

"I don't know if I can even walk." Brujia stated weakly.

"Don't worry. You can fly." Hexe replied.

"Not on that broom. My nose is finally clearing and with this memory loss spell and cold pills, I feel terrible."

"But look on the gloomy side. You have your head back." Hagatha retorted." Now we must get things prepared. I know that we should have a Sabbath under a full moon, but that is out. Yes, we should also have it at midnight, on the Witching hour, but we have to compromise. Since Brujia doesn't feel well, we will have to walk, so she won't have sinus problems. We could make a effigy of Arian and put nails into it but, of course, we would need a piece of clothing, hair, nails or something personnel to work with to torture her but we still need her alive for Sebastian's body."

Brujia searched through her pockets. "I have consecrated candles, incense, herbs, and geometrical shapes such as circles, triangles, and a pentagram."

"Brujia!" Hexe screamed. "That's only used for beneficial spells! Where has your mind gone? Are you still sick from the memory loss spell?"

Hagatha complained. "For our summons we need an athame. You know: a long black handled knife of steel or iron used for drawing magic circles on the ground to cast ritualistic spells, or a sword. We need the witch's rod, a censer or small dish or smudge pot used to burn the incense, wood, etc. A chalice or cup, a pentacle, which is a circle of wax, metal, clay, or wood inscribed with a pentagram, of which is a five pointed star inscribed into a circle."

"But," Brujia added. "We must call upon the four elements, fire, air, earth and water."

"We know that." Hexe retorted." I think you have a memory problem. Why are you telling us what every witch knows?"

"The athame or sword has the alliance with fire. The censer with air, the chalice is associated with water and the pentacle with the earth but, unless we acquire these items, we can't have a Sabbath." Hagatha groaned." We should have twelve witches and our lord, for the count of thirteen. We need an offering for our lord so he will return or offer us powders, ointments, and an instrument of evil. But, what can we offer him? (Canned food, some raw meat, and spices with cold pills.) I would be laughed at. It just won't do! What can we do, Sisters?" Hagatha disclosed.

Hexe added. "If only there was a holiday that we could meet other witches. The most important are: 1). Walpurgis Night or Beltane on April 30^t, 2). Halloween or Samhain on October 31st and 3) Candlemas or Oimelc on February 2nd. What day is it? Is it March 21 or September 22 for the vernal and autumnal equinoxes or is it June 21st or December 21st for the summer or winter solstices. "

"It is July 20th, you fool!" Hagatha grunted. "The only holiday that would come close is Lammaes or Lughnasadh on August 2nd. We won't find anyone with this date. We are doomed! We can't even use our Book of Shadows which outlines the ethics, beliefs, traditions, and techniques of Witchcraft."

"So what do we do, just sit here Hagatha?" Hexe protested.

"No! "Hagatha shrieked. "Maybe we can purloin the items? We will slither about in the night. Look Sister, over there, do you see? Uncle Horatio's neighbors are getting into their car. Did I use the correct term Sister? They must be going out this evening. Perfect! Let's just wait for a half an hour and we will break into their home."

"It seems safe." Brujia suggested." How do we break in?"

"Fool, just break the window." Hexe shouted.

"But, Sister, there is a wire and a label stating that this is protected by Home securities. What does that mean?" Brujia pondered.

"Let me see that," said Hexe." She is right. The place is wired."

Hagatha screamed. "I'll just zap the wire with a lightning bolt. It might burn out." Hagatha zapped it. The alarm burst out ringing loudly. "Oh, oh!" She zapped it again and the system went dead. "That's better!"

"Let's wait. I hear a horrible sound approaching us." Hexe breathed heavy.

"Let's make ourselves invisible." Hagatha yelled.

All three went for Brujia's pocket trying to get the toad. However, the toad jumped out into the bushes.

"After him!" Hexe screamed.

All the witches jumped into the bushes after the toad. Brujia was the quick handed one and captured him as the police arrived at the scene. One policeman saw strange bodies squirming in the bushes. Then suddenly the bodies disappeared.

"What the? I saw someone over there, Sir." The first officer pointed.

"Well, where? I don't see anything. "The other officer replied.

The first officer ran to the bushes. "I could swear I saw, forgive me, gypsy clothing in this bush."

"What are you saying? Look, we must call in. Let's look around the building for anything suspicious. "

"Hey, It seems an electric short occurred over here, a melt down with the wire by this window. Yet, there is no forced entry. Do you think it could be just a short and this could be a false alarm?"

"I can't explain it. Should we check the grounds again?"

"Why not? Do you think it warrants a surveillance, Sir?"

"I guess so?"

"I will radio in. All right?"

"All right."

"Sister! How will we get into the house? "Hexe's nerves frayed.

"Why do you always worry? I have a perfect idea." Hagatha consoled.

"What is it?" Brujia crawled over to her.

"I will make an illusion and get rid of them."

"But, what?" Hexe whispered.

"It is going to run away?" Hagatha laughed.

"What is?" Brujia expounded.

"This." Hagatha replied." Observe their car, is that the correct term, Sister?"

Hagatha pointed her finger. A lightning bolt burst out going through the rear windshield towards the ignition, which started the car with an electric spark.

"I don't see it drive away." Brujia stated.

"But, why?" Hagatha stared confounded.

"Don't forget the gears." Brujia added.

"Oh, yes. How could I forget?" Hagatha sent another lightning bolt towards the car breaking the glass, yet, targeted at the gear so it pushed it back one notch. The car drove backward hitting its back tire on the curb and continued over the sidewalk.

Hexe rebuked." Does everything you drive go backwards!" Hexe sent another lightning bolt through the car to push the gear to drive. The car drove off careening down the street.

"Sir, they must have used explosives. I heard it and then they stole our car."

"Let's go after it, but radio in for back up."

"See Sister, we have won. Let's break into the house while we can." Hagatha rejoiced.

Brujia jumped out of the bushes as they all went to the backyard. Hagatha broke the sliding glass door with another lightning bolt, which sent the glass flying. They entered.

"Observe! We need some candles." Hagatha confirmed.

Brujia took some candles out of her pocket and lit them using her index finger as she passed them out.

"This is furniture? Brujia, why are you sitting on that chair?"

"Hagatha, this chair is so comfortable. Why don't we stay here while we wait?"

"Because, you big buffoon. The owners will return. "Hexe shrieked.

"Oh." Brujia groaned.

"Look, I found a sword on the wall. It looks old, but the design is wrong. I think the term is authentic. It seems five years old." Hexe rejoiced.

"Good, I found a chalice. It is a brandy glass but it will do. Maybe this bottle of brandy would be nice for the master." Hagatha suggested.

"I found an incense burner. "Brujia added." What is this room? "They entered the kitchen.

"I don't know. What is in this box?" Hexe opened the refrigerator. "My, it is cold. Can this be cold storage? This would be nice for our master but how could I take it with?"

"What shall we offer our master?" Hagatha wailed.

"How about jewelry? There must be some upstairs in one of the bedrooms. I found some." Hexe rejoiced.

"Good Hexe, very good." Hagatha recommended.

Light from every direction streamed into the house. "We got you surrounded. Come out with your hands up. Remember, we have tear gas."

"We are surrounded, Sisters," Hexe screamed. "They have those muskets pointed at the house. What is tear gas?"

"That did it! I am not giving these items up." Hagatha retorted.

"What shall we do?" Brujia groaned.

"I will put a spell on them, to sleep!" Hagatha voice crescendoed.

SLEEPING SPELL OR POTION
To summon unconsciousness as if dead.
Like comatosis in the head
A hypnotic spell to induce some rest
As if in hibernation, sluggish at best
To drowse and slumber in repose
Somnolent of one's intimate woes.

"Too bad this spell can't be sent by the witch's rod." Hagatha pointed her index finger towards the floor directing the spell at the police.

As the words were spoken, a mist came forth like violet dark clouds enveloping everyone while men tried to run away from it. It rushed like volcano lava and as thick. Nothing could stop it, resulting, as it cleared, with fifteen men strewn on the ground, unconscious. Not one radio signal could be made.

Brujia was elated, "How extraordinary!"

"I haven't seen that in ages. I enjoyed it. Let's go!" Hexe gleamed.

The three witches took their items wrapped in tablecloths and left the house. Hagatha kicked one of the officers' shoes to see if they were completely asleep.

"Shall we, Sisters?" She headed towards the lake.

Hexe yelled. "Hurry! It is almost the Witching hour."

"Let's prepare!" Hagatha took the athame or sword and drew the huge circle upon the ground.

Hexe took the citronella candles, the only candles she could find, placing them on the outskirts of the circle. Brujia started the fire with the wood she found in the center of the circle. The censer or incense burner was lit on a small pedestal. Hexe filled the chalice with brandy. She set it with the pentacle onto the pedestal. Instead of the witch's rod, a wooden rod had to take its place.

"Brujia, what are you doing? "Hagatha croaked.

"I got these dolls. You know the Sabbath needs twelve witches, well, we are only three." Brujia replied.

"If I didn't see it, I wouldn't believe it. "Hagatha muttered.

Hexe called. "The Witching hour is approaching. Sisters!

The three witches made a circle around the fire. Hexe complained." What are these dolls doing here?"

"Oh, they make Brujia feel less alone. Let's continue."

"We call upon the four elements: Fire, Air, Earth and Water."

The three witches then went into their incantations as they danced around the fire.

Hagatha continued. "We call upon the four elements and the order of twelve."

Hexe threw some incense upon the fire as large flames of crimson emanated forth. Then from the fire, a red mist engulfed all three witches as they continued to dance and sing in Latin.

Hagatha then showed the offerings consisting of the jewelry, brandy, and food saying "Sorry that it cannot be more."

Brujia then threw some ingredients into the fire causing the color of the fire to turn a yellow green, which reverted to a blood red cloud oozing.

"We call upon the Evil one, our lord of Darkness, to help us in our endeavors." Hagatha wailed." Help us."

An orange cloud started to emerge slowly as a face could be distinguished. The face was completely red with two horns growing from his head. His eyes started to open revealing a burnt yellow with green color swirling inside. The face augmented larger and larger, one of the witch's head sizes could match the size of one eyeball.

"Oh, Evil one, My lord!" as Hagatha, Brujia and Hexe bowed again and again for his coming and his approval. "We offer this to thee. Please help us, Oh Lord, for we have been betrayed by mere mortals."

Hexe continued. "We need guidance and help to take back what was once ours, Oh, Lord of Darkness! We have given our souls to thee. Help us! Tell us what has become of Sebastian Simons. Did he perish and where is he?"

The face made contortions as if to speak. The voice was harsh and deep, which could scare a soul by it's very sound. "No, he lives!" Fire came out from his mouth as the words emerged out from his lips.

"What do you mean he lives?" Hexe tried to remain calm.

"A soul named Arian has saved him and his family, taking them to the Realm of Twilight."

"Oh, say that it can not be!" Hexe wailed.

"It is true!" The devil's voice hissed.

"How can I get him back?" Hexe cried. "Arian, you will die for this!"

The devil continued. "They have concocted the debitum naturae or the death spell for witches. Beware! They will know of a lightning bolt protection spell and the like."

"Can you foretell if we live or die?" Hagatha inquired.

"I leave that challenge to you! "The devil professed.

"What can we offer you that could tempt you to help us? "Hexe groveled.

"Nothing that you have could tempt me, but for your future service, I will help thee. To prevent them from freeing Arian you must destroy the pedestal! You must acquire another emerald to do this. The size must be very large. I will give a magical athame for each of you, one witch's rod, and another instrument of evil consisting of a small vial, so that you can conquer them. Now leave me!"

"Thank you, Thank you, Oh, Lord! "All the witches cried in unison, bowing again and again, still giving praise.

The face started to fade as the fire extinguished itself by the dripping of the blood from the image that had left.

Hexe screamed uncontrollably yanking her hair. "I should have known! That Arian! I can't handle this. I will butcher you and watch you die!"

Hagatha tried to soothe her. "We have other problems, they have the debitum naturae! But, let us be happy we have our athames, one witch's rod, and an instrument of evil."

Brujia said. "Maybe we should give up! I don't want to die!"

Only the stars danced upon the night as daylight approached, it being of the wee hours of three AM.

Sebastian lay totally awake unable to sleep. Arian mused through his thoughts. He could hear his children breathing as they fell asleep. He reviewed every instance he could with Arian especially when he kissed her. His thought to himself, how not even Marisa ever caused such longings in him? He wanted to spend every moment with her. He checked the clock on the mantelpiece. It chimed three AM. "How will I function without any sleep? Maybe If I ask Arian? She might know something for insomnia. "

He crept out of the bed trying his best not to wake the children. He accessed the doorway. He opened it carefully. He hoped the door wouldn't creak to give himself away. He also had to think of Uncle Horatio. He seemed to have ears that were accentuated to every sound. Sebastian didn't want to deal with him after no sleep. He knocked softly at Arian's door.

"Arian," Sebastian whispered." Do you know what to do about insomnia? I can't sleep at all."

"Sebastian?" Arian whispered back.

Sebastian heard Arian with her silken robe hastened to the doorway. The doorknob turned. His heart quicken its pace as he beheld Arian in her robe with a long braid of thick, dark hair sensuously draped as it went past her waist.

"Are you all right?" Arian whispered.

"I can't sleep." Sebastian admitted.

"Oh." Arian said smiling. "Would you want to hear a lullaby to make you more drowsy?"

"I would love to, but Uncle Horatio has ears. You know what happened before."

Arian smiled again. "I don't have any warm milk which is what is usually prescribed to induce sleep. You look terribly tired. Maybe I should console you sitting on the sofa in your room with the children sleeping in their beds. Then Uncle Horatio can't say anything and we could be together. We really need our rest considering what we are up against."

Sebastian whispered, "I love you so much. How do you think we can get married? Uncle Horatio is a retired sea captain. Maybe, if we had a row boat on the lake, he could marry us?"

"Sebastian." Arian whispered." You have not even asked me yet. Besides, we are still in our night attire."

Sebastian absent-mindedly conceded. "Oh, I knew I forgot something. Arian," he dropped down on one knee," will you marry me?" He looked patiently into her eyes for an answer.

"Yes, I will. I love you for eternity. How could I ever refuse you?" Arian's heart rejoiced.

They kissed nothing would part them. They smiled at each other.

"Come." Arian pleaded." You need some rest. I will have to teach you fencing tomorrow plus we have to come up with a strategy. There are so many things we don't know in this twilight except the certainty of our love, so not another word. We will go to your room and sleep on the sofa with the children."

Sebastian agreed. He and Arian opened his door quietly. They slipped in and left the door open for her honor's sake. She took off her robe, as they lie down on the sofa together, and used it as a cover for the both of them. Sebastian held her close and soon fell asleep. Arian fell asleep too after so long a solitude she was with him at last.

Sebastian's arm fell asleep. He couldn't understand why because his head was on the pillow. He gazed down to see Arian asleep on his arm. He tried to stretch it slightly when he checked to see if she was awake. Her eyes met his and they kissed again.

Arian smiled and whispered. "Good morning."

Sebastian said. "Good morning."

"What time is it?" Arian spoke quietly in his ear and kissed it.

"Don't start." Sebastian warned her.

She looked guiltily up at him and smiled as if to say innocently, me?

"It's six thirty AM."

"Oh, my. I must bake the bread." Arian remembered. "Or you will not have any."

Just then Selena and Lucien woke up staring at Arian and their father on the sofa.

Sebastian noticed them. "I can explain. This is your new mother to be."

Lucien jumped up from his bed. "I knew it." He ran to Arian" I just knew it."

Arian embraced Lucien while rising from the sofa. "Oh how I love you all."

Selena pondered, "And what about me?"

Arian traversed to the bed and embraced Selena too. "I love you two very, very much as if you were always my own. You are beautiful treasures of my soul."

Arian pulled at her night robe that Sebastian still lay on. "Please excuse me. I must make breakfast. I must wake Uncle Horatio so I can use the food in Uncle Horatio's house. Giselle wrote me that it is kept, please correct me if I am wrong, in a refrigerator, which is a strange box that cools food?" She glanced at Sebastian for confirmation.

Sebastian nodded.

Arian ran to kiss Lucien and Selena. "I am too happy even for words. I would get you ready but your father will do that." She kissed Sebastian again.

He held her there for a time and smilingly let her go.

Arian blushed crimson and departed.

"Why did she blush, Daddy?" Selena asked.

Sebastian answered, "I believe she is a little self conscious, but it will pass. I am going to ask your thoughts about the decision because it affects you just as it affects me. Lucien?"

Lucien stared directly at his father. "I approve father. She is so beautiful and she loves us. I can tell."

"Selena, what is your opinion? I love you very much. I want to know if you are happy about this matter?" Sebastian asked earnestly.

"She loves us. She sacrificed herself to save me from that ugly witch." Selena replied." She always kisses me."

Sebastian hugged both his children, "You mean the world to me and it will include Arian. Let's pick some flowers for her in the garden when we are ready. Oh, I better shave. Come let's be off." Sebastian heard running footsteps, followed by a knock at his door. Arian opened the door. She was dressed in a beautiful white silk brocade dress with lace trimmings.

"May I come in so I can kiss you and then make your breakfast."

"Please. You look beautiful and you are so fast."

Arian apologized. "I know it is not ladylike to run but I am so late. Where are my children?" She looked at Sebastian again.

"Here we are!" Lucien and Selena answered her.

Arian kissed and hugged them. "You are so precious to me. And where is my charming cavalier that has swept me off my feet again?" She ran to Sebastian and fully kissed him with such tenderness that he couldn't think straight at all." If I don't hurry, you won't have breakfast. Oh dear, I am so happy." Arian waved good-bye. "Adieu, until breakfast. I better wake Uncle Horatio." She softly closed the door. She then knocked at Monsieur (Uncle) Horatio's door.

"Yes, who is it?" Uncle Horatio stated.

"Forgive me for waking you. It is I, Arian." She spoke softly.

"I will be with you in a minute." Uncle Horatio went to the door. "Arian, you look lovely in that. What can I do for you?"

"I would like to ask you if I could use some of your food supplies at your home? I am sorry to ask, but I don't usually feed so many. I am in short supply. Giselle has written that you hold perishables in a refrigerator. I could use the transport spell to rid your house of smoke and transfer what I need here. Do I have your permission? I want to make breakfast special."

"I don't mind, not at all." Uncle Horatio assured her.

"Thank you." Arian curtsied. "Please go back to sleep." Arian descended the stairs.

Uncle Horatio repeated what Arian had said. "Special. What has Sebastian done?" He walked to Sebastian's door and knocked.

Lucien answered. "I am coming, who is it?"

"Your Uncle." Uncle Horatio replied.

Lucien opened the bedroom door. "Good morning, Uncle."

"And where are you off to? You are dressed so early." Uncle Horatio implied.

"I am supposed to pick flowers with Selena for our new mother." Lucien responded promptly.

Uncle Horatio practically choked. "What?" He gasped.

Selena put on her shoes and continued. "Daddy couldn't sleep so he brought Arian to our room, with us. They slept on the couch together so all of us would be safe."

Uncle Horatio blanched white. "You run along now and pick some flowers, while I will stay here and have a few choice words with your Father. Make haste and be careful."

Sebastian was shaving when he saw his Uncle with a very stern look of disapproval upon his face coming towards him.

"Good morning, Uncle. What brings you here so early? "Sebastian stopped talking seeing the mood Uncle Horatio was exhibiting.

"You! I thought I could trust you more than that. From what I hear from the children, you should be ashamed of yourself. It is outrageous with children about. I am so shocked I am at a loss of words except these. You are a rogue!" Uncle Horatio blurted out. "Your Father wouldn't even approve!"

"Dear Uncle Horatio. I proposed to Arian last night, and she consented to marry me. I couldn't sleep so for honor's sake we fell asleep on the couch with the children. So the only thing that happened was that I kissed her and held her all night which for me was ecstasy. I told her that you would marry us being a retired sea captain on a rowboat on the lake. So stop shaking. You will upset your metabolism. She loves me!"

"It is still not as proper as I thought. But I can understand. She was alone for three hundred years. My God, I can't even imagine being alone so long. Do the children approve?" Uncle Horatio queried with some concern.

"They said that they approve. We shall see. How did they sound to you? You would be considered an ally if they did disapprove." Sebastian scrutinized his Uncle carefully.

"They seemed ecstatic on choosing flowers for their new mother which was a direct quote." Uncle Horatio confirmed.

"This means so much to me." Sebastian, lost in happiness, looked in a daze.

Uncle Horatio stated. "Sebastian, you have to be reasonable. You have to snap out of this daze. There are three venomous witches after you in particular and they don't care who gets in the way. How are we going to solve this problem if all you can do is think of Arian? They pose a real threat. How do you think that we got here, in the Realm of Twilight? What about telling your sister? Would she even believe us? I don't know if it is not a dream? Would you believe it?"

"You are right. We will have to wait for the wedding. Arian did mention that she was going to teach me fencing and something about the out come of twilight, which I fell asleep and didn't hear it. What did she mean? Well I am ready. I better check on the children."

"What about me? I am not ready yet." Uncle Horatio answered.

"Hurry." Sebastian responded.

Harpsichord music echoed through the house. Arian played out of sheer happiness as the intricate pieces were played with such ease revealing the spirit of anticipation and excitement from one accompaniment to another.

"Excuse me, Uncle Horatio. I don't want to be parted from her. I must get the children. I told them to pick the prettiest flowers."

"Lost your head again." Uncle Horatio shook his head. "You are a hopeless case." He smiled and then hastened to his room to get ready.

Giselle flew with Lucien and Selena in choosing flowers for Arian while they ran through the gardens.

Arian implemented the transport spell to vacate the smoke from Uncle Horatio's house. She had it exit by the chimney as not to bring too much attention. Though, with the witches in constant observance, detection was questionable. Arian focused on the box that contained the perishables. She transferred the refrigerator in its entirety but noticed too late that a black line detached rather forcibly from the wall as it popped out. It landed by the stables because she wanted it not to be too obvious. She pondered on how out of place this metal object was. Its height matched hers. How does one open it? It wasn't locked and there was an edge. She thought to herself. Lucien, she will ask Lucien. Now where were the children? She did not have to look hard. She heard the laughter echoing in the garden. She knew of a short cut so she hastened towards them.

Sebastian waited in Uncle Horatio's room for him to get ready and noticed Arian emerging from a secret door covered by ivy whispering to the children as they earnestly tried to conceal the flowers behind their backs. She kidnapped them rushing away. "Uncle Horatio, what is she up to?"

"I beg your pardon, I didn't catch that. You were talking to the window." Uncle Horatio reiterated." I am ready. Let's have breakfast. I am famished."

"I will meet you downstairs. It seems I will have to pick my own flowers." Sebastian hurried.

"Very well," Uncle Horatio shook his head again.

Sebastian chose red roses as he ran around from the front so as not to be noticed by anyone. He slackened his pace when he came to the dining room in route to the kitchen. He heard Arian in utter amazement about something? But what! Uncle Horatio seemed to be talking but he couldn't decipher it. "Arian?" Sebastian announced himself. "Good morning, I had planned to come with the children but you seemed to hurry them away? " He presented her with the roses.

Arian rushed up to him kissing his cheek." Good morning." She took the roses as tears came to her eyes. "It is not a mystery. It is just when I transported the refrigerator, I had no idea how it opened or of the strange things it contained. So I needed help for your breakfast this morning. It is ready on the dinning room table. Shall we? I should put these in water."

Sebastian gazed into her eyes. "Let me kiss you again."

She complied while blushing again in his arms.

Uncle Horatio noted. "Arian, he is so smitten on you, he has lost his head. Oh by the way, congratulations on your betrothal." Arian smiled back. "Thank you." She walked arm and arm with Sebastian to the dining room as she held onto the children by putting the remaining arm around both of them while still holding the roses.

Uncle Horatio walked in with Giselle on his shoulder.

Sebastian held out the chair for Arian while Lucien did so for Selena who adored the attention. Uncle Horatio seated himself.

Sebastian commented." The dining table setting looks beautiful. The silver platters of French bread, fruits with sugar icing, the deviled eggs, and bacon strips. Served with hot coffee or tea with cream and sugar, even butter."

"Please serve yourselves. Everything looks so rich; I probably am not used to it. So I will have my usual, oatmeal with fruit. I apologize." Arian glanced at Uncle Horatio." Oh, I forgot. May I call you Uncle Horatio?" Her eyes entreated him with a hopeful smile.

"Of course you can." Uncle Horatio replied.

Arian rose from the table and kissed Uncle Horatio's cheek and then re-seated herself.

Now Uncle Horatio seemed to be very touched that Sebastian stated. "Now who lost whose head?" His eyes mocked his Uncle.

Uncle Horatio smiled. "I see what you mean. What is on the agenda for today?"

Arian, who helped the children with the dishes and poured the milk suggested. "A fencing lesson followed by how to fly a broom, followed by incantations and how to solve the riddle."

Both Lucien's and Selena's eyes brimmed with excitement.

Lucien commented. "Sounds great! When can we start?"

"You must finish your breakfast. You will need it for energy." Arian smiled.

"I like the broom part the best." Selena reminded everyone.

"I think this will be quite exhilarating." Sebastian stated.

They finished breakfast while Arian placed all the dishes, utensils and leftovers away. She had help, even with Sebastian, who asked what he could do. While they made semblance in the kitchen, which took forever for Lucien, they made their way to a field close to the courtyard.

An area none of them had seen before. It was close to the far side of the house. Arian opened the doorway of an adjoining stone building where an arrangement of swords, foils and rapiers had been mounted on the wall. Arian grabbed a light one. She opened a cabinet where face masks, padding and leather gloves had been stored on shelves.

"You will be needing all of this gear. Padding is placed over the chest and shoulders. Gloves, for your hands, will be worn because you will be cut by the rapier's edges and the point. Facemasks are obvious to protect your heads. Please put them on while I change." Arian urged.

"What are you going to wear?" Selena asked." Maybe I shall change too."

Arian smiled. "I have a long gown which is impractical for fencing. However, with your modern attire it allows you more freedom in movement. I will be in my undergarments and boots. If you will excuse me I will change in here."

Sebastian had a broad smile. "We will await you.'"

Uncle Horatio stated. "Steady. Let 's put this gear on." He looked over the equipment.

Arian emerged in a corset over a gathered shirt and slip with boots that went from her feet to her knees.

Sebastian held his breath as he admired her.

"Let's begin. When you practice slowly, you learn faster. I will show you the basic movements in which you will practice including lunges. We will start in how to hold your rapier. The hilt is used to protect yourself in case your opponent tries to cut your hand off."

Selena gasped.

"It is a blood thirsty business but for protection one has to learn." Arian stated. "The -blade cut is similar to knife cuts. You realize how bad it is only afterwards. Here I will demonstrate on these candles that are on the table." Arian slashed at the candles, which didn't seem to be effected. She then pounded the table with her foot and the candles split in two halves and vertically falling in sections onto the table.

Lucien was in awe, as did the rest of them.

Uncle Horatio stated matter-of-factly. "This is what you are going to marry? She seems quite handy with that thing."

Lucien shouted. "I want to learn!"

Arian recollected, "I know when my father taught me, I was just as excited as you are. Please position yourselves at an angle, in that way the less of a target you will be. Let's go outside. The fresh air will cool us when we exert ourselves."

They followed Arian to the adjacent courtyard, where effigies stood lined up. Focused down the middle stood a large wooden target with red for the bulls' eye in the center followed by other colors.

"When you fence, you do it in cold blood. It means you kill not based on a rush of emotions but with the analysis of how to combat your opponent." Arian summarized, "and remember, to be equiponderate or balanced."

"Arian!" Hexe's voice rattled the Realm of Twilight as thunderbolts flashed through the sky. "I will kill you in any excruciating way possible for taking Sebastian away from me! I will cut your entrails out and set them on fire when you are still alive." Hexe screamed violently and then cackled.

Arian said matter-of-factly, "Prepare, I await you, till honor is satisfied."

Selena cried still hearing Hexe laughing and ran to her father. Both Uncle Horatio and Sebastian were stunned at the evilness pouring out in the vile threats. Lucien kept staring at Arian who didn't seem to be perturbed at all.

Arian admitted, after Hexe finally stopped screaming, while looking at Sebastian. "It was always a matter of time, but when you are attacked, the best defense is a good offense." She threw her rapier behind her as it penetrated the center of the bulls' eye on the target. It swayed from side to side from the effort that was exerted back and forth rhythmically.

Sebastian marveled. "Impressive."

Lucien opened his mouth like a codfish watching the rapier still swing back and forth.

"Shall we continue?" Arian spoke calmly.

Sebastian commented. "Show me how, so I can do that." He gave Selena to Uncle Horatio so Selena could feel still secure.

Arian demonstrated to Sebastian how to stand and slowly gave him instructions on how to throw the rapier in the same manner. Arian brought him twelve rapiers for Sebastian to practice. The first one he threw hit the target. It was not the bulls' eye but close enough.

Arian replied. "I am very impressed for a beginner. Maybe I have underestimated you. I am very proud of you. Please continue."

Arian then went to her new daughter, to hold her and comfort her. She hugged Selena and tried to coax her to try to pick up a rapier but, Arian noticed that Selena was too upset so Arian held Selena in one arm trying to give instructions to Uncle Horatio who was next. Lucien then followed, he was very proud of Arian and wanted to be just like her.

Arian then went back to the regular lesson. She had Uncle Horatio hold Selena for a little while, as Sebastian and Arian started.

Arian demonstrated saying. "You should hold your rapier or foil like this for this practice, so that one can not knock it out of one's hand. *En garde,* "as she showed the basic steps and she gently provoked Sebastian to fight. At the end Sebastian seemed to feel quite comfortable with the foil, as if he had known before.

Arian replied. "Monsieur, you seem to remember. I am quite taken with you. You have impressed me greatly. Maybe, you would like your old sword better. You always told me, it gave you more balance." She handed the sword from her own hand showing it. "See, you had it engraved. I use it constantly here." She handed it to Sebastian.

Sebastian picked it up and saw the engravings stating. "The property of Alexus Simons." Sebastian just stared at it.

"Let me spend more time with Lucien and you should duel with your Uncle. Selena?" Arian inquired. "How do you feel? Do you want me to hug you again?"

Selena appeared calmer, but answered. "All right I need another hug." She ran to Arian.

"My, my, those ugly words upset you so. I wish I could make you feel better but I must help Lucien. Come, let's go together."

Uncle Horatio stated. "You seem to be doing the best out of all of us! Even Lucien is doing better than I. I am so upset!"

Sebastian lunged at his Uncle, making Uncle Horatio lose his foil. "Touche'!" Sebastian repeated.

"Maybe," Uncle Horatio said, "I will hold Selena so I will feel better."

Arian noticed a sad pupil and told Lucien, "Go, duel with your father. I will try to coax Uncle Horatio a bit."

Lucien ran to his father as Sebastian welcomed the challenge.

"Uncle Horatio," Arian curtsied and replied." Please, don't feel so bad. You just need some coaxing. Let me work with you. When one makes mistakes one learns better."

"You seem to be a philosopher too." Uncle Horatio tried again.

"You are doing better, but maybe we should have some refreshments." Arian grabbed Selena and picked her up into the air and then pulled her towards her close. "Let's try flying, I know nothing on the topic. I brought the brooms out this morning. I have the spell written in my pocket. Shall we go to the house for some lemonade?"

Lucien ran to Arian. "Yes," he replied gingerly.

Arian brought Selena to Sebastian. "Can you hold her while Lucien and I put the swords away?"

Sebastian kissed Arian's cheek as he picked up his daughter.

Lucien and Arian picked up the swords as Uncle Horatio walked towards Sebastian.

"This insult is no joke. I am still shocked by those words. I hope you are the best swordsman possible." Uncle Horatio whispered.

"I will do anything to protect my family." Sebastian held Selena to cheer her up.

Arian and Lucien joined them. They all walked towards the house as Arian carried her dress with her.

"Where should we practice?" Lucien became inspired.

Sebastian suggested. "In a place where there are as few trees as possible so that we won't be entangled in them." He looked at Arian to name the place.

Arian smiled. "That would mean the meadow area. There is lots of grass and some soft earth and hardly any trees. Maybe I should prepare a quick lunch. I don't how long it takes us to become proficient at it."

All of them went to the kitchen as Uncle Horatio and Arian made the sandwiches and Sebastian poured more lemonade.

"This is going to be fun." Lucien became more excited.

Sebastian and Uncle Horatio held the brooms and Arian carried Selena. Selena exhibited more excitement being more relaxed.

Sebastian placed one of the brooms on the ground reciting the spell. The broom responded as it vibrated and hovered over two feet above. Sebastian approached it carefully. Arian and the rest of the family also examined it closely.

"Be careful." Arian kissed his cheek.

Sebastian looked at her with longings but the excitement enthralled him as well. He picked up the broom and held it tight as he sat upon it. The broom took off. Sebastian breathlessly maintained his balance while flying. "I am going to try to land this thing," as he braced himself.

The broom responded to his thoughts. The broom slowed and then stopped about three feet above the ground so that he could get off with ease.

Lucien ran to his father. "May I go with you?"

"Certainly." Sebastian placed Lucien in front of himself so Sebastian could have a better hold of his son.

Uncle Horatio took another broom and recited the spell and got onto his. "Let's go together. Sebastian, you can pick up the pieces if I fall."

Sebastian laughed. "No, you will do fine. Your thoughts control the speed and the landing. So go slow. Sebastian with Lucien took off. "Now, Lucien, use your thoughts to direct the broom for yourself."

Lucien said proudly. " All right, Father!"

Uncle Horatio absorbed in the scenery almost hit a tree as Sebastian rushed past him grabbing Uncle Horatio's broom so that he would miss it.

"Thank you. " Uncle Horatio flushed.

Both Sebastian and Uncle Horatio landed as Arian gave Selena to Sebastian and Lucien went to the last broom and recited the spell. Lucien and Arian got on the third broom together.

Arian replied. "I am ready. You will fly. I will be the passenger."

"Oh," Lucien blurted. "I love flying. Maybe, I should become a pilot and fly planes."

"Planes?" Arian was puzzled. "Do you mean plan by the Greek word Platanus or platys meaning broad as in leaves or the word plane as in flat, level, or even. Lying on a surface that is plane, from the Latin word planus?"

"No," Lucien stated. "I mean an airplane."

"I am at a loss." Arian felt antiquated. "Please, explain. I will be asking you for so many things." Arian spoke gently. "I really need you."

Lucien expounded. "It is an aircraft heavier than air, that is kept aloft by the aerodynamics forces of air upon the wing driven by jet propulsion. Well, that's what my father says. I don't really understand it. It is a machine as big as a house yet long not wide, which holds passengers on it while it flies between continents. That is how we flew from our home in Montreal to London."

Arian stared amazed. "From Montreal to London. My technology has improved to actually fly. But, why does you Father live in Montreal? Did he offend a monarch to be sent to a colony?"

Lucien seemed surprised. "What monarch? Do you mean a butterfly?"

"No," Arian stated. "In the genus butterfly there is a species called Monarch. However, the monarch I am referring to means a King."

"Oh, I guess you wouldn't know but Canada is a country not owned by England anymore."

"Oh," Arian stated in a matter of fact. "I thought it was owned by France. Well, let us enjoy the ride. It is beautiful up here." Arian held onto Lucien's waist.

Selena finally cheered up. "Daddy, I love to fly. Can we take the brooms home so we can play and fly with them?"

Sebastian replied. "I don't know if we destroy the witches, if the witches' brooms will work, but, it would be fun." He held on to his Selena with such pride.

Sebastian saw Lucien and Arian coming closer towards them as he flew parallel to get along side them.

"Are you enjoying yourself?" Arian beheld him with such loving eyes.

"Yes, immensely, so I guess we must go on o the spells. "Sebastian said regretfully.

Lucien reiterated. "Arian wants to know why we live in Montreal? Arian thinks a King banished you there, being a colony, because you offended a monarch. Did I say that correctly, Arian or should I say Mommy?"

"Yes, you did." Arian blushed.

Sebastian's eyes met hers. "Arian, my father moved us there due to a job opportunity. He was a curator for the museum. There are not so many Kings and Queens that even have power now, but of course, you wouldn't know that. I love you. You will learn all about it soon enough." His eyes mocked her.

Uncle Horatio just flew by. "My, this is fun. I don't even want to stop. But, I am sure that is what you are contemplating, isn't it?"

"Yes," said Sebastian. He started the landing run.

Lucien followed his father, as did Uncle Horatio. They all dismounted and picked up the brooms and headed towards the house. Arian made some tea and snacks as they entered the spell room by the secret passage. The children loved going through any secret passage. Giselle flew with them telling Arian everything that she had over heard by her chirps. Arian brought the crystal ball.

"So, there you are." Sebastian had waited impatiently for Arian. "What took you so long?" His eyes were fixed upon her so one could feel the connection that drew them together.

Arian whispered. "Sebastian," as she tried to attract only the attention of Sebastian and Uncle Horatio, not the children. Arian forlornly gazed at the children who were playing with Giselle.

"What is it?" Sebastian's anxiety grew.

"Giselle told me that the witches know everything about the spell, debitum naturae and that the Devil has given them magical athames, which are swords that correlate with fire being one of the four elements. They also acquired the witch's rod with extra magical elements. The Devil told the witches to acquire the largest emerald to destroy the pedestal."

"There is such an entity as a Devil?" Sebastian seemed shocked.

"Well maybe he was a demon. I can't explain it." Arian responded. "However, with the witch's rod, the witches can conjure themselves a crystal ball. Let me see in the Anthology how to create one, under the letter C." Arian scanned through the pages. "According to the Anthology, the only way to fabricate one is to acquire this list of substances. (Please refer to the footnote.) It is listed in the text that the substances are infrequent and paranormal. The witches would require the use of their laboratory along with their substances for its creation."

Sebastian interrupted. "What if they could access this crystal ball through their newly acquired witch's rod to do whose bidding let alone steal it?"

Arian perused the fine print under the activation spell of the crystal ball. Arian's eye's scrutinized the minuscule lettering. "The sanctuary spell prevents any intervention from the witches through the witch's rod."

Sebastian pondered. "But the sanctuary spell is negated by the full moon. If only we could have the crystal ball adhere to only our commands."

Giselle chirped wildly flapping her wings while pointing at the adjoining page. Lucien tried to calm her by petting her. "See! This print is so small, I will need a magnifying glass."

Uncle Horatio commented. "Lucien, I have one in my pocket. Here you are."

Three persons and Giselle attempted to read the Anthology of Magical Spells.

"It says." Arian adjusted her head to attain more light. "A encircled acquisition clause."

Selena asked. "What is that?"

Sebastian smiled wryly. "I think we have found what we are looking for."

Arian read out loud:

ENCIRCLED ACQUISITION
To constrain the unforseen's accessibility
Repressed or cloistered from availability
Deliminate your global portal
From all intruders including mortals
Exculpate your exclusive rights
By avowing your assertion through ones sights
Retinal variations will ensure
Ones biased inclinations shall endure.

Arian still seemed confounded.

Sebastian elucidated. "I believe the crystal ball can obtain our retinal images from the user's eyes to only channel the crystal ball's use to only us. So that if the witches attempt to interfere, excluding jamming which takes all three of them at once, with our crystal ball after the sanctuary spell will be removed by the full moon, they will be banned."

Arian carried the witch's rod and the crystal ball to enact the spell.

Giselle chirped again while Arian listened diligently.

"According to Giselle, Cassandra is worried. Whoever Cassandra is?" Arian's curiosity was now aroused.

"Oh my God, Cassandra." Sebastian felt guilty.

"Who is Cassandra? Is she Uncle Horatio's daughter?" Arian queried.

"No." Sebastian replied. "She is my sister. I was supposed to call her on our first night at Uncle Horatio's."

"But, that was seven days ago." Uncle Horatio mentioned.

"I have to call her to tell her that we are all right."

"How does one call her? Don't you write to each other using the mail?" Arian expressed.

Sebastian tried to explain. "Now, we have fiber optics that use or convey speech over distances by converting sound into electrical impulses. But, I would have to transfer to Uncle Horatio's house to call her."

"Well," Arian suggested." Maybe if you told the crystal ball where the address is and that you want to speak using electrical impulses to your sister's telephone, it might work. It is worth a try?"

"But what should I say?" Sebastian seemed worried.

Arian was at a loss. "If you tell her the truth, not even I would believe it. It is too fantastic!"

"Well, let's see if I even get through." Sebastian repeated the address in Montreal as he concentrated on his sister's phone. The phone rang. "This is Sebastian Simons' residence and also Cassandra Simons, please leave a message at the tone. Beep." Cassandra, this is

Sebastian. I know this is inexcusable not to call you but urgent business has come up. We are all right and so is Uncle Horatio. We will call you back as soon and when ever possible. Please do not call us at Uncle Horatio's. The phone is unattended at the moment. We all love you very much and we are very sorry to inconvenience you. Sebastian."

"If I were your sister," Arian explained." I would have ominous or foreboding feelings but that is the truth. Well, I guess we better get started. Arian accessed the Anthology of Magical spells and looked up the subject of love potions. Nothing was listed so Arian indexed "Affaire de Coeur or the Affairs of the heart as she recited.

AFFAIRE DE COEUR
Caressed by a whisper, as fleeting as the breeze
Impassioned by expressions inferred by ease
More than complaisant, touched by blush
Frail by beauty, softened by a hush
Flamed as sensuality with petals of a flower
Perfumed in intervals of hallucinating powder
With the elixir of illusion, concealed as a disguise
Transfixed as one beholds, to fool ones eyes.

"My, this is so romantic." She stared into Sebastian's eyes. "At least the beginning lines of the stanzas are. My, if you heard these words Sebastian, you will be in deep trouble. Hexe will never let you go for I would never want you to leave me. Sebastian, there is a footnote: This spell can not be sent via the witch's rod. It must be splashed or poured directly on the intended. The intended must see the usurper. Exception can be made by dousing the love potion again on the victim to change its mate. Let's see if there is an antidote. My, my, here it is. Maybe, we should brew some."

"What is it?" Sebastian seemed compelled.

Arian recited.

AFFAIRE DE COUER ANTIDOTE
To keep your lover always at bay
Use musk from a skunk and run away.

"Perfect!" Arian expressed. "The cross -reference or prerequisite, is used with an atomizer. See shelf number 28. I better go and retrieve it right away. I think this would work on anyone, not just a lover, but who knows." Arian went for it. Sebastian held onto her hand, stopping her.

"You don't have to retrieve it yet, the bottle probably smells from great distances." Sebastian added.

Both the children and Uncle Horatio laughed very hard.

"Maybe, you should wear it around your neck Monsieur, just in case." Arian teased but Sebastian turned her around so that she faced him and held her there as he kissed her. She started to melt.

"Excuse me, Sebastian, but we need your mind on the problem at hand." Uncle Horatio stated.

Sebastian let Arian go. She needed Sebastian to steady her as she leaned against him still weak. "Well," Sebastian suggested. "We need a spell to fight against those ghastly lightning bolts. Here it is." He recited.

PROCTECTION FROM LIGHTNING BOLTS
A burst of brilliance between two clouds
A flash expelled as lightning goes through the shrouds
Effusing flex may strike the ground
Conducting the accumulation or deficit in electrons found
Use iron filings suspended, diverted down
So if discharged at its' potential, it bounces around
Like a liaison ousting, which is quite profound.

"It has a cross-reference. Each of us needs a witch's rod."

"Speaking about witch's rods," Arian interrupted. " Since the witches acquired one from the Devil, let's look it up in the Anthology."

Sebastian searched under the letter W. "Witch's rod," Sebastian continued. "A magical device that utilizes magnetic electron flux. Micro-molecular molecules are created or transferred. Thoughts or electrical impulses change atoms, which changes their matrix using the universal laws of physics, gravitation, and telekinesis. Known only to life forms from outside or from the ancient ones. Note: the witch's rod universal rules state that the witch's rod can not destroy or negate their own power from their own kind which includes the protection of the owners of the witch's rod. When copied, the duplicates will lose their potency as time expounds. Their life expectancy as a whole, lasts several thousands of years."

"Ancient ones?" Uncle Horatio whispered quite spooked.

"We must know all the possibilities. I wonder which ancient ones. However," Arian conceded, "we should write all these spells in a book so one can carry it with you." Arian retrieved some handbooks to write all the spells that they needed in alphabetical order.

Sebastian turned to the spell, Exodus from the Realm of Twilight. He recited the poem. Sebastian then turned to Arian. "Do you think that there are certain moonbeams that can transverse through a stone, but what stone?"

Arian's eyes lit up with a thought.

"What is your mind pondering on?" Sebastian moved towards Arian who was still copying the spells. Uncle Horatio helped in the recopying since he felt in the way reading the spells.

"Giselle gave me the idea. Why would the Devil tell the witches to destroy the pedestal, which is needed in my escape? To do so he told them to use a very large emerald. The rings that we wear are the crux of the spell."

"You mean moonbeams will transverse through the emerald and give an ion wave that will direct us towards the ethereal and the beyond. This is vague." Sebastian brought the Anthology closer to Arian so he could be next to her. Arian's smile met him as they sat sequestered together.

"Comfy! "Uncle Horatio smirked.

"Yes," Arian said demurely. Arian focused on what Sebastian was pointing to on the page. "A threshold eau of a pond. "Eau is the French word for water. The water of a pond, Uncle Horatio, is there a pond or a lake near you that could correspond to this spell?"

Uncle Horatio's eyes opened. "Yes, there is a lake right near by my house. Does this mean we will dive at midnight to find the pedestal under water? Oh, God, I know I like the sea but I don't dive well. I have ear problems. Oh, no."

"The children are fatigued. I will put them on the sofa and play on the harp to lull them to sleep. We had a busy day. I don't think they would want supper by the way they droop. But, I will ask? Do you want some supper or do you want to rest?"

Lucien replied. "I am hungry."

"Well, Messieurs and Mademoiselle, Please excuse me. I will return with some refreshments."

Sebastian read the poem and remembered the definition of emeralds followed by the cross-references "Pillars of Hercules." He used the dictionary for the definition of the word pedestal. Definition: The foot or bottom support of columns, pillars. "That's it!" He said to himself." So the Pillars of Hercules will recompense, which means something given or done in return for something else: example reward."

Arian descended the stairs with an entrée of roast pork and mashed potatoes.

Sebastian immediately stated. "I will help you."

As twilight approached, it drizzled waking the witches who were up all last night in the summoning of the Evil one. Soaking wet with the freezing droplets, Brujia sneezed again.

"Must you do that!" Hexe wiped it off her arm. "It's bad enough I am wet with the cold drizzle. You send shivers all over me. Hagatha get up. How can you sleep at a time like this?"

Hagatha yawned. "I am so tired. I could sleep through anything."

Brujia sneezed again. "I think I am really catching a cold. With this drizzle I seem to be worse."

Hexe stated. "Isn't anyone else cold? Oh, I forgot both of you are fat."

Hagatha stared at Hexe. "Well it has its advantages. I am not cold. Can you hold your head so that your teeth stop chattering? It is unnerving."

Hexe responded. "I have no control over it. Where do you think we could steal a huge emerald? Hagatha?"

"I believe." Hagatha remembered. That jewels, large ones, were very prevalent in India."

Brujia asked, "How far is that? Maybe we could walk there?"

"Oh no." Hagatha contradicted. "You fool, India is on another continent, if I know my geography. "

Hexe commented. "Really?"

Hagatha lamented. "Why do I have you as sisters? Why? Why? Why?"

Brujia interrupted. "I don't want to hear that. We could say the same for you. So we forgot our geography. We also have been dead for one hundred years."

Hexe inquired. "How could we locate an emerald close by? It would take too long to go to India anyway."

Hagatha replied slowly. "We will use the witch's rod provided by the Evil one. So my dears, we fly."

Brujia had to submit herself to fly on the ragweed brooms again. "Why didn't we ask for brooms?" She wailed. "I know I'll ask the witch's rod to create one, I am sick of being allergic." The new witches' brooms appeared.

The witches flew over London for approximately one hour.

"Confounded, the witch's rod hasn't even signaled us yet. Aren't there more emeralds around?"

Hexe surveyed the area. "I don't recognize anything anymore. All I see are buildings. How boring."

Brujia sneezed, crashing into Hagatha, still having her cold, making the witch's rod drop from Hagatha's hand.

"Can't you look where you are going? I dropped the witch's rod on account of you. The witch's rod landed on that great building over on the roof. You great buffoon." Hagatha cursed.

Hexe stated. "I will retrieve it. I noted where it fell." She dropped down from the sky and landed on an immense building. "There you are." She noticed that the rod changed color from brown to green." Hagatha, Brujia," Hexe signaled with the rod.

Hagatha rejoiced. "We found one. This is glorious."

Brujia sneezed again. "Well, if I had not crashed into you, you wouldn't have located one."

"If you think you are going to take credit for this, consider, I would have located it anyway." Hagatha maintained.

Brujia made an ugly face.

"Oh you can be so childish at times." Hagatha complained.

Hexe waved. "How long are you going to argue? We have a signal from the witch's rod."

"Yes, we know." Brujia answered back.

Hagatha asked. "What is this place?"

Hexe flew to the ground level and returned. "The British Museum, Hagatha."

Brujia pondered. "Do you think it has something to do with musing or singing?"

Hagatha held her hands on her head." Of course not! It is for antiquities and science items. Why don't you study more?"

Brujia retorted." I have to do all the cooking, while you bury yourself in books which make me sneeze."

Hagatha lamented. "Only you would come up with an answer like that one."

Hexe contemplated. "We have to break in again so we better change to be invisible. Where is the toad?"

Brujia recalled. "Flying always makes toads sick so we will have plenty of spit."

Hagatha uttered." Um, there are guards about, I can see them inside and out from the entry."

"All right toad, spit!" Brujia pressed the toad. She anointed herself and her sisters while reiterating the spell and they all became invisible.

Hexe read the entryway out loud. "The Museum is closed on Mondays."

Hagatha pushed Hexe. "Who cares." She zapped the lock with a jolt of electricity from her finger two times because she remembered home securities, in rapid succession. It remained silent. She held the witch's rod outward to ascertain the variance of its color. "The deeper the green color will indicate the correct direction to be taken."

Brujia stared at all the stairs. "We will be walking forever. I am even prepared to fly through this."

Hagatha whispered. "With all this paraphernalia, you would undoubtedly crash and bring all the guards down upon us, so be patient."

"These steps keep going down. If I have to walk another flight, I will throw up." Hexe turned slightly green.

Brujia said. "Let's rest for a bit." She leaned on what she thought was a wall but instead it was a display case containing an Egyptian sarcophagus. Because of Brujia's weight, she cracked through the glass and the old wooden veneer of the sarcophagus. She fell in coughing and sputtering as a huge cloud of dust sprang forth.

Hexe retorted. "Oh my it seems to be occupied."

Brujia stated. "There is someone in here. One of his arms fell off. Help me out of here!"

Hagatha replied. "It's too tight for you. We will have to break you out. I hope the guards don't come. Hexe help me. Yank her arms while I will hold the sarcophagus and be quick."

They finally got Brujia free while she constantly sneezed.

Hexe cried. "You smell awful. Stand over there so I can breathe."

Brujia was trying to dust herself off.

"Quiet, someone is coming. Quick, stand away from the sarcophagus, Brujia. That is where they will investigate." Hagatha's eyes looked up in dismay." Come." She pushed her down another flight of stairs thinking that being invisible they could be concealed. However, they left a trail of dust footprints.

Two guards hastened to the scene.

"My God! This sarcophagus is totally demolished." The first guard shouted.

The second guard ran down the flight of stairs a little bit. "Hey, look over here." He called to the first guard." Dust footprints. Do you think the mummy escaped?"

The first guard stated. "Let's call for backup. I don't want to follow a mummy this late at night. He seems to have forgotten an arm."

"Stop being gross and make the call." The second guard yelled.

Hagatha pushed her two sisters running down and across through another corridor. "That was close. Brujia, stand off a bit. The smell is atrocious."

Brujia stated. "If you think you have it bad, I am wearing it!" She kept shaking her arms to dispel the smell.

Hexe cried. "It is not working. You waste your efforts on trying."

"Enough, They are coming." Hagatha whispered.

Brujia replied. "What shall we do? I thought we were invisible."

Hexe stared down. "It's the dust! Make a wind with the witch's rod so it will disperse from us, Hagatha."

Hagatha commanded the witch's rod. "Blow the dust off us!" The witch's rod complied and blew the dust away.

At the same moment the guards pursued the trail of dust footprints when they were blasted with a gust of wind.

The first guard screamed. "It is the mummy's ghost. Let's get out of here!"

"I am with you!" The second guard ran as fast as he could.

"Good riddance." Hagatha announced. "We finally have sometime to recollect and get the emerald." She held the witch's rod out which pulsated a deep color of green. "We are getting closer."

Hexe rubbed her hands together just thinking of holding onto the stone. "It's over here! It is just as you said. This emerald on display belongs to a maharajah."

"How nice. Steal it, we don't care who he is. He probably stole it too." Hagatha commented.

Brujia sneezed again. "I think you better look above it before you steal it. It seems to have some beams like a circle around the display."

Hexe tilted her head upwards. "I will just zap it." When she did so, it flared back and hit her stunning her finger." Oh! It hit me. I feel tingles all over."

The alarm sounded.

"Not again." Hagatha screamed. She took the witch's rod slashing at the beams that ricocheted away while she snatched the gem. "Run you fools."

They hid behind an Egyptian artifact display that was in glass. When the guards ran past, the witches were invisible.

Hexe breathed easier. She glanced at the display. "Hagatha." She whispered. "These artifacts have the hallucinating powder used in the love potion spell. I can smell it."

Hagatha still out of breath stated. "I am too excited. I can't smell a thing especially when Brujia is so close."

Brujia scoffed. "I am sorry, Hexe. Do you even know the love potion spell? You can't look it up. We don't have the anthology."

Hexe spoke softly. "I memorized it so if I ever had the chance to catch Sebastian all I would have to do is make the ingredients."

Brujia said. "Of course, we have to go through all this trouble so you can have a fling. How dumb!"

Hexe screamed enraged. "You don't understand anything do you!"

"Stop this instant. Aren't we in enough trouble? We don't need to have more befall us." Hagatha threatened." Just steal the ingredients and let's be off. I grow tired of this."

Hexe zapped her finger as the lightning bolt cracked the glass case and promptly stole the ointment, the hallucinating powder and the vial, which contained the elixir of illusion.

Another alarm sounded.

"Oh!" Hexe stated. "How do we get out of here? I am a bit lost."

Hagatha glanced about. "I don't know either. But we can call for our brooms to come to us and exit through the sky light above us."

Brujia commented. "That is thick glass, Hagatha, maybe you should zap it first."

Hagatha conceded. "You are right."

She called for the brooms mentally. When the guards saw that the brooms were flying in the air. They evacuated.

Hagatha pondered. "What has got into them?" They followed the guards to the exit."

Upon their return in the dead of night, they made a fire for warmth and tried to brew the love potion.

Hexe complained. "We need a larger cauldron. My ingredients will boil over."

Hagatha stated. "We don't have any and I want to conserve the witch's rod so just make the potion with smaller amounts of ingredients, as long as the ratio is correct, who cares. How much shall you need?"

Brujia answered back. "More than she could ever make."

Hexe screamed again.

After dinner Arian cleaned the table to go back upstairs to wash the dishes and so forth. She left them again.

Sebastian returned to the Anthology of Magical Spells to see if a spell existed to rid magical powers on the one who wanted to use it. He thumbed through the index under p for powerless, but there was no listing. Sebastian thought very hard when he saw that Arian had come back down the stairs.

"Are you staying?" Sebastian asked.

"I forgot the napkin holders. I will return when I am finished with the kitchen work. How are the children?" Arian smiled again at him.

"I think they are taking a nap. Uncle Horatio is still voraciously copying the spells. While I ponder on powerless." Sebastian sighed.

Arian came closer and whispered. "Try impuissance: Lack of power or weakness." She caressed his cheek with her hand.

"Your vocabulary astounds me. You bewitch me too." Sebastian whispered.

"I must finish this, I will return." Arian smiled again teasing him with her eyes.

Sebastian watched her ascend the stairway again. He turned to the index under I. Impuissance, and there was the spell listing:

IMPUISSANCE

Degressed from nervelessness becoming decadent
Crippled, hampered as waning to beckon it
Dwindled by diminishment in size
Unbeknownst, like a surprise
Inundating within a stifling force
Gravitating all the power in its course
Quailing to retrogress
Especially when under duress.

Cross-reference: Use in conjunction with the witch's rod. Note: It only works in parallel universes, not in reality. The spell only removes magical protection resulting in conventional attire and weapons.

"Here, Uncle Horatio, is another spell for you to copy." Sebastian confirmed.

Uncle Horatio languished. "Another one. I wish I had my lab top. My hand is tiring. You know it is not just one copy, it is several."

"Do I detect a note of complaint?" Sebastian questioned.

"Um," Uncle Horatio stated. "I only hope that I copied them correctly or the spells won't work."

"Please Uncle Horatio, make sure they are correct. The implications are deadly." Sebastian warned.

"Yes, I know." Uncle Horatio agreed. "It's a dreadful business."

Arian came down the stairs seeing two sleeping children on the couch and Sebastian buried in a book while Uncle Horatio held onto his hand from writers' cramp.

Arian stated. "I think we should all get some rest. You really look like you need it." She rubbed Sebastian's neck and shoulders.

"Don't stop that feels good." Sebastian relaxed while Arian rubbed him.

"I agree." Uncle Horatio relinquished his quill pen. "I keep dripping the ink all over the place." He watched Sebastian being massaged. "Who is going to sleep where?"

Sebastian turned and stared at his Uncle and Arian.

Arian answered. "This is our last night because tomorrow will be a full moon. In which case, I thought that Sebastian with the children and I would be in the master bedroom so I could have my intended family together, maybe for the last time, if you don't object, Uncle Horatio."

Sebastian didn't realize that it was the last night before the full moon.

Arian continued. "I want to thank you for your diligent work in trying to release me from the Realm of Twilight, however it turns out. I will never forget any of your kindness or of Giselle's undaunting work so that we could get this far. I am fearful of your safety as well as my own."

Sebastian drew Arian into his arms. "We will do our utmost best to win so you can be my wife which I want so very much. I love you."

Arian held onto him.

Uncle Horatio came up to them. "Of course, I do not object. Who could, seeing you." He smiled to ally her thoughts. "Forgive me."

Arian smiled back. "I do forgive you. I love all of you. You are my only family in the whole world, now."

Sebastian suggested. "Let's go to bed. We will think a lot better in the morning." He went to carry Lucien while Arian picked up Selena.

Arian asked. "Uncle Horatio, please extinguish the candles and take Giselle up. We seem to have our hands full."

Uncle Horatio smiled. "Of course. Come Giselle." Giselle flew to Uncle Horatio's shoulder and chirped.

Everyone went to his or her own rooms. Sebastian removed his and the children's belongings from his room and walked to the master bedroom with Arian, who in the meantime had changed Selena to her nightgown. Lucien changed in the rest room. Sebastian changed behind the screen while Arian arranged Sebastian's and the children's belongings into her armoire. Lucien emerged from the rest room and Arian went in to change to her nightgown.

Lucien hopped into bed. "This bed is so big, you really can't fall off of it."

Arian smiled. "How do you want the arrangement?" She stared at Sebastian.

"Well, I am a bit biased. I would like the outside followed by Arian followed by Selena followed by Lucien on the other side." Sebastian hinted.

"Oh." Arian smiled. "It is fine with me."

They went to bed. After about one hour, Selena turned to Arian.

"I am sick. I feel like throwing up."

Arian immediately grabbed Selena and took her to the rest room.

Sebastian glanced at Lucien; they were the only ones left in the bed. "This is not good."

Lucien shook his head. "I don't think anyone will get any sleep tonight."

"What could have made her ill?" Sebastian asked Lucien.

"I don't know. She was very upset about the witches." Lucien stated.

"It must be nerves." Sebastian added.

They all could hear Selena throwing up, while Arian held her head and washed her face.

Sebastian got up. "How is she doing in there? "He opened the door.

Arian responded. "Not well. I think she is too nervous. She told me while she undressed that she doesn't want to lose anyone. Why can't the witches go away."

Selena looked at her father. "I am sick."

Sebastian came to her. "It will be all right. We will try to make you better."

Arian said. "Maybe, if I give her crackers to absorb the acid, excuse us."

Sebastian held the door for them as they descended the stairs.

Sebastian spoke to Lucien. "Try to sleep if you can. Arian will probably keep her down stairs so that we can sleep." Sebastian heard a knock at the door. "Who is it?"

Uncle Horatio asked. "Who is sick?"

"I really admire your hearing. You should have been a detective." Sebastian stated. "Please go back to bed. I will go and check on Selena and Arian. Sleep Lucien."

Lucien acknowledged. "Yes, Father."

Sebastian walked Uncle Horatio to his room. "I think Selena is having a reaction of nerves from what the witches said, unless she has a fever. Whatever the cause, keeping you up won't help. I do appreciate the concern."

"I just hope she will be better, poor little thing." Uncle Horatio sighed." Good night, I say that in jest. You won't sleep. I know you."

Sebastian nodded as he descended the stairs in search for Selena and Arian. They were located in the kitchen.

"Did the crackers work?" Sebastian asked Arian.

"I don't know. She threw up again before I could feed her. She doesn't have a fever, which is good unless she gets one later." Arian searched Sebastian's eyes." Is Lucien asleep?"

Sebastian shook his head. "Uncle Horatio also inquired so everyone in the house hold is awake."

"Oh." Arian whispered while holding Selena wrapped in a blanket in her arms.

Sebastian noticed Arian didn't have a robe. "Are you cold?" I could get your robe?"

"No, it is not necessary. It is less to clean if Selena throws up again. Why don't you get more rest? I will look after her. She knows you care. You have been taking such good care of her or she wouldn't have turned out so beautiful." She looked at Sebastian intensely." I love you."

Sebastian couldn't resist, he walked towards Arian and held her as close as he could while trying not to disturb Selena. He kissed her neck. He held her for quite some time regretting to let her go. Arian was completely weak.

Selena reiterated to her father. " I am sick Daddy. I am going to throw up."

Arian went for the bucket and held Selena as Sebastian held Selena's head up a bit as she wretched.

"Please, Sebastian get some sleep. You need your strength for our problem at hand. Everything depends upon you. Please rest at least."

Sebastian regretted leaving her. He kissed Arian again as he went upstairs. He opened the bedchamber's door quietly and noticed Lucien was fast asleep. He lay down carefully. He then heard a violin being played with the most beautiful Vivaldi concerto no. 12 in G major .The music was so calming and cheerful. Arian played to Selena to make her feel better. The piece was followed by Concerto no 1 in B flat. The music was so enervating as it lulled and relaxed him to sleep.

　　　Selena was finally asleep. Arian had been with the child for six hours. The crackers must have worked. Arian quickly picked up Selena carefully and went upstairs to her room. She placed Selena on the sofa and tucked her in. Arian then went towards Sebastian. He was asleep. She knew that look as she bent over and kissed his cheek quietly. She used to do that with Alexus and it still worked. When she kissed his cheek very close to his mouth, Alexus as did Sebastian smiled. Arian then kissed Lucien and he did the same thing. Arian went to her writing desk and wrote for thirty minutes in her diary. She then rose and snuggled up to Selena, covering herself up as she collapsed from the long night.

CHAPTER 10

THE SILENT TEARS

    Sebastian had a good night's rest. The music worked so completely but where was Arian? How was Selena? Sebastian stared around the room. His eyes focused on Arian's picture. That dress is beautiful, he thought to himself. Lucien stirred a little, yet he was still asleep. Sebastian sat up quietly to see if Arian had even come up. There she was, still holding onto Selena who was sound asleep on the sofa.

    Sebastian got out of bed. Arian was not covered so he took his robe to cover her up. He engulfed her into it. She is beautiful, as he stared at Arian, sleeping. He thought to himself, she must be tired. I didn't even notice her come up. What time is it? He looked at his watch, five in the morning. Maybe, I should try to sleep a bit more, but, instead, he went to her picture, as he stared at it again. I wonder? Would Arian mind if we took the picture with us? I don't want to leave it here. He then noticed her vanity items. Her crystal cut perfume bottle had a fragrance, which he craved. She didn't wear eye makeup which was probably not done at that time .He surmised that her eyelashes would even be longer. His eyes focused on the beautiful writing desk. What a lovely book, it didn't have a title. The white leather book had embossed pink and red roses with violets surrounded in ivy leaves. Etched around it was gold leaf.

    He opened the book, Arian Simons' Diary. My arrival in 1699! Sebastian knew it was wrong to read it but there was a picture of the chateau with himself and Arian, drawn as if it was a photograph, which captured him as he marveled at the skills that Arian possessed.

    He perused through it. It started when she found the Chateau Quintessence was designed for Alexus Simons' prison. To make Alexus comfortable this home had been created as an exact replica of Alexus's in every detail. His clothes for he would need a wardrobe were magical so it couldn't wear out. It contained everything he would need. Of course, he would have been exposed to the love potion so Hexe would at least be an illusion like Arian, so even my clothes are here as well as my painting.

I am now writing everything from my entire life in chronological order since I am imprisoned here for a lifetime or more. Only twenty-three years of my life had normalcy. Sebastian saw her life, as an ambassador's daughter. The exotic places she visited and lived at. (Every chateau she had spent time in or embassy). All the people she could remember in detail had been drawn, as were the cities. It resembled a photo album. Alexus was drawn everywhere as was her father, Dorian, and Uncle Cecil, which included her cousins, Antoine and Alain De La Vega. One page alone consisted of a picture of Alexus dueling Alain. Alain was a very handsome man even at forty. Sebastian still raged to himself of what that man had said to Alexus.

As the years go by, my references, which were the last touch of reality was marked every day in the diary to try to find out what the date was. My life at Quintessence had been basically of starvation, for I have never done gardening in my life. My first years of purgatory had gone by and Dorian's birthday approached. What seems odd was, I found this crystal ball in the witches' basement. I could see my Alexus only when he kissed someone; I was so happy that I could even see him. He kissed our son. My, had Dorian grown. I will draw his picture. He is seven years old. Sebastian shocked noticed that it looked exactly like his son Lucien. Sebastian kept on reading. I long to see my family. If only I could return. Every injury I have, no matter how painful, I eventually heal. There is no escape from this place. I tried to set goals for myself for I can not waste my time with sorrow. I practiced my fencing, my music and my languages. There are many books that I study to take my thoughts away. I have found a magical bird named Giselle. She is my only companion. She even learned to write when I taught her.

Sebastian flipped through the book seeing the date 1820. Alexus had reincarnated. I didn't believe it since I am Catholic. I felt my Alexus when he died in 1745. His soul came to me to tell me that he still loves me, and how, he has tried to rescue me, but failed. He told me, that he can't stay and that he regrets leaving me here. He asked me to forgive him, as a soul. His new name is Aramis De Valmy. He was born to French parents in the Loire Valley. He is a nobleman. I have read some literature on reincarnation, but I am astounded and shocked still. My thoughts have gone back to 1699. Why do I remember now? When I was struck with lightning, I could hear Hexe say that I would see all of my Alexus's lives of everyone who he loved and all his children. Is this what I am going to endure every one hundred and forty years approximately? Aramis is just born. I see his parents. What am I going to see next! I still can't believe I am 134 years old.

Aramis is 16 years old and has kissed his first girl, as I always do, I drew her, It saves time rather than writing. Aramis will marry Jacqueline La Pagerie. She is beautiful and I can tell he really loves her. At least I am happy for him. But I am in total agony. She will be a good wife, if it wasn't for her having my Alexus, I guess I would have liked her for a friend. I don't want to exist like this. My tears fall so freely. I can not vouch for the ink. This page is soaked. I will have to draw their wedding on another page. I know it is not his fault. If my complete lives were placed as a lineage. What would I see? It's just whenever he kisses her I see it. My heart is truly breaking.

Sebastian had tears for Arian as well while he read this narrative. He continued. Aramis is very handsome and I see lots of his good and noble qualities as my Alexus, his sensitive hands, his wit and his concerns. I love him still. All I have to do is see his eyes of which one sees his soul. Immortally is awful. One must die otherwise one's thoughts never change, new ideas never emerge and objectivity runs away. The worst for me is yet to come. I would like to have my son once again in my arms. I thought I couldn't have anymore tears, but I will see all his children. I wonder at times if I am mad or insane. How can I tell? I have read every book in this house twice! I compose my own music, for I get bored on just the same thousand I know by heart. I also draw everything to keep myself sane but am I?

I thought I couldn't have anymore tears, but I am wrong. He has just gotten twins, a boy and a girl. Here are their pictures. They are beautiful like always. His daughter is named Isabeau, and his son is named Andre. Hexe has visited me in the crystal ball to announce that Aramis has just had another boy named Phillipe. I must admit my Alexus and Aramis has always been faithful. Here is the picture. The only time I have peace is when Alexus or Aramis are in between lives of reincarnation. My heart should be stronger since by this time I am 169 years old. I still lament I only had my Alexus for four years out of 169 approximately 1/36th of the time I have been imprisoned.

When Aramis died, he didn't visit me. Does one remember all your lives and could you then visit the souls one leaves behind? I thought I could at least see his soul again to talk to someone but I am denied. Oh, how I long for my death! Sebastian stops for a moment gazing at Arian sleeping. He turned the pages again and sees his new name as Sebastian Simons with his baby picture of 1964. Shock still filled his soul.

My Alexus has been born again. His new name is Sebastian Simons. I always loved that name, Sebastian. It is a derivative of Augustus, the first emperor of Rome. The year I guess is 1964. My calculations have been imperfect. I should have practiced more. He is handsome like I thought he would be. At 16 he kissed his first girl. Here is her picture. Sebastian skips as he read. Sebastian had just married Marisa Harris. She is beautiful. Yet, I think he sees her beauty more than her character, she is selfish.

I shouldn't be upset, but why does he have to look like my Alexus exactly. I thought with all the time that has gone by I would handle this life of his better. Marisa is too cold. He shouldn't have married her. I even liked Jacqueline better.

Lucien, Sebastian's first child with Marisa is born I could be wrong but I believe the date is 1992? Why did Sebastian choose that name of Lucien? My son, Dorian's middle name was Lucien. He mimics my son Dorian exactly. I know from my heart that this Lucien has my son's soul. Lucien's soul just speaks to me. I shouldn't cry so much now, for time does heal, but since this child looks exactly like my Dorian and has Dorian's soul. I want to hold that baby so much. I would love to hold my Alexus. The feeling this Sebastian gives me has made my tears return. Marisa doesn't even like children, which upsets Alexus/Sebastian. My Alexus/Sebastian is not happy. I feel sorry for him and myself.

Sebastian stopped reading as he skipped parts. Two years later I see Sebastian with his new daughter, named Selena. That was the name I was going to give my second child, which the witches killed. Here is her picture. This Selena gives me the same feelings when I was with child the second time, with the same soul, why? This life of Sebastian has given me more tears imaginable. The children that I was torn from have a mother who doesn't like children. The children do not deserve that but maybe Sebastian will make up for that. This Marisa, I will never forgive her. She has made my Alexus/Sebastian very unhappy. He doesn't deserve this either. I cry for him and myself. It is raining here as it buffets against my window. It seems to know my feelings exactly.

All of a sudden I only see Sebastian kiss his children. What has happened! Where is Marisa? Who is taking care of those precious children of whom I long to have.

Sebastian skips until he sees the end of the diary notation. Selena is feeling better, the music and the crackers must have worked. She is a bundle of nerves, which I think might have caused her illness. I have just gone upstairs. It is four in the morning and I must kiss my Sebastian and Lucien. They always smile if you kiss the side of their cheeks just like my Alexus always did when he slept. I have drawn them for the last time today, for it is already morning, which might be my last day alive. How will I tell Sebastian? Sebastian continues to read. If I leave the Realm of Twilight, I can not find anything about a cross-reference for survivors. Of course, that is if Sebastian discovers the key to release me. Will I age my three hundred years when I go into reality and change to dust? Also, I must go through the anguish of being hit by a lightning bolt, which is questionable if I will survive while I cross to reality from the Realm of Twilight. How can I transverse it? As I watch them sleep, how do I say goodbye. We have come to a full circle. I can't sleep for this might be my last night of life. How I have longed for an end to my misery. I never thought that I would have or be near my Sebastian again. To be held in his arms with such ecstasy in his embrace, to have found them at last, only to lose them again. Mon Dieu! I will give myself the last rights and play a piece for my funeral. I have talked to Lucien who has told me that cremation is cheaper, I really wish I didn't have to burden them. I must sleep now. It is four thirty. This will be my last entry, in this book of three hundred years to date. This book has been my sanity. I wish I could see my father again, but where can he be, reincarnated into someone else? To the ones I love the most, Sebastian, Lucien, Selena, Giselle, who is forever faithful and Uncle Horatio, who I hope will help my new family. Adieu. Adieu my loved ones.

Sebastian, in shock, had no words to say. He stared at Arian who slept near Selena.

Arian woke up as she partially rose trying to focus on the mantel clock to see the time. It was six in the morning. She turned her head and saw Sebastian. "Sebastian " She quietly spoke. She saw him reading her diary, "Sebastian." Arian got off the sofa and ran to him. "You read my diary. I never thought, I couldn't express, I am so sorry. I never thought that anyone would read it. If you don't want to talk, I understand. But I want to say I love you. You must be cold, here let me put your robe on you. "

Sebastian had tears in his eyes.

"Your past lives and reincarnation must shock you. It shocked me too since I am Catholic. I will take Selena and put her to bed. I must make breakfast. Sebastian, if I kiss you would it help?" Arian placed his robe over him. "Yes, I know you like a book, but now you know me like a book as well. Sebastian, maybe you should lie down. You are in shock. Let's go." She touched his cheek ever so gently." I love you please lie down. Maybe I should get you a brandy?" Arian became desperate, she sat on him." What is ailing you? You must confront it, Sebastian." She kissed him gently." I guess I will leave you to make your breakfast. I can't seem to get through!" Arian tried to go but Sebastian held her hand. He appeared upset. "Sebastian." Arian kissed him so passionately. She knew his venerable spots being married to him once. It worked he responded to her as he kissed her the same way. He held her even closer as tears fell from his face.

"Arian." Sebastian finally said." You can't die on me. I have hurt you so much. I am so shocked."

"It is not your fault. If I put my lives with the men I would have been forced to marry, it might be the same. For in my life time there was only duty to whoever was chosen for you. Finance and security was the only thing that was important. Love was supposed to follow, or maybe respect."

"How can you forgive me?" Sebastian held her so close to him." Do you know for certain that you will die? I need you and our children need you. I never should have married Marisa. I never loved Marisa like I love you. I found out too late, about her real character. You are the most important person in my life, besides the children. Let's go to the book of Anthology. There must be something we can do."

"Sebastian, I have looked. It doesn't mention survival for I want to stay with you as well. Let me hide that book before the children read it. I can't deal with you and the children being so upset. I can't have everyone crying, including myself."

Sebastian held her tighter.

"Sebastian, let's go and look at the Anthology book again." Arian took her diary and opened her drawer. She threw the book in it and locked it. Sebastian finally let Arian go as he held her hand. They left the room. They quietly walked to the spell room. There was Giselle.

Arian greeted her. "Good morning, Giselle what is wrong?"

Sebastian seemed even more depressed.

Giselle chirped.

"Oh my God!" Arian cried.

"All right, what did she say?" Sebastian implored.

"The witches have acquired a two hundred and fifty carat emerald which will certainly out power ours." Arian expressed fear.

"Steal it!" Sebastian said provoked." We can use the transport spell!"

Arian obtained the witch's rod as Sebastian went for his handbook and recited the spell as Arian waved the witch's rod using the crystal ball.

Hagatha and Hexe had the emerald in-between them as they slept. When suddenly, Hexe awoke seeing the emerald become transparent, then translucent and then disappear as Hexe jumped to catch it, but failed.

Hexe screamed loudly." No!"

Hagatha yelled. "What is wrong with you? Do you want me to die of shock?"

"The emerald has been stolen by Sebastian and Arian. What can we do?" Hexe 's fury raged within her.

"Oh my! It took us so long to acquire that one." Brujia responded." I guess we will just have to get another one!" She went back to sleep.

"Do something Hagatha!" Hexe wailed.

"It is impossible now. I would need the crystal ball as well as the witch's rod to steal it and the sanctuary spell still protects everything within its circle. We will have to think about it later. I am too tired. We must have our rest for tonight's business. So let's sleep!" Hagatha reaffirmed.

"I am going to sleep too!" Brujia commented.

Hexe wailed again as she screamed louder." It's not fair!"

Arian rejoiced." We did it!" She kissed Sebastian as she held the emerald in her hand.

Sebastian held her so close as they searched for the word for immortality in the Anthology. They both flipped the pages. "There must be a list here somewhere. I can't lose you. I love you too much."

"Maybe the crystal ball could help by locating the correct word. It isn't immortality or the lack of it." Arian replied, not wanting to hurt or ever leave Sebastian.

The crystal ball focused on the word sopravivenza.

Arian expounded. "That is the Italian word for survival."

Sebastian turned to the letter S. There it is sopravivenza. Then he crossed referenced it with the exodus spell. See page number one thousand five hundred and forty six. Life expectancy with the duration in the Realm of Twilight being one hundred years is very poor only twenty percent. Sebastian eyes began to tear.

"I am doomed. I have been here three hundred years. "Arian sighed quietly.

Sebastian seemed more desperate. "What if we use the lightning bolt protection spell? Your survival will improve. "

Arian scanned Sebastian. "Let's look at the cross reference."

They both turned to the page of the lightning bolt protection spell. Sebastian read aloud. "A survival rate would improve to sixty percent depending on where the lightning bolt strikes or other electromagnetic variations. We are going to douse you in it. I need you too much."

"I will do almost anything to be with you." Arian kissed him so tenderly while Uncle Horatio called.

"Sebastian, Arian, are you down there?"

Sebastian did not want to stop holding Arian. He wanted to be alone with her and not be disturbed.

Uncle Horatio called again. "Is there anyone down there? I hear breathing."

"Yes," replied Arian regretfully. "Are Selena and Lucien awake?"

"No," Uncle Horatio stated." I was wondering why would you be down here?"

"We are here because Giselle told us that the witches have obtained an emerald that would exceed ours. Therefore, Sebastian and I stole it by using the transport spell. Also the life expectancy for myself returning is twenty percent, so Sebastian wanted to use the lightning protection spell and douse myself in it so the percentage will be sixty percent."

"What?" Uncle Horatio ran down." Oh God, we can't have that. The children love you, as do I, not to mention, this gentleman here has been in love since he saw you, though, maybe he won't admit it. He probably will admit it a day later. Aren't you cold? Shouldn't you be wearing something warm?"

"No." Arian declared. " Both of us are upset especially when I told him this morning. That is why we came down here to find the cross-reference. "

"Well, what shall we do? Sixty percent is better than twenty percent. But those still are dangerous odds." Uncle Horatio exhibited his nerves being as upset like everyone.

"Don't tell the children. I can't handle everyone crying. I guess I should have mentioned it earlier but I wanted to find out for myself before, in order to prepare you. What time is it?" Arian glanced at Uncle Horatio and Sebastian.

Sebastian observed his watch. "It is six thirty in the morning."

"Oh my, the children. I must go up, Sebastian." She kissed him. "You must cheer up for Selena's sake. Selena was sick for six hours and I only had one and ½ hours of sleep. Selena is a bundle of nerves from Hexe. I must start breakfast." She kissed Sebastian again, "I love you. I have all my confidence in you. I will survive!"

"Sebastian, where did you steal this emerald? This is really huge. "Uncle Horatio stared astounded.

Sebastian watched Arian ascend the stairs. "We stole it from the witches. I better get ready and see the children, excuse me."

"I'll go with you." Uncle Horatio followed.

Arian kissed the children trying to get dressed as Sebastian entered the room watching his family. Selena blew her father a kiss, which inspired Sebastian to blow a kiss back.

Uncle Horatio conveyed a very disturbed perspective.

Sebastian rushed towards him. "You will upset the children, let's talk outside."

Uncle Horatio seemed beside himself as Sebastian ushered him away into the hall.

"You know more than you say." Uncle Horatio added.

"Do I? Arian stated the main problem. It is her ability to survive the change from immortality to the Realm of Reality. As far as we comprehend from the exodus spell, the Pillars of Hercules emerges from where we know not yet. A large beam will come forth, reacting with Arian somehow altering her life with a sixty-percent chance if she douses herself with the lightning spell. She has endured such agony. I know, because I have read her diary since 1699. She can see reincarnations of my soul with other marriages of previous life times as well as my recent one. How did she stay sane for three hundred years, I do not know. I have never read anything so sad. I want to protect her from any more pain. I love her so much. I have never thought I could, except with her. She knows her odds and accepts it as life. She has such courage as she dotes on the children." Sebastian spoke in a very low tone. "She expressed to me that she can't handle it if the children know. So no matter how sad, we have to have the appearance of being normal. I presume that since she had this endless loneliness, she is willing to accept her fate. Her last entry was to have finally found us at last only to lose us again."

Uncle Horatio was speechless and just shook his head.

Sebastian commented. "She knew all along and yet her only wish was to end this dilemma without harm coming to us which with our involvement would be uncertain. She has sacrificed herself for me. Just the thought of Hexe having me for eternity, makes me feel absolutely disgusted and abhorred. So there is only one resolution. I will save Arian even if it means my death. I can not endure to see her in any pain."

"Don't say any more Sebastian or I will break down." Uncle Horatio stated. "This whole business is so exhausting and we haven't started with the assault."

"The only thing I want are those witches dead! And I will succeed if it means my whole life and that of my family. If Arian can be strong, so can I, you must excuse me. I want to be with my family. So let's dress and solve this dilemma. "

Uncle Horatio put his hand on Sebastian's back." Let's accept the challenge. I hate them too!"

Sebastian saw Lucien in Arian's arms as she hugged him while Selena jumped up and down on the bed wanting to be taken too. Arian held both of them smiling. She glanced up at Sebastian. "We missed you." Arian's eyes bewitched him with such a look.

Sebastian had to hug Arian while holding his children too. "Come we have lots of planning to do. I am tired of anyone threatening my family, which I hold so dear. So shall we dress? I better hurry up. Has Giselle any more information? She has been so faithful."

Arian shook her head implying a no whispering, "I love you," in his ear. "I better get breakfast ready and I have two volunteers, don't I?"

Lucien immediately said. "What will we do?"

Arian held Sebastian's hand so he could not change as she placed his arm around her waist and turned to kiss his nose in which he didn't expect.

Selena lamented. "If only I was taller, I could kiss Daddy's nose too!"

"Now I have two bewitching girls." Sebastian held them." But I must change, so if you will excuse me."

Arian shook her head as she teased him. Selena immediately copied what Arian did, smiling too.

Sebastian spoke to Lucien. "Engage your mother and sister for me. I must change."

Lucien asked. "What shall I do?"

Sebastian gave Lucien a hint. "How about breakfast?"

Arian smiled. "Ah ha. I know it would be coming soon." She brushed her lips across his cheek teasing him again." I will be waiting for you. I haven't done that for three hundred years. We must practice fencing again. This time we will go for the coup de grace. You will not think of me as Arian, but your worst opponent because only then does one succeed in learning to be ruthless as you will ever get. Don't be afraid of hurting me. I know exactly what to do. Promise me. "

Sebastian still held her and whispered. "I promise. I want to kill them more than you do for what they have done to you."

Arian put her finger on Sebastian lips. "The children, "she whispered in his ear as she hugged him." I won't keep you. Come let's make breakfast we have another busy schedule." She embraced Lucien and Selena as she eyed Sebastian smiling.

Uncle Horatio was at the door as Arian opened it with two little ones.

"Good morning Uncle Horatio."

Sebastian stated. "You're done?"

Uncle Horatio said. "And what have you been doing?"

Sebastian said hastily. "I have been detained by my family." He gazed at Arian holding his children walking them down the stairs.

Uncle Horatio quickly closed the door. "While you were being hugged by your family?"

"Uncle! How do you manage to hear everything!"

"Never mind! I have drawn up this marriage document. You must do it here in the Realm of Twilight. No one would ever believe her age anywhere else."

"You forget, she has her marriage certificate in her diary."

"Well, that's a start. We could use the same format. Imagine how touched she will be when we have the ceremony in the chapel. I can't see you parted from her either. I even spoke to Giselle. She will chirp at your wedding. So if you will get the license form while you change and pick some flowers, we can surprise them at breakfast."

Sebastian pressed Uncle Horatio's hand. "I will bet she will cry."

Uncle Horatio smiled. "They always do."

Sebastian tried not to cut himself shaving. He missed his razor." How would the document look like?" Sebastian thought to himself.

Uncle Horatio commented. "Lucky for you I print reasonably well. How are we going to fake the blood test?"

"I don't think we can. Maybe the witch's rod can figure it out. Where will you state that the license took place?"

"I think it should state it at my residence, after all Quintessence is not in Reality. We have to do it on the sea or I am not licensed to do the ceremony and then from there transfer the wedding to the chapel. We will call the ship Quintessence. Why not!"

"I better select the roses while you finish up." Sebastian ran down the stairs two at a time.

Arian was making the tea, while Lucien arranged the plates and saucers.

Selena peeked out the window. "Daddy is picking roses again. Should I wave to him?"

Arian shook her head. "He is trying to surprise me."

"But I can see him." Selena pointed.

"You will find that a surprise, to be special, you just ignore the little things, as your father dashes about the garden. It's better that way."

"Oh." Selena contemplated.

Lucien put the breakfast on the cart while Selena played with Giselle. Giselle winked at Arian.

Arian asked with a puzzled look. "Giselle, what do you mean by winking?"

Giselle chirped. "You will find out soon enough."

"Since when do you keep secrets?" Arian asked.

Giselle chirped again. "I had to promise Uncle Horatio and Sebastian. They want to tell you. It is a surprise."

Arian's interest rose but at that moment Sebastian came in with a beautiful bouquet of roses. She froze in anticipation.

Sebastian came closer. "Let's be married. Uncle Horatio has drawn up a marriage license and is waiting for us on the boat on the lake to join us in holy matrimony."

Arian cried while she jumped into Sebastian's arms kissing him repetitively. Lucien and Selena joined them as they held her.

Sebastian presented her with a bouquet as he offered his arm. Sebastian held her as she practically fainted. "Arian, are you all right?"

"I am too happy."

"Now, there are a few things I have to explain. Uncle Horatio can only legally marry us on the water, so we will have the actual ceremony on the lake on a little boat. So everyone will have to stay put on the boat or we will capsize. After that, we will go to the chapel so I can kiss you as my legal wife followed by breakfast. What do you think?"

Arian kissed Sebastian unable to contain her happiness. Giselle chirped to explain that she needs a veil and that they should hurry because Uncle Horatio is waiting by the lake. Arian held onto her loved ones and then ran upstairs to get a veil. She returned looking absolutely beautiful. They all walked towards the lake to see Uncle Horatio smiling back at them.

"Since I was a navel captain, I will load the boat so that we don't have any problems once we are on the lake. So, Lucien and Selena will enter and stay at the back, while I will go to the bow, followed by Arian and Sebastian, which will be at the center. Watch your step, the boat sways as well as goes up and down." When everyone was aboard, Uncle Horatio pushed the boat away from the small peer with a paddle and rowed to the middle of the lake. "Now whatever happens, don't get up. We don't want to douse Arian on her wedding day."

Giselle, who was on Uncle Horatio's shoulder, chirped beautifully.

Uncle Horatio asked. "Arian, will you take Sebastian as your lawful wedded husband?"

Arian gazed at Sebastian. "I do."

"And you, Sebastian, will you take, Arian as your lawful wedded wife?"

Sebastian held Arian's hand and looked directly into her eyes. "I do."

"Then with the power vested in me, I call you man and wife. Please exchange your rings, your emerald ones and then you may kiss the bride. I must add carefully so not to disturb the boat."

Sebastian asked Lucien to give him the ring while Arian asked Selena to hand her Sebastian's ring. They exchanged rings. Sebastian carefully removed Arian's veil and kissed Arian very softly. Arian was so touched as tears fell from her eyes. Arian then carefully kissed Selena and Lucien behind them. Arian then leaned very carefully and kissed Uncle Horatio.

Sebastian had rose petals in his hand and threw them over the small boat as he held Arian's left hand securely in his. Uncle Horatio rowed back to the peer. They disembarked all holding one another as they made their way to the chapel. Arian anointed all of them with holy water as they entered. There, Sebastian kissed Arian again. Arian sang French songs while Arian's joy had to express itself. Her voice echoed through the chapel as she sang one after another. Sebastian held her as she sang as both could feel their heart beats together.

Uncle Horatio stated. "If only I had a camera."

Arian gave Uncle Horatio a quizzical look. "What is that?"

Sebastian explained. "It is a devise that captures images on an emulsion film which is light sensitive. It takes pictures like you would do paintings."

"Astonishing," Arian seemed impressed as she held onto Sebastian." Breakfast is cold I am sorry to say. We will need it for our long day. Words cannot express my happiness at this moment. I have all my loved ones."

Uncle Horatio responded. "I am sure we can resurrect breakfast."

All of them went to the dinning room.

After breakfast, merriment of excitement was in the air as Arian played Pachelbel's canon in D on the violin followed by dancing with Lucien and Selena while singing.

"As frivolous as this seems, we have no time to lose to practice our fencing. So why don't you practice the basic moves till I change?" Her eyes were even more flirtatious than ever.

Sebastian had to hold himself back. He knew that the danger presented by the witches had to be dealt with.

When Arian emerged she carried two foils. She faced Sebastian and Lucien. "Please approach me and begin."

Sebastian asked. "Do you mean you will take both of us at the same time?"

Arian affirmed. "That is precisely what I mean. Make your lunges count gentlemen. Do not be afraid. I have done this countless of times before with my cousins from Spain."

Sebastian stated. "Very well, come Lucien she is quite handy with that." He stared at Arian. "Aren't you."

Arian smiled as her foils blazoned in the sun. "Selena if this upsets you, just bury your head into Uncle Horatio and hold tight. In time you will adapt."

Arian faced her opponents as they advanced. She made counter moves very easily. She coached them on the choices of moves, which would be better depending on the circumstances. She apologized when she touched Lucien chest pad. "I am very sorry Lucien, you are out." She hugged him." I am very impressed with your performance. You can't compare yourself to a person who has hundreds of years of experience. " Now, it was between Sebastian and herself. "En garde, I will be as provoking as I can." Arian affirmed.

Sebastian had a feel for fencing as if he had done it before. So he did his best but Arian kept coming. He thought he had her cornered but Arian did a double backward flip out of the corner and came at him again. He thrusted forward forcing Arian's foil out of her hand but she used her boot flipping the foil upward, caught it and came after him again.

Lucien was in delight. "I want to be just like Mommy."

Sebastian had to think hard. Two can play this game he thought. He approached again but when Arian lunged as he countered, she kissed his cheek. This caused Sebastian to be off guard. Arian somersaulted and had him at point.

"Touche'." Arian countered.

Uncle Horatio complained. "You cheated. Kissing is not allowed."

Arian smiled. "When you deal with your life, that is what you do. Besides, how could I not with such a handsome opponent? I am impressed with your performance as well. Are you sure you haven't remembered it from a previous life?" Arian dropped her foil. "Let's go back to basics. Would you help me up?"

Sebastian pulled Arian towards him kissing her fully on the lips. Arian almost fainted with weakness. Sebastian had to support her.

Arian appeared dazed with Sebastian. "I can't think straight. I must sit for a while. I will hold Selena for a bit while you practice with Lucien or Uncle Horatio."

Sebastian walked with Arian to Uncle Horatio, Selena and Lucien.

Uncle Horatio stated. "I never thought sword play was so hard. It certainly takes a lot of stamina."

Arian smiled holding her Selena. "And how are you?"

Selena responded. "I was fearful for both of you."

Arian said soothingly. "You know that your Father would never hurt me and I would never hurt him. You are so fragile my little precious one. Here, I will hold you while Uncle Horatio can practice instead of protecting you." She glanced up at Uncle Horatio thanking him.

Uncle Horatio smiled. "What is an Uncle for?"

Arian studied Sebastian's face. She knew that look too well." Sebastian," Arian beckoned him.

"Yes, Arian." His look didn't change.

"Maybe after practice and after the strategy we could give the children and ourselves a nap so we will be fresh for this evening?"

Sebastian secretly smiled catching her meaning fully. He tilted his head towards Uncle Horatio.

Arian motioned Sebastian closer. "Oh, I know a very secluded spot and a secret passage out of the house from the master bedroom." She whispered into his ear.

Selena whispered into Arian's other ear. "What are you whispering about?"

Arian responded immediately. "Love nothings. Married people say it all the time."

Sebastian kissed both Arian and Selena. He turned to watch Lucien practice with Uncle Horatio, knocking Uncle Horatio's foil from his hand.

"Touche'!"

Arian commented. "Very good Lucien! I am sorry, Uncle Horatio. You have too relaxed of a grip. I think you are too concerned not to hurt anyone. How kind, but you see the outcome."

Uncle Horatio saw them whispering and he secretly smiled, too.

In the meantime, Hexe ranted and raged about the stolen emerald. "How Arian will pay for this." Hexe stalked back and forth seething with fury.

Hagatha stated. "You will wear yourself out. Surely we can find another."

Hexe shrieked back. "It is the time factor!"

Brujia held her hands over her ears. "We know. But look at it this way. The full moon is tonight. We could steal it back from them. They won't have a sanctuary spell for protection."

Hexe scoffed again. "If they can purloin the emerald ring from us, how many other spells will they use against us? I want to narrow the odds. I have waited too long while he kisses Arian instead of me! How will I stab at thee, Arian, with poison."

Hagatha suggested. "Let's hold a séance and see what they have been doing?"

Brujia interrupted. "But séances are usually held at night. Tis morning?"

Hagatha sputtered. "So we will hold it in a cave so it seems dark. That should do, shouldn't it?"

Hexe jumped up excited. "I will get the small cauldron and the fire wood."

Brujia seemed doubtful. "But you need sulfuric acid fumes. The Sibyl inhales the vaporous fumes so that she can hear from mother earth the predictions."

Hagatha reiterated. "We still have some of the hallucination powder from the Egyptian jar. We can make do. It has a derivative containing sulfuric acid."

Brujia continued. "I don't know. I have never dealt with it before. We are not sure if it works. We haven't tried it yet."

Hexe countered. "Of course it will work as a love potion and for the sulfuric acid fumes. I can smell the ingredients are correct."

Brujia stated. "It's not for me to say."

"Stop this. It is pointless. There is no one we could try the love potion on because they would pursue us continually like a lovesick dog. Who needs that when we have to fight for our possessions as well as our home with the addition of Sebastian." Hagatha added.

Brujia sulked saying, "Yes, Hagatha."

Hexe expounded. "Let's go. The cave is about a mile from here."

Brujia conjectured. "I am not going to carry all this and also walk. Let's fly. I sneeze anyway from my cold."

Hagatha replied. "You are correct. It is just too much to carry."

They appeared as quite a spectacle in the sky with their ingredients flying behind them because they forgot to use their cloak of invisibility spell. Several car accidents occurred as it snarled up the traffic.

The cave resided near the lake as the water lapped into recessed pools spilling off the main wave. It drained again down the cracks as fissures percolated its way back to the lake. The drippings from the stalactites augmented as they went deeper into the cave.

Brujia sneezed again. It echoed through the caverns as it rebounded from the walls.

Hagatha complained. "Why didn't you take your cold pills? Your sneezing is only louder in here."

Brujia retorted. "They make me so drowsy. I can't think straight."

Hexe sniffed. "This cave has mildew. That even makes me sneeze."

Hagatha stated. "That's perfect, two of you who sneeze. Then let us be quick about it. Brujia you can set the cauldron over there and make haste."

Brujia set the wood in a pile. From the stand she hung the small cauldron dangling in the middle. She enlarged it with the witch's rod. She tried using a flint to light the wood but at the same moment a drip of water from the hanging stalactite quenched it. Brujia counted the frequency of the drops so she could rub the flint in the opposite time the drop would fall but her timing was a bit off.

Hagatha interrupted. "Brujia, dear."

Brujia replied. "Yes, Hagatha."

Hagatha continued. "What are you doing?"

Brujia stated. "Lighting a fire."

Hagatha remained calm. "I see that."

Brujia asked. "Then why did you ask?"

Hagatha said exasperated. "Why don't you use a lightning bolt from your finger instead of fooling around with the flint and water drips. Doust thou comprehend?"

Brujia smiled. "Oh, of course."

Hexe sneezed just when Brujia finally lit the fire and blew it out. "Sorry Hagatha."

Hagatha lit the fire. She couldn't wait for Brujia any longer. "There. Now, let us put some water, the hallucinating powder and the sulfur granules and mix until it boils."

Brujia sighed. "Do you know how bad sulfur smells. It is worse than rotten eggs. "

Hagatha turned and faced Brujia. "What kind of witch are you?"

Brujia defended herself. "Well, after falling into the sarcophagus with that mummy, my nose has gotten very sensitive to foul odors. I just can't take them anymore."

Hagatha lit a few torches." That would be the right spot for just enough gloom," she announced. "Now, we shall begin. Take the athame and make the circle. Get the chalice and the censer and place it over there, Brujia. Get the pentacle and the candles and light them around the circle."

Brujia retorted." Why are you just telling us what you want us to do, we know that already. Why don't you help us? We are doing all the work!"

"Quiet! This must be perfect!" Hagatha contested.

Hexe kept the fire burning evenly boiling the contents in the cauldron. "There." She joined the others.

"We call upon the four elements: Fire, air, earth and water! Awaken the spirits. Awaken Oh Goddess, Oh Hecate, sister of ours. We need more help." The witches now started to dance around the fire, faster and faster. Brujia tossed in a magical herb into the fire as it flared. The flames crescendoing higher as it reached the cave's ceiling.

"Oh, Hecate, a Sorceress of time from the ancients. We call upon the Sisters of Sisters. We need your advice. Oh Sibyl, oh oracle, that tells us life and death." The witches called out.

Brujia then threw in the sulfur as she complained." Oh!" She then held her nose.

Hexe screamed. "Stop that. You insult us."

The flames from the sulfur intensified. The color turned green and then a midnight blue. A face emerged. A Greek face, like a Greek or Roman mask from the theater of Pompeii. The mask had no eyes, just holes for the eyes, nostrils and mouth, which revealed itself. The mask was made of gold!

Oh Hecate, Goddess of the Moon, Earth and the Underworld, Realm of the Dead, now, of sorcery and of witchcraft. We beg you! We appeal to you. We beseech you. Help us. Tell us what we need to know. Your words are your wisdom." They called.

The blue midnight mist augmented as the glitter sparkled within it shining, like magic. A siren voice of silver spoke out. "Have you consented on going through with this venture?" The holes for eyes now had a silver light piercing the darkness out towards the three witches.

Hagatha bowed. "We have, oh Sibyl!"

"You should think twice!" Hecate's voice reverberated. "I see danger!"

"What kind of danger?" Hexe queried.

The Goddess mask changed her direction towards Hexe. "This man, Sebastian, is very brave and good. He has married his former wife from the past, Arian." A hologram of Sebastian and Arian holding each other, as Arian sings in the chapel, exuded from Hecate's head, like a thought. Then, as it got free, it turned into a bubble displaying a live movie as the bubble floated around the cave.

Hexe cursed.

From Hecate's head another bubble exuded as she spoke. "They have: the debitum naturae spell (the bubble broke off), the lightning protection spell (another bubble), the expulsion spell, the impuissance spell, athames, the transformation and anti- transformation spell, the anti-love potion spell, along with the encircled acquisition spell to prevent anyone from ever using the crystal ball in their possession and maybe more. They are very creative."

The bubbles floated around the cave as each spell in the bubble was printed in its' entirety, scrolled on a page. Hexe basically stared at Sebastian and Arian for it displayed what was actually happening at this very moment. Sebastian was kissing Arian.

Hexe cursed again.

Hagatha groveled. "What do you suggest? Oh Wise one."

Hecate's silver light changed to a vibrant violet, expelling from her eyes as the blue mist and the bubble holograms intertwined in the cave. "This is a challenge! Both sides are somewhat equally matched. The balance or scale can tip either way. Caution is wise. With the debitum naturae, death is completely permanent. There is no escape from the Pit of Tartarus. If Hexe wins, Sebastian's hate is so great; the love potion will not work. You must make it stronger. Have you made the correct poisons for Arian or the others? The suspension poison spell is the best. It is like a spider's venom, keeping its victim fresh for any use for the body or soul. If Sebastian can not be won over, do you plan to kill him and then resurrect him later?"

"Yes." Hagatha confirmed." We have already thought of it."

"Your fate is sealed! To the last I still caution thee, beware!"

"Oh thank you for your prophecy, Oh Hecate. We are greatly in your debt." Hexe confirmed.

"I, Hecate, prophesize, live as time, but even time has an end. Beware. Death may be at your shoulder." Hecate's mask became translucent. The violet light ceased. The bubble holograms broke as the blue midnight mist engulfed the mask and transformed it to black smoke, then to white smoke and then clear, as if nothing ever existed with no traces at all.

"Sister," Hexe beckoned. "We have lots to prepare. Sebastian will not have any peace till he surrenders to me, and he will. He will! Brujia, collect as many spiders as possible. I need them for the suspension poison spell. Go on!"

"Why do I have to collect them? Why can't you?" Brujia retorted.

Hexe continued. "You know that you have the fastest hands. How else did you catch all those bugs for the toad? Go on!"

"Oh, all right, I'll make an attractant to lure them down, but I am not touching them or extruding their poison. That is your job!"

Hexe shouted. "Well, just don't stand there! Make haste!"

"Sister. We must protect ourselves. You know the transformation we need. I won't explain, just in case Arian or Giselle is spying on us." Hexe and Hagatha winked at each other.

Hexe smiled. "That will be perfect, Sister!"

Hagatha continued. "Now, sister, we still have to strengthen your love potion. It is the hallucinating powder that we must add more to. We will quadruple it! And if we have to kill Sebastian in order to win, so be it. We have Selena to trade her soul to resurrect him. For I know what you want to do to Arian."

"What about the emerald?" Hexe complained.

"Don't worry!" Hagatha reassured Hexe. "When we capture Sebastian there will be no time to save Arian. Even if he does save her. We shall be there as well. I know the survival rate is twenty percent at one hundred years. Arian has been there for three hundred years. The lightning bolt will kill her. There is no doubt. That will be fun to see Sebastian lose her again like last time."

"Well," Brujia announced. "The attractant worked. I have three hundred spiders. I am giving them to you, because I am not touching them."

"Brujia." Hagatha screamed. "We need more exotic spiders, not these plain ones. Have you no mind at all!"

"Look." Brujia retorted. "I just put the attractant out. I can not tell what types of spiders live here to be exotic! I was lucky that any spiders came. Beggars can't be choosy!"

"Now, let me see. What spells do we have for our strategy." Hagatha recalled. "Well, we have our athames, transformation spell and invisibility spell. Sebastian and Arian probably thought of the impuissance spell, so if you go to Arian, you would be on your own, Hexe. I know you are a good swordsman, but so is Arian."

"With my hate for Arian, I will be victorious. My hate has spanned the ages for I lost Sebastian with his past lives as much as Arian has. Lucien will be saved. I could love him as well, when he gets older, but Uncle Horatio and Selena will be suspended. For Arian, I will smear poison like arsenic or strychnine on my sword so once stabbed, it will give Arian as much pain as possible. I am actually looking forward to our duel if necessary."

"Well, I am still worried. "Hagatha continued. "We also have the love spell along with the sleeping spell. We can jam the crystal ball communications but we will need all our minds to accomplish that. Although it could prove difficult since we all will be fighting. Oops, I almost forgot the illusion spell. We also have the witch's rod. Maybe they don't know all it's properties, which is a better protective agent against lightning bolts, like a shield."

"Oh, we must get rid of that Giselle! I will scorch that bird for all the trouble she has given us!"

"Good." Hagatha replied.

"Oh," Brujia groaned." I found some exotic spiders so I have done my chore. I am resting."

"You know Hexe, Uncle Horatio is not so bad looking. We will save him for me. I rather fancy him and he might even give me children. Even though, he did call me ugly. What was his last life's wife's name, Elizabeth?"

"Oh yes." Hexe recalled.

Arian inquired. "Is anyone thirsty? The sun is getting higher and we still have to create an illusion and a strategy. Maybe we should go back?" She stared at Sebastian." Do you think that we need more practice time? I don't want anything to ever hurt you. I love you so much."

Sebastian's eyes concentrated only on her holding Selena. Arian looked so fetching holding their Selena." Let's go. We must think of a strategy."

Arian gave Selena to Sebastian as Arian started to pick up the foils. Arian then returned to Sebastian. "Sebastian, we should try how heavy the athames are to see how more difficult or easy they are to work with. We will do that in the spell room."

Lucien pivoted making a somersault and had Uncle Horatio at neck point. "Touche'!"

"My." Arian turned to Sebastian. "Our son certainly learns fast like his Father." She gazed into Sebastian's eyes. "But," Arian continued," Uncle Horatio needs some cheering up. I better go, Lucien." Arian called." You are now becoming my knight in shining armor, but you know your Uncle is a little out of conditioning to even try that maneuver. We must cheer your Uncle up."

"Never mind," Uncle Horatio acknowledged. "I will hold Selena. She seems to be more of my side of the family."

Sebastian ran over with Selena. "Lucien, I am so proud of you. That shows enthusiasm and skill. Maybe we should practice more with the athames together. Come let's go into the spell room where we can duel in the basement." Sebastian suggested.

"Maybe, Sebastian and Lucien should go to the Realm of Reality instead of me, while I will stay with Arian and Selena in the Realm of Twilight!" Uncle Horatio commented.

Arian poured the refreshments as they all navigated into the kitchen and then they continued to the spell room. Arian brought a lot of fruit, if anyone wanted it.

Sebastian checked the Anthology reading the properties of what an athame possessed. Arian nestled closer to Sebastian for her curiosity was aroused as well. He held her as they perused together.

Sebastian read aloud. 1) The athame is associated with fire. It can send a corona flare or burst of energy like the sun at its victims to bombard them. 2) When the sword clashes, be careful of the sparks, they can singe. 3) It can emanate a smoke screen to camouflage oneself and ones opponent. 4) Special athames (from the devil) can fight on their own if the owners athame is knocked out of their hands.

Uncle Horatio obtained the three athames. "They are as light as the rapiers or the foils. At least that is good news." Uncle Horatio handed one to Lucien, to Sebastian and then to Arian. "Maybe you need to feel the weight as well."

Sebastian did some practice maneuvers and pulled Arian towards him. "Let's try it over here."

Arian and Sebastian faced each other. Sebastian started with a lunge. Arian countered it. Both were fighting hard. Arian explained slowly how to do the somersault. Sebastian tried it and succeeded but Arian flipped out of the way.

"Now I will show you how to do the flip. There is a harness that I will put you into, so one doesn't hurt oneself." She latched Sebastian into it. "Now, let me explain how to do it." Arian explained as she demonstrated it slowly." I will use this rope to counter your weight by a pulley, which is attached to the harness, if I see there is a mistake. Therefore, if you would land on your back, we will pull on the rope to keep you suspended in the air. I don't want any accidents. Uncle Horatio, I will need you for a counter balance. Please hold onto the rope that I am holding onto. I will need your strength. We are ready, Sebastian. Don't feel foolish. Everyone starts like this."

Sebastian tried it and succeeded.

"Well." Uncle Horatio stated." I am proud of you. But you are probably remembering it from your past life."

Arian exuberated as she told him to do it again so it would be like clockwork.

Sebastian felt at ease with it. Arian kissed him every time he succeeded. This inspired him. Lucien was next; however, Uncle Horatio refused to do the flip.

"I am too old for that." He promptly replied.

Giselle flew down towards Arian. Arian had to duck to avoid collision. "What is the matter? Why are you so upset?"

Giselle chirped uncontrollably.

Uncle Horatio stated. "Bad news. Things always get worse, never better."

Sebastian consulted Arian. "What is she saying?" Giselle kept on chirping.

Arian contemplated seriously. "The witches have consulted Hecate."

"So who is Hecate?" Sebastian countered.

"She is the Goddess of witchcraft, sorcery, of the Moon, the Earth and the Realm of the Dead."

"Oh God!" Uncle Horatio blurted.

"The witches are making a stronger love potion, four times stronger for you, Sebastian. They will butcher me and use strychnine and arsenic on the sword to make me suffer. They will save Lucien for later, so they can have you both, Sebastian and Lucien (as lovers). Selena will be suspended. The suspension poison spell is derived from spiders' venom and enhanced to keep the victim immobilized so their body and soul are in a stasis. When they need any body part or soul they utilized it. The poison is administered by a blow gun with poison darts."

Sebastian cursed. "Damnation." Arian placed a finger gently over his lips. Sebastian pulled Arian towards him and held her.

"There is more." Arian said hastily.

"What could be worse than what you have just announced." Uncle Horatio complained.

Hagatha stated that I would not survive the exodus spell and that they can't wait to see me die. However, they are happy we don't know about the witch's rod that can create a shield against lightning bolts. That is good news for me. Yet, there is more bad news."

"What can be worse?" Uncle Horatio expounded.

Arian continued. "They can concentrate and jam our crystal ball communications. They will kill Giselle and that Hagatha was going to poison you, Uncle Horatio, with the suspension spell but one could say that she is smitten with you and she wants you, Uncle, as her lover! She wants children from you as many as possible. She is trying to look like (as an illusion, mind you) of your latest wife, Elizabeth, even though you called Hagatha ugly."

"Oh God!" Uncle Horatio seemed as if he would have a coronary.

Sebastian expressed shock as he picked up his children, Selena and Lucien.

"I think I am going to throw up. I have such abhorrence that I will do anything. I will learn to flip and to do somersaults, maybe, more sword practice. Why Hagatha? Out of all of them she is the ugliest one. And what do they mean by my latest wife? She is the only one."

Selena cried. "What does it mean as a lover?"

Arian explained. "A lover means the way one obtains children. You will understand when you are older. You are too young."

Selena stated. "I want to go home, Daddy!"

Arian went to Sebastian to hold onto their children too.

"What about this love spell? If it is four time stronger, we must counter it." Uncle Horatio became excited to the point of panic. Arian mentioned there is a fermenting substance that was used for the entry into the Realm of Twilight to become immortal. The witches will have to use that again. When we read the spell, it was not mentioned, therefore, it must be under immortality. But first, let's look up the lightning shield from the witch's rod, under W for witch's rod. Uncle Horatio still rattled on as he kept saying. "I should have been more focused and learned better. Because it is my life, oh, my death. I must spend my life doing that with that hag for eons of time?"

Arian walked to Uncle Horatio. "We all must confront this situation." She hugged Uncle Horatio. "I couldn't see my Alexus/Sebastian or my family go through this, so I took the lightning bolt instead. Please, try to control yourself and focus on the problem at hand. You should lash a piece of wood to your spine because it needs stiffening! We will combat this!"

Uncle Horatio, being held, felt better as he tried to calm down. "I am all right, I am just a bundle of nervous.

Arian asked Sebastian. "According to Giselle, what do you want to focus on in this Anthology. We have the following: a love elixir that is four times it's strength, the witch's rod in making a lightning shield, the anti-cloak of invisibility, the anti-transformation spell, the anti suspension spell and the poison. As for the antidote to strychnine, which is a colorless crystal obtained from nux vomica, I already know of the antidote. It is potassium permanganate. The antidote to arsenic, which is a silver white powder, is to dilute it with large amounts of water or a soothing substance like egg white, cream, pulverized charcoal, tannic acid, or milk of magnesia. This is common knowledge since poisoning was widely used in my time and, of course, not to mention an illusion to fool the witches."

Sebastian upon hearing the seven choices stated. "You are amazing. I would never know about poisons. Let's start with, is there any antidote to the love elixir?"

Arian turned to the page. "The cross reference states if the ingredients have been augmented to four times its strength the antidote is useless. (Good luck)."

Uncle Horatio's stomach turned. "How can this be an Anthology of Spells without an antidote?"

Arian 's eyes met Sebastian's. She shook her head towards Uncle Horatio and sighed. Sebastian held Arian, Selena and Lucien closely towards him.

139

Sebastian stated. "Well, let's go on." He turned the Anthology to the witch's rods and read out loud. "Witch's rod: It enacts a variety of spells. See listings with a star after it." Sebastian checked the listings as he came to l for lightning." The witch's rod can be made into a shield of protection against lightning, which will endure instead of chance encounters with the lightning spell. It will deflect them away including assaults by coronas delivered by the magical athames. See shelf number 239 for stored shields." Sebastian whispered into Arian's ear. "This might solve our other dilemma with the Pillars of Hercules." He tightened his hold around Arian's waist while rubbing his cheek against hers.

Arian spoke as a matter of fact. "Knowing how the witches are, they will cloak themselves to be invisible and then strike. They were informed by the Evil one and by Hecate that we have the debitum naturae. They won't want to expose their skin to be killed. They would probably wear a suit of armor. I am familiar with the parts since I was exposed to it when I was small in my mother's house in Barcelona. The head is the helmet. The covering over the face is the beaver followed by the neck, gorget, the shoulder, pauldron, breast plate, the gloves or gauntlet, the hip or tasse, the thighs are the cuisse, then the knee piece, the shin or greave and the last is the shoes which are the solleret."

Sebastian's curiosity rose. "What was your mother's maiden name?"

Arian answered. "De La Vega."

Sebastian remembered. "Ah yes! How could I forget?"

Selena smiled. "How will we undo the cloak of invisibility, Daddy?"

Sebastian hugged Selena since she hadn't started crying yet. "Let's see." He turned to the page in the Anthology. "If you remember, the cloak of invisibility uses toad spit. So we shall look up the anti- cloak of invisibility.

ANTI-CLOAK OF INVISIBILITY
To undo or expose the unforeseen
Into tangible shapes discerned from what has been
Sprinkle spectral dust to divulge or unveil
It always attaches to silhouetting one for betrayal
Unmasked, they know not of their being exhumed
Believing themselves cloaked, still assumed.

Giselle pointed to the shelf number for the spectral dust. Lucien took it off the shelf and handed it to his father.

Sebastian took it from Lucien. "Thank you, Giselle and Lucien."

Arian rubbed Lucien's shoulders. She smiled and kissed his forehead. "I believe the witches have this leather belt with pockets that seem to be numbered so that you make a list of what you have and accordingly, place it in the corresponding number. They are located next to the witch's rods.

Uncle Horatio said. "To think this is your ninth day of vacation. Isn't it exciting?"

Sebastian recalled. "Uncle, we can't change the past. We have to go on, no matter what. Let's look up the anti- transformation spell, so we can change them into something we can handle as well as the transformation spell." He read out loud the anti- transformation spell:

ANTI-TRANSFORMATION SPELL
Reduced back into ones absolute soul
Condensed to be changeless despite your goal
Undeceiving from what portentous fallacies profess
Add denaturation powder, steamed and possessed
Immutable, as it holds firm and fast
Making the pretender static and constant to the last.

Lucien asked. "What is denaturation powder? Does is break magical bonds?"

Sebastian perplexed answered. "To say the truth, I do not know or understand most of these spells or materials listed here. It is a mystery. Most of these spells are deadly. Take for instance the memory loss spell. If one accidentally inhales it, we are doomed. We better check out an antidote to the memory-loss spell just in case.

ANTIDOTE TO THE MEMORY- LOSS SPELL
To heighten one's knowledge in one's head
To stimulate retention before it goes dead
Supplement with oxygen to magnify recall
Enhancing perception what increases it all
Peppermint sprigs leaves one reminiscent
Inhaled perspicaciously, bubbled like effervescent
To improve one's wit, to preserve reason
Amplifies enlightenment in every season.

Uncle Horatio looked up the listing of the shelf for the oxygen and peppermint sprigs and placed it on the table. "What is next, the anti-suspension spell?"

Sebastian checked. "Yes, you are correct, Uncle." He thumbed through the Anthology once again." Don't look Selena. I know how you hate spiders."

All eyes, with the exception of Selena's who took her hands and covered her face, focused on the diagrams and procedures to extracting spider venom. It even explained the ratio of body weight to the concentration needed. The average amount of spiders collected would be approximately three hundred. The spell suggests using an attractant to collect the exotic spiders. Upon harvesting, place the venom at room temperature. It spoils if it is too hot. Use with a blowgun and darts reciting:

SUSPENSION SPELL
Once circulating through thy veins
Cessation of feeling quenches thy pains
Heartbeats diminish to an indistinguishable hush
While hindering your life force in a rush
Intermittence is shunted, retarding delay
Siphoning the will, lulled away
Remission results, keeping one semi-permanently at bay

Antidote: heat the victim gently if immediately poisoned in a tub of water. If one waits to long, use the anti-suspension spell.

Arian had tears in her eyes. "No one will do this to any of my family." She kissed Selena and Lucien. She leaned on Sebastian who was speechless. Arian found a healing spell so she could focus on something other than spiders, the healing spell:

HEALING SPELL
Brew rosemary and thyme to bind they wounds
Use chamomile tea internally so that it will soothe
Make a poultice salve about thy chest
To extract the sickness from thy breast
Amend thy spirit with positive vibes
Recuperative in nature so to survive
Add electrolytes to insure the cure
Mix very well so you can endure.

Reading something about healing made Arian more calm. "Sebastian, you were saying something about creating an illusion with Uncle Horatio. What is it?" She gazed into Sebastian's eyes.

He smiled at Arian. "I have thought on this carefully. We are going to use videos."

Arian reiterated. "Videos? What are videos?" She searched Sebastian's eyes intently for some kind of clue.

Uncle Horatio beamed. "That is perfect. We could shoot a sequence flying about and the witches, who, know nothing about it, would never know."

Arian seemed a bit impatient. She placed her arms around Sebastian's neck looking directly into his eyes and said. "Please explain. I don't know either."

She was so bewitching he kissed her softly on her cheek stating. "Videos are like television, which converts light rays into electrical signals for modulation upon a radio carrier wave or for transmission over wires. The television receiver reconverts the signals into electron beams that are projected against the fluorescent screen of a kinescope or picture tube, reproducing the original image. Video designates the picture portion of a telecast, as distinguished from audio or the sound portion. It is placed on a magnetic tape on which electronic impulses can be recorded for later playing."

Arian tried to comprehend what Sebastian stated. "I am still at a loss for words, for instance, television, electronic signals, modulation, radio carrier waves, wire. Shall I go on?"

Sebastian smiled. "You astound me. Most people wouldn't even catch all the words and block them out, but not you. I love you so much. Well, in simple terms, it is a device that captures the light images that you see onto a magnetic tape. When you rewind the tape back to the beginning, it plays back exactly what you had first seen. So you have the moving images for as long as the tape lasts. He drew Arian into his arms and hugged her."

Arian seemed amazed. "I never could have imagined that. I would love to see one."

Sebastian concurred. "You will because you will be the one taking the video of us."

"I will, but I never did it?" Arian reaffirmed.

"It's easy. I will show you." Sebastian reassured her. "We better get your video cam and tapes, Uncle. Do your batteries need charging because we can't charge them here?"

Uncle Horatio pondered. "I don't remember. We will have to check it out when we get there."

Arian brought the witch's rod to transfer Sebastian and Uncle Horatio. She caressed Sebastian's face whispering in his ear. "Please take care, both of you." She smiled at Uncle Horatio.

Sebastian winked. "We will be fine." He hugged Arian, Lucien and Selena. He then walked to where Uncle Horatio stood as Arian, using the witch's rod, recited the spell thinking to deposit them into the kitchen as they vanished from sight, while the children waved.

Arian hastened to bring the crystal ball back to insure their safety with Giselle on her shoulder. Both children stared at their familiar house that Uncle Horatio still had not moved very much furniture into it.

Sebastian asked Uncle Horatio. "Where did you put it?" He surveyed the house again. "You know I never realized how eight foot ceilings compare to the chateau?"

Uncle Horatio concurred. "Now since you mention it, it is a bit confining. Oh well, here it is in the closet. We are in luck the batteries are fine and here is an empty tape."

The phone rang.

Sebastian listened to the message. It was Cassandra.

"Uncle Horatio or Sebastian. Please explain your last message. I am worried sick. I have a notion to come and ascertain the facts for myself. Maybe a police inquiry might help. I don't know anything. Sebastian, answer me!"

Sebastian obligated to his sister picked up the phone. "Cassandra. I just heard your message. We are all right for now."

Cassandra implored. "Sebastian, you are there?"

Sebastian stated. "I just came in. I can not stipulate more. Do not and I repeat do not come. I have enough to consider with the children's safety, others and myself. Who, I promise I will explain. For my peace of mind, stay where you are, safe. Promise me."

Cassandra pleaded. "My God. What is happening? What others? Is this line tapped?"

Sebastian said calmly. "If you love me, which I know you do, please don't ask any more questions. I cannot explain any more than I have said. Please take care of your nerves. When all of this is over, perhaps you will understand. I hope you do. I love you. Good bye."

Uncle Horatio commented. "I don't think that calmed her down a bit. You really handled that with flair."

Sebastian hung up the line. "What could I say. That a three hundred old or older witch wants me for a lover and will butcher my family."

Uncle Horatio replied. "Very awkward."

Sebastian reminded his Uncle. "There is a witch for you too or have you forgotten."

Uncle Horatio winced upon the memory. "Don't say any more or I will be sick."

Sebastian picked up the video cam and tapes and waved to Arian who he knew watched from her crystal ball to transport them back into the Realm of Twilight. Arian repeated the spell while concentrating and waving the witch's rod to place her Sebastian right in front of herself. When he arrived, she ran up and hugged him again. He held her there while he beckoned his children, who ran just like Arian, up to him and after he hugged them too, he stated. " Did you hear Cassandra. I hate it when I can't explain."

Arian acknowledged. "We heard. There is nothing we can do at the moment. How does this video work? It looks so small."

Sebastian showed Arian how to insert the tape. He placed it in Arian's hands and made her look into the view. He pressed a button while the cam was running and the view changed to close up or far way with the telephoto lens. Arian couldn't believe what she saw. She focused with a color view.

Arian took the two hundred and fifty-carat emerald and gave it to Lucien. "I want the children to have this. They can use it to send lightning bolts at whoever for protection. It is also to be used for our illusion to lure the witches away so you can seek them out. Please explain how we can accomplish it?"

Sebastian responded. "We will video tape us flying in pursuit of the exodus spell. So actually we should be taking the view in the Realm of Reality not in the Realm of Twilight."

Arian nodded. "Why don't we look at Reality in the crystal ball then use it as a virtual image for the illusion spell to make our surroundings like Reality here in the Realm of Twilight. Shoot the video. That was your term of flying about so they will think that you are in Reality when you are not."

Sebastian marveled at Arian. "You have a very good grasp of things. I couldn't have stated it better myself. Shall we?" He offered his arm to Arian who took it.

Arian told Lucien and Uncle Horatio to bring the witches' rod, brooms, crystal ball, emerald, convex mirror, the video cam and spells, while she picked up Selena. They hastened outside. Arian took the crystal ball concentrating through it to see the Realm of Reality outside of Uncle Horatio's house. She then thought of the surrounding area of the lake. While the crystal ball held that image, Arian placed the convex mirror to take the crystal ball's image as a virtual image. She then recited the illusion spell placing the image of Reality in front of them at the meadow. It materialized just as commanded.

Uncle Horatio, Lucien, Selena and Sebastian were utterly amazed. Arian was pleased it worked.

Uncle Horatio stated. "If only the movie industry could do this, they could save millions of dollars in set costs."

Sebastian replied. "I don't think they would believe us either. We might as well shoot the flying sequence. Lucien, you will fly the broom for Arian so she can take the video, as she will also hold onto Selena. So Arian will be in the back with Selena in front of her and you, Lucien in the front flying. While Uncle Horatio and myself with the emerald, will fly as you take the video. Understand."

They all nodded.

Uncle Horatio replied. "Won't this be fun. Your first marriage video sequence of two men flying. How endearing, not even the bride is seen. How will we explain this to Cassandra?"

Sebastian shook his head. "A most unusual day. I loved the part where I marry you, Arian." He stared at her. "We better fly. Is everyone ready?"

Lucien answered. "I am and Mommy has both of you in focus in the video cam."

Arian had to manipulate the video single handed so she could hold the broom and Selena making sure Lucien guided the broom.

Sebastian was going to give the signal to everyone when he stated. "Oh, by the way, the video cam also records sound, so don't say anything while we fly."

Arian blinked. "It does? You never told me."

Sebastian agreed. "I know. It was an afterthought. You do it so much you don't think about it."

Arian waited, like the rest of them, for the signal. Sebastian waved his hand and flew the broom with Uncle Horatio flying behind him. Lucien followed as Arian, holding onto Selena, took the video. Sebastian hovered about the lake taking the exodus spell out and then resumed while the others followed. They returned and Arian stopped the video. Sebastian examined the video from the beginning.

He smiled at Arian. "This is excellent, Lucien's flying and your footage. Usually beginners can't take good pictures, but these look professional." He kissed her cheek. "I am proud of both of you." He rubbed Lucien's head." I am famished. Can we eat?" He stared at Arian.

Arian smiled at Sebastian asking, "What would you want?"

"I am not fussy. Sandwiches are fast."

Arian took Lucien and Selena, curtsied and said. "We will return shortly in the dining room. Come Giselle, you must eat too."

When they were out of sight, Uncle Horatio stated. "Let's go over the strategy again and again. I don't want Hagatha or anyone hurting us. Remember, we must destroy the fermenting substance for the spell of immortality, so they can't use it on us."

Arian called. "Here have a late lunch. It is two thirty in the afternoon and there is so much we still must attend to."

Sebastian and Uncle Horatio appeared as hot sandwiches and soup with tea was offered.

"How did you do that so fast?" Sebastian marveled.

"I knew this day would be the most trying so I prepared ahead time, in order that I could spend more time with you." Arian responded. She portioned the soup from the tureen with a ladle. "Uncle Horatio, maybe the food will put you in better spirits."

"I am worried about this fermenting substance. How should we destroy it? "Uncle Horatio added.

"Burn it." Sebastian stated coolly." It's the only way. "

Arian helped the children as she placed more hot French bread from the serving cart to the table. "I kept it warm." Arian replied as she offered it to Sebastian.

"The strategies start like this, " Sebastian replied," with the illusion first. The witches will be invisible so we won't see them. We will also be invisible, we as in, Uncle Horatio and I."

"How can I tell what will happened to you?" Arian whispered. " Especially when I can't see you! I will be moving the illusion around the countryside and around the lake, but the moon doesn't show until seven thirty in the evening. So, the emerald can't summon the Pillars of Hercules with the witches. Therefore, what should I do in the meantime? Oh, I just thought of something, Sebastian. I will ask the crystal ball to focus on your emerald ring to locate you. We will start at 7:00 PM. I can alter the tape's duration by rewinding. The illusion then can fly backwards."

"I suppose since that is all the footage we have, that is all we can do. Yet, if we find the witches, you can make the illusion go around them instead, to drive them off in tangents." Sebastian thought." We must communicate with two crystal balls. I must know what is happening to you on your side, Arian. You will have the impuissance spell so the witches will not be able to use their magic, but that doesn't hinder them to inflict pain. What if you took the antidote before Hexe can stab you with the poison? Would that make you sick?" Sebastian's eyes showed concern.

"Yes, Sebastian, it would make me sick. The antidote only works when you have ingested or are inflicted with the poison, except the milk of magnesia, which is good for upset stomachs and a myriad of other remedies. But, if you want, I could put the healing spell on me to cheer you up. Remember, Sebastian, your emerald ring can also send out lightning bolts. If you lose, your athame, use the emerald. It is activated by your thoughts like the witch's broom."

"Let's list what the children have for protection." Sebastian remarked." First) Lucien will have an athame to protect himself and Selena. I know I can count on you, Lucien." Sebastian showed admiration for his son." You also will have Arian's protection as well as Giselle's help. Second) Selena will have the use of the emerald, which, when activated, sends out lightning bolts as Arian has mentioned. Third) Lucien, Selena and you, Arian will have one witch's rod. Fourth) Both of you will have the transfer spell to escape. Fifth) All of you will have the crystal ball, especially if Arian is fighting, which I hope will never be, if I can help it. To continue, you have Sixth) one witch's broom. Seventh) The children will each have the expulsion spell and Eighth) the memory-loss spell along with their spell book."

Arian interrupted. "I think they should also have the lightning protection shield to prevent darts used by blow guns. Nothing is going to touch my babies. Forgive me, Lucien and Selena, I get emotional when you are concerned." She rose to hold them.

Sebastian smiled lovingly at his new wife.

"What am I assigned to do Sebastian?" Uncle Horatio put in.

"We will have to play it by our wits. If we can discover the whereabouts of the witches, who are invisible, we could put the anti-cloaking spell on them. This will be tricky. Arian can detect me being invisible with the emerald but we don't have enough emeralds to go around to detect you. So you must stay very close to me, Uncle. We will have between us a lightning bolt shield spell and a protection spell including the invisibility spell. So I don't even know if I will even see you. We will have to try it out and review the Anthology on that."

Arian stared at Sebastian." Sebastian, I have emerald jewelry upstairs to equip everyone with an emerald. Why didn't I think of that before? I don't wear jewelry because nothing can last three hundred years. I just leave it upstairs. Let me retrieve it." Arian rose, curtseyed and left the room.

"How thoughtful." Uncle Horatio smiled touched by the thought.

Arian returned momentarily as she placed a necklace around Uncle Horatio's neck. On the chain hung an emerald ring. It was very petite with diamonds. "The only other emerald is this seal of office. I would have given it to Uncle Horatio, but it is too heavy, if one thinks of all the rest he has to carry. So I must give it to Lucien. This seal belonged to my Alexus/Sebastian being the Earl of Sussex. It is rather cumbersome. Would you like to examine it, Sebastian?" She brought it to him.

Sebastian was amazed of the weight." Lucien." Sebastian asked. "Can you handle the weight of this?"

Lucien rose and walked towards his father. "My it is heavy. I will try."

Sebastian placed the seal around his son's neck as Lucien first sank and tried to stand upright. "Use it as an emergency, Lucien. Selena, you will use the other one but please, do not lose it. We must return that one to its original owner. "

"All right. " Selena responded.

"Shall we go back to the spell room, to see if this invisibility spell and anti-cloak spell really work?" Sebastian suggested. When everyone left the table, Arian quickly cleaned up and brought an apple strudel down to the spell room.

Sebastian noticed her entrance with the strudel. "What is the occasion?"

"For one thing, it's our wedding. Will the wine do? I have juice for the children. Oh! Sebastian, you are putting toad spit on our son."

"Lucien volunteered and if it makes our children invisible to the witches the better." Sebastian elucidated.

"You are right but, oh." Arian sighed.

"I don't want that on me!" Selena complained.

"Father's orders. No choice." Sebastian replied giving her a stern look.

"Oh!" Selena pouted.

Uncle Horatio volunteered to anoint her. "Come Selena, let's try it on."

Arian had just cut the cake slices and poured the refreshments when she noticed Lucien had disappeared. "Oh, now I can't even see who I am offering the cake to!" Lucien, unseen, suspended the plate, while the cake was being devoured bite by bite. The cake vanished. "Do you like it Lucien?" Arian countered.

"Yes, very much. May I have another slice?" Lucien replied with an unseen twinkle in his eye.

"Yes, Lucien but you will have to help yourself." Arian responded. "Sebastian, you don't have any hands. I don't know how far I can offer this plate? Can you see yourself Lucien or your father's hands?"

"Yes, Mommy. I can see myself and Daddy's hands."

"That's amazing! How does Selena look? She is almost finished." Arian wondered.

Lucien replied. "She looks more opaque without the toad spit and translucent with the toad spit.

"I am touched you called me Mommy, but let me read the Anthology on the cloak of invisibility. If a group places the spell upon themselves, they will see each other because the spell was placed approximately at the same time. However, others that placed the spell upon themselves at a different time or on a different group at the same time will remain invisible between each other. Arian then gazed at Lucien. Arian's eyes were misty. I would hug you, Lucien, but I can't see you. Sebastian, you are holding your fork without hands. It looks so incredible, even the emerald ring disappeared. I will take the crystal ball to see if I can locate you. I only see your ring."

"Arian," Sebastian whispered, "the strudel is delicious."

"Really!" Uncle Horatio rebounded. "I must try some."

Selena or an invisible person 's cake was disappearing, as was the apple juice. "It is delicious Mommy." Selena added.

Arian offered the wine and then scanned the Anthology to see the duration of the spell. "It lasts for twenty four hours." Arian replied." We will also put it on Giselle. She will need a tiny lightning shield. I couldn't have my Giselle scorched."

"Mommy, may I have another slice?" Selena asked.

"Of course." Arian smiled. "Sebastian your wine, if you please."

Sebastian took the crystal glass from Arian's hand as he kissed her on the cheek.

Uncle Horatio commented. "This is extraordinary. What is the recipe? I love it."

Arian blushed as she got out the spectral dust." All right. I am going to find you .I hope you have finished your cake." Arian took a pinch of spectral dust to conserve it as she listened. "Oh, I think I have you." She heard the children scurry. "I hear you, so don't get upset if I catch you." Arian waited. She threw it in the opposite direction of the noise and got them both with one sprinkle.

Lucien was numb from shock of discovery. "How did you know we were here?"

"A mother's intuition. I am sorry but I couldn't waste the dust." She held them to console them. "The spectral dust makes whoever has toad spit on, change to a fluoresce apple green. You glow in the dark."

Sebastian enjoyed this scene turning Arian with one hand so she would face him. He held her and then grabbed the children as one unit. Arian placed her head on Sebastian chest and stayed there enjoying every moment. She then stared into his eyes.

Uncle Horatio said. "Look over there."

"There isn't anything there." Sebastian added. Everyone looked.

"There isn't any strudel left either." Uncle Horatio blotted his mouth with his napkin.

"Oh." Arian smiled. "You know, Sebastian. That poison, the debitum naturae is so dangerous even I am afraid of it. If the wind blows, it could rebound on us. Even wearing leather gloves would not protect you but be absorbed instead. If only we had a substance that was impervious to moisture."

Sebastian expounded. "We can use plastic gloves."

"Plastic?" Arian repeated. "What is plastic? There is a Greek word plastikos meaning form."

"It is a combination of various nonmetallic compounds synthetically produced used by polymerization which can be molded into various forms and hardened, being moisture resistant." Sebastian explained as he took the witch's rod to obtain plastic gloves from Uncle Horatio's kitchen drawer. "Here they are. See!"

Arian held them. "They will be perfect. I guess now I will place the potions, which are held in vials, into the belts with the spell books that we copied. How does the transforming spell work?" Arian confirmed.

"Let's try it." Sebastian turned the page for the transforming spell. He took the witch's rod and recited the spell, concentrating on a quill pen which turned into a clear ball point pen.

"What is it?" Arian marveled.

"A 20th century pen." Sebastian remarked.

"This is a pen? The ink is that thin line inside of it. How can you activated it?" Arian mused.

"Take the cap off and write with it." Sebastian suggested.

Arian bemused said. "Oh." Arian wrote with it on a sheet of paper." I don't have to dip it into the ink. I am impressed especially with your video cam. My, have I missed out. Can you turn this pen into a live animal or other item?"

Sebastian took the witch's rod and pointed it at the ballpoint pen and recited the spell again .The ballpoint pen metamorphosed into a monarch butterfly as she rebounded away.

"Oh, how gorgeous. You must transfer her outside but what a romantic thought. I am so touched, Sebastian. Thank you."

Sebastian directed the butterfly out by the window.

Arian beheld him so lovingly." Oh." Arian glanced at the time. "It is four thirty in the afternoon. We better rest for the moon will be out at seven thirty in the evening and at 7:00 P.M. we must start the illusion. I also have to feed you something for the long night to come." Arian became quite sad." We must gather everything we need. The belts with the poison, potions and spell books. Not to mention bringing, the shields, athames, witch's rods, crystal ball, brooms and plastic gloves. I have potions, videotape and cam, crystal ball, witch's rod, one broom, antidote for poisons, which I will leave with the children. If anything happens to me they will transfer it. I know my Lucien. Let me think plastic gloves, emeralds and shields. I even have a shield for Giselle. As for the impuissance spell, oh Sebastian, you must conjure a tiny witch's rod for Giselle." Giselle flew towards Arian as Arian coaxed her. "The only spell you will carry is the impuissance and the memory loss spell." Arian asked the witch's rod that Sebastian had in his hands, "witch's rod, please devise a spell vial belt for Giselle." It materialized in Arian's hand. "Here Giselle, the belt goes around your waist and the vials like ammunition can be pushed out by your beck and grasped by your feet" She petted her ever so gently.

Sebastian pointed the witch's rod and conjured up tiny witch's rod. He stared at it amazed.

"We will transfer all this up when you will have to leave." Arian whispered. "I thought we could have more time, but that isn't always possible. Shall we go? I want to show you something." Arian stared at Sebastian as she held Lucien and Selena hands. "Uncle Horatio, please extinguish the candles." They departed.

"What is it?" Lucien's excitement grew.

"You will see." Arian eyed them. They all followed her upstairs into Arian's bedroom.

"There it is, a secret passage." She pressed a button as the panel slide to reveal the passage.

"Oh, another secret passage!" Lucien said with glee.

The passage was adorned with wallpaper in patterns of roses and ivy and was lit by petit sconces. She took Sebastian's hand. "I wanted us to be alone together, but that seems impossible now. It leads to a secret garden outside the grounds that the family never saw. My Alexus/Sebastian was an architect by hobby and built this home for me. This estate resembles slightly the chateau that was my home in France but prettier. He worked out every detail and constructed this secret garden for us to be alone." They past fountains adorned with beautiful statuary as the tall chestnut trees etched the outlines of the surroundings of the lake and off to the side stood a Greek- temple, but circular. The garden replicated the parterres of Versailles as the park sprawled in every direction. Swans swam passed on the lake as the children just ran enthralled with the beauty.

Sebastian couldn't speak. He was so taken with the beauty. Arian stopped a moment as she pointed to another statue and the boats on the lake.

Uncle Horatio spoke up. "So this is the rendezvous from this mornings practice?"

"Yes," Arian shyly replied." I knew you caught us whispering. I have no luck." Arian 's eyes just stared at Sebastian.

"Uncle, could you leave us alone, please." Sebastian held Arian so close.

"Oh, of course. I will play with the children. I want to see what is around the bend." As he left, his grin augmented.

"This is so beautiful. I am so taken by the gazebo and the lake. This place is so perfect. I really regret it as well that we have so little time." Sebastian kissed her so tenderly." I really wish I married you yesterday. Don't think that I haven't thought about it ever since I held you for the first time in my arms trying to get that witch from strangling you." He kissed her again as Arian melted in his arms. They stared at each other as they walked towards the gazebo by the lake's edge. They enjoyed the view.

"I thought this site would calm everyone's nerves. I come here to collect my thoughts and to dream of the past, for that is all I had for three hundred years."

Sebastian held her closer trying to console her. He caressed her face gently, which changed the mood .All she could think about was Sebastian. She smiled at him so radiantly.

Suddenly lightning bolts tore through the sky as they rocketed. Hexe's voice boomed as she rasped. "Sebastian, I will have thee by tonight for certain, prepare. You will see Arian die and you will be mine at last. Trust me. You will come to me. You will! You will!" She laughed louder and louder.

Sebastian, shocked from the outburst, held Arian closer. Selena burst into tears and the children with Uncle Horatio ran into the gazebo for shelter. Lucien's eyes were large. Arian held her arms open as both the children ran to both their parents.

"I hate that woman. I mean witch!" Uncle Horatio blurted out.

Arian picked Selena up as Sebastian held Lucien.

"I never win. Just when I get the family calm, this has to happen." She turned and buried her head into Sebastian's chest.

Sebastian held his family very close. Even Uncle Horatio stood closer.

"We must rest." Arian suggested. "Let's go to our room." Arian led the way while Sebastian picked up Lucien.

They walked back to the chateau. When they entered Arian's room, Selena stopped crying. Arian placed her on the bed. Sebastian placed Lucien there as well. Sebastian sat on a chair as Arian went to the harp.

Uncle Horatio just stood aimlessly at the doorway. "May I join you?"

Arian smiled. "Oh, of course, you may. Why don't we all lie down, while I play the harp. Music always calms the nerves. Uncle Horatio lay down on the sofa. Sebastian lay down with the children. We will all have quite a long evening ahead of us. I will play the Concerto in B flat op 4 no 6 by George Frederick Handel. It is a beautiful piece. It always transcends ones soul." She started to play. The music released the stress as it relaxed and delighted the listeners. The children were falling asleep. Sebastian laid more relaxed on the bed staring at Arian admiring her and her bravery. Arian then picked up a piccolo and played Vivaldi's concerto in C major. As Sebastian became sleepier, she sang lullabies. It did the trick. Sebastian like everyone else fell asleep.

Arian slipped away out of the room to make dinner. She stopped a moment as she gazed at Alexus's picture with their son, Dorian. She went to the kitchen. She had dinner all ready as she spent the time talking to Giselle. She ascended upstairs towards the family. She crept into the room quietly as she beheld her family in peace. She first went to Sebastian glancing lovingly at her family. They were sleeping so deeply. She finally had to disturb them.

"Sebastian, Sebastian." She gently touched his face. Sebastian's eyes met hers. They kissed. "We must rise. Dinner is ready. We have only one hour before the offensive begins and I must, for superstition sake, light candles for all us to pray for our souls."

Sebastian seemed upset. "That's all the time we have left!" He stared into Arian's eyes. "But, you haven't even rested at all."

"I know." Arian conceded. "Come Lucien and Selena. We must rise now and eat for our strength tonight. There isn't much time. I made you roast beef with mushrooms in a sour cream sauce, mashed potatoes, salad and I baked our wedding cake. We must be brave." Lucien stared at her. "We will finally finish this business and move to our future. I know, for the honor 's sake of my family, it will finally be satisfied. Come on." She said it calmly and cheerfully. "Let's go."

Sebastian got up. Selena sleepily rose with Lucien. Lucien could sense Arian's bravery. He admired her. Arian hugged the children taking them down the stairs. She paused to eye Sebastian. "Please." She spoke softly. "Wake up Uncle Horatio."

Sebastian went to his Uncle. "Uncle, Uncle, dinner is ready. We only have an hour left. We have slept for some time. I will meet you downstairs. I want to be with Arian."

"Huh, oh. Doesn't that girl ever sleep!" Uncle Horatio seemed amazed. "Sebastian, this will soon be it. I am nervous. How does Arian do this? She has nerves of steel."

"She certainly does. But after three hundred years of purgatory, there will finally be an end of it. Please Uncle, I want to be with Arian."

"Oh, I am sorry Sebastian." Uncle Horatio said softly. "Oh, Sebastian did you burn that fermenting substance?"

"Yes, I did. I don't want to last for eternity with that witch. I want eternity with Arian!"

"Good, good. " Uncle Horatio commented.

The dinner table was gorgeously laid out. The wedding cake had real roses on it, ever so small. The icing was whipping cream. There were flowers everywhere.

"Arian." Sebastian eyes sparkled with amazement. "The table is beautiful." He seated himself. "You have changed your dress. That dress is the one in the picture in our room."

Arian smiled as she wound a music box that played baroque music in the background. "I am so happy it pleases you. Good evening Uncle Horatio."

"Good evening Arian." Uncle Horatio stared at her. "This is wonderful. Where did you get all this energy? My you look enchanting in that dress."

Arian smiled again. "Thank you Monsieur." She curtsied. "I hope everyone got some rest. All of you worked so hard today. We certainly did a lot of things from our wedding to swordplay, to flips and somersaults, to spells of invisibility and back and to transform a pen into a beautiful monarch butterfly. This day is one of my happiest days I have ever spent, especially marrying you, Sebastian, besides acquiring these two precious souls of which I have always wanted since long ago. I am quite enraptured. We have made our strategy and we will all do well. Good luck to all of us tonight. Let me cut the cake or should we cut the cake together, Sebastian?"

Sebastian rose. "Let's cut the cake together. My, that dress is so lovely on you. I have to restrain myself. It is so distracting. You look exactly the same as the day that painting was commissioned."

"Thank you." Arian smiled. "I had to think of something to make this evening a success. Shall we? "

Giselle flew around the room expressing her happiness for Arian. Arian winked at her.

They held the knife together as they cut the slices of cake. The first one went to Uncle Horatio, the second to Lucien and the third to Selena and of course Giselle got one. They cut the last one for themselves as they tried to feed each other holding the fork together as they laughed.

"I am afraid dinner is finished. Let's go to the chapel so I can light the candles for us and our future." Arian pulled Sebastian's hand towards her. With her other hand she took Lucien's. "Lucien please take your sister's hand." She dragged them out of the door towards the chapel. "Please, Uncle Horatio follow us with Giselle." They were running as she dragged them. She anointed them with the holy water. Then she set six candles on the altar and lit them singing a prayer. It rebounded echoing throughout the halls, being so lovely it encouraged their hearts.

"We are ready, now. Everything is prepared. I used the transfer spell to obtain the witch's paraphernalia."

Sebastian and Uncle Horatio put on their belts and gathered their brooms, witch's rods etc.

Arian embraced Sebastian kissing him ever so tenderly. She stared in his eyes. "Waiting three hundred years was worth it. By having you here with me again, each second is so immeasurable and precious. I had no idea that we would ever meet." She then turned to Uncle Horatio. "Having the pleasure to be with you again is an honor. I know both of you must like each other immensely, otherwise, you wouldn't be here. Your joviality and your concern have always inspired me. I know you will both do well. Good luck tonight. I will hold you close to my heart as long as I live. Sebastian, I love you and you, Uncle Horatio."

Arian picked up Selena. "Kiss you Father good bye Selena." She held Selena closer to Sebastian to kiss him. Selena kissed her father as she started to cry.

Lucien hugged his father very hard and Uncle Horatio. He had tears in his eyes. "You are coming back, aren't you?" He choked as he spoke.

Sebastian said very positively. "I am coming back Lucien, Selena and Arian." He walked up to them, and kissed each one. Arian was the last. "Take care of your mother and your sister, Lucien."

Sebastian returned to Uncle Horatio. Arian took the witch's rod and recited the spell as Arian gave her last loving looks at them. Sebastian's eyes were fixed on his family. They disappeared.

CHAPTER 11

COUP DE GRACE

In the Realm of Reality, twilight enhanced its hues as it lost its dominion to the oncoming night. No clouds were visible as the clarity sharpened the endless view. The forth-coming moon would only too soon show its glow onto the lake and surrounding forest. The anticipation could be felt vibrating through, expediently seeking some kind of release but yet, unfulfilled, it intensified. Sebastian examined the sky through Uncle Horatio's parlor window. He checked his spell book copy. It was written alphabetically as was the number corresponding to the vials in the belt along with the athame, crystal ball, witch's rod and witch's broom. Sebastian's only thought was to rid himself of the witches. He viewed the crystal ball to coordinate the illusions with Arian on the other side. He beckoned Arian. Arian immediately appeared in the crystal ball. He noted her attire. She was in her fencing boots, corset, slip, belt and shirt with two rapiers and two daggers. She placed the plastic gloves on and then her leather gloves over the others. He couldn't see the children.

Sebastian asked Arian. "Do the children have the cloak of invisibility on?"

Arian attached her belt around her waist. She carried the crystal ball, the spell book, the video cam, her own witch's rod along with the debitum naturae and a few other vials. Arian promptly answered. "Yes, that is why you can't see them. Believe it or not they are next to me as is Giselle. She also has toad spit on. The children have all their equipment. If they didn't wear their emeralds, I could not detect them. Adding extra toad spit negates the spectral dust so if the witches find out, they can re-disappear, it is not very good for us, is it?"

Sebastian sighed. "Lovely. They could do that."

"Luckily for me you don't have it on so I still can see my handsome husband." Arian stared at Sebastian." Where is Uncle Horatio?"

Sebastian stated. "Uncle Horatio is drinking a brandy to quiet his nerves."

Arian smiled. "Oh." She noticed Uncle Horatio coming into the parlor. "How are you?" Arian mused.

Uncle Horatio added. "A bit better after the brandy."

Arian nodded. "When do you want me to start the illusion? We have about ten minutes of footage. I noticed when I rewound the tape backwards, while viewing it, that the children with the toad spit on, makes the images jump. Since the witches will also anoint themselves when they follow the image, the picture will jump or it will vibrate a bit, which means the witches are closing in."

Sebastian thought. "That is odd. All right. Start the illusion where you and I fell off from Brujia's broom, and where Hexe tried to imitate Selena. I will anoint myself with the toad spit and sprinkle the spectral dust there. You shoot the illusion footage with the witch's rod. The illusion will stir up the dust and other cloaked entities going through should be seen. The moon will be coming up soon. So please be ready. I love you."

Arian's eyes met Sebastian's. "I love you too. Please take care of yourself and your Uncle." She watched Sebastian and Uncle Horatio disappear. Arian timed the ten minutes as the full moon radiated its moonbeams eloquently. She used the illusion spell as she played the video cam into the convex mirror to the exact spot that Sebastian indicated in the Realm of Reality. The image of Sebastian flying with Uncle Horatio flew past the spectral dust.

Three cloaked witches meticulously scanned the images carefully.

Hexe contemplated. "What do you think? Do you believe they can out fly us? This will be easier than I thought." She gleamed.

Brujia confused. "Well what type of strategy do you want to use, Hagatha?"

Hagatha composed herself. "Hexe and I will pursue them. You, Brujia will remain here in case they double back. Obviously, they want to rescue Arian first."

Hexe along with Hagatha flew right into the spectral dust. Only Brujia, who had orders to stay, noticed that both of her sisters turned fluorescent apple green in shapes of armored knights so that the debitum naturae could not be used upon their skin.

Brujia thought to herself. "Oh my, they flew through spectral dust! Maybe what they pursue are illusions? But how can I warn them?"

Sebastian along with Uncle Horatio also noted Hexe and Hagatha's apple fluorescent green silhouetting shapes.

Sebastian spoke to Uncle Horatio, "Brujia didn't fly by, so she is still cloaked and she must have seen that her sisters are uncloaked. Do you think she can warn them?"

Uncle Horatio stated. "Your guess is as good as mine."

Sebastian whispered into the crystal ball. "Arian, I know you can hear me. Have the illusions fly back through the spectral dust. Brujia is still cloaked."

Arian whispered back. "I can see Hexe and Hagatha. They have almost caught up with the illusions. I am running the tape a bit faster so they think they have the advantage of secrecy. I will put the images back where you are so that the dust will blow back on Brujia if she is there."

The blue moon rose to its full clarity. From what Arian detected, she could see where Brujia was located. She glanced about her, in the Realm of Twilight and she saw the children as well as Giselle. She then focused on Sebastian who was invisible before. He now was visible just as Uncle Horatio. The blue moon negated the cloak of invisibility. She spoke to Sebastian through the crystal ball.

"Sebastian." Arian pleaded. "The blue moon negates the cloak of invisibility. I see all of you and I see the children with Giselle. It doesn't work. Brujia is behind the tree and you are by the lake."

Sebastian noticed Brujia from where Arian described her. "So much for invisibility."

Arian stated. "I will have the illusion come to you so that the witches will be confused who to attack. Prepare."

Hexe and Hagatha followed the images of Sebastian and Uncle Horatio as Arian had the images come back to Uncle Horatio's house. Arian had the images hover, when Hexe and Hagatha realized there were two Sebastian's and two Uncle Horatio's and that none of then were cloaked.

Hexe suggested "So now there are two of you, Sebastian, so much the better. You shall succumb to me forever. It is just a matter of timing. If you want to play with illusions, I will give you all the ramifications of hell, who are at my disposal, my loved one." Hexe raised her arms as she commanded the dead from the abandoned gravesite to writhe into view as they filled the sky with ghostly shapes.

Hagatha motioned that she will give the signal to move, with her athame, which glowed in its still apple green fluorescent light through its entire length. Brujia and Hexe waited.

Uncle Horatio, the real one, tried to keep from shaking as more and more spirits occupied the sky.

Sebastian got his vial for the expulsion spell, if inundated by spirits; he would use the witch's rod, which would deliver the spell.

Hagatha screamed signaling with her athame. "After them you fools!"

The spirits rushed at both Sebastian's and both Uncle Horatio's.

Sebastian used the witch's rod for the expulsion spell as he aimed it on the oncoming onslaught of spirits while using his athame to spout out smoke so that he and the real Uncle Horatio would be cloaked. Arian had the images of Sebastian and Uncle Horatio rush Hagatha and Hexe right through the spirits.

Seeing the image of Sebastian and Uncle Horatio coming for them, Hagatha and Hexe fired their athames with bursts of flames to stop them. But they still came for them as Arian maneuvered them away from the flames but still at them.

The wind from the expulsion spell dissipated a lot of the spirits. Uncle Horatio aimed his witch's' rod at a number of them as well. Luckily for Brujia, she was behind a tree, as she had to hold onto the trunk. The wind was so strong her broom broke up thrusting Brujia up onto the branches. But her sheer weight from her armor sent her crashing to the ground. Brujia lifted her beaver so she could sneeze from all the dust as it echoed within her suit of armor.

Brujia complained. "Oh, did that hurt!"

Hagatha holding onto her head, shaking. "Oh, Brujia has lost her broom. She won't be much help since she can't fly. Why? Why? It is up to us, Hexe. The bumbling fool! If I create a broom for her with the witch's rods even with all that wind, I don't know if she will be able to grab it."

Sebastian ordered Uncle Horatio. "Attack Brujia, since she is more vulnerable while I engage Hagatha and Hexe. Arian is already using the images to disrupt them."

Uncle Horatio swallowed hard. "All right. What shall I use on her?"

Sebastian suggested. "Use your athame to get her on the run. So if she runs, she won't use her athame on you and then put the memory-loss spell on her, if you can."

Uncle Horatio responded. "Very good."

Sebastian stated. "Good luck, Uncle."

Uncle Horatio flew towards his quarry, Brujia. Brujia started to run in-between the trees. Uncle Horatio thought to himself. For someone that buxom in a suit of armor, she is doing quite well. The flying got tricky when Uncle Horatio crashed into a tree, losing his athame in the lake. Brujia changed directions and came after Uncle Horatio for his broom. Uncle Horatio tried to focus as he saw two and half Brujia's coming towards him. He grabbed for his broom, witch's rod and shield, when he noticed that many of his vials of spells were broken. He checked if it was the debitum naturae. Luckily it wasn't. He took off his belt just in case when Brujia started slashing at him with her athame. Uncle Horatio instantly picked up his shield while screaming for Sebastian. "Help me! Help! Help!"

Arian could see it in the crystal ball. She picked up the two hundred and fifty carat emerald using her witch's rod, she made the emerald send lightning bolts aimed at or in-between Brujia and Uncle Horatio. After warding off Brujia, Arian sent some at Hexe and Hagatha so Sebastian could start his attack. Arian sent another lightning bolt at Brujia's athame destroying it. "That should even the odds." Arian spoke to her children.

Brujia wanted Uncle Horatio's broom. She ran at Uncle Horatio who was still amazed that the lightning bolt destroyed Brujia's athame. Brujia's beaver was up. All Uncle Horatio could see was Brujia's red face puffing from the exercise. He turned to run onto his broom but Brujia yanked if away. Uncle Horatio yanked it back as they had a tug of war.

Hexe and Hagatha flew in disarray to avoid Arian 's lightning bolts. Sebastian welcomed the diversion while he expelled the rest of the spirits with the witch's rod. He decided to make another athame because he had two opponents just like Arian had done in the practice, He had to carry one athame under his shield, which proved cumbersome but he had no choice.

Hexe cursed. "Just wait until I kill thee, Arian, your time is almost over. I will kill you in the most excruciating way possible." Hexe attacked Sebastian as her athame sent flames out to burn him alive if she had to.

Hagatha came at his flank while Hexe made a frontal assault. Sebastian fired his athame to cancel the flames that were fired by Hexe while buffeting them off in space. He rammed Hagatha with his shield hitting Hagatha in the head. Hagatha was not prepared for Sebastian's venomous strength of hate. Hagatha's head was jarred from the blow. She was dazed even with her witch's rod she could not utilize it. Sebastian slashed at Hagatha's broom sending her into a spin when Hexe came up from behind. Sebastian double flipped with his broom to get away, shocking Hexe's attack. He shot another lethal corona at both Hexe and Hagatha as it followed Hagatha's broom singeing the edges.

Arian sent another lightning bolt at Hexe. Hexe had to move fast first from the corona and next from the lightning bolt.

In the meantime, Uncle Horatio wrestled with Brujia. She proved the stronger of the two as she yanked the broom from Uncle Horatio's hand. So to get it back, Uncle Horatio whacked Brujia's backside with the witch's rod causing Brujia to drop the broom while Uncle Horatio jumped on the broom, grabbing his belt and flew off. Unfortunately, Uncle Horatio miscalculated the height looking back to see what had happened to Brujia and was upturned by a low lying branch knocking him off his broom once again. Uncle Horatio groaned as he turned himself over. His clothes snagged on the underlying wood debris. He yanked to free himself to see Hagatha almost crashing into him as she broke her fall over Horatio's former position.

Uncle Horatio screamed. "Oh, my God! Not you!"

Sebastian stared downward at Uncle Horatio screaming for help. Shaking his head. "What next?"

Arian had to focus the lightning bolts at Brujia who was closing in as Uncle Horatio pushed Hagatha away from him.

Uncle Horatio screamed. "No, no!"

But Hagatha didn't let go of him as she tried to put the love elixir on him. "Stand still my love."

Arian now materialized into Uncle Horatio carrying an athame. She slashed at both Hagatha and Brujia. She singed through Hagatha's armor as Hagatha screamed in pain. Brujia broke off the attack but Arian flung her dagger right through Brujia's beaver as it held Brujia's head to a tree. Arian went for the kill at Hagatha seeing Brujia incapacitated. But Hagatha took what was left of her broom and flew off still holding her chest from Arian's attack. Arian sent a corona at the brooms' base breaking it into two as Hagatha, unsupported, fell.

Sebastian attacked Hexe sending coronas from both athames to ward off her athame's corona as he flew at her at high speed. Hexe flew away trying to rescue Hagatha from falling. She caught her and flew erratically away using her athame for a smoke screen to conceal them.

Arian had to dissipate back to the Realm of Twilight as she exerted too much energy. She stated to Uncle Horatio. "Finish her off."

Uncle Horatio took his debitum naturae from his belt. But Brujia didn't wait. She tore out the dagger from the tree, releasing her helmet and ran off. Uncle Horatio noticed that his spell book was soaked from the broken vials. He couldn't read a thing, being wet, the ink ran.

Uncle Horatio stared in disbelief at his spell book. "Oh, oh!"

Sebastian called through the crystal ball. "Arian. Where are you?" He couldn't locate his Uncle.

Lucien answered. "Father, we are safe but Mommy is saving Uncle Horatio. Hagatha almost doused him with the love elixir."

Sebastian unbelieving stated. "What, she was to protect you." He saw Arian dematerializing back to the Realm of Twilight drained. "How are you?"

Arian said. "Your Uncle is a disaster. You better find him." Both Selena and Lucien held onto her as Arian hugged both of them.

Hexe tended to Hagatha. She made Hagatha lie down so she could assess her wounds. Arian gouged out most of the breastplate down to the skin covering her collarbone. Hagatha bled. Hexe pointed the witch's rod repeating. "Heal thy wounds." Hexe asked. "Hagatha, how do you feel now?"

Hagatha had very shallow breathing. Moving her chest to breathe was too excruciating. She spoke in spasms. "I think I am a bit better, thank you."

Hexe cursed. "For all the pain you have caused in my sister, I shall give you it in triplicate Arian. I swear!" Hexe commanded with the witch's rod. "Brujia!" Brujia transported next to Hagatha." When Brujia appeared she realized how bad Hagatha was.

Brujia cried in shock. "My, Arian almost killed you! How are you?"

Hagatha moved slightly stating. "We will have to use illusions to fight Sebastian for I need to rest. We could use Boreas, the North wind. With winds buffeting them, their strength will be vanquished so we can save ours."

"Good, you do it, Hagatha." Hexe affirmed. "But I will kill Arian now. Why not attack Sebastian's most vulnerable spot, his children and his new wife. My vengeance has been roused seeing you suffer Hagatha. If you will excuse me, Arian has only minutes to live. Take care of Hagatha, Brujia," as Hexe created another witches' rod for Hagatha, taking hers.

Hagatha held Hexe's hand. "Arian is treacherous. Maybe you shouldn't go alone."

Hexe reiterated. "I am consumed with hate. She better beware. For her luck has run out. I will finish it this time. She won't interfere again. She will wish that she never saw me!" Hexe dissipated into the Realm of Twilight.

Hagatha grasped Brujia's arm. "I feel foreboding. She is too hateful. She will make errors."

Brujia said. "Hexe can not be reasoned with and I can't leave you like this."

Hagatha suggested. "Let's make the North wind illusion."

Sebastian used the crystal ball to locate Uncle Horatio. He seemed to walk in circles about the lake. The reflection of the full blue moon imparted beauty into rapture as the moonbeams floated sensually over the water rising and falling in endless patterns of calmness.

"Uncle Horatio!" Sebastian called. "Are you all right? Here, I have another broom. Arian made it for you with the witch's rod."

"Thank God, an ally!" You don't know how glad I am to see you. If it were not for Arian, I would have been done for." Uncle Horatio sighed from relief." Hagatha fell almost on top of me. I heard and felt her proximity of her fall. God is she heavy! I feel awful especially when she said. "Stand still my love." I think I will have a coronary if I see her again."

"Uncle, get a grip on yourself." Sebastian commented. "It's not over yet. They are regrouping for more trouble."

Uncle Horatio confirmed. "Arian really gave Hagatha a blow. She bled from her breast plate."

Sebastian's concern rose." Hexe will probably be vengeful. I better check with Arian." Sebastian focused back to the Realm of Twilight as he tried to contact Arian but what he focused on was Hexe as Giselle dived down with the spell of impuissance on Hexe's head. She was successful.

Hexe cursed. "Giselle, I will burn you in infernal flames of Hell for this."

Uncle Horatio turned blanched white. "Sebastian, forget about the Realm of Twilight. Look behind us!"

A colossus eminence sprang from the lake as a frosted jagged-edged creature expanding to forty feet in height blocked Sebastian's view. Discernible arms with a bearded head of ice still forming augmented in width. His breath spouted ice spicules maliciously spewed as winds' fury from Hell.

Uncle Horatio hyperventilated. "I think this is not the first death that I will die from tonight."

Sebastian pulled at Uncle Horatio. "Let's not wait for it to grab us. We better distance ourselves until we know what it can do."

Torrents of wind filled with stinging ice gushed past as they tried to distance themselves. But they were blown in every which way as the North wind, Boreas, made his way closer to his prey.

Uncle Horatio shouted to be heard. "Go get him, Sebastian. I have all the faith in you."

Sebastian tried to calm himself but all he could say was. "Thank you."

Boreas first bombarded them with another wind of frost like daggers towards Sebastian and Uncle Horatio. The shield protected them but for how long? Sebastian guided the witch's rod and pointed it at Boreas using the transfer spell. He recited it quickly. All the ice spicules reversed direction back to Boreas. Boreas became angry and sucked the wind back down his throat sucking both Sebastian and Uncle Horatio towards his mouth. The brooms were not strong enough to fight it. Sebastian pulled his broom straight up towards the stars as Uncle Horatio gasped.

"Help, oh God!" Uncle Horatio was sucked into Boreas' mouth.

Sebastian, horrified, ordered his witch's rod to transfer Uncle Horatio out of there. Uncle Horatio came through Boreas' nose and out straight up to the sky holding onto his broom and an athame as he finally approached Sebastian.

"Are you all right? "Sebastian called out concerned.

"Yes, oh thank you. It seems all I do is panic. My heart throbs. I am not well. This fellow's innards are like walls of frost. I almost suffocated in him if it were not for you, dear Sebastian." Uncle Horatio kept holding his chest.

Sebastian then aimed his magical athame firing a flamed corona to see what effect, if any, it would do. Boreas blew the flamed corona back at Sebastian and Uncle Horatio.

Uncle Horatio replied "I think you have gotten his attention."

Sebastian pulled Uncle Horatio down as the flamed corona just past them. "Too close, Uncle. Let's use the athame from different angles and form another flame corona but augment the flame with the transformation spell and consume him."

Uncle Horatio said. "For all it's worth, let's melt this thing."

Both Sebastian and Uncle Horatio flew out perpendicularly, respective, of their target as they sent two simultaneous flamed coronas at Boreas. Then with the witch's rod and the transformation spell they augmented the flame twenty times its original size. The flames were too big for Boreas to blow away. To make it even more difficult, Sebastian created another corona and enlarged it transferring it inside of Boreas. He was consumed, melting into oblivion back into the lake screaming piteously. Being consumed he came after Sebastian and Uncle Horatio running as fast as he could to engulf them with the flames and water of which he reverted.

Sebastian pulled Uncle Horatio with him as they were flying faster to avoid the confrontation. Boreas, since he was melting, blew the flames from around him towards Sebastian and Uncle Horatio so if the water could not drown them the flames would burn them as well.

Sebastian turned his broom around to face his opponent as he told Uncle Horatio to get out of the way. Sebastian transformed himself as large as Boreas holding his shield and athame he hacked the rest of Boreas into pieces.

"Well." Hagatha yelled. "You can't consume me! Hexe should be fighting with Arian or killing your children by now while you still have to confront me!"

Terror struck Sebastian's heart as those words tore at him.

Hexe was still wiping off the impuissance spell that Giselle doused upon her. She tried to use Hagatha's witch's rod but it lay there dead from any incantation as well as her broom. She cursed again. "I will find you!" She tried to send a lightning bolt at Giselle but her finger couldn't send one. She cursed again. "And when I do, You will die, I swear."

Arian faced Hexe. "I have been waiting for three hundred years for this moment. So don't waist your breath on idle talk." Arian had two rapiers and two daggers. She assumed her stance of attack. "En garde, I speak as if you are civilized, of which you are not."

Hexe screamed. "You die now. I want to rejoice at your excruciating death."

The two opponents exchanged blows but Arian, wary of Hexe, stayed well out of reach in case Hexe would do something unexpected. Hexe was surprised of Arian's skill as she tried to stab at her but Arian got out of the way each time. Just as Hexe thought that she could corner her, Arian maneuvered miraculously flipping away again. Arian knocked Hexe's powerless athame down and stood on it while Hexe viciously thought of how to retrieve it. She blew poisoned darts at Arian while Arian thwarted them away as they came too close. Arian advanced while Hexe threw more daggers at Arian.

Lucien and Selena hiding in the secret gazebo saw Hexe and Arian combating blows at one another. Lucien concentrated hard to reach his Father through the crystal ball. Sebastian heard Lucien's voice and immediately picked up the crystal ball. It focused onto Lucien as Selena clutched onto her brother.

Sebastian asked. "What is wrong?"

Lucien responded. "Mommy is fighting with Hexe. Hexe is throwing poison darts as well as daggers."

Instinctively Sebastian said. "How is your mother? Is she all right?"

Lucien replied. "She is advancing on Hexe's position despite what Hexe does."

"Oh God!" Sebastian felt sharp pains in his chest as he was filled with anxiety.

"Now Mommy has thrown her athame at Hexe's heart. Mommy is running towards her with the debitum naturae."

"Yes, Yes, what is happening?" Sebastian pleaded.

Lucien stated. "I will send you an image from Mommy to you."

Sebastian stared. Arian was about to open the vial, when Hexe sprang back to life using the athame that was stabbed in her, against Arian.

Hexe screamed. "I am immortal. Every time you think you can kill me, I come back!" She laughed." Too bad for you."

Sebastian wanted to keep watching but he heard strange sounds of thunder clashing about, as he had to draw his attention from Arian and the children to see what Hagatha was planning to do. He reverted back to his size of six feet and five inches.

Uncle Horatio flew toward Sebastian's side. "You better get a look at this. Each time their illusions become worse."

Dark thunderous clouds appeared from the clear sky obliterating the glowing blue moon with the menacing gloom. The thunderclouds took shape as arcs of lighting bolts ripped through disrupting time and space.

"This is it." Uncle Horatio sighed. "Our lightning bolt spell won't handle this."

Sebastian stated. "Does this have a name? The North wind was called Boreas. We could ask Arian but she is fighting with Hexe in the Realm of Twilight."

Uncle Horatio gasped." Not with that evil, wicked, nasty, venomous witch of evil!"
Sebastian concluded. "You are getting repetitious, Uncle."

Brujia asked Hagatha while Hagatha was still creating the next illusion. "Since your witch's rod was rendered useless from the impuissance spell, I will summon its own return to the Realm of Reality as well as Hexe's broom. Well, lets see if I remember the puissance spell. How does it go "

PUISSANCE SPELL

Swayed from impugned uncertainty
Pertinaciously recoiled to instill its ability
Osmosed efficacy from tottering dominions
Unrepressed by squelched nisus as a resilient minion
Nimiety capacity assimilated
Nigh tangency, thoroughly infiltrated
Redeemed and amended from being taunted
Totally expressed, omnipotence undaunted.

"That should fix it." Now," as Brujia examined her vial, "is this all of the love elixir? We don't have very much of it."

Hagatha answered. "When we concentrated it to four times its strength, it condensed in size so use it when the opportunity arises which hopefully will be soon. Uncle Horatio is just the perfect target, the bumbling fool."

Brujia told Hagatha. "Hexe is not doing very well. Arian has already killed her once."

Hagatha alarmed ranted. "Arian is so treacherous, she should have been a witch."

Arian confronted Hexe again as they were dueling back and forth. Arian sliced through Hexe's armor to her clothing.

Hexe screeched in fury. But when Hexe did, she heard Selena scream with fear.

Hexe gleamed. "Your adopted children are nearby. How unfortunate for you if I find them."

Arian attacked with more fury talking under her breath so that Lucien could hear." Please stay as quiet as you can."

Hexe countered. "You forget Arian. I have excellent hearing. The children are by the lake in the gazebo." Hexe ran to access the walkway. Arian had to run after but instead she materialized in front of the children because of the emerald rings the children had on.

"How long have we been dodging these lightning bolts? The last one practically burned my broom. It is not flying well." Uncle Horatio complained.

Sebastian used his witch's rod to transform Uncle Horatio's broom into its proper order.

Uncle Horatio, now flying better, stated. "Thank you, Sebastian. This weather is getting worse. Does magic work in the rain?"

Sebastian wondered. "I hope so. The rain is coming down in torrents."

Uncle Horatio sneezed. "It's a plot to tire us out and I must conclude it's working."

Sebastian agreed. "We could use a transformation spell on us to keep us vigil and refreshed."

Uncle Horatio added. "Will it hurt?"

Sebastian said. "Let's try it on." Sebastian transformed as well as Uncle Horatio. "How do you feel?"

"Better. I am amazed." Uncle Horatio replied.

Sebastian thought. "Hagatha's injury must be serious. Why else do we have these illusions? I should check on Arian and the children. He took the crystal ball to see Arian with two children behind her. Hexe threw waves of darts and daggers at them. "Oh my God! Sebastian held his breath. "I have to go back."

Uncle Horatio stated. "I think not. Look below us!"

Up from the lake a whirlpool encased both Sebastian and Uncle Horatio sucking them into the bottom of the lake to drown them. They were completely submerged unable to breathe. The water's strength was unfathomable. Sebastian utilized his witch's rod to encase himself and Uncle Horatio in a very large bubble of air so at least they could breathe.

"Now what shall we do?" Uncle Horatio sputtered.

"Let's make the bubble float to the surface so we can escape." Sebastian acknowledged.

Uncle Horatio smiled. "Very good."

Sebastian felt a foreboding. He wondered what would be at the surface. He readied his athame for the worst as well as the witch's rod.

Hagatha asked Brujia. "Be prepared with the love elixir. When they surface, we will be ready for them."

Brujia and Hagatha flew over the lake in anticipation of what would follow.

Arian was fed up with Hexe. She aimed and plunged her dagger into Hexe's heart. Hexe screamed in agony as it penetrated deep into the chest. Arian then grabbed the witch's rod speaking to Lucien. "Please recite the transfer spell and get away. Do it, Lucien!"

Lucien complied. "Yes, Mommy." Arian watched them both being transferred, Selena and Lucien, into the house. She threw the witch's rod along with so that as the children left, they would have the rod to be able to transfer again.

Hexe came back. "This time you will have the pain!"

But Arian attacked Hexe before Hexe could finish her words. She slashed hard. She knocked Hexe's athame out from her hands again. She was relentless, even for Hexe who seemed tired. Arian slashed again at Hexe's neck but at that same moment Hagatha transferred Hexe back to the Realm of Reality, so she could have her Sebastian. Lucien felt Arian's presence in him as she materialized with the children. "Let me see the crystal ball, Lucien." Lucien relinquished his hold on it.

Lucien informed Arian. "Father and Uncle Horatio are in a bubble of air because they were encased in water."

Arian immediately scanned the surface to see two witches waiting for their prey like spiders. Arian spoke to Sebastian through the crystal ball. "Sebastian, they are all waiting for you to float to the surface so they can put the elixir on you."

Sebastian cried. "Arian are you all right? I was so worried for you."

"Sebastian, make illusions of other bubbles, so you and Uncle Horatio can escape." Arian suggested.

Uncle Horatio ranted. "They are waiting for us! Oh God. Oh, God!"

163

Sebastian used the witch's rod creating thousands of bubbles. He then focused upon the witches' position using the crystal ball on the surface so he could navigate their bubble far away. He then ordered the bubbles to burst at the witches like waterspouts as they surfaced elsewhere.

In the meantime, Hexe appeared into the Realm of Reality. Hexe gasped. The bubbles, thousands of them, doused all the witches. They flew higher to escape, barely seeing where they were flying.

Hexe screamed. "It's Arian. She has informed them. Now, my Sebastian has gotten away again. I hate her so much!"

Hagatha absolutely soaked added. "You would have died again. She almost chopped off your head. You can't win. She out matches you, Sister."

Hexe raved. "It's not true. I would have won!"

Brujia reminded Hexe. "Arian would have killed you three times, Hexe. Give up, Arian is better."

Hexe contested. "I can't think straight when I hate her so much. But, I will win."

Hagatha stated. "Denying the truth will get you killed. I won't have it. I will kill Arian. You trap Sebastian. Let's locate him first. Arian is trapped. I can deal with her later. We must stay with the original plan."

Sebastian eavesdropped on the witches' conversation. He spoke to the witch's rod. "Make Uncle Horatio and myself invisible so that the witches will not detect us with their witch's rod."

Uncle Horatio relaxed a bit. " Do you think the witch's rod can do it?"

Sebastian continued. "At least we could try. Arian is safe for the moment. She can rest from Hexe's attack." Sebastian asked the crystal ball to focus on either himself or Uncle Horatio. The ball only showed a blank. "This might work."

"I am relieved." Uncle Horatio answered. "But, I am seeing lightning bolts in the sky."

Sebastian asked the crystal ball to focus on the lightning bolts. It revealed Arian using the emerald (two hundred and fifty carats) on the witches. Sebastian stated "Arian is firing at the witches again, we better help her."

"That did it." Hagatha cried." We will all kill Arian, then Sebastian will come to us. We won't have to look for him."

Hexe smiled gleefully. "Good. I want her to die an excruciating death."

Brujia mentioned." You never even got close to killing her."

Hexe warned her sisters. "Giselle put the impuissance spell on me. I couldn't even use my magic."

Sebastian could not risk the witches' attack on Arian. He would rather sacrifice himself. He contacted Arian with the crystal ball. "Arian." Sebastian whispered. "Use the illusion spell with the video cam and aim it towards the witches. I won't let them come after you. I love you too much to risk you and the children."

Arian responded. "I will do so right away." She looked at him and then got the video cam aiming it at the convex mirror to make the image come at the witches.

Hexe focus above. "I see them. They are above us." She took off in hot pursuit while Hagatha and Brujia also followed, trying to out fly them.

Brujia asked Hagatha. "How come we see them now when we couldn't focus on them before with our witch's rod?"

Hagatha responded." Why do you always ask questions? But, you know you do have a point! What should we be following?"

Brujia answered. "I don't know. I am just tired of the whole thing."

Sebastian had Arian take the witches through the trees where he had a rope to hinder their flight so that they would topple off. He would fly over them and splash the debitum naturae on their skins even if he had to expose their skins, flailed if need be. He was determined.

Uncle Horatio waited on his broom behind the thickets of trees, where the witches would land. He was trying to calm himself by taking several deep breaths but nothing seemed to work. Sebastian on his broom waited for the precise moment to pull the rope. He saw the virtual image of himself and Uncle Horatio whiz by followed by three witches. Hexe was in the lead, followed by Hagatha and Brujia. Sebastian pulled the rope. All three of the witches fell tumultuously upon the ground. Sebastian flew over them with his athame. His debitum naturae was carefully opened and he had his spell book of which he would recite the transformation spell to get the witches' armor off. He succeeded as the witches tried to get up from their fall without their armor. Uncle Horatio gazed at his spell book. He forgot that when he crash-landed, the vials of spells soaked his spell book causing the ink to run. Uncle Horatio was above Brujia on his broom trying to make sense of the spell that he had to say. Brujia yanked Uncle Horatio off his broom as the two of them wrestled on the ground. Brujia whacked Uncle Horatio down with the back of her hand and got her elixir out and doused him.

Sebastian was about to pour the debitum naturae on Hexe when he heard Uncle Horatio in ecstasy cry out.

"Brujia, I love you! Come my love. Don't be shy."

Hexe grabbed her athame as she contented with Sebastian who still had the open vial of the debitum naturae.

Arian didn't lose a second. She grabbed the emerald to shoot lightning bolts at Hagatha so that Sebastian combats only one witch rather than two as Brujia ran away from Uncle Horatio who pursued Brujia half crazed.

Brujia screamed. "He loves me instead of you, Hagatha. Help me now! Hagatha, don't leave me with him." Brujia climbed a tree despite Horatio's advances." Please, Hagatha, this isn't fair."

Uncle Horatio used the witch's rod and made a rope. He lassoed a tree branch as he swung up to her. "I found you my love, come to me."

Sebastian was just about to pour the debitum naturae on Hexe for he had knocked her athame from her hands.

"Now, Sebastian." Hexe stared at him." My Love. Put that down. You will love me soon. I promise."

"Never!" Sebastian said vehemently displaying such anger.

Hexe, in less than twenty seconds reverted into a huge black panther showing such venom, as she jumped at Sebastian with her fangs out and her teeth ready to bite. Sebastian jumped back as Hexe jumped away and reverted back into herself with a broom and flew away. Sebastian held his breath for the poison almost touched his skin when he jumped back. Where was his Uncle? Sebastian couldn't locate him. "Uncle." He screamed. "Where are you?"

Sebastian turned as he gazed across the way to see his Uncle swinging on a rope trying to catch Brujia." Oh, my god." Sebastian placed his hand to his face. "He has been doused with the love elixir." He grabbed for his crystal ball. "Arian, have you seen my Uncle?"

"Yes, Sebastian. I couldn't save him. I couldn't materialize fast enough. I am sorry but he is keeping Brujia away from Hexe and Hagatha more than he did when he wasn't in love. It seems for him, that love makes him brave. Sebastian, they are probably regrouping. Be careful. We all love you ever so much."

At that moment two electric bolts came very close to Sebastian. Sebastian surrounded himself like a protective sphere with the lightning protection shield. The witches sequestered him with his protection shield away like a bubble being pulled upwards towards the thunderclouds.

"Arian! " Sebastian called out but the crystal ball went dead due to the electrical interference .He dismounted from his broom standing motionless within the sphere Sebastian stared in disbelief. He was inside a thundercloud where the electricity exploded in waves in different parts with such colors producing the hugest lightning bolts, which created deafening thunderclaps. The crashing together of the electrical bolts inside the voluminous cloud arced. Lightning burst forth rushing past the bubble with such force. The thunderclaps sounds were staggering as Sebastian held his ears from the pain it gave. The clashing of the lightning simulated a visage of the sections of a brain during synapses, with the electrical discharges. It was frightening as well as difficult to escape. The witches undoubtedly waited for him.

Arian and the children gazed upon the crystal ball. She explained to the children about lack of communications with Sebastian. "It is the electrical interference. How is Sebastian going to get out of there?" Arian worried. She asked the crystal ball to focus on the witches.

Hagatha gleamed. "We will finally get him now. He will have to come out of there sooner or later, and when he does, we will be ready for him. He can't shoot his athame that well even if he has two of them. For we will send a large lightning burst in front of him that will blind him, as we will capture him in the process. By then, we will douse him in the love elixir and he will be yours to the end of time."

Arian took the witch's rod. "Come I will send you to your Father. I will materialize a moment later."

Sebastian saw his children transfer. Selena hugged her Father witnessing their surroundings while clutching him tightly. Lucien hugged his Father as well and stared at the lightning tearing forth.

"Why are you here?" Sebastian inquired hugging them back for he missed them.

Lucien announced. "Mommy is coming. She will materialize, so we can talk to you without the electrical interference."

Arian materialized into Sebastian, as Sebastian held her there not letting her go.

"I always have so much pleasure when I feel your presence within me." Sebastian whispered.

Arian blushed as she turned around to kiss him. "The witches are waiting for you. I am at a loss to help you. I could transfer you with us or do you have any other ideas?" She stared into his eyes so concerned. "We can' t communicate with the electrical interference's."

Sebastian held her." I have an idea. Where are the witches precisely."

"They are forty feet below you in a straight line."

"How large is the cloud?" Sebastian continued.

"The cloud is eighty feet wide and two hundred and eighty feet high. "Arian gazed into Sebastian's face.

"I will take the witch's rod and create two large magnets on either side of the cloud. One magnet being the cathode being the negative force, while the other the anode being the positive force. I will suspend them into the air turning their magnetism on at the same time. That will pull all the positrons towards the cathode and all the electrons towards the anode, splitting the clouds' electricity. Then before I turn the magnets on, I will also create invisible iron filings that will not be felt and place them on Hagatha and Hexe. So when I turn this on, Hexe and Hagatha will be attracted to the cathode and will short the system, burning them or shocking, them, or maybe even killing them. Then I will attack them, what is left. So I guess you must go back."

"Must I?" Arian kissed Sebastian while holding onto Lucien and Selena. They were all in awe staring into the heart of the cloud. "Be careful. Please steer yourself out of danger. I think I require another kiss." Arian's eyes bewitched him.

Sebastian gladly obliged. He kissed and hugged each of them.

Arian took the witch's rod transporting the children to Giselle, to make sure that they were safe. Arian held Sebastian and dematerialized away. Sebastian missed them already.

He employed the witch's rod to create the cathode and anode and the invisible iron filings placing them on Hexe and Hagatha. He made a flash of light so bright that he escaped without detection. At a safe distance he turned on the magnets simultaneously. The most extreme clap of thunder burst forth as it echoed through the cloud. The tearing of electrons disseminated the cloud apart as lightning bursts exploded everywhere. Hagatha and Hexe were drawn to the cathode at such speed that they impacted the cathode as the electric arcs expounded. Both witches appeared unconscious. Their attire of the armor kept the electrons buzzing around them. Even their hair was singed. However, their protective spell saved them from death. Sebastian attacked them taking his witches' rod to transfer them into their normal attire for the debitum naturae. He flew hard to pour the poison onto them. He just reached Hagatha when suddenly both witches disappeared.

Sebastian swore. "Damnation! Where did they go? Arian!"

Arian answered. "Brujia has saved her sisters with her witch's rod. They are on the surface in the tree groves close to the Uncle Horatio's house towards your left. Forgive me, it is my left which is your right. They are badly hurt. Prepare for another illusion. I miss you already, Sebastian. Let me find your Uncle. He is walking in the forest calling Brujia. Please take cover. This night seems endless."

Sebastian quite concerned inquired. "Are you tiring? You never rested and you didn't sleep last night."

"I know." Arian sighed." But fear of the unexpected drives me on. Maybe, if you are good in archery you could create a bow and arrow and shoot the poison at them. Your Uncle's chimney is a protected spot, be careful."

Sebastian flew to Uncle Horatio's chimney and took the witch's rod out.

In the meantime, Brujia complained. "You almost got killed out there. It is a miracle that you are alive, with such a lightning bolt. Have you seen yourself? Your hair is singed. It is amazing; you're not bald. Let's give up. This isn't worth it. Both of you have a fried appearance. Hexe, why don't you find someone that likes you. It would make life easier."

Hexe only cried. "How is my hair? My Hair!"

"Well, you still have some. It is just hard to find. I am even amazed you two have skin. This man means business. He hates you. You killed his child while imprisoning his wife for three hundred years. Don't think Arian didn't tell him, she has a diary. Knowing that, he in this lifetime has fallen in love with her again. In the meantime, you almost killed his Selena, hurt and threatened his Arian, in which he will hate you the more."

"Oh shut up! My hair! I look awful! I must make myself beautiful. Give me that witch's rod, Brujia!" Hexe snatched the witch's rod.

"I already said that it is past the power of magic! "Brujia contested." Hagatha, how are you feeling. You are too quiet. Is your chest hurting?"

"No," Hagatha replied. "I am very tired but I know you inoculated Uncle Horatio. Where is he?"

"I tried to lose him. I even put him in armor so he can't follow me so quickly. You better do something, so that he will go for you. I don't want him!"

"I know, I will give us a refreshing spell." Hagatha expedited her witch's rod. All of them felt better.

"Brujia, my love, come to me. I have finally found you." Uncle Horatio professed.

"Oh, no!" Brujia wailed.

Sebastian had the witches in his sights when Uncle Horatio burst onto the scene protecting the witches from Sebastian's arrow. Uncle Horatio was becoming inconvenient. Brujia was safe. She had her armor on. But Hexe and Hagatha had their usual attire.

"Brujia! Please come to me. I know you love me."

"Hagatha, do something." Brujia shrieked as she ran behind Hagatha.

"I know you are playing with me. Being hard to get my Love? You will find I have no fear. I will not forsake you! My heart beats just for you. You tantalize me. Excuse me, Hagatha. You are in the way. I want your sister, not you. You are not for me. Now Brujia, I know you love me."

Sebastian was getting sick from this tiresome dribble.

"Horatio." Hagatha demurely beckoned. "You love me, not this flit of a girl. Kiss me!" She pointed to her mouth. "Hexe, persuade Horatio to stay put!"

Hexe, who had made herself beautiful again, came closer to Uncle Horatio.

Uncle Horatio felt danger. "Brujia, please come to me! I don't trust your sister."

"Never!" Said Brujia exasperated.

Sebastian worried. Hexe was getting closer. He thought. That's good but if I miss, then Uncle Horatio will be in danger. I must try it. Sebastian aimed and fired. The arrow would have hit Hexe in the arm but Uncle Horatio moved his arm and it hit his Uncle's armor instead, instantly bouncing off.

"Oh God." Sebastian called out. "Thank God he is covered in armor."

Uncle Horatio disappeared. Arian transferred him out of the way as Arian whispered to Sebastian. "Try again." Arian's image empathized through the crystal ball. "Your Uncle is safe. I placed him in the forest. Your Uncle is open to suggestions and may harm us."

Sebastian aimed again as Hagatha and Hexe ran for their lives. Brujia ran behind the trees. Hagatha transformed herself back into an armored knight, as did Hexe. Sebastian used his athame to mist his escape.

Hagatha's fury rose." Hexe, he almost killed us again. He is too smart for us. We will send our athames to attack him and we will kill Arian now. Let's go. I will fight her first. Then, when you have an opportunity, you will stab her and make it quick. Brujia will make sure our athames will aim its strikes to make each blow count to really keep Sebastian busy."

"But." Brujia cried. "Why don't we give up?"

"Never!" Hexe saucily snapped." I want my Sebastian."

Arian gazed in the crystal ball. "We must prepare, Lucien, you must, at any point of danger, protect you and your sister by transferring to a safe place." She held the children ever so tightly. "I love you so much. I will contact your father, Sebastian? What is happening to you? Are you all right?" The crystal ball focused on Sebastian. He was fighting two athames and his own Uncle Horatio as Brujia orchestrated everything with the witch's rod. "Oh no, not his Uncle too! Giselle are you ready? I must prepare." Arian appeared desperate. She was past angry. She sent using the three largest emeralds, a colossal lightning bolt against Brujia using the crystal ball to aim.

Brujia saw the lightning bolt coming, as did Uncle Horatio. He flew to her to save his love. Sebastian's blows were strong as he broke one of the magical athames. It fell to the earth lifeless. Sebastian transferred himself to Arian's side, everyone ran to him.

"How did you know that we need you? The witches will be here soon. Where can I hide the children?" Arian held Sebastian not wanting to let him go. "Will the athame come across to the Realm of Twilight?"

"It can't, not unless it has the witch's rod with the transfer spell. That athame can wait for me. I must protect my family." Arian didn't want to let Sebastian go as she kept scrutinizing the crystal ball.

Arian cried. "They are here! We can't fight them in the house. There isn't any space. Giselle be careful." They gazed in the crystal ball seeing Giselle diving at Hagatha and dousing her whilst Hagatha's embitterment fumed. The impuissance spell made her useless. Hagatha attempted to send lightning bolts but nothing came out of her fingers.

"Hexe is hiding. I will engage Hagatha. You get Hexe, Sebastian. You will be my surprise as Hexe is Hagatha's." Arian kissed Sebastian so tenderly. Sebastian didn't let go." We must go." Arian peered into his eyes. He kissed her again as they kissed the children. Arian ventured out to meet Hagatha.

"Show yourself or are you afraid?" Arian announced.

"Me, afraid of you? Don't make laugh." Hagatha dealt the first blow. "Curse your soul! You hurt my Hexe!"

"I know she is here with you. You never play fair." Arian won again. Arian made every strike count. "Why don't you fight me both together?" Arian flipped to see Hexe in the corner of her eye. "So there you are. How brave, here to stab me in the back!" Arian lunged at Hagatha. She struck so hard that Hagatha's athame fell from her hand. Arian stood on the athame. Arian stared at Hexe. "So why don't you finish me off? Obviously, the impuissance spell is not on you, so why are you waiting? Get it over with!"

"No, we must torture you very slowly. Where should I start?" Hexe laughed.

Sebastian ordered the witch's rod to transform Hexe's armor off as Hexe screamed, trying to revert back. Sebastian threw his athame at Hexe. Hexe transformed herself into a wall using Hagatha's, witch's rod. The athame bounced off. Sebastian created another athame for himself as Hexe reverted back to herself as they fought again.

Hagatha ran for shelter while Arian undauntedly pursued after her.

Uncle Horatio, nevertheless, rescued Brujia. He reached her at the last moment on his broom dashing away from the lightning bolt as it exploded missing them by inches.

"Leave me alone. Thank you for rescuing me, however, you are becoming annoying. If you do love me, you would respect me. Leave me at the house and go away." Brujia was blunt.

"But, Brujia, my love?"

"I will thank you again but leave me alone."

Uncle Horatio flew her to the house. "I am doing everything you ask of me. So why don't you marry me? We could have a church wedding here by the lake. Isn't it romantic?"

"You have delusions of grandeur, but not with me. I am not your type. You must get over me or else!"

"What are you saying or else? What must I do to prove my love?"

"Where is Sebastian? He must have transferred to the Realm of Twilight. Oh no, Hagatha will kill me."

"No she won't. I won't let her harm a hair on your head."

"Why me? Oh God! "Brujia wailed." Oh well, if you love me, promise that you must find Sebastian and bring him to me. You must tie him up with this rope. Now go. I will transfer you to the Realm of Twilight with me. Be good or else! If you can't find Sebastian, bring me the children. Wait! Let me rephrase that, not our children but Sebastian's children. I am going to be blunt! Understand!" Brujia recited the transfer spell. Both Brujia and Uncle Horatio transferred across. "I will wait here for your return. Bring whoever you can."

Uncle Horatio proceeded into the house to find the children. He knew where they would be hiding, in Arian's room. He ran upstairs then hesitated as he slowly turned the door handle. "So there you are Lucien. Come to your Uncle."

"No." Lucien cried pushing Selena behind him." Stay away! You are not yourself. You love a witch!"

"Now Lucien, she is not a witch, she is a person."

"No, you have forsaken us by having a love elixir on you. You are supposed to love Hagatha, not Brujia .You saw the wrong witch but, they will change that once they have you." Selena blurted.

"I never thought you would say that, Selena, you trust me, don't you?"

" No!" Selena grasped the memory loss spell and threw the vial at her Uncle." Don't breathe Lucien. Giselle, save us!"

Giselle pointed her witch's' rod and transformed the children's size so that Giselle could accommodate them. They mounted as Giselle flew out of the window. Uncle Horatio sputtered and coughed.

"Who am I? I must open this window more. I must get some air. My do I have a headache! I need more air. Who am I? Where am I? Who should I call? Oh my God, I am sick."

Giselle watched from a tree and made her tiny witch's rod clear the air in Arian's room from the memory loss spell.

Uncle Horatio walked down stairs and out towards Brujia." Oh, my love. Who am I? I know you, for I am so much in love with you. Your soul just talks to me. My, you are beautiful."

"Oh no! Someone dispensed the memory loss spell on you. It lasts two days, I should know. Your Giselle doused it on me. My, how time flies. Well, you are no use to me now!"

"But, don't you want me! I love you, but I don't know who you are."

170

"That is ridiculous! I would have never thought that the love elixir would be so strong that the memory loss spell can't even help you forget. I must go and find Hagatha."

"But, don't leave me alone, my love." Uncle Horatio pleaded as he followed her.

Sebastian had Hexe cornered as they fought furiously.

"My love, why can't you understand? I need you. You would be very happy with me. I could give you anything you want."

"Don't ever call me your love and all I want is Arian and my family, never you." Sebastian knocked Hexe's athame out of her hands.

"Sebastian, you can't kill me. Your conscience will tell you that it is wrong." Hexe started to throw daggers at him. "These daggers are filled with the love elixir, my love. Try to avoid them."

Sebastian protected himself with the lightning shield as he stood on her athame. "Try again! I will have no regrets only relief that this has ended." He started to recite the spell for he knew the debitum naturae by heart as he opened the vial.

Hexe was still throwing daggers. Sebastian buffeted each one while balancing the poison with his other hand. Suddenly Hexe's athame grew to five times its size knocking Sebastian off his feet. This caused Sebastian to spill some of the poison, which touched his gloved hand. It soaked the leather glove as he tore the leather glove quickly off. He covered the vial. The athame kept growing as Sebastian tried to buffet the blows. But the athame could fight by itself. Sebastian knew Hexe was going to murder his Arian, as now there would be two witches. Hexe's athame was relentless.

Brujia found Hagatha cornered when Arian finally discovered Hagatha's hiding place. Arian had her spell book opened and took her vial of debitum naturae as she recited the words.

"Hagatha." Brujia cried." Here, have my athame." She tossed it into the air.

Arian couldn't reach the athame. It was tossed too high for her to reach it. So Arian ran towards Hagatha to stab her with the rapier, which she threw at her, when she knew the range, before Hagatha had time to catch Brujia's athame.

Hagatha screamed. "Help me, Brujia. Kill Arian. Throw your daggers! Do something!"

Brujia took out her daggers as Uncle Horatio wrestled Brujia to the ground.

"You can't kill Arian if that is her name. I won't let you." Uncle Horatio professed.

"Let go you buffoon!"

"No. I won't let you kill her. She is my niece. I think, I am not sure."

Hagatha still waited for the athame to come down; however, Arian's rapier hit Hagatha's heart. Hagatha screamed in agony.

"Hagatha." Brujia wailed." I will save thee!"

"Don't think I will give you up." Uncle Horatio gleamed. "You are so close to me now."

"That did it!" Brujia yelled. "This is it! I have had enough of you!" Brujia recited the transformation spell, as Uncle Horatio manifested into a stone armored knight.

Giselle used her witch's rod and changed Brujia's athame into a plain sword.

The sword fell into Hagatha's dead hand. Hagatha regenerated back to life again. Arian read the spell expediently trying to open the vial of debitum naturae while Hagatha was pulling the rapier out of her heart. Arian closed her vial pulling out her second rapier from her scabbard

"I will kill you for that!" Hagatha bewailed. "This time it will be the end for you. You have hurt me for the last time!"

"En garde!" Arian composed her stance as Arian threw her dagger at Brujia with such force that Brujia's helmet dented knocking her out cold. Brujia swooned to the ground.

Hagatha, knowing how Arian fought, kept her distance as they struck blows. Brujia still lay unconscious.

Giselle created with the witch's rod a lightning protection shield for Arian as she observed daggers coming towards her. Arian caught the shield in her hand.

Lucien and Selena atop of Giselle stared down while Selena clutched her brother. "I am out of the memory loss spell, Lucien. I threw both vials at Uncle Horatio. And Giselle seems to have lost her vial when she attacked Hagatha."

"That was smart. What other spells do we have?" Lucien abated.

Selena sobbed. "The expulsion spell, but that means they would only come back again. Let's call Daddy to help Mommy."

Giselle instead flew them to Sebastian. Sebastian used all his strength to break Hexe's athame. It fell in two pieces, dead on the ground.

Sebastian witnessed Giselle deposit Lucien and Selena towards their father. She corrected their size. "Where is Mommy? I must find her quickly!"

Lucien explained. "Mommy is fighting Hagatha and that Uncle Horatio was turned into stone because he prevented Brujia from killing Mommy with Brujia's daggers."

"I must go to her. How does Mommy materialize into people? You, Lucien have seen Mommy do that, explain."

"She concentrates very hard on the emerald ring to make herself materialize into people, but it takes a lot of energy. That is all I know."

Sebastian rubbed Lucien's head. "Stay with Giselle. I can't lose either of you." Sebastian concentrated but it failed. He tried again. It didn't work. He became desperate. He put all his strength but nothing happened.

Lucien cried. "Mommy is being bombarded with," as he viewed the crystal ball with Selena, "daggers like bullets coming towards her from Hexe. Mommy is still fighting Hagatha. Mommy sees the daggers coming. She is taking her shield to protect herself. They all missed except for one. She was stabbed in the stomach but she is still fighting Hagatha. Mommy has pulled out the dagger from her stomach. She is throwing the dagger back at Hexe but she missed. Hexe only gloats while she laughs. Mommy is bleeding!" Lucien and Selena started to cry.

Sebastian absolutely enraged utilized a Herculean strength to materialize into Arian. He could feel her agony as she still fought Hagatha. Arian's eyes were tearing from the pain. She shuddered from the anguish but fought. Sebastian's sword became Arian's as they struck Hagatha's athame with such venom that even Hagatha backed away. Arian and Sebastian were back to back. Sebastian was so exhausted from materializing into Arian.

"Sebastian, you have come at last to your lady's aid, but too late I am afraid. Arian's poison will get to her in a moment." Hexe gleamed.

Sebastian had tears in his eyes as Hexe took her athame to send a corona at Arian. Sebastian turned to face Hexe and the corona as Arian countered to face Hagatha. Hagatha struck another blow.

"Arian!" Sebastian called. "How can you fight with such pain?" Sebastian sent his corona towards Hexe's to obliterate the other. Now, Hexe and Sebastian were striking blows. Sebastian and Arian were still back to back.

"I must." She gasped from the pain." I must protect my family."

Brujia was coming to as she slowly rose but sunk down again.

Arian threw the rapier at Hagatha striking her in the heart. Arian was defenseless. She collapsed to the ground in pain as she doubled up. Sebastian hit Hexe's athame breaking it. He threw another dagger at Hagatha to keep her where she was. He took his athame and transformed it to five times its size. Hexe mounted her broom to escape while Sebastian with all his might threw the transformed athame at Hexe cutting off her head. He hastened to open the vial repeating the spell as he ran and poured it on her.

Hexe's head returned unto her neck as she screamed in such agony. "I am dying and I am in such excruciating pain." She screamed again." Sebastian!"

Giselle, in the meantime traced back her steps and found the memoryloss vial. She flew towards Brujia dousing the memory loss spell unto her. Brujia awoke to see Hexe dying as Hexe was shrinking becoming mottled and misshapen, shriveling into dust, screaming from the top of her lungs due to the pain. The dust, like a vortex, twisted away to the Pit of Tartarus. The witch's rod remained on the ground where she was beheaded.

Brujia didn't wait, not knowing who that was, grabbed a broom and Hexe's witch's rod and flew away to God knows where.

Sebastian held Arian. Arian was crying silently, but started to sing French prayers, the same ones he heard in the nightmare (the glimpse of the past). It was like the last rights. Arian eyed Sebastian and then at Hagatha to warn him. Sebastian had to get Arian's belt to obtain the other vial of debitum naturae. Arian bled profusely from her stab wound. It must have cut an artery. The blood was all over Arian, which brought tears to his eyes, but he had to hurry to kill Hagatha.

Hagatha had resurrected herself as she panicked hearing Hexe's cries. She was still powerless. She fled to avoid Sebastian. Sebastian created a bow from the witch's rod. He dipped the arrow 's head into the poison. He recited the spell out loud and aimed the bow towards Hagatha. He pulled the string. The arrow flew fast and sure towards Hagatha's back. She screamed in agony. She too became mottled, misshapen, shriveling into dust as she vortexed away, with such screams as would shake the soul.

Sebastian immediately rushed to Arian but the children and Giselle were already surrounding her. Lucien held Mommy's hand while Selena embraced Mommy's head, cheek to cheek, crying profusely. Giselle held in her foot the healing spell vial as Giselle opened the spell book with her beak for Sebastian to recite.

Arian shook uncontrollably from the pain. Her facial expression was suppressed, restrained and tightened. Her breathing was spasmodic as she kept her jaw fixed so she wouldn't scream to upset the children. Sebastian took the healing spell from Giselle's foot and recited it while pouring the vial's contents over the puncture wound, which was soaked in blood. Arian winced and jerked in pain upon contact. Sebastian waited for a result. The blood didn't' spurt out, it oozed slightly and then ceased as it healed.

Giselle pointed to the spell book at the symptoms. Sebastian held Arian's other hand squeezing it and kissing it as he restrained himself emotionally so he could think rationally. Since Giselle didn't get a response from Sebastian, she conducted her witch's rod to change a blade of grass into a pen, and wrote in the spell book. Please give the antidote immediately these symptoms are only the beginning. They will be worse very soon. No one noticed. So Giselle carried her spell book opened to the page that she had just written and flew to Sebastian's face so he could read it.

Sebastian with Giselle before him sighed. "Oh my God!" He looked for the number to the vial that corresponded to the antidote, one for arsenic and the other for strychnine. He held Arian's head. "Here, can you take the antidote? Your jaw is so restrained I am afraid I will hurt you by making you take the antidote. I know you don't want to scream in front of the children but we will understand."

Arian peered at Sebastian and then at Selena. Sebastian got the hint and held his Selena while trying to give Arian the antidote in her hand. But she turned over throwing up blood. Selena screamed, as did Lucien. Sebastian put the children aside and held Arian's head taking his handkerchief to wipe the blood from Arian's face and tried to pour the antidote on the side of Arian's mouth so she would ingest some but she wretched again turning on her side before he could give her any.

Sebastian grasped the witch's rod saying. "If you can heal do so, don't' leave me confounded."

Arian stopped throwing up. She turned toward Sebastian. She breathed a bit easier. Sebastian held her and made her take the antidote. Both Lucien and Selena held her.

Giselle wrote to Sebastian. These symptoms will go on for some time. You should keep her warm for she will have chills, spasms, fevers, pain, and emesis.

Arian tried to say words but all she could do is form words. "I love you."

As Sebastian held Arian she flushed with a fever. "I love you too." He kissed her forehead. "Come I will transfer all of us including Uncle Horatio, who is now stone, back to the house. I will nurse you back to health. I remember that you always go through the pain, but since you are immortal you can't die. Hoping that assumption is true, we have one day to make you better and the last day for the exodus spell so that I can have you for my wife, with unknowns still to face. But let's start by making you as comfortable as possible." He kissed her hot cheek. You are burning up. I think I better give you a bath to bring the fever down. He held the witch's rod and transformed everyone with the exception of Uncle Horatio, who he deposited in the foyer, to Arian's bedroom.

Lucien closed the window so that the chilled air would not effect his mother. Sebastian lay Arian on the bed and removed her boots.

Sebastian told Lucien. "Wrap your mother in blankets while I get the boiling water. He used the witch's rod for he wasn't going to waste time and wait for the water to boil.

Giselle rested on her perch.

"Selena." Sebastian called. "Change for bed, you too Lucien. I will stay up with your mother."

Selena ran to the restroom while Lucien changed behind the screen.

Sebastian pointed the witch's rod to the bathtub. "Fill this with hot water." The water poured out of the rod miraculously. Sebastian felt if the temperature was correct. "Lucien and Selena, I will be going back and forth with Arian to the restroom and bed, so you both will sleep on the couch. Kiss your mother good night while I kiss you now. I am sorry we might disturb you depending on how sick your mother is." Sebastian tucked them in and kissed their foreheads. "I love you. Both of you were very brave. I am very proud of you. Now I better take care of Mommy. I hope you will be able to sleep."

Arian opened her night table drawer and grabbed her handkerchief. She placed it in her mouth and screamed through it to muffle the sound while doubling up and shaking. All of them dashed back to Arian. Sebastian tried to hold her while replacing the blankets back on Arian.

"Lucien." Sebastian stated. "Keep the blankets on your mother while I get the witch's rod and the crystal ball."

Lucien along with Selena tried to keep the blankets on as Arian convulsed violently. Sebastian quickly returned with the witch's rod and the crystal ball. He asked the witch's rod to assess Arian's condition and write the words from the crystal ball to sheets of paper so they would know what is happening. Sebastian waved the rod over Arian. The crystal ball illuminated with an incandescent light as words sprang forth onto the page.

The symptoms displayed are the reaction of the poison causing internal hemorrhaging from all her organs. It is caused by another poison that is unfamiliar, probably from the Devil's ointment as an instrument of evil killing immortality. Prognosis is very poor.

Giselle read the prognosis too.

Sebastian asked the witch's rod/ crystal ball. "Can you stop the bleeding? Can you heal her?"

The words on the page stated: to some degree.

"What is her blood type?" Sebastian pursued the rod.

O positive was written on the page.

"I am O positive." Sebastian thought out loud. "I will have to give her a transfusion. She can't keep losing blood and fluids." Sebastian asked the witch's rod to analyze his blood to see if it matched Arian's by examining for other antibodies and antigens that could effect the transfer. "If I describe the implements used for a transfusion can you duplicate them?" Sebastian waited impatiently for the rod to respond while he drew what he needed.

The crystal ball wrote yes.

"Make the duplicates to what I have specified in the drawings and for now please do all you can for Arian." Sebastian requested.

The implements materialized on the night table.

Sebastian asked the witch's rod. "Can you monitor five hundred milliliters of blood in the transfusion?"

The crystal ball wrote yes.

"Arian." Sebastian held her. "I am going to give you some of my blood. I will have to insert this needle into you vein in your arm as I do so to mine. I am sorry to have to hurt you but you need blood. We are the same blood type, if you can understand." He kissed her forehead.

Sebastian lay down next to Arian. He held the witch's rod telling it to monitor five hundred milliliters. He took a cloth moistened with alcohol as he used alcohol on both needles, which were attached to plastic tubing on either end. The needle's gauge was sixteen so the transfer would be fast. He found his vein. He held the needle to his vein and punctured it while not transversing the vein's wall. Blood filled the tube quickly as he let the blood drops fall to insure that Arian would not get any air injected into her vein. He had Lucien pinch the tubing as he then inserted the needle into Arian's arm while he had Selena hold Arian's upper arm steady so she wouldn't not jerk away and pull the needle out. He instructed the rod to monitor the five hundred milliliters as he lay next to Arian.

Sebastian noticed that Arian didn't jerk away, so he spoke to Selena. "Please give Mommy water to dilute the poison as much as possible."

Selena obeyed her Father bringing the ewer of water from the bathroom and a glass, which she filled. She held Mommy's head as Selena removed the handkerchief from her mouth. Selena placed the glass to Mommy's lips.

Sebastian urged Arian." Please drink as much water for me. I love you so much."

Arian attempted. She drank half a glass.

Sebastian kept saying. "More."

Giselle flew to Sebastian with a note. Stop the transfusion. You have given five hundred milliliters as per the witch's rod.

Sebastian asked Lucien to pinch the tube again. He took more handkerchiefs and held it tightly over the needle insertion and pulled the needle out of his own arm. He asked Lucien to hold it, as now he would do it for Arian's arm. He twisted a handkerchief and tied it on Arian's arm. Then he did the same for his own. He asked the witch's rod to heal both puncture wounds.

Arian managed to drink two glasses of water while Selena held her head.

Selena then placed her cheek on Mommy's and kissed her crying. "Mommy, Mommy please get better."

Sebastian asked Arian. "How are you feeling now? Can you talk?"

Arian glanced at him but shook her head to say she could not.

Sebastian questioned the witch's rod. "Has the transfusion helped or not?" Sebastian rose from the bed a little faint but he had to see how the witch's rod would respond.

The witch's rod stated she has stabilized a bit.

Sebastian asked the witch's rod to re-heat the water for the bath and light the fireplace. He carried Arian to the bath followed by two children." Maybe you should try to sleep. You really had an eventful day."

Both Lucien and Selena said. "We want Mommy!"

Sebastian set Arian down behind the screen in the bundle of blankets. He attempted to undress her with Arian's advice while the children held the blanket over her. The corset was especially tricky. To undo her hair from her ringlets and pins confounded him. The length of her hair fell passed her knees. It was so thick and soft with a fragrance of her perfume that lingered which he wrapped in a towel. Her skin was soft and caressive. She waxes, he thought to himself. Arian's eyes seemed dull and feverish. He asked Lucien and Selena to watch her while he got more blankets, pillows, and Arian's nightgown. Returning he placed the blankets and pillows next to the fireplace. He placed Arian's nightgown on the screen. Concealed only by a blanket Sebastian placed her as is in the tepid bath water that was heated by the witch's rod. Sebastian had the children keep another blanket tautly over the bath while he bathed Arian carefully to remove the blood. Sebastian drained the water with Arian still in as he enveloped her with another blanket to lift her out laying her behind the screen.

Giselle stayed with Arian like a protective guardian.

"Here, Lucien and Selena, sleep next to the fireplace while I dress Mommy over by the screen." Sebastian stated gently.

Both children obeyed instantly.

Sebastian removed the wet blankets and draped Arian in her robe while still on the carpet to dry her thoroughly. He placed the nightgown close to make the transfer quick. He replaced her robe as he beheld her petite elegant form quickly placing the nightgown over her head and over her silhouette. Arian was beginning to shake from the chills again. He instantly put more dry blankets over her and situated her near the fireplace close but not too close to the children who stared up with concern. He obtained a basin in case she had to throw up. He lay down besides her holding her close. He asked the witch's rod again for an update on her condition.

He checked the written page with heighten interest. It stated: Give her milk of magnesia to coat her stomach and more water to dilute the poison. She has a temperature of one hundred and three degrees, so place a cold compress on her head. She seems a bit more stable.

Sebastian asked very quickly to the witch's rod. "Is there a possibility that Arian could die?"

The witch's rod wrote. Her diagnosis appears still questionable even with the transfusion. Make her drink more water and milk of magnesia to flush her system.

Sebastian got the water and the milk of magnesia. He tried to make Arian drink but it proved difficult since she fixed her jaw so tightly from the pain. Sebastian put the glass to her lips saying. "Please, Please, drink more!"

Arian did what Sebastian pleaded her to do. She gasped. "Take me to the rest room."

Sebastian carried her gently but quickly and didn't leave her. She had blood in her urine. He wanted her to lie down again and make her drink to replace her body fluids but she threw up again. He made her drink a glass of water so the taste would go away. She cried in his arms unable to keep silent any longer.

Lucien and Selena heard Arian crying and came to comfort her as Arian held Sebastian. They all held her. Sebastian made her lie down and offered her to drink again.

Sebastian ordered the witch's rod. "Please update her symptoms."

The witch's rod wrote. She will fluctuate as the toxins course through her system for the rest of the night.

"Can you boost her immune system or stop the toxins?" Sebastian questioned again.

The witch's rod wrote on the page. Everything that can be done was done. The outcome depends on the patient.

Sebastian stated. "Wake me every fifteen minutes with an update on every organ while I rest along side her. He made the children sleep by the fireplace after kissing them saying. "Your mother needs rest just like you do."

Arian had a change of temperature. She was cold so he placed more blankets on her as he held her head on his lap while he sat up so she could have the freedom of movement for her pains. Arian stopped crying too exhausted to continue.

The witch's rod obeyed its' commands waking Sebastian every fifteen minutes. But soon Sebastian was too exhausted to wake up.

The clock chimed at six AM. It had the ring of silver bells as it counted endlessly the time. Sebastian woke. He was stiff from sleeping on the floor in the rest room with the fireplace. He looked at Arian. She wasn't in contortions. She lay very quiet, blanched white like porcelain. He reached out his hand to feel her head if she had a temperature. She was ice cold.

"Oh my God! Was she dead and I fell asleep and didn't notice?" Sebastian was terrorized to a point of apoplexy.

CHAPTER 12

EXODUS

Ridden with guilt he blamed himself. "How could I have slept through this?" He thrust out his hand to feel for a pulse. He couldn't feel one. He got up quickly but quietly, lest the children would wake up. "How could I explain?" His heart tightened as panic-stricken he uncovered Arian to listen to her heart. But his own heart pounded so fast he couldn't hear anything. He caressed her cheek to try to rouse her. She didn't move. He whispered to her desperately, "Arian, Arian, wake up please," into her ear, shaking her gently.

One eye peeked open staring at him followed by the other eye as pain crept back into her face.

"Thank God your are not dead!" Sebastian kissed her cheek gently as she felt his tears fall on her face. He held her clutched to his chest. "Did you just fall asleep?"

Arian whispered. "Yes."

"I am so sorry, but I had to know. How do you feel? What can I do for you? Please say something? I can't lose you. I love you."

Arian said soothingly. "Shh. I will be all right. I am so exhausted." She managed to raise her hand to his face to calm him but she let it fall too tired to sustain it." Please let me rest. I am too weak to speak any more."

Sebastian covered Arian up very gently as he lay next to her not holding on because she had so much pain, but close to feel one another's warmth. He slept for another four hours. It now chimed ten AM. He woke again as he checked Arian. Her breaths were shallow but steady.

Giselle flew to him with a note. Sebastian read. I have made breakfast with my tiny witch's rod if you and your children would care to have some. Please put Arian to bed. By the way, Uncle Horatio has a crystalline tear. I think he is unhappy being stone. Here are other items that you must attend to. There is the witch's athame waiting to kill you in the Realm of Reality. There are many daggers of poison lying about. Not to mention a missing broom, Hagatha's witch's rod, an athame, broken vials of potions including the debitum naturae and a spell book to be eradicated. You must help your Uncle. Brujia has the memory loss spell that I had placed on her but she will be back for she can sense the magic that is located at Quintessence. The exodus spell should be reviewed .The last item is to read the witch's rod updates on Arian and good morning.

"Thank you Giselle. You are very helpful and informative. We couldn't have gotten as far as we did without you and I am indebted to you." Sebastian gave her a very serious look displaying his heart feelings.

Giselle chirped cheerfully and watched Arian from her perch.

The children were still asleep. So Sebastian transferred the children back to the couch and Arian back into a cleaned bed. (Sebastian had the witch's rod clean it from all of Arian's blood.) He perused the updates on Arian. It did update every organ: blood pressure, hematocrit, urinalysis, serum chemistries, and blood typing. Sebastian smiled when he read that she could still have children. It finished by stating that the patient was stable. "I am impressed at your capabilities witch's rod. I even thank you."

Sebastian poured himself some tea. He spoke out loud. "It would be nice to have a updated newspaper." A newspaper instantly appeared. The headline read, still missing a two hundred and fifty-carat emerald stolen from the British Museum. No traces found. Sebastian choked on his tea. He commanded the witch's rod to polish off all the fingerprints and return it at once to the British Museum. The emerald dissipated as Sebastian followed it with the crystal ball to the case where it was kept. He saw the face of the guard just staring at it, pointing with his shaking arm unbelieving of its reappearance. Sebastian scrutinized the list Giselle gave him. He asked the witch's rod to obliterate the witches' athames, daggers, poison on the premises of the Realm of Reality and the Realm of Twilight. He ordered the debitum naturae along with the other entire potions etc. to be placed back at Quintessence in the cellar where the witches' substances were kept as well as the spell book. With that accomplished he poured tea for Arian. She needed fluids. He walked quickly and knelt beside the bed placing the tea on the night table as he felt Arian's forehead. He took the witch's rod and gave Arian a refreshing spell so she would feel better. He kissed her forehead gently when he noticed that Arian was not alone, two children were in bed with her. Both peeked out from underneath the blankets guiltily.

Sebastian stated in a whisper. "How did you get there? Weren't you sleeping?"

Lucien whispered back. "I had to check on Mommy, so Selena and I sneaked into Mommy's bed. She is breathing very deeply so we didn't disturb her. We had to know."

Sebastian asked. "How are both of you?"

Selena responded. "I am very happy that Mommy is still alive." Tears ran down her cheeks.

Sebastian reached over to calm Selena with a touch. "Shh, Mommy is better. If she was awake, I would give her some tea, but she really has to rest. I have never seen anyone that ill before. I was just as worried as you were. Are you still tired or would you care for breakfast? Giselle conjured it up with her witch's rod."

Lucien's eyes lit up at the prospect.

Sebastian carried Selena carefully out from the blankets while saying to Lucien. "Be as quiet as you can." Lucien slipped out. Arian didn't even wake she slept soundly. Sebastian still holding Selena quietly rose and offered breakfast to the children. They all stared at the newspaper. "While you eat, I will take a bath and change. Please be quiet. Do not disturb your Mother."

Lucien promised. "We won't."

Sebastian hugged both of his children. "I am so proud of you both. I love you both very much."

"Daddy." Selena hesitated." I threw two vials of the memory loss spell at Uncle Horatio. Does it mean that he will forget for four days instead of two?"

Sebastian alarmed repeated. "Two?"

Lucien tried to explain. "Selena was afraid. I don't think she meant to throw two vials."

Sebastian smiled seeing how Lucien was protecting Selena, who bent her head toward the carpet upset. "We will just have to fix it. According to Giselle, a crystalline tear formed from his eye on his helmet. She believes that your Uncle is not very happy."

Selena put her hands to her face. "Poor Uncle, what should we do?"

Sebastian held Selena who kept staring into his eyes. "First we have to find a spell to transform your Uncle from being a stone statue back to life. So after all of us are washed and dressed, we will bring the Anthology of Magical Spells up into the bedroom and try to solve the mystery."

Lucien asked. "Do we have to change Uncle in the sequence of the spells that had befell him or can it be mixed up?"

Sebastian contemplated. "I would tend to believe in the same sequence from the most recent to the love elixir, which I already checked was not-removable. It is still not safe. Brujia is still at large, so I designating one of the witch's rods to keep a vigil just in case. We have to go over the exodus spell tonight when the moon is full just in case the spell is more complicated. We all want Mommy to come with us. Please have breakfast. I will pour the tea for you. Giselle has set a warming plate underneath, so your eggs and toast will stay warm. Be careful. Don't burn yourselves. I will have a quick bath and be with you in fifteen minutes. Enjoy. It's a beautiful day."

Selena smiled. "All right Daddy."

Lucien nodded as he ate a piece of toast.

Sebastian walked past Arian on the way to his bath. Arian was sound asleep. He checked her forehead again, no fever. He picked up the witch's rod and asked. "How is Arian fairing?"

The witch's rod wrote from the crystal ball. She has improved. She is in a stable condition.

Sebastian smiled a sigh of relief. He touched her forehead and went to take his bath.

The children finished their breakfast and then they checked on Mommy. Lucien walked quietly followed by Selena. Arian lay on her side on the edge of the bed. She encountered two sets of eyes staring at her.

She smiled still exhausted. "How are you?" She stretched her arm to hold them." Come into the bed, one on each side. Lucien, help your sister up for I cannot."

Both of them joined her as she put an arm around both.

"Have you been fed?"

Lucien snuggled up against Arian's chest. "Yes, Father said Giselle conjured up breakfast for all of us."

Selena held Mommy's cheek against hers and snuggled against Arian's chest from the other side. "Daddy said we should be quiet and not disturb you so we won't talk much."

Arian understood what Sebastian really meant and said. "Oh, then we should follow what he says. I am very tired so if you want to lay with me, we can rest. But if you want to do something else quietly that will be all right. You have boundless energy. Brujia is still out there so don't go outside, for me. Promise."

Lucien replied. "We promise."

Selena nodded. "I want to stay with you."

Arian smiled. "And you, Lucien?"

Lucien said. "I want to stay with you too Mommy."

"I see. In the drawer next to my bedside is an architectural work, done by my husband, Alexus Simons. You can see his designs while I sleep. I will have Selena move to your side, Lucien, so both of you can see it."

Sebastian enjoyed his bath, so instead of fifteen minutes, it was already a half an hour. "Oh my, what are the children up to?" He thought to himself aloud. I better check. He opened the door quietly to see what the children were doing but they were not at the table, couch, or anywhere in the room. Where could they be? He walked into the room to see Arian's foot dangling out from the edge of the bed. He smiled. She must be hot. I hope she doesn't have a fever. He glanced at the bed to see the children leafing through a leather -bound volume while lying next to Mommy.

Lucien looked up to see his Father silently staring at both of them. "Don't worry Father, we are very quiet. Mommy said we can do this so that we can follow what you said."

Selena smiled flirtatiously at her Father just like Arian had done several times before, imitating her actions precisely.

"So you have found my weakness, Selena. As long as Arian rests, I am happy. I know both of you love her as I do. So let's not say another word. I will just place her foot back in the bed in case she gets cold."

Sebastian lovingly peered at Arian, who seemed to be asleep. He gently placed Arian's foot softly in between the blankets. When he checked her again, she smiled at him. All he could do is squeeze her hand tenderly. "I am sorry to have awakened you, though it is not the first time." He smiled back. "How are you?"

"Exhausted, but I am so happy. My loved ones are here including Giselle. I see you hovering over me on your perch."

Giselle chirped.

"I am going to feed you." Sebastian insisted. He walked to the table and brought the oatmeal that Giselle had prepared. He returned with a chair next to the bed. "The witch's rod is so convenient for me. I don't have to clean or do any domestic chores like you were doing. Magic does spoil one." He asked the witch's rod to warm the oatmeal." That should help your stomach and it tastes better than milk of magnesia." He placed a small spoon full into Arian's mouth, who took her medicine like a good girl." What are the children reading through?"

Arian swallowed and stated. "It is the architectural works of my husband, Alexus or you in the past. It was his favorite hobby. May I ask what you do now?"

Sebastian smiled. "I am an architect."

Arian smiled. "I guess I shouldn't be surprised."

Sebastian expressed. "I would like to see that book too. But how is it here, wouldn't it be in the library?"

Arian perceived his point trying to avoid his eyes. "It is always at my bedside. For it was his life. I guess I am just too sentimental. I love you. You seem so dashing this morning instead of fighting witches you are in a more domestic scene, feeding you wife and children. May I ask you the time?"

Sebastian checked his watch. "Almost eleven A.M., which reminds me. We have to do something about Uncle Horatio. Giselle said he has formed a crystalline tear. He isn't very happy. I left him in the foyer downstairs. I also think that we should try a trial run with the exodus spell in case something else occurs that we are not prepared for. I am not going to risk any time with only three appearances of a blue moon. So I will treat you with the witch's rod. We must have you better. I need you too much." He took the witch's' rod again and refreshed Arian." I hope this magic doesn't run out, or I would have lost you last night. How do you feel?"

Arian stretched her arms. "Better, much better. I would like a bath too."

"I will assist you, Madame Simons." Sebastian smiled." Lucien and Selena, I will have the witch's rod make hot bath water in the adjoining bathrooms so all of you can wash. I will help you Selena. I don't want you to slip or fall. So take the witch's rod to watch over you and have it summon me to put you in and out. Let's go." Sebastian carried Arian to the bathroom. "What do you want to wear, another night gown?"

Arian smiled. "No. I think you can manage putting on one of my gowns. I can be on the chaise lounge. Obviously we will be examining the Anthology of Magical Spells for Uncle Horatio."

Sebastian was about to fill the bath with hot water when he asked. "How are you?"

Arian stated. "I am not that tired as before. I feel normal. If only we had more time." She gazed at Sebastian flirtatiously." How long does Selena take for her bath?"

Sebastian smiled. "About a half an hour. What are you up to?"

Arian smiled. "I don't need a bath, so what do you think. If you got her in the bath about now and then a half hour later."

Sebastian grinned implicating her meaning. "I think I better put Selena in for her bath."

Arian whispered in Sebastian 's ear. "I will be waiting."

When Sebastian returned, he locked the bedroom door. He saw Arian gazing out of the balcony with only a silken sheet draped over her showing her petite bare shoulders and back like a living sculpture. She returned his stare and blushed.

They were finally together at last.

The witch's rod knocked at the master bedrooms' door.

Sebastian lamented. "I believe I have to pick up Selena." He kissed Arian. "You know you are still blushing. The children will suspect something."

Arian kissed his ear. "Do you know of a spell that stops one from blushing?"

Sebastian murmured. "No, I better dress. I don't want Selena to catch cold or you. You better dress too, Madame, though I don't want to leave you. I love you more than life itself." He kissed her again and again. "I can even feel you blush. Will you be all right? I know this is one of my happiest days of my life." Sebastian got up to dress.

"You don't know how long I have waited for you. Three life's times and now you are mine. But I feel sort of guilty about Uncle Horatio. This is one instance he could not interfere."

Sebastian smiled again. "Yes, I know!"

Both of them laughed.

"How do you put this corset on? It looks complicated." Sebastian asked.

Arian showed him smiling jubilantly. "I love you."

"Yes, and how do I know! I don't know if I can think straight. All I can do is smile because of you." He swung her up into the air, caught her, and kissed her tenderly. He smiled back at Arian as he unlocked the door and hastened to Selena's room. "I apologize for the delay. I had trouble dressing your Mother. I hope you are not cold."

"No, Daddy, I used the witch's rod to keep the water warm."

Sebastian helped her out. "Here let me wrap you up in towels. I left your clothes here. Please dress now. I will check on Lucien. Lucien." Sebastian called. "Are you all right?"

Lucien came up from the stairs stating. "I checked on Uncle Horatio. He appears to be very uncomfortable. He was stuck at attention all night."

Sebastian felt even more guilty patting Lucien's head. "I am touched by your concern for your Uncle. Let's get the Anthology of Magical Spells." When Sebastian entered the dining room to open the secret wood panel passage that lead to the cellar, Giselle flew to Sebastian's shoulder.

She chirped holding a miniature crystal ball. It revealed Brujia entering the premises of the garden.

Sebastian responded. "She senses the witches' paraphernalia. Come Lucien, stay with me. Let's retrieve the witch's athame and the debitum naturae. Giselle, you warn Arian and make sure Selena is with her."

Giselle flew upstairs.

Sebastian armed as well as Lucien strode out into the foyer past Uncle Horatio when Brujia ventured in.

Sebastian kept Lucien behind him and threatened. "En garde." He held his athame. "You will die!"

Brujia nonchalantly replied. "I think not!" She waved her witch's rod at Uncle Horatio. "Defend me against them!"

Uncle Horatio reverted from stone back to life dressed in his suit of armor miraculously armed with an athame.

Sebastian immediately took the hilt of his athame and smashed it against Uncle Horatio's helmet so hard that it dented the armor. Dazed, Uncle Horatio fell in a clang of metal to the floor.

Upon hearing the commotion, Arian 's voice called. "Sebastian! Lucien! Are you all right?"

Sebastian glanced up to see Arian holding onto Selena carrying a rapier and the witch's rod. On her shoulder was Giselle, who carried vials of spells as they stared down from the staircase railing.

Sebastian asked Brujia. "Why are you here?"

Brujia complied. "You have what I seek, my magic. I will not let you keep it. It is mine. I will be back. You can be assured of that!" She disappeared in a black puff of smoke.

Arian ran to her husband and son embracing them. "She is going to be more trouble."

Sebastian held onto Arian who was still holding Selena as he embraced Lucien. He breathed easier." Well it solved one problem. We don't have to find a spell to change Uncle Horatio. But Brujia always manages to manipulate him against us. How can we change him back from being a pawn?"

Arian asked. "How hard did you hit him?"

Sebastian pondered. "I don't know. Just the thought of him being used against us infuriated me. I better get the witch's rod assessment now." Sebastian ordered the witch's rod to diagnose him. He read the printed words from the crystal ball out loud. "An uncomplicated concussion. Luckily the helmet absorbed the blow or it would have been worse."

Sebastian with the help of the witch's rod transferred Uncle Horatio back to his own room in his normal attire. He used the witch's rod to heal the concussion. He elevated his Uncle slightly at the head and shoulders with pillows while he drew the curtains to keep it dark. He also administered an ice pack by the witch's rod onto Uncle Horatio's head. "We better find a spell so he can't be manipulated. I will have to tie him to the bed just in case. I am sorry that I have to do this Uncle, but my family comes first." He ordered the witch's rod to watch him and inform him if he comes to as well as if Brujia shows up. Sebastian with his family closed Uncle Horatio's door. "Let's go to the Anthology of Magical Spells to find a spell to have Uncle return to normal."

When they arrived in the cellar, Sebastian consulted the crystal ball. "Can you detect a witch?"

The crystal ball responded in writing that it could detect magic so theoretically it could detect a witch, however, Brujia has the cloak of invisibility on, therefore, it was unable to focus on her.

"Alas!" Sebastian inferred. "They always manage to escape us."

Arian caressed Sebastian's cheek. "You did your best."

Sebastian's eyes flashed with remembrance and smiled at Arian, who promptly blushed.

Selena asked. "Why are you blushing, Mommy?"

"Oh am I? I must be thinking of something that triggered it. But I will be fine. Thank you for your concern. " Arian held Selena's cheek tenderly.

Lucien noted. "Maybe the spell is under un-manipulation?"

Sebastian secretly smiled hearing Arian's explanation for her blush. He turned to Lucien. "Let's see."

UN-MANIPULATION

To divert from ones original with outside help
Influenced by altering means, uncontrollable to thyself
To utilize an objective opinion
Instead of being governed by exploiting dominions
To no longer be bridled by subjugation
Curbed only by its confrontation
Wield thyself with the absolute truth
Abated by honesty or soothe.

Use with the witch's rod.

Sebastian reiterated. "We could try it. It couldn't hurt."

Arian wondered. "His last spell was the transformation spell, then the double memory loss spell, and then the love elixir spell. So we should transgress back in the same order. The memory wit spell should be first. Shall we try it? It is twelve in the afternoon. I should feed you."

Sebastian countered. "Let's use the witch's rod, time is running out."

Arian took the witch's rod and thought of a menu for their lunch. "Well, it should be on the table waiting for us. My, this is too easy, but you are right. We don't have the time." Arian appeared nervous. "We still have to think of the exodus spell."

Sebastian consoled Arian. He was worried too. They all ascended the stairs. Lunch consisted of tomato soup, warm sandwiches, and left over wedding cake with tea prepared on the table. Arian ordered the dishes to be cleaned with the witch's rod, as they hurried to see Uncle Horatio. He was awake in his bed, tied up, and thoroughly obstinate. Sebastian knocked at the door.

"I don't want to talk. I am too upset. To think I am tied up." Uncle Horatio blurted out.

Arian replied soothingly. "It is not your fault, it is mine. I couldn't materialize fast enough to save you from Brujia's love elixir, or do you remember, probable not."

"That's right. I really don't know you. Who are you? But I do remember this girl had blood all over her. I was a statue and nobody even offered me a blanket. There was a lovely girl who changed me from a statue to return me to life. You assaulted me on the head and probably tied me up. Oh by the way, you tie a wicked knot of which I am unable to undo. I am not talking to you!" Uncle Horatio turned around as best as he could and wouldn't even face Sebastian.

Arian touched Sebastian's hand to try to make amends so that Sebastian would feel better. "Uncle Horatio, please understand." Arian persuaded. " Tell me what were you going to do to your nephew, Sebastian, before Sebastian gave you a blow on the head?"

"I really don't want to talk to you either."

Arian walked around to face Uncle Horatio." Please, try to remember. Your headache should be a little better, besides I have lunch for you. Would you care to eat something?'

"That's another thing! I am not treated correctly. Not even fed!"

"Uncle Horatio." Arian pleaded. "Here, tell me the truth. Weren't you going to defend the woman you love? It was she at the door who transformed you?"

Uncle Horatio pondered. "Yes, I was going to defend her from this person." He pointed to Sebastian.

"Why?" Arian continued.

"Because, I love her. She is a lovely person."

"No." Lucien interrupted. "She is a witch. She is the ugliest thing for she sold her soul to the devil."

"Lucien." Arian said softly. She placed her hand over his shoulder gently. "Not now." She returned her attention to Uncle Horatio. "I must tell you the truth. You have a memory loss spell placed on you and a love elixir to love the woman who transformed you from a statue. She also made you into an armor knight. You are open to suggestions so that you don't have a mind of your own. I know this is difficult to reason out, because at this moment, you are not objective. If that woman would ask you to kill me, would you?"

"Of course not, that would be wrong."

"So why were you going to attack my Sebastian?"

"That is different. I was protecting her."

"From what! "Arian faced him.

"I don't know." Uncle Horatio answered perplexed.

"Sebastian, let's put the memory wit spell on him. It might help."

"You can't do that! What am I, a laboratory animal!" Uncle Horatio protested.

Sebastian stated in a matter of fact voice. "I am sorry Uncle, but we have to do this to you." Sebastian recited the spell." To heighten ones knowledge in ones head." He continued using the witch's rod.

A pink cloud hovered over Uncle Horatio's head as the cloud went into Uncle Horatio's nose and out of his ears as a white gas.

"Sebastian? Arian? What is happening to me? Oh my God! I want to hide. I am in love with a witch that manipulates me! I can't stop it! I want to die. Oh my God! She is ugly and I love her. I almost hurt all of you. I am despicable. Don't look at me!"

Arian tried to console Uncle Horatio. "Welcome back." She kissed his forehead and hugged him so tenderly. "We understand. Don't say anything against yourself. I want to thank you for protecting me from Brujia." She hugged him again with tears in her eyes.

Uncle Horatio hugged her back as the children came to greet Uncle Horatio. Sebastian put his hands on his Uncle's shoulders giving him a shake.

"Let's feed you." Arian replied. "We still have some wedding cake. I am sorry we didn't feed you earlier, but Sebastian with the witch's rod and Giselle helped me, otherwise I think I would have died last night. I was very close to it, especially because of the poison. After you eat, we will see if the un-manipulative spell will work on the love elixir. We will hope so, for we miss you the way you were." She hugged him again.

"You said my Sebastian. Didn't you Arian?"

"Yes." Arian stared directly at his face.

"So, Sebastian and you?"

"Uncle!" Sebastian's eyes flashed. "This is not the time as usual. Besides, you are compromising a lady's honor. Oblige me and drop the subject." Sebastian engaged his Uncle. "Or shall we talk outside!"

"Oh!" Uncle Horatio said quietly.

Arian blushed quietly as she smiled at Sebastian, knowing that he was defending her honor.

Sebastian walked towards Arian whispering. "I love you." He held Arian around the waist.

"Why is Mommy blushing again?" Selena asked.

"Mommy has been just married. Married women do that." Sebastian embraced his daughter and re-enforced Lucien with a loving gaze.

"Let me bring you some tea." Arian spoke softly. "Brujia is still at large, so we better put the un-manipulative spell on you."

Sebastian recited the spell using the witch's rod. "Do you feel better Uncle?"

"I can't tell! But I left you alone again and."

Sebastian interceded. "Uncle! We are married! Don't say another word."

"What is going on? I don't understand." Lucien implored.

"Let's leave! We will be in the spell room." Sebastian countered. He knew that Arian probably would blush as he tried to protect her. Sebastian told the witch's rod to untie his Uncle.

"All right." Uncle Horatio conceded. "I must freshen up."

"Will your Uncle be all right? Arian peered at Sebastian trying to ascertain more. "Can we trust him?"

"I told the witch's rod to only listen to the direct family. The rod will watch my Uncle very carefully just in case. I can't risk anything." Sebastian informed her.

"What was Uncle Horatio implying?" Lucien asked.

"We are now lovers, Lucien, because we have pledged our love to each other for a life time. That is what marriage is, respect, love, and the sanctity of children. I love you as my very own. You will understand it better when you are older. It is just in my time, subjects with this implication, were not mentioned in public, one had to be more discrete. I can't explain it any better, dear Lucien."

"Oh." Lucien stared at his father.

"Your mother is right." Sebastian smiled at his son. "Now we must concentrate on the exodus spell."

Lucien pressed the button to the secret passage way towards the spell room.

Sebastian searched for the exodus spell. He reiterated." Upon a blue moon where moonbeams derive."

Arian leaned closer to Sebastian. "It all depends on tonight or tomorrow. I wish I could come with you. Do you think Brujia will interfere with my release?"

Sebastian replied. "She," he whispered, "at this point probably doesn't remember. But tomorrow, her two days will pass. Do you think, Arian, that you could materialize in me and use the refreshing spell to keep us company?"

Arian smiled. "We could ask the crystal ball?" She nuzzled her head on Sebastian's chest holding him as she stared into his eyes.

Selena burst forth. "Can we come too? You can't leave us alone, if Mommy is going."

"I was planning on both you and Lucien to accompany me, as well as Mommy. So let's ask the crystal ball if it is possible for Arian to accompany us. She could materialize and use the refreshing spell to sustain herself."

The crystal ball lit up, writing: "Yes, provided she does sustain herself with the refreshing spell, however, the duration of this trip is three hours. She might not last and will have to return to the Realm of Twilight."

Arian expressed joy. "I will be privileged to stay with you for a few hours, but does that imply there is a part two of the exodus that we don't know anything about?"

The crystal ball answered as it proceeded to write it down. "Yes, first you will have to extract the clue to recompense the Pillars of Hercules. This is a map, then one has to decipher the map to hasten an escape."

Uncle Horatio appeared descending the stairs munching on his sandwich as he also read the crystal ball. "There is another map. That's not fair."

The crystal ball countered. "This is how it has been through time. There is no other explanation."

"Will we be able to figure it out Sebastian?" Uncle Horatio sighed in disbelief.

Sebastian answered. "We must! Maybe the witch's rod can help us? The witch's rod was very informative with Arian's health."

"When will there be another blue moon?" Arian asked the crystal ball. "Just in case I can't escape this time."

The crystal ball responded. "The next blue moon is in six months."

Arian's eyes welled up in tears trying not to cry.

"Six months!" Sebastian gasped. "Don't upset yourself. I will stay even if I have to get another job. I won't leave you ever!"

Lucien and Selena started to cry. Arian hugged her children. Sebastian came up to all of them and held them.

The crystal ball responded. "You are lucky. It doesn't always come every year."

"Oh Sebastian." Uncle Horatio whispered." I still feel bad about last night. Don't tell a soul. Promise me. I looked ridiculous swinging on that rope. Maybe, you didn't see that."

"We saw you Uncle! You were very brave in saving the woman you love. Everybody saw you Uncle. We all had crystal balls."

"Oh God! How embarrassing! I will never live it down."

"But." Sebastian continued. "How is your head? I really didn't think but reacted, when Brujia told us that you would defend her."

"I have a slight headache. I can't even trust myself, Sebastian. That is the worst thing in my entire life, not knowing if I will betray my own family. I can tell that the children don't trust me. I can understand, but it hurts. Isn't there anything you can do for me, Sebastian?"

"Sebastian." Arian called. "If we could use an illusion of Brujia and make her say something to see if Uncle Horatio listens to her, we could test if the un-manipulation spell works. It is worth a try."

"How will we get a picture of Brujia?" Sebastian pondered.

"I will draw her from memory and we will make an illusion. The only problem is," as Arian started to draw, "to mimic her voice." Arian drew Brujia diligently with a pencil. She asked the witch's rod to bring her paints down from her room. Arian added colors. Sebastian and the children watched with amazement as every detail emerged, even Uncle Horatio marveled. "Now." Arian stated. "I will ask the witch's rod to enlarge the picture and to mimic the voice. Let's make the illusion."

"Sebastian, what are you going to make the witch's rod say? I don't want to do anything stupid like I did last night. I am becoming afraid." Uncle Horatio paced up and down. "What am I going to do?"

Sebastian and Arian along with the children traversed to the other side of the room to discuss what suggestion to give Uncle Horatio to perform. If he did what Brujia asked, they would have to lock him up again.

"What is taking them so long to choose? I am almost at wits' end just like last night." Uncle Horatio spoke to himself.

Sebastian suggested. "Let's make him use the cloak of invisibility. Lucien can throw the spectral dust in the anti-cloak spell to find him. So when our illusion of Brujia will suggest this and if Uncle Horatio disappears by using the elixir of invisibility which is located on the table, we will have to lock him up again."

"Poor man." Arian lamented "You know Brujia is still out there."

Sebastian said soothingly. "Don't worry, the witch's rod is on patrol and so is Giselle. If Brujia decides to steal the substances she needs I have ascertained the anti-transfer spell." Sebastian recited:"

ANTI-TRANSFER SPELL
Unable to convey
So that nothing will ever stray
Impeded so one can't depart
Not consigned away like art
Un-transportable to remain
Unceded so to stay the same.

And I have already put it in place."

Arian gazed into Sebastian eyes. "How clever of you." She kissed his cheek. "What happens if she tries to purloin the substances?"

Sebastian smiled. "You mean steal it."

"Yes, I mean steal it. "Arian rephrased. "What effect would it cause with the use of the transfer spell?"

"The power of the transfer spell and the power of the anti-transfer spell would cause an earthquake."

"An earthquake!" Arian repeated. "I haven't heard of an earthquake since 1692 at Port Royal. Port Royal was the capital of Jamaica situated at the entrance to Kingston harbor. Half of the city went under the sea followed by a tidal wave, which devastated the rest. There were so few survivors, basically from the prison, located far away on the outskirts of the city where the terrain was above sea level. Of course, my second cousin, Antoine De La Vega, being a pirate, wrote me all about it. The reason for his disclosure is that he lost so much money in the venture."

"A pirate?" Lucien and Selena repeated.

"Yes, his diary is here somewhere. He probably was hung. He was very adventuresome and notorious while noted for being an excellent swordsman. He never married, but, never mind."

"My." Sebastian professed. "Adventure practically gallops in your family."

" You are just as adventurous. You are my cavalier, who rescued me." Arian focused at Uncle Horatio. "Uncle Horatio seems worried. We better hurry this up." Arian suggested.

All of a sudden, the chateau started shaking violently. Lucien and Selena ran to their parents. Sebastian grabbed Selena and Lucien with Arian pulling them under the table for safety. "Go for cover!"

"Oh." Uncle Horatio called back as he scrambled under another table.

"How long will this last?" Arian queried. "It seems to be getting worse."

The substances started to fall off the shelves.

Arian held onto Sebastian, "What if the memory loss spell fell down? We could all forget. Should we stay down here?"

Sebastian held unto Selena as Arian held onto Lucien. "Brujia must want her substances very badly. That is why the vibrations are getting worse." Sebastian added.

"Will the chateau last? You, being an architect could access the stress levels." Arian expressed.

"I don't think that in the 17th century they built stress factors for earthquakes. So to estimate, maybe two more minutes before the building will collapse."

Arian searched Sebastian face." We will be buried alive. Do you have the witch's rod with you, Sebastian, for I do not?"

"No, Arian, but maybe I can call it." Sebastian concentrated his thoughts and the witch's rod appeared.

"Thank heavens." Arian became calmer. "But, why couldn't the witches do that?"

"Maybe," Sebastian analyzed," there is a distance factor or maybe they didn't know all its capabilities?"

The building still vibrated and then all of a sudden it ceased.

Sebastian was the first one to check the room.

Arian called. "Is it safe, Sebastian?"

"It would seem so." Sebastian implied.

"What broke?" Arian rose while taking the children from under the table.

"The cloak of invisibility. Luckily we have lots of that."

"How can you see the vial if it disappeared?" Arian responded.

"I know what was on the table." Sebastian replied. "Witch's rod, repair all the damage, if there is any before Arian finds it, please!" He whispered.

"Shall we make the virtual image?" Arian inferred.

"Yes." Sebastian replied.

Arian took Brujia's picture and had the witch's rod enlarge it until Brujia was to size.

She used the illusion spell and the witch's rod to mimic Brujia's voice. Brujia appeared (the illusion). The voice spoke to all. Selena and Lucien stayed with their parents. Uncle Horatio, knowing that it was a test, perspired profusely with tense raw nerves accenting his white pallor in his face.

The illusion spoke. "Uncle Horatio, take the cloak of invisibility and place it on thy self. You will be more useful to me!"

Uncle Horatio felt compelled because he liked Brujia; yet, he didn't retrieve the vial that held the spell of invisibility.

"Do you think the un-manipulative spell works?" Arian entreated Sebastian.

Brujia said again. "Get the vial of invisibility, Uncle Horatio. Now! I command you!"

Arian gasped and pulled Sebastian's arm. "There are two Brujia's. She is here!"

Sebastian replied exasperatedly. "What happened to the witch's rod patrol?"

Giselle flew down to warn them of Brujia.

"Maybe the witch's rod can't warn us as fast as Brujia can appear!" Arian noticed Giselle as their eyes met while Sebastian held the witch's rod.

Uncle Horatio observed two Brujia's. "Arian, how did you do that?"

"We didn't." Arian and Sebastian reiterated simultaneously.

"Do what I say, Uncle Horatio or else!"

"I know that voice. You can't order me around. I am over you. Thank God! You never treated me very nicely, after all I did to help you. So go away!" Uncle Horatio insisted.

"I have a better idea." Brujia pointed her finger at Uncle Horatio, reverting him into a statue of stone. Then she pointed her finger to her illusion as it exploded in an array of golden dust. She faced Sebastian, "I want my magical substances or else. They are not yours. So give them to me! I care not if you live or die. I would prefer to forget this instance even though I know you killed my sisters. The memory loss spell should last two days; however; I seem to be immune. So give me my substances. Now!" Brujia demanded.

Sebastian tried to maneuver to get closer to his children.

"You are the most dangerous one, Sebastian. Answer me. Will you give me all my substances? Or else, I may let you live?"

"Would you ever be so considerate?" Sebastian abated. "You are rather conniving. So please, leave the premises."

"What will you do to me? I want my substances or magical ingredients. I give you two minutes to discuss it or else!"

Arian's eyes met Sebastian's eyes at that moment Brujia sent a cloud of silver smoke towards Sebastian and his family as Selena ran towards her father instead of letting Sebastian counteract the cloud with his witch's rod, which would have protected them. Lucien ran to his father as well. Selena jumped into Sebastian's arms hindering him completely as Lucien clutched his leg. Arian did a backward flip, to get out of the way, knowing what the cloud could do. Sebastian had no time to respond. Selena didn't let go. All of them except Arian turned into stone.

Arian flipped again as Giselle with her small witch's rod created an athame. Arian jumped to catch it as she ran with all her might towards Brujia to smite her.

Brujia shocked, used her athame sending a corona around Sebastian and family. "Watch them burn! Now, give me the substances or Sebastian and family will crack from the heat and die."

"Giselle! "Arian screamed. "Save them!" Arian's blows were powerful. Arian delivered vigorous assaults with ruthless fury. Her tears welled forth in her eyes as she made every blow count.

Brujia used her magic fabricating another athame. She struck with two of them as she utilized both sides. Giselle then created another athame for Arian. Both opponents fought hard. Giselle tried desperately to douse the fire but Brujia sent another corona towards Uncle Horatio.

"If you burn the chateau, you will burn your substances. This will all be for nothing."

"My substances have a high boiling point so they won't burn. But, I will kill you for murdering my sisters!" Brujia raved.

Arian tried to concentrate on her opponent, but seeing Selena with copiously amounts of tears springing forth upon her cheeks of stone only made Arian emotional. Even Lucien had tears in his eyes. "That did it you die! How dare you hurt my family! You are dead!" Arian vowed.

"Give me my substances!"

"Never! Why, so you can kill someone else!" Arian struck so hard that one of Brujia's athames broke. "Giselle use the witch's rod to stop the fire."

Brujia pointed her finger and almost killed Giselle sending a lightning bolt towards her, which started another conflagration. Flames swept over to Sebastian and the family.

Brujia hurled a barrage of poison daggers at Arian, which was strapped to her side.

Arian cringed, lamenting. "Not those poison daggers again! " Giselle tossed her a lightning protection shield just in time so she could protect herself. "Giselle, get the impuissance spell quickly."

Brujia panicked instantly turning into an armored knight. Arian reciprocated by sending lightning bolts towards Brujia's head so Brujia couldn't see, using her emerald ring. Brujia closed her beaver or visor. Arian threw her athame at Brujia's neck, which knocked Brujia down flat on her back. Giselle dropped the impuissance spell into Arian 's hand as Arian ran and poured it through the beaver before Brujia could use more magic against Arian. Brujia tried to get up. Brujia permutated into a large python ready to crush Arian but the impuissance spell caused Brujia to revert back to herself without the armor. Arian slipped from the potion that spilt on the floor as Brujia took the flat of her athame and struck it across Arian's face losing it from the recoil of the blow. Arian fell down onto her back as the blood dripped from her cheek. Brujia pounced upon Arian.

Brujia tried to draw out her poisoned dagger from her belt to stab Arian in the heart but Brujia had trouble extracting it because she still had to restrain Arian's arm, which clasped the athame. Brujia had to encompass Arian's movement by crushing Arian's chest. Arian, with all of Brujia's weight tried to free herself with one arm so she could push away. Arian became desperate. Arian managed to take her free hand and with her fingers she plunged them into Brujia's eyes.

Brujia screamed in agony as she tried to gouge Arian's face and succeeded. Arian pulled away from her. Brujia retaliated and kicked Arian's head as she rose to prevent her from escaping. Brujia tried frantically to find any athame to plunge it into Arian's heart. Brujia located it not being too far out of reach. While she bent to pick it up, Arian reeled on the floor from her pain emanating in her chest, her head, and her gouged face. Giselle flew and threw the debitum naturae into Arian's hand. Arian still laid there in agony as Brujia raised her athame still covering her eye as she plunged the athame with all her might aiming for Arian's heart. Arian rolled out of her way as the blade missed her by inches. Arian opened the vial. Simultaneously Brujia tried to extract the sword that she had driven into the floor being caught between the rectangular stones. Brujia changed directions as she finally freed the athame trying to cut Arian's head off as Arian got up to her feet with difficulty. Arian threw the vial at Brujia as she recited the spell by memory. The vial struck Brujia.

Brujia screamed in agony saying. "Oh Hexe, Oh Hagatha, help me!" Brujia then turned mottled, misshapen, and shriveled as she kept screaming in agony. She turned into dust as she vortexed away.

Arian hastened to Giselle. "Give me the witch's rod." She ordered the witch's rod. "Stop the fire!" The fire ceased. "Giselle, are you all right?"

Giselle chirped.

"I am in agony." Arian cried." My face!" She kept wiping off the blood." Even my teeth hurt! She kicked me so hard my ear feels like it tore off, not to mention my chest and lungs. My God, just look at my Sebastian, Lucien and Selena!" Arian burst into tears.

Giselle chirped and motioned to use the witch's' rod to heal her.

Arian clasped the witch's rod. "Please heal me and wash my face." She took her handkerchief to dry herself. Arian ran to Sebastian and family, taking the witch's rod. "Please transform them back." But nothing happened. Arian repeated saying the same thing but the witch's rod did nothing. Arian turned to Giselle. "What is wrong? What did Brujia do! That witch!" Arian said in disgust. "Witch's rod what is the problem? Why doesn't the transformation spell work?"

The witch's rod with the crystal ball printed out. "There are three spells at work, so that the transformation can not take place."

"What do you mean? You can't decipher it! There is a transformation spell and a lasting spell or an endurance spell. "

The crystal ball printed out. "I still can't decipher it due to the third spell which hides the name of the second spell."

"Oh my God, my family!" Arian's tears fell more readily down her cheeks. She took the Anthology book searching for an endurance spell. Giselle nuzzled Arian's face while on her shoulder chirping softly trying to console her.

"There isn't any endurance spell or lasting spell. I have looked for immortality and there is nothing mentioned with the transformation spell." Arian held the witch's rod. "Can you read my Sebastian's thoughts, so he can help me think. Please, if you can, please, print it out."

The print out came as follows: "Are you all right! I am sorry I got frozen like this but Selena jumped into my arms as you can see. I couldn't react fast enough with her clinging onto me. I am so angry with myself for leaving you defenseless. I let you down. My thoughts are harder to form the longer I am in stone."

"I would have done the same thing if she had jumped to me, Sebastian. It is just the last time I saw a cloud coming towards me, it was green, transferring me here to the Realm of Twilight. So I knew I must jump away quickly. Please, don't be angry with yourself. My babies are crying and I can't endure it. I need you to help me figure out this second spell, Sebastian."

"I can't think straight. It is very difficult to think at all when you are in stone." Sebastian's thoughts printed in the crystal ball.

Arian went to Sebastian to hug him. "I hope all of you can feel this." She kissed each one of them. "Selena, please don't cry. I get too emotional and I must think. Be my brave girl, you are in your Father's arms. Oh, Uncle Horatio, I am sorry if I am ignoring you. I know this is the second time you are in stone." Arian propped the Anthology book closer. "Come Giselle, Please keep me some company." Arian scanned at the transformation spell again. There were no footnotes to be seen. Arian looked next at the time. It was 5:30 PM. "I have been searching for four hours!" A filigree key fell out of the Anthology book. "A key! What if there is a spell lock. That is what the veiling spell was concealing," Arian read under S for Spell lock." There it is.

SPELL LOCK
To secure any spell from being tampered
Conjuration interlaced instilled and hampered
Clasping the spell with the filigree key
Pretend to turn it while reciting enchantments to thee
Evocation pronounced seals the decipher
Unable to be charmed by any further magical cipher.

A spell lock works only with a special filigree key. Pretend to turn the key as you recite the spell lock along with the transformation spell, which will release them as musical notes will emanate. "Giselle, this might work!" Arian used the filigree key as she recited the spell. She turned the key as musical notes emanated. Sebastian changed from stone into flesh as he collapsed still holding onto Selena on the floor with Lucien still clutching unto his leg. Arian ran to all of them. "My Sebastian, Lucien and Selena! Talk to me. Are you breathing? Sebastian, please say something." She hugged all of them. "Sebastian! My God, please, breathe! "Arian pointed the witch's rod. "Make them breathe!" Sebastian's eyes finally focused on Arian as he took his first breath as if he had suffocated, as did the children. Selena finally got to cry out loud as her tears fell. Lucien clung to Arian, as he cried too. Arian eyes teared as she went to Sebastian still holding Lucien. Sebastian looked exhausted. He propped himself up to kiss Arian. Sebastian's eyes were tearing. Arian couldn't stop kissing all of them. She also picked up Selena with her other arm. Giselle kept chirping to make Arian notice Uncle Horatio.

"Oh." Arian cried. She turned towards Uncle Horatio. "Oh, how could I forget. I can't blame you for being angry with me. I must rescue him, Lucien." She put Selena back into Sebastian's arms. Lucien didn't let go so she carried him to Uncle Horatio to rescue him.

Uncle Horatio finally breathed as he too had tears in his eyes. "I am upset, but I understand. Thank you Arian!"

Arian kissed Uncle Horatio's cheek while Lucien still clung to her. Arian knew Lucien was traumatized so she rocked Lucien like a baby in her arms kissing him so tenderly as she now walked to Sebastian. Sebastian held Selena as Arian kissed Sebastian each holding a child. Arian felt weak.

"Let's all go to bed and rest. We have two hours before the full blue moon and I am going with you. I will have dinner ready by the witch's rod not like last night. I want to lie down too. We must refresh ourselves. Oh, Sebastian." Arian held him again. She took the witch's' rod and all of them were in Arian's room. She wanted to put Lucien into the bed but he didn't let go so Arian sat in a chair with Lucien in her lap. Sebastian placed Selena with Arian.

Selena said. "Don't let go either. I want to hold you and Mommy."

Sebastian knelt holding his family. Sebastian replied." I am exhausted. I love you but I hated to see you in such pain by that witch! I never want to let you go. But I felt so incapacitated and useless with my performance."

"Never say that! Selena needed you. It was totally unexpected. You had no idea Selena would hold you with such fear that stopped logic. If she had run to me, instead of you, the situation would have been reversed." Arian consoled him.

Sebastian kissed her again. "I guess we should get some rest."

Arian smiled at Sebastian blushing. "You always leave me so weak. Oh, Uncle Horatio, are you feeling better?"

Uncle Horatio, who was lying down on the sofa, waved being so tired from the ordeal, signaling that he was all right.

Arian tried to get up. Sebastian rose helping Arian hold two children in her arms as she walked to bed, with one on either side.

Sebastian replied." Witch's rod awaken us within an hour, please."

Sebastian couldn't get very close except by holding Arian's hand as they all fell asleep.

Giselle slept on her perch.

An hour went by like an instant. The witch's rod prodded Sebastian as it attempted to wake him up. Sebastian, still being exhausted, pushed the witch's rod away from him, but it didn't stop bothering him. It was relentless. Sebastian woke.

"All right. Thank you, I am sorry, I didn't want to wake up." Sebastian checked his watch. The witch's rod went away as Sebastian stared at his family. Arian was awake. "Arian, didn't you sleep?"

"No, I couldn't, not with these two on my chest, Sebastian. My chest is completely numb. I can't feel a thing, but I dare not wake them. They are so stressed out. How are you? I miss you. I can only touch your hand."

"I never felt so useless. I almost lost you again." Sebastian interceded.

"What awaits us in the Realm of Reality, frightens me." Arian whispered. "At least I will be able to be with you for a while. When I get too exhausted, I will take the children with me. I hope they will last. I even need a refreshing spell now. I have a migraine headache worrying about all of you."

Sebastian rose and stretched towards Arian. "Maybe I should take these bundles off you, Madame?"

Arian blushed again. "I am sorry. I can't help it. All I think of is you. I must feed you. Why didn't I ever use the witch's rod for dinner before? I could have been with you even more. I really regret that, Sebastian." She stared at Sebastian expressing all her heart.

Sebastian gently rubbed Lucien's head. "Lucien." Sebastian called softly. "I regret this, but we must rise. Lucien."

Lucien's eyes opened slowly as he still clung to Mommy. "Do we have to?" Lucien's voice whispered.

"I am sorry, yes. Mommy 's chest is asleep. She needs a blood supply. Come, we must go soon to the Realm of Reality to help Mommy."

Lucien slowly rose, but he didn't want to let go. Sebastian went to the other side to wake Selena.

"Selena." Sebastian whispered in her ear. "It is time to get up. We must go soon."

Selena's eyes went to her Father. "Do we?" She slowly replied. "Can't we all stay home. I want to stay here with all of us."

Arian pulled Selena towards her as she tried to escape the bed holding Selena.

Sebastian replied. "Does my lady need help?"

"Yes, desperately, otherwise, I will remain here."

Sebastian grabbed Arian who carried Selena still in her arms, as he assisted her.

"Thank you, I could never have managed it by myself." Arian demurely replied with such tenderness.

Sebastian wanted to kiss her for that, but the time was getting late. He smiled at her with loving eyes.

Lucien walked towards Mommy as he held her again. They all peered at Sebastian.

Sebastian winked at Selena while trying to cheer all of them. The witch's rod knocked at the door announcing that dinner was served.

"Sebastian, may I ask? Would you please wake your Uncle Horatio? My hands are tied." Arian eyes pleaded. "Giselle, please join us."

Sebastian smiled as he called. "Uncle! We must arise." Sebastian shook him gently.

"Oh, what! Do we have to? I am so tired. I guess we do if you look at me like that. Oh well. Lets go." Uncle Horatio got up. "My, I am glad the witches are gone. Maybe we will get some peace. How hard will this be? We have been inundated with horror for days!"

"Don't scare the children. We all had enough for today." Sebastian mentioned.

"Oh, Oh, of course not." Uncle Horatio sighed.

Sebastian and Uncle Horatio descended the stairs to the dinning room.

Arian greeted them. "Good Evening, Messieurs, Your dinner awaits you. My, the time flies away so fast. We have a half-hour." She turned to Sebastian.

Sebastian seated Arian next to him not across the long table. Sebastian sat at the head of the table while holding Arian's hand for a moment. He wanted Arian to be close to him.

"Sebastian." Arian spoke. "Is it cold when you fly on the witch's broom? I am worried about the children catching colds. The children are a bit stressed and that makes them more susceptible. I can't risk that."

"Maybe, we will ask the witch's rod to bring the children's sweaters from Uncle Horatio's place."

Lucien asked. "Can we all be on one broom. I want to be with you and Mommy since, Mommy will materialize later."

"I am sure I can adjust the broom to accommodate all of us." Sebastian focused on his Uncle." We must bring all of the spell books."

"You can forget about mine. When I hit that tree, I smashed practically all of my potions on my spell book which caused the ink to run through. That is why I couldn't do anything right. While I tried to decipher those spells, Brujia got me! What a disaster."

Sebastian smiled which made Arian so happy. She caressed his cheek as she collected the dishes. Arian replied. "Witch's rod, please clean the dishes and put them away. Thank you. Here, are the sweaters." Arian helped the children dress. "Witch's rod, please obtain the following. Spell books, expulsion spell, witch's rod, lightning protection shields, emerald seal, anti- memory loss spell, cloaking and anti -cloaking spells, anti- transformation spell, transferring spell, healing spell and sleeping spell. Also please bring an athame, just in case and the crystal balls. I am even a bit nervous, Sebastian." Arian whispered. Arian placed the witch's' belt around her Sebastian with a crystal ball. She offered a belt to Uncle Horatio, who put the belt on himself.

"Arian, aren't you going to wear one?" Uncle Horatio implored.

"No, I will be with Sebastian, though I will carry a witch's rod. We will even take Giselle." Arian utilized the witch's rod and designed a birdcage for Giselle that could be tied around ones waist. She took the witch's rod again. "Are we all ready?"

Lucien replied. "I must adjust the birdcage a little so Giselle and I won't collide."

"Selena, please hold on tight. I know your Father will keep a good grip on you. Sebastian, Uncle Horatio, would you want to bring your jackets? I will have a shawl draped around me."

Sebastian admired Arian wearing the mohair shawl. It draped around her beautiful shoulders. He wanted to hold her, but he had to be practical for what lay before them. "Yes, Arian." Sebastian responded.

Arian asked the witch's rod to bring them their jackets. They instantly appeared as both of them put their jackets on. "I will transfer you now. The full blue moon approaches." Arian read the spell as Sebastian mounted the enlarged broom at the end with Selena in the center and Lucien at the top. Giselle swung in her birdcage from Lucien's waist. Uncle Horatio had the regular size broom. "I will be with you in a little while." Arian recited the last refrain.

Arian viewed the crystal ball diligently to see where Sebastian was. They landed in front of Uncle Horatio's house. Once that was established, Arian materialized into Sebastian.

Sebastian could feel her as she energized within him. It always gave him such sensations. Sebastian prepared to hold her waist the moment he could grab her. "I have you at last, Madame." He held her waist as he could feel her blush again in his arms. Arian half turned to kiss him while now holding onto Selena and Lucien. Sebastian held her head as he lingered on her lips. Arian smiled so radiantly, while he hugged her. She nestled into his arms.

Sebastian retrieved the exodus spell from his pocket as he started to read the stanzas again.

"Where to, Monsieur Sebastian?" Arian teased him as she turned her head to wink at him. Selena now nestled against Mommy as Lucien got closer to his sister.

It was 7:30PM. Sebastian took out Alexus/Sebastian's huge emerald seal. The moonbeams seemed to collect and deviate themselves towards the center of the emerald into resonated tones. The moonbeams still collected. Arian, Lucien and Selena all turned their heads to watch it. The emerald maintained its collected moonbeams, as the sound became higher pitched as if filling a glass of water, to the brim. The emerald became alive by vibrating so violently that Sebastian had to use both hands to hold onto it. The center of the stone emanated an emerald green light, into the sky that shot up straight into the heavens. The light slowly dissipated as the ions exuded into a sine wave, darting out towards the night.

Sebastian called. "Hold on, we are going to have to move fast to catch up with that sine wave. The broom shot forward like a bullet as Sebastian forced it to traverse as fast as it could move.

"How can you control the speed? "Arian queried. "We are traveling extremely fast, for me anyway."

"I must follow that beam before it disappears. It is traveling faster than we are. The speed is controlled by my thoughts." Just when they caught up with it, the beam reverted and turned the corner.

"Where is Uncle Horatio?" Arian gasped.

"I can't wait for him! The beam is pulsating so fast that I can hardly see it to keep up with it." Sebastian concentrated very diligently.

Arian took the crystal ball from Sebastian 's waist to see what had happen to Uncle Horatio. Selena and Lucien expressed their joy by the sheer speed of the broom.

"There he is! He missed the turn and kept on going straight. Now, he has stopped. He just realized that he missed the turn." Arian suggested." I will transfer him to be with us using the witch's rod." Arian recited the transfer spell.

Uncle Horatio appeared. "Oh, here you are. I first couldn't get the broom to start. Then I missed the turn and oh, well, you know the rest. I am sorry but I am afraid to fly fast due to my accident rate."

The children burst out laughing. All of them passed a ruined castle, in the distance. Its fortress walls jetted out against the clouded sky, silhouetting its loneliness among the hills. Lucien pointed it out to them. At that moment, a red ruby beam sprang forth to join the emerald beam as it intersected, and became one beam, being striped. They both traveled as one, like a sine wave (green), the other like a cosine wave (red), racing their way across the sky. The new beams traveled faster than before as it attenuated. It now transversed faster.

"Will we be able to keep up with it, Sebastian?" Arian marveled.

"I will make sure. I don't ever want to lose you, my lady." Sebastian assured her.

Arian could feel the tension in Sebastian, as she leaned closer to him.

Lucien announced "It is turning again. Are we making a circle?"

"I do not know my Lucien. "Arian responded.

"The beam is going straight up!" Lucien expressed excitement.

Arian exclaimed. "Sebastian, is this the stanza. Through the ethereal and to the beyond.

We are quite high up!"

"We will follow it." Sebastian said determined.

The steep climb caused everyone to shift towards Sebastian.

Arian whispered into Sebastian's ear. "I hope we don't fall off. Is the weight situated that we could, because the children are sliding towards me and I am sliding towards you."

Sebastian affirmed. "I will keep a good grip on all of you."

The beams ricocheted at the base of a cumulus cloud skipping along causing deflections as the beams separated and twisted together. It hit ice particles as they hissed melting instantly. They plunged back toward the earth as Sebastian diligently followed it with Uncle Horatio.

Uncle Horatio stated. "I think I lost my stomach some time ago."

Lucien commented. "It is aiming for the lake!" He tilted Giselle's birdcage to make her upright.

Selena held her hands so it would cover both eyes. "Daddy, I don't want to look. I think I may be sick."

Lucien pleaded. "Not on me!"

Arian quickly took the witch's rod. "Remove Selena's nausea away, please." She waved it over Selena." How do you feel, Selena?"

Selena answered. "Better."

Lucien responded. "Thank you Mommy."

The beams hit the water spreading across with its colors making a fluid grid. The longitude and latitude lines remained stiff as the ice particles from the cloud transported with the beams generated a topographic substance solidifying as structural sections of light blue crystal emanated from the water of the lake. It constructed itself. It harnessed energy from the beams swirling and churning the water as the edifice emerged. Columns with entablatures upon crystalline floors rose in height. The columns were connected with arches, which interlocked the coffered vaulted ceilings. Half an hour elapsed and it still was forming.

Sebastian recalled. "This structure reminds me of the baths of Caracalla at the calidarium."

Arian rested against Sebastian as she became drained. "That was a beautiful structure. I remember the frigidarium with its great open air natatium or pool."

Sebastian noticed Arian tiring while she nestled into his frame. "You were there?" He quickly manipulated the witch's rod to put a refreshing spell onto Arian knowing how much energy the transfer expended upon her.

She glanced at him touching his cheek. "You are so attentive my cavalier. My Father, being an ambassador had a position in Rome."

The children, while she rested, watched spellbound at the crystalline topaz blue temple, as the vibrations pulsed throughout.

Sebastian asked. "Shall we fly in? It is pointless to stay out here."

Uncle Horatio hesitated. "Do you think it has finished constructing itself yet? Maybe, we shouldn't just rush in. It looks a bit electrifying."

"Arian has a limited time. So we should take the challenge." Sebastian confirmed. "Let's go." He made his broom fly into the temple.

Uncle Horatio followed, not wanting to stay outside by himself either. "Very well."

They flew past the columns into the center of the building as huge crystalline doors opened as they passed and shut sealing them in.

Uncle Horatio felt trapped. "The doors have sealed us in. Should we do something?" He fell silent when he saw Sebastian.

Sebastian focused his attention ahead of them as all of them stared at the huge crystal ball located in the center of the chamber. Above them a crystalline dome of blue let the blue moonbeams coalesce into the crystal ball which etched into it only colors. It revealing a fluid map of the structure in three dimensions spanning the entire crystal ball. They all dismounted.

In the scripture one could read. Your immortal soul enters here to encompass the journey to The Pillars' of Hercules. Enter when the beams open the portal.

Arian turned to Sebastian and the children. "I guess I have to enter it alone since I am the only one that is immortal. Sebastian, I have written you this letter." She removed it from her corset. "I was going to give it to you at a more opportune moment but I think I want to give it to you now. You are so precious to me. Lucien and Selena let me kiss you."

Sebastian rushed to her. "I don't want to let you go alone. Here take the crystal ball so at least we can communicate." He embraced her and kissed her.

Both Lucien and Selena had tears in their eyes.

Lucien pleaded. "Don't go Mommy, we need you!"

Selena started to cry.

Uncle Horatio held her hand with a grip of steel. "Maybe you shouldn't go. We don't know anything about it."

"Dear Uncle Horatio. I have been too long immortal. I want to be with Sebastian and my children. If I don't go, I will always be separated. I will have to risk it for the ones I love." She kissed and hugged both of the children. She ran to the portal.

Sebastian stopped her. "Arian!" He held her. "Let's use the witch's rod to explain what will happen, if we all go. After all, if there is such a thing as reincarnation then we all have immortal souls."

Arian embraced him already feeling faint. "Please ask."

Sebastian asked the witch's rod. "Can we all go since souls are immortal?"

The witch's rod wrote the reply in Sebastian's crystal ball. "Yes."

"That did it, we all go." He kissed Arian as she clung to him. Both children ran and hugged her. Even Uncle Horatio sighed with relief and then realized the he had to go in the crystal ball portal as well.

The beams opened the portal as the hiss of high intensity electricity sparked through the edges. The circular opening enlarged for their passage. A flight of crystalline stairs descended through the water going deeper into the lake. Yet, no water flowed at them as they saw the levels of water above them while they descended into the crystalline building.

Arian held Sebastian with one arm around his waist while her other held Lucien. Sebastian carried Selena. Sebastian had altered his broom and Uncle Horatio's to be very small so he could put them into his pocket. Uncle Horatio walked very close to Sebastian's side checking his surroundings carefully. When they reached the foot of the stairs another portal opened. The moonbeams lit the entire chamber.

Three figures were in the chamber larger than life. One figure spun threads. Another one separated the threads measuring it out depending if it was short or not. The third with sheers cut the thread.

"We are the Goddesses of destiny." Atropos spoke. "Your life Arian, has been extended for more than three hundred years. It can be longer. Do you really want me to cut it short? Most would want to live forever. You are unusual not to want to. Does love rule you so much?"

Arian concentrated to see slight flickers through the thread as it vibrated in a resonance. Arian stated. "I love my Sebastian and my children. I want to live a life equal to theirs for everyone must accept the inevitability of death even immortals. For they just die long after normal lives do, but die they must, so immortality is just a perception depending on ones time frame of life."

"Well stated," Clothos responded, who spun the thread. "But to find The Pillars' of Hercules and withstand it's power of change maybe another matter."

Lachesis, who measured the length hinted. "Actually it was supposed to be Alexus, excuse me, Sebastian whose life was to be extended but Arian interceded. Nevertheless, here is the verbal map one must follow to journey to The Pillars' of Hercules. Depending on the outcome, the thread that I hold in my hand will be measured and cut by Atropos. Your fate has been sealed." She handed Arian a velum parchment neatly folded. "Adieu."

Uncle Horatio asked. "How do we leave?"

The three Goddesses' images faded into their pedestals as the light dimmed back to the blue moonbeams. The chamber doors opened revealing the stairs ascending back to the crystal ball portal.

Arian leaned heavily on Sebastian as she obviously had overstayed her time in the Realm of Reality. Sebastian invoked the witch's rod to revive Arian while both children clung to her wondering what would happen tomorrow.

Sebastian stated. "Please wait while I read the transfer spell so we can transfer rather that fly back to the Realm of Twilight."

Arian opened the map. It had strange symbols.

Lucien glanced at it and turned the sheet from its normal orientation to its side. "If you turn it, it could be hieroglyphics."

Arian explained, "It is old Greek. That is how they write and the orientation is horizontal. I have not deciphered old Greek in ages. I just hope I get it right."

Sebastian responded. "We all do." He saw the anxiety written in the children's faces.

Uncle Horatio leaned on the blue crystalline wall checking his watch. "It is ten thirty. It took three hours and now the map is in Greek. The Anthology of Magical Spells was hard to understand as it was."

"Uncle," Sebastian whispered. "You are upsetting the children."

Uncle Horatio clarified. "But Arian reads Greek. That's good, for I do not."

"Thank you Uncle. We all feel so much better." Sebastian glanced up to the ceiling. Here is the transfer spell." He noticed Arian was fainting. He held her tightly as he used his other arm to wave the witch's rod. "Selena and Lucien hold onto your mother too. I want all of us to be together." He recited the spell placing all of them into the master bedroom.

He carried Arian to the bed placing her very gently while waving the witch's rod to revive her. She opened her eyes. He could see how exhausted she was but she smiled as she held her arms out to hold him. They were joined immediately by the children.

Lucien propped up Selena and crawled to where Arian was lying so he could hold onto her while Selena cried holding onto Mommy's waist. Lucien had a combination of Daddy and Mommy while they hugged, but he didn't mind as long as he held Mommy.

Uncle Horatio announced. "Good night. I think I will retire and leave you. Why did the fates have to say all that in front of the children? You are not going to get much rest. I will let myself out. Oh, where are the candles? I don't see well in the dark."

Sebastian replied. "At the door are the candles and the flint lock, Good night, Uncle. Let's get ready for bed. We have to decipher what Arian will translate from the Greek verbal map." He carried Arian to change while both children followed. "All right, each of you will change behind the screen while the rest of us stays by the fireplace. When you two are done, I will change Mommy and myself while you stay by the fireplace. In that way we all get to have Mommy. Lucien, you change first. I will light the fireplace and get the bed-clothes with the witch's rod."

The clothes miraculously appeared as the fireplace lit itself. Selena snuggled into Mommy while Sebastian held Arian whispering in her ear. "What did you write me?"

Arian smiled. "Open it and read to yourself."

Sebastian examined the scented ribbon parchment that was sealed in red wax impressed with the seal of the Earldom of Sussex. He carefully opened it and read to himself.

To my precious love, Sebastian. (For your eyes alone)

Embraced by your tenderness, charmed with rapture,
Impassioned with delight for me to capture,
The ecstasy of your love, endearing and enticed,
Sumptuous in depth, esteemed and blessed more than twice,
Fondled with pleasure, embellished as a treasure,
Devoted with such sentiments as sacrifices your leisure,
Redeemed and adored as cherished in forever,
Transcended through time, captivated by being together,
Sensuousness revered with symphonies of variation
Beautiful and graceful, exquisite in all it's adulation.
PS The only thing I desire in life is to be with you.
Love Arian.

Tears of joy fell from his eyes. He was so touched that all he could do was kiss her even though she held Selena who was in between them. Arian never knew how long Sebastian could kiss her until now. Even Lucien returned and Sebastian still was kissing her while she blushed. So Lucien kissed what was left on Mommy's face too.

Selena whispered to all. "I need some air Daddy. I am squashed."

Sebastian stopped not wanting to. "I am sorry Selena. I miscalculated about you being there. Selena it is your turn to change."

Arian gasped for breath as she smiled lovingly at Sebastian while still being kissed by Lucien. She kissed Lucien back. "My I need to catch my breath. I love all of you."

Selena got up to change bringing her clothes. "I am going now Daddy." She responded.

Arian held Lucien since now it was his turn. He gazed up at her in admiration.

Sebastian refolded his letter carefully. He pressed it to his lips and spoke to Arian. "Are you feeling better?"

Arian smiled again while holding Lucien. "Yes with all of this attention, I am the luckiest person in the world, all because of all of you. Lucien what did you do with Giselle? I seem to have lost track of her."

"I let her out of her bird cage. She is on her perch as usual." Lucien promptly responded.

"Thank you Lucien. You are so thoughtful. "Arian hugged him while catching a glimpse of Sebastian's worry.

Sebastian being pensive again asked. "What do you suppose is in this?" He picked up the velum parchment with the Greek symbols on it. "How do you know if one can translate it correctly if it is old Greek? I couldn't tell. Luckily you can."

Arian concurred. "I haven't practiced it in ages. But it seems logical that since they are Greek that they would write in their own language of the times."

Selena ran up to Arian. "I am dressed now for bed."

"Yes, we can see." Arian embraced her." Now we," peering at Sebastian, "must change. Come and sit by the fire."

Sebastian carried her while Arian caressed his neck. He questioned. "How do you manage to pull your corset on and off all by yourself?"

"I stand by two mirrors while it is still loose and pull. To remove it I hold my breath very tightly and try my best like you are doing and undo a cross link at a time."

"You must have patience like a saint. I rather kiss your neck." Sebastian did so very tenderly.

"Maybe you need our help." Lucien answered." I am very good with knots."

Arian smiled. "You are a bit too serious and the children need to go to bed. Let me remove this while you change. Thank you Lucien but I will manage."

He guiltily acknowledged Arian by nodding. "I am just thinking of your letter." He turned her slowly and kissed her fully on the lips as she blushed.

Selena affirmed. "I think we undress faster than you."

Sebastian had to stop himself. "Yes, you are both correct. Forgive me for causing the delay." He hastily undressed and put his night shirt on while staring at Arian who finally managed to remove her silk gown and corset." Allow me." He removed the rest and placed the nightgown over Arian.

Arian pulled Sebastian with her, to where the children waited by the fireplace. "It is past eleven, to bed, all of you."

Sebastian attended the fire so it still would be warm for the next morning. He gazed at the blue moon shining in as it made patterns on the floor of the master bedroom. Arian helped Selena onto the bed while Lucien jumped up by himself. She tucked both in kissing their cheeks. But Selena wanted to be kissed again. Arian obliged kissing both of them equally. Sebastian then hugged the children good night. He then waited for Arian to get in as he stayed at the edge holding her closely and nuzzling her ear and forehead with his face. "Good night." He whispered.

Arian turned around and kissed him fully on the lips. "Good night." She whispered back. "I could kiss you all night but no one would get any sleep."

Sebastian answered. "Don't tempt me, Madame."

Arian smiled at him. "I love you. Good night Monsieur." She felt Sebastian's arm around her waist pulling her into him.

The clock chimed at five in the morning when Sebastian opened his eyes haunted by what would happen to Arian. She slept soundly next to him as she snuggled into his chest. He kissed her forehead and held her in silence. He could hear the children deep in sleep as he relished the moment of having his family for now safe.

Giselle flew towards Sebastian with a note carrying it with her foot and placing it into Sebastian's hand. He nodded and read. "Good Morning! Please ring the bell if you desire breakfast, which I will have the witch's rod prepare. I think that the earlier you start to decipher the fate, which was given to you, the better. I feel foreboding. Please do not upset the children more than necessary."

Sebastian whispered into Arian's ear. "Arian," he said softly.

Arian stared up into Sebastian's eyes and kissed him slowly and tenderly as she made her way across his face as quietly as possible.

Sebastian whispered when he could get a chance because Arian kissed his mouth and lingered delicately on the corner, which she knew was one of his weak points. "You are flirting."

Arian smiled back saying, " I know it from your past and it still works." She continued.

Sebastian held her softly mentioning. "Giselle thinks we better decipher the fate because she feels a foreboding. I am haunted by it too so the earlier we know the better."

Arian stopped and peered into Sebastian's eyes sadly.

"Don't look at me like that. I can't stand seeing you so distressed. So let's leave the children sleep and brush up on your Greek. Giselle will have the witch's rod prepare breakfast when she hears the bell ring." He stopped. He could see the tears welling up in Arian's eyes. He held her face softly nuzzling his nose against hers. It helped. She relaxed in his arms." We will conquer this together. I will never leave you and you will never leave me willingly. So let's tackle the problem." Sebastian got out of bed quietly practically picking up Arian at the same moment. He placed her gently on the carpet. "Choose what you want to wear while I get ready. I will be waiting," his eyes teased her as Arian blushed.

Arian quietly knocked. Sebastian opened the door. "Please enter Madame."

Arian slipped past placing her clothes and his on the chairs. "It's so nice with the witch's rod. Imagine, instant hot water." She filled the bath.

Sebastian smiled. "We have it in our century so you will get used to it." He was shaving as he watched Arian preparing to wash in the bath draping her long hair out of the way placing it up and pinning it. "It is so nice not to see you sick. I hope I never have to see it again. When you were hit in the face with the flat of Brujia's sword, I was so furious that I couldn't save you. She also kicked you in the head. She had what was coming. I feel no regrets. Thank God for the witch's rod that can heal you, like it did with the three poisons that the dagger stabbed into you." Sebastian paused seeing Arian leaving the bath with her hair up with the exception of one strand accenting along her back." My, you are beautiful. Oh, you are blushing, again."

Arian repeated. "Three poisons."

"Yes," Sebastian affirmed." The witch's rod assessed that the third was the Devil's instrument that can kill immortality, but you were too sick to understand all that was said at the time. Here let me get you a towel."

"Thank you," Arian smiled." I guess that is why Hexe gloated so wickedly."

"I better check if the children are awake. Please stay by the fire since you are wet." Sebastian spied to see. "They are still asleep." He watched Arian taking the pins out of her hair as it fell past her waist. He walked up to her saying, "Good morning." He held her." Do you need help with your corset since I am available?"

Arian stated. "You can probably pull it tighter than I, but then I will need help to get it off tonight."

Both of them stared at each other at the mention of tonight, which still remained a mystery. They kissed to calm each other down, soothed by each other's embrace.

"I shall leave you and wake the children." Sebastian smiled. He closed the door quietly. He walked to the bed staring down at two sleeping children peacefully resting. He whispered just above their ears. "Lucien and Selena. It is time to rise."

Lucien opened his eyes upon hearing his Father call him. "Yes? Is it time already?"

Sebastian softly stated. "Yes, we want to decipher the fate. Did you sleep well?"

Lucien noted that Selena was still asleep. "Yes. It is so nice that Mommy was not sick and that everyone is safe." He got up quietly and hugged his Father. Sebastian responded instantly hugging his son.

Sebastian whispered again." Selena, it is time to get up. "

Selena turned and put a pillow over her head. "Already."

"Come, I will help you down from the bed. Your brother is up."

Selena peeked out from under the pillow while Sebastian gently picked her out of bed and hugged her. "Good morning. Let's bundle you off to the bathroom."

Arian hugged Lucien as he picked up his clothes. He hugged her back with concern.

"Mommy, how do you feel now?"

"Dear Lucien, I am fine. Your Father has seen to that already. The water is hot so if you need to adjusted it, command the witch's rod."

Lucien went to take his bath.

"So Selena, I see your Father has you in his arms, saving a damsel in distress. I will make the adjoining bathroom available for hot water for your bath." She opened another door to the adjoining chamber. My Alexus/Sebastian thought of it just in case two people wanted to take a bath at the same time that the other room's bath would have two accesses."

Sebastian was surprised. "You never mentioned it before. I seem to find out more and more about this house. I just thought it was a closet."

Arian stated. "In time you will know everything, if not more. I am the one who has to catch up with three hundred years of knowledge to the present. Selena, I will help you with your bath while your Father will ring for breakfast. Please wake your Uncle so he won't be late for breakfast."

Sebastian smiled. Arian 's countenance with Selena in her arms beckoning him with her eyes was so beautiful. He held both of his girls. "I await your return." He rang the bell and walked to Uncle Horatio's chamber and knocked.

Uncle Horatio answered. "I am coming." He opened his door. "Good morning Sebastian and how are you and your family?"

"All of us are very well. And you, Uncle?"

"I slept well. It was harder the previous night standing up like a frozen statue." Uncle Horatio replied.

"Uncle, please join us for breakfast which is now being prepared by the witch's rod under the guidance of Giselle. I am sorry to have woke you so early, but Giselle and I have forebodings about the fate's letter."

"Um, speaking about a letter, what did yours say? It was scented." Uncle Horatio hinted.

Sebastian smiled broadly. "Here read it." It was in his pocket as he handed it to his Uncle.

Uncle Horatio read the passage. "My God does she love you."

Sebastian beamed. "She loves me. I never had it written before. She writes it so eloquently. It's so touching. It makes me speechless."

Uncle Horatio stated. "What if she dies."

"The thought just tears me apart. I will do everything in my power to protect her or sacrifice myself in the endeavor, which leaves you and my sister in charge of the children if both of us die. I have never been so fulfilled and loved in my entire life. I have never been so happy and contrasted with such tragedy either. She was at her deathbed when you were a statue. She convulsed with such pain, throwing up blood, screaming in agony. There was blood in her urine. That is why we couldn't change you back from being a stone statue."

Sebastian gazed into the master bedroom as he saw Arian; swinging Lucien in circles as Selena tried to catch him running after in circles too.

Sebastian smiled. "Look at them. The children adore her and call her Mommy. She has protected and loved them so much. We are a family."

Uncle Horatio patted Sebastian's shoulder. "Then let us now take another challenge. What will that letter from the fates make us do?"

Sebastian whispered. "We shall see."

Giselle flew up chirping.

"Oh, excuse me," Arian interjected." But Giselle had informed me, that breakfast would be cold if we don't go down now. Good morning, Uncle Horatio, I hope you slept well. Do you have a headache?"

"No Arian, I am fine. I will be ready shortly." Uncle Horatio winked at the children. "Good Morning."

"Good morning Uncle." They said. Lucien and Selena ran up to him and hugged him.

"My I have missed this." He hugged them back." Well, I don't want to be late so I better hurry. See you in a minute." Uncle Horatio closed his door.

Sebastian offered his arm to Arian while holding his hand out for Selena while Arian offered her hand to Lucien. They descended the stairs followed by Giselle to the dining room.

Arian mentioned. "I am so spoiled. I don't have to prepare breakfast. It just suddenly appears. Thank you, Giselle."

"Where is that letter from the fates?" Sebastian asked.

"Where I usually keep letters." She gazed at Sebastian and blushed.

"Oh," Sebastian smiled.

The table had fresh fruit and flowers which scented the room. The sunlight glittered through the crystal chandeliers and the candleholders giving off rainbow patterns on the walls reflected by the mirrors. Arian poured the tea and served the dishes.

Arian remarked. "How pensive you are. Maybe we should serve lunch outside by the gazebo by the lake. We could feed the swans. I am sure Giselle took care of all the things that I had not attended to since you came. I didn't have the witch's rod then. I can't imagine ever being alone. You have filled my life with so much happiness these past few days. It's like looking back at an empty dream that never was. So to keep my family, I better translate this. If you want to run through the gardens, it is a perfect day."

Sebastian rose to hold her. "I will take the Anthology of Magical Spells up and check out more about lightning while I sit with you in the library for company. I will not miss a second without you. I am just as eager to know what befalls us."

Lucien and Selena also came to their Mommy and hugged her. "We will stay with you. We can read about you cousin the pirate."

Uncle Horatio quickly added. "I will edit that book with you just in case it gets too revealing!"

"That will be comforting to know." Sebastian shook his head." Is this Antoine De La Vega?"

Arian nodded her head. "Do you disapprove? Really, there is nothing we could do about it then either. My Father stated to anyone who asked. Never heard of the man.'"

They all laughed.

Sebastian asked. "How notorious was he?"

"Very, was all I got out of my Father. Being an ambassador in the court and hearing about Antoine stealing funds, his reckless behavior with a price or bounty on his head of 2000 Louis, not to mention ransoming the Governor's daughter, was quite embarrassing."

"My God!" Uncle Horatio denounced. "It is shocking. What a rogue!"

"Haven't I heard that line before?" Sebastian eyed his Uncle.

"When did you call Sebastian that?" Arian sounded alarmed speaking to Uncle Horatio.

"When he didn't know that we were engaged." Sebastian insinuated. "But I clarified it immediately."

"You should know Sebastian is entirely honorable." Arian confirmed. "I better translate." She rose to go to the library. "Please witch's' rod, clear the table and please clean the dishes and the house. Thank you."

"All right. Sebastian, I am asking for your apology so I can have some esteem from your lady." Uncle Horatio stated.

"Your apology is accepted. " Sebastian conceded.

"Good." Uncle Horatio replied." Your honor has been satisfied I guess. No duel."

Lucien puzzled asked. "What is going on? Did I miss something or is this going to be the lecture of wait until you are older."

Both Sebastian and Uncle Horatio laughed.

"Yes," Sebastian concluded to Lucien. "This is one of those explanations."

Selena gave a quizzical countenance. "I don't understand."

Lucien added. "And you won't with a explanation of wait until you are older, either."

Arian sat at the table in the library with her old Greek lexicon besides her murmuring in French. She leafed through the lexicon repeatedly, shaking her head. "Mon Dieu." She translated the following:

Abstract:

To alter from immortality in the Realm of Twilight back to the Realm of Reality one must obtain these devices which are protected from anyone who would use it for ill purposes with deadly consequences.

A quest to locate a xenon flash tube.

A quest to locate the crystal-like potassium dihydrogen phosphate and a neodymium doped glasses.

A quest to locate an yttrium target.

Upon deliverance of these devices to the crystalline temple of the fates, they must be in a proper alignment to recompense The Pillars' of Hercules.

With the third blue moon and the proper alignment of the crystal, the pillars will appear. Assembly of the devices will activate a light amplification by stimulation emission of radiation or laser.

Once an excited state, by a wavelength of a certain frequency, amplifies to a stimulation emission. The photons impinge to release by moving back and forth between two parallel ends or mirrors corresponding to the polished ends of the Pillar, which is made of either rubies, which is corundum, like emeralds or sapphires. The ends can be coated with a highly reflective non-metallic film, which denotes a resounding cavity.

The result is a coherent light beam creating a monochromatic light with little divergence, which means all the waves are in phase. If aimed at an yttrium target, x-rays are achieved.

Once they emit, they will revert from immortality back to reality into a finite lifetime. Etc.

Arian stopped translating the Greek words not believing the contents and implications. She did not understand the device (The Pillar of Hercules) but she did understand to acquire the constituents would endanger anyone with deadly consequences. Was it worth it? Was all that they encompassed simply another means of death or separation? She should never have involved them." It would have been better if Sebastian had never known me, for him, it would be less painful. What have I done?" She spoke all of this out loud in French with tears running down her face. She inspected the room. Sebastian had left the room with his Uncle to search for another spell to cure lightning bolts so the only witnesses were the children. She ran to them kissing their foreheads and spoke to them still in French. "I need to get some air. Please, forgive me." She fled to the garden.

Lucien told Selena. "Please follow Mommy while I get Father. Something is wrong!"

Selena eyes flashed with fear unable to move.

Lucien grabbed his sister. "Come with me we will both get Father." He dragged her calling. "Father, Father! Please come. Something is wrong." He ran to the dining room to open the secret passage to the cellar.

Uncle Horatio spoke to Sebastian. "Did you hear something? I distinctly heard Father."

S. and S. Antonson

Sebastian alarmed ran partially up the stairs to see both Lucien and Selena eyes wide open in terror. "What is it?" He wondered.

Lucien replied. "Mommy speaks only in French. She kissed us crying saying Mon Dieu and ran into the garden. What is wrong?"

Selena nodded. "I was so scared I couldn't move so Lucien took me. Daddy what will happen to us?"

"Uncle, could you make a snack for the children, while I find Arian and sort this out." He turned to the children." I will find her and explain, Lucien and Selena," he hugged them." It will be all right. We will sort this out. Excuse me." Sebastian grabbed for the crystal ball and witch's rod to locate her just in case she would be in an area unfamiliar to him. "Uncle!"

"Oh, of course. Let's see what we have to divert your mind off this questionable reaction of your mother. Shall we?" Uncle Horatio said soothingly.

Sebastian located her with the crystal ball. She was in the gazebo watching the swans skimming through the water of the lake while holding onto a pillar as her tears dropped into the lake one by one and then streamed. Giselle was on her shoulder caressing the tears away from her eye with the feathers from her wing while softly chirping. Sebastian went to the library to see for himself what Arian translated while trying not to let Arian's crying effect him. Luckily she wrote the translation from old Greek to English. He read it in its entirety as far as she translated. The Pillars' of Hercules was an alien laser. He spoke to himself. "Oh, my God!" Each of the intricate pieces to excite the laser was protected by deadly consequences. And if they were found and aligned, the outcome would be a laser beam at x-ray levels of radiation, which meant certain death, if anyone was hit by one. He waved the witch's rod to transfer Arian and Giselle back to the library. She materialized in the center of the room with Giselle. Upon seeing Sebastian she ran to him apologizing to him in French. She buried her head into his chest while holding him very tightly. She cried soaking his shirt with her tears. He held her quietly saying, "Arian, I have read your translation. It is a laser. We have them in our century. They, I believe in this sense was used for telecommunications by the definition of The Hercules' Pillars, but it achieves x-ray levels which means high levels of radiation, which are extremely dangerous. Not only that, to combine it into a laser, the parts are protected by God knows what. But no matter what, I will do it for you. You have sacrificed you life for three hundred years. So it is my turn to sacrifice for you. My mind is made up. To be finally with you for a normal life means everything to me. There is no more to be said." He kissed her as she stared at him.

Arian murmured in English. "If you had never seen me you wouldn't have to sacrifice yourself as you want to do now. You have children that depend on you, which is more important than I, (a ghost of your past). You must think of them and your future. I wouldn't know how to support them. They, if you died, would be living with a timeless ghost in the Realm of Twilight with no preparations for their future only love for them and magic. They need you."

Sebastian countered. "You are not a timeless ghost. You are my wife. How much more can you sacrifice. You are now my life. I could never exclude you ever. Knowing you, I would rather die than be parted from you. You rule out my Uncle, who will give them the reality, while you will take care of them spiritually. I have to think of them with their mother. Allow me to

210

fight for your honor and the hope of our happiness. We will conquer this together. I swear. I don't want you to suffer as you did for three hundred years."

Unbeknownst to Arian, Sebastian, and Giselle, the walls had ears for the children as well as Uncle Horatio overheard while peeking in from the doorway until Uncle Horatio bumped into the door handle which clicked.

Sebastian who was still comforting Arian, securely in both of his arms spoke. "Why don't you come in instead of listening in the hall."

CHAPTER 13

INEXTRICABLE

Both Lucien and Selena eyed Uncle Horatio for giving them away.

"Sorry." Uncle Horatio flushed while he held his head.

They entered the library as Lucien ran to Arian and his Father.

"What does it say that made Mommy cry?" Lucien murmured.

Selena held out her arms wanting to be taken. Arian noticed, hinting to Sebastian by changing her position, so that he could see the constraint in Selena 's face, tighten and pale, hopeless with anticipation which made her look so forlorn that Arian had to pick Selena up while she held out a hand to Lucien to embrace him.

Lucien continued. "Please explain."

Arian elucidated. "I really don't know if I translated it correctly but, your Father has to face three majors obstacles. If he succeeds, then he has to assemble this monstrosity together to activate and recompense The Pillars of Hercules. Your Father is determined, for my sake, to rescue me. But it is so dangerous. I can not dissuade him. I have wasted enough time. I must translate more because it will take all day. First we have to obtain these objects. Therefore, I can't go with your Father. We will have to remain here. You, Selena and Lucien, will be watching the crystal ball, while I decipher the rest of this."

"What is it Daddy?" Selena asked. "What is this machine?"

Sebastian smiled as he came closer to her. "It is a solid phase laser."

"What is that?" Arian seemed puzzled.

"Lasers have a multitude of functions for instance, from measuring distances, to the intricately of eye and cranial surgery. They even weld and are used in the military for telecommunications."

"But, a solid phase laser, Sebastian? What are we delving into?" Uncle Horatio expressed shock.

"Now, since we know that its' about lasers, we need radiation protection or black body like they use in the Stealth bomber. I will use the crystal ball and the witch's rod to assist in Arian's protection."

"But," Uncle Horatio interrupted. "What are we facing and how do we put together a solid phase laser? I am not an engineer!"

"Not now, Uncle." Sebastian touched his Uncle's shoulder." Let's ask the witch's rod and crystal ball for some advice and then I will go into more details."

Arian huddled in between her two children hugging them as she continued her translation. "Here, why don't you two look at my picture book. I drew these pictures of all cities that I visited. Maybe, you might recognize them. I know it is hard to concentrate when so much is happening, but, pictures are always entertaining."

Selena turned the pages. "My what city is this, Mommy?"

"Oh, this is Brussels. Does it still look like that?"

"No, not exactly." Lucien commented." But I have only seen pictures since Daddy had an assignment there. This building was in the picture."

"Sebastian," Arian called. "Here is the first deciphered challenge that you must conquer. I must find where, in the Realm of Twilight, the ancient elm tree is. We could ask the crystal ball?"

Sebastian hastened to Arian, as Sebastian read the riddle aloud.

OUEST I

From the ethereal now imprisoned, where time and reality cease
Energy from within, will exude in bursts, will then be released
Harassed from beyond, bathed in waves, so not to correspond
Hidden clandestinely, unless recklessness is depended upon
With the zenith of the sun, make a 90° angle left of the ancient elm tree
This will be where the quest for what one construes as a starting for thee
64 paces due east, look for a centerpiece of bronze
From hence, 86 paces to the west, towards the lake and ponds
Sail across, if one can not step, until the count is correct
From the center of the lake, plunge and pull the latch direct
As it opens it reveals, a subterranean portal
Traverse it, if you dare, merely being mortal
For this is the portal of disremembrance
Giving one a sense of disembodied semblance
Pursue to undermine its' infinity
Which only can end its' own morbidity
With a spark of hope, you may achieve

Your goal at last which can upheave
Resulting in a hydrogenous aftermath.

"I am impressed Arian, you really translate well."

"Sebastian?" Arian focused her eyes so tenderly at him. "A hydrogenous aftermath means a flooding end. There is no way out of this except by magic. Even if that works, I fear for you and Uncle Horatio."

Sebastian held Arian in his arms. "We will succeed."

"But Sebastian," Arian interrupted. "I have never seen the centerpiece in bronze and I have been here for three hundred years."

"Please Arian, my mind is made up. You never looked for it either." He hugged her to bestow confidence. Sebastian knew that his strength would always calm her as she melted in his arms. "What time is it?"

Uncle Horatio answered."11:00A.M. Sebastian."

"Crystal ball and witch's rod, where is the ancient elm tree?"

The crystal ball revealed the site.

"I have seen that tree. It is twenty miles away from here." Arian rejoiced. "Sebastian, "what will you need?"

"I will ask the crystal ball and witch's rod. First, we need a sextant, so I will be accurate with the degrees."

"May I go with you for part of the journey? You will be on the lake where we could say adieu."

"Why not!" Sebastian smiled. "The first part doesn't seem dangerous."

"Let's refresh you both." Arian suggested." For your journey, I will ask the witch's rod to make sandwiches and select the wine so I know you will have enough energy. Sebastian, please take the athame with you, besides the witch's rod, the crystal ball and the witch's brooms."

Sebastian, fully prepared, told the witch's rod to transfer all of them to the ancient elm tree. Sebastian had the sextant as they patiently waited for the zenith of the sun.

"Are we at the correct coordinates witch's rod and crystal ball?"

The crystal ball indicated to Sebastian that he was correct.

Arian held Selena and Lucien's hands with a worried anticipation. The sun was at its zenith as the light rays came directly down upon Sebastian. He took the angle at 90° left of the tree.

Arian now had the pages that Lucien carried while she continued reading the instructions out loud. "Take 64 paces due East Sebastian."

Sebastian paced them out as the others followed. Sebastian responded. "Is this where the centerpiece of bronze should be?"

"Yes, "Arian replied. "But, I don't see it. Could it be buried?"

"Witch's rod and crystal ball," Sebastian commented." Where is it?"

The crystal ball indicated. "You are standing on it approximately one foot down."

"Please, reveal it." Sebastian continued.

The ground opened itself up like a grave revealing a beautiful engraved bronze star with angles inscribed over it.

Arian called out. "Now from hence, 86 paces West towards the ponds."

Sebastian could only take 76 paces as they ran out of ground. "We must travel by boat." Sebastian ordered the witch's rod to create one. "This is it. We must part now." Sebastian uttered regretfully.

Arian ran to kiss Sebastian with such sensations even he felt weak. He held her tighter but slowly released her as he hugged Lucien and kissed his forehead. Arian carried Selena towards her husband. Selena kissed her Father and started to cry.

"Selena has my sentiments exactly." Arian whispered.

Selena wrapped her arms around her Daddy's head and didn't let go of him.

Sebastian said quietly. "Selena you are only making this worse."

Selena was determined. "I need another kiss."

"Very well. "Sebastian kissed her as he pulled her hands away.

Arian held her." I love you."

They all turned their attention towards Uncle Horatio. Arian kissed his cheek. Uncle Horatio hugged Lucien and Selena.

"Good luck, Messieurs, I wish I could come with you but, I must decipher the rest. I can't express the immense love I have for you. I am so proud of both of you for being so brave and caring for me, adieu my loved ones."

Selena still cried as Sebastian counted 10 more paces. He pulled out Arian's pages as he silently stared at Arian waving at the edge of the pond.

"Witch's rod, make us a submergible with a retractable arm to open the latch." The submergible appeared as Sebastian and Uncle Horatio entered into it. Sebastian still stared at Arian holding Selena as both he and Arian waved.

"I hate good byes." Uncle Horatio cast an emotional glance.

"Uncle, I need your mind to help me search for the latch. I don't see it. Crystal ball show me where it is!"

Arian took her crystal ball while addressing Lucien. "You and Selena will watch the crystal ball while we will return home. Tell me everything Lucien." Arian transferred them to the library.

"Daddy is looking for the portal." Lucien reported.

"Please constantly watch the crystal ball. I must decipher this, even though; I would rather see what your Father is doing. Here, please eat your lunch." Lucien grabbed for a sandwich, as did Selena. Arian pressed herself hard to finish her task.

The crystal ball first displayed the latch encrusted with practically everything.

"Well," Uncle Horatio stated. "This quest would be nowhere without this crystal ball. Who could see that latch? Oh, be careful Sebastian, when you open that thing. Who knows what will come up? Here, let's have some wine." But, as Uncle Horatio tried to open the bottle, the pressure exploded the cork as it doused its contents back at Uncle Horatio and Sebastian. Sebastian turned facing his Uncle dripping from the wine. Uncle Horatio uttered. "This wine doesn't travel well! It must be the pressure. Here is your sandwich Sebastian."

Sebastian held his temper while he asked the witch's rod to clean up the mess. Uncle Horatio staunchly held out Sebastian's sandwich.

Lucien and Selena burst out laughing.

"What is going on?" Arian implied.

"The wine bottle's cork, due to the pressure, just exploded, dousing Daddy and Uncle Horatio. But, Daddy kept his temper. They are now going to open the latch to the portal."

Arian hastened to see what the portal held inside.

Sebastian maneuvered the retractable arm as he attempted to open the latch. The arm slipped repeatedly. Sebastian tried it again. It was lifting. The air suction, once the latch swung up, pulled the submergible into the labyrinth subterranean tunnel. The water miraculously was expelled out and the latch resealed. Torches lit the passages.

"I guess," Sebastian implied," we can escape from this, Uncle and walk or ride our brooms to the next destination."

"Here, Sebastian. You should eat your sandwich first. We need the energy."

Sebastian took the sandwich as he read to himself. "Transverse, if you dare, merely being mortal."

"Look," Uncle Horatio pointed." What is glowing in front of that hallway?"

"Beware," echoed through the tunnel as a marble plaque lit up saying. "This, is the Portal of Disremembrance."

"Crystal ball," Sebastian asked. "What is disremembrance?"

The crystal ball responded as it revealed the word oblivion.

"Oh!" Uncle Horatio disclaimed." Maybe we should ask the crystal ball, what it is first, before we enter? We might as well prepare. Sebastian, this is terrible!" They scanned inside. "There is no way we can deal with this. Let's go back."

A force field of beams blocked them while protecting the entranceway.

"No," Sebastian concurred." The beams are the morbidity, but what triggers the collapse of the dome inside is what puzzles me?"

"Mommy, Mommy, Daddy is going to approach a crystal dome and there is water completely surrounding the outside of it, if it collapses, how horrible!" Selena cried.

Arian dropped the pen as she stared at the crystal ball. "Mon Dieu! Witch's rod, can you finish this translation for me with the crystal ball?"

"No." The crystal ball revealed. "My memory only refers to Latin, not old Greek. To achieve this, one must find the witch's rod from the ancient Greek times. This rod would be buried too deep for me to extract. Besides, there is a curse upon it that must be deciphered to release it. I can not help you."

Arian sighed in despair. Arian couldn't concentrate, so she stared at the crystal ball to see her Sebastian. Arian called him. "Sebastian, what can I do to help you?"

Sebastian glanced at the crystal ball. "Arian, the electric beams are not the problem. This dome is as large as Rome's dome of the Pantheon. Yet, this one is made of crystal. It is about 170,625 cubic feet. The foundation is composed of 15 foot high and 24 foot, thick ring resting upon a highly resistant clay base. The dome, at the summit, is 5 feet thick. This thickness increases towards the drum, where it exceeds 20 feet. The dome structure penetrates one third of the way into the drum ring, which thus has an inner height of 70 feet and an outer one measuring 99 feet. Going upward, the material used for the wall gets lighter and lighter. Obviously, in the center of the floor of this dome is a pedestal, where the xenon flash tube resides. But, if one takes it, there must be a projectile that shoots straight at the dome to crack it with devastating results. Witch's rod dispense the electric force field beams."

The beams ceased as Sebastian and Uncle Horatio ventured closer to look inside of the chamber.

"Can there be anything on the floor that can trigger the projectile?" Arian questioned.

"Witch's rod respond to Arian's question." Sebastian ordered.

The witch's rod and crystal ball wrote. "The floor has traps everywhere. The only safe area is the circumference where the wall resides."

Arian supplicated. "Your brooms are the only way in but what are you going to do to prevent the water avalanche?"

"That is not so difficult." Sebastian explained. "I will use the witch's rod to construct an inner cement dome that is not as large with a metal mesh to ensure its reinforcement. If the cement breaks, we can avoid the destruction a bit better than the hydrogenous aftermath."

"Sebastian, can the witch's rod do that? Aren't you expecting a bit much?" Uncle Horatio expressed.

"We shall see. Witch's rod, create the scaffolding, to counteract the thrust of the vaulting. Also when you add the concrete use metal meshing to reinforce it. Start with the walls. In order to alleviate the thrust of the concrete, please pour as you proceed, ring by ring, so that each ring is dry before receiving the weight of the one above it. The mixture must be lighter and lighter as one approaches the top, insert double masonry braces like a vaulting ribs, use as a dilation joint, so that the walls can settle without cracking."

Sebastian on his broom flew directing the witch's rod's progress as a second dome emerged while torches were added so one could see.

"Is it dry Sebastian? "Uncle Horatio queried. "This is quiet impressive. You should make more buildings like this. Imagine the construction costs. You would be rich."

"Uncle, I can't do that! Besides, I am only doing this for Arian."

Arian asked the crystal ball. "What will cause the projectile to fire?

The crystal ball showed the xenon flash tube.

"If one could counter balance it, would that prevent the projectile from firing?" Arian wondered.

"No," The crystal ball responded.

"There is nothing you can do, Sebastian. When you pick up the tube, nothing can stop the projectile!" Arian confirmed.

"Maybe," Uncle Horatio replied." We should wear a helmet to protect ourselves."

Sebastian was flying on the broom in circles inspecting the new dome for stress. "The dome is completed." Sebastian asked the crystal ball. "Can we use the transfer spell to escape out of here?"

The crystal ball wrote. "Yes."

"If we take the xenon flash tube, can we transfer out of this place?" Sebastian abated.

"No." The crystal ball stipulated.

"No?" Arian repeated. "But how do they escape out of there?"

The crystal ball displayed. "The same way you got in."

Arian continued. "How large is the projectile?"

"As large as a usual canon ball. For the pedestal is the cannon."

"Oh my God, Sebastian! Did you hear that." Uncle Horatio replied nervously.

"Can the witch's broom fly through water?" Sebastian asked.

"Yes," the crystal ball reaffirmed.

"Witch's rod, can you design a plug for the canon out of wrought iron?"

"Yes," the crystal ball wrote.

"Do so." Sebastian countered.

Arian whispered. "Be careful Sebastian, I love you."

Sebastian smiled." I will be all right. Uncle Horatio, stay close to me. Please!"

"Don't worry. I will stay like glue."

Sebastian replied. "Stay close to the exit until I reach you." Sebastian flew towards the pedestal. He flew at top speed as he picked up the xenon flash tube with one hand and replaced it with the plug using the witch's rod." Please pound in the plug, witch's rod."

The plug was driven in deeper. Sebastian and Uncle Horatio flew expediently out of the chamber knowing the plug would only give them seconds. The cannon exploded spewing the shrapnel out cracking the cement dome .The fractures and fissures split the cement as the tremendous pressure exuded while cement chunks fell from the ceiling creating slight cracks on the crystal dome. The pressure increased causing the crystal dome to start to trickle slowly as the pressure rifted, it cracked the clear crystal dome. The pressure of the weight of the water from outside of the dome caved it's way in demolishing what was left as the water fissured in avalanching down towards the passage ways and onward. Tons of water cascaded down making its way towards Sebastian and Uncle Horatio. They were both flying at top speed.

Arian gasped. "Sebastian, the crystal dome gave way and all that water is coming towards you!"

Sebastian responded. "We have just past the mile and we are coming towards you as fast as we can. I can't fly this broom any faster."

"Crystal ball, will the water catch up to my Sebastian?'

"Probably." The crystal ball wrote.

"Is there any short cut they could take to alleviate this?"

"No." The crystal ball demonstrated.

Arian held her breath as they watched the horror unfold. "Is there a barrier you can construct to slow the water?"

"Yes."

"Do so, as many as necessary!" Arian demanded.

Barrier after barrier, were placed to block its way, but the pressure made them collapse. However, it did give more time to Sebastian and Uncle Horatio.

Sebastian heard a rumbling sound like a wall of water coming straight towards them. Sebastian tried to fly faster, yet, as they passed a tunnel in front of them that joined their passage, it transversed with a water wall, submerging Sebastian and Uncle Horatio.

Uncle Horatio screamed. "Our situation has not improved." Uncle Horatio was swept away crying out. "Sebastian!"

Sebastian gripped his broom holding his breath maintaining his course as the water completely engrossed him.

"Sebastian!" Arian called out. "Your Uncle is lost. I will transfer him here. You are on your own."

Sebastian waved concentrating only on the exit ahead.

"Witch's rod transfer Uncle Horatio here, please." Arian spoke quickly.

Uncle Horatio appeared dripping on the carpet. "Oh, thank God! Arian! I was about to drown."

Arian asked the witch's rod. "Please bring towels for Uncle Horatio and also dry his clothes."

Everyone stared at Sebastian. Sebastian harnessed the witch's rod to open the latch of the portal as he held onto his broom tightly to buffet through the lake. Sebastian emerged from the lake into the air as he flew home finally catching his breath.

Arian waited for him as he alighted off his broom and into her loving arms. The children were all over him. Uncle Horatio patted him on his shoulder.

"My, I thought you would be wet but your flying must have dried you off, my brave cavalier." Arian kissed him.

Sebastian picked up Selena and implored." Witch's rod, take extremely good care of the xenon flash tube." The witch's rod stored it away. Sebastian picked up Lucien with his other arm. Arian embraced them all. He gently placed Lucien and Selena down, as Arian watched him lovingly. Sebastian eyes only focused on Arian's eyes but Uncle Horatio whacked him on his back.

"Sebastian, I am so glad you made it home." Uncle Horatio said relieved.

Sebastian smiled, but his mind went back to Arian. "What is next?"

Arian lowered her eyes full of concern. "It only gets worse."

"Worse!" Uncle Horatio was taken aback.

"Yes, you are going through a live volcano to retrieve a potassium dihydrogen phosphate crystal and a neodymium doped glasses, if I got it right."

"What?" Uncle Horatio repeated.

Sebastian confirmed. "Yes, Arian did translate it correct for the solid phase laser."

"Let me place a refreshing spell on you and your Uncle. Maybe, you should eat something. We all saw what happened to the wine. Come and relax here on the sofa, Sebastian." Arian pleaded.

Arian had Sebastian and Uncle Horatio rest while she offered both more food and more wine recently prepared by the witch's rod. The children were offered a snack.

"What time is it?" Sebastian pondered.

"2:30PM, we must go to the mountain starting with the bronze centerpiece." Arian sighed regrettably.

Sebastian stood up as Arian held him closer with the children. Arian ordered the witch's rod to transfer them to the centerpiece as she handed the transcription to Sebastian. Arian held the children by the hand staying close to him.

QUEST 11

Up through the mist of a mountain with time
Hidden caverns with diverging paths will align
Start with the bronze centerpiece from the first rhyme
Focus upon the line of cypress and pine
Go north 100 paces to the mountain's base
Turn clockwise at the hour of three on the sundial's face
An entrance will open if one presses the crystalline stone to the right.
Enter quickly for the entrance seals itself by night
Beware of the sulfurous fumes which attacks with a blast
Like Pompeii's mount Vesuvius from the past
Run quickly for it is timed in five minute intervals or less

That will suffocate and glue your esophagus at best

To avoid the ooze of molten lava step only on the stones of magic which controls

Keep to the left narrow tunnel as it inclines towards your goals

Your goal is within reach in the caldera delicately placed.

So as to disturb it, will be dangerous, so do make haste.

Sebastian read aloud. "Go North 100 paces to the mountain's base. Turn clockwise at the hour of three on the sundial's face. An entrance will open if one presses the crystal stone to the right."

"Here is the crystal stone." Lucien replied as Selena ran to touch it.

"The stone is a peridot." Arian declared. "I guess this is where we must part again." Arian hesitated remorsefully. She kissed Sebastian again so tenderly. "I love you so much. "

Lucien and Selena kissed their Father.

Sebastian replied. "I love all of you so much but I must go. Good bye." He kissed them again.

They all hugged Uncle Horatio. "Good bye." He quoted.

"Be careful, all of you." Arian waved as Sebastian pressed the stone to the right as a passage emerged from the cave.

"My, it already stinks!" Uncle Horatio reluctantly entered it.

"Be careful of dragons." Selena added.

Arian noticed a small lizard like creature at the entrance of the cave. "Sebastian, Selena is correct. See." She pointed at the creature. This is a dragon larvae."

Sebastian followed Arian's gaze. "Arian, that is just a salamander. Dragons don't exist, only in myths." He teased. "But I will be careful." Sebastian echoed.

"You think there is a dragon in here, Sebastian?" Uncle Horatio pondered.

"Stop that! It is not mentioned in the poem, but if you see one, tell me about it." Sebastian smiled.

Arian utilized the witch's rod and the transfer spell to get home. "What is happening, Lucien?"

Lucien said. "They are talking about dragons."

"Oh," Arian smiled, "I must transcribe this next quest."

Sebastian read out loud again as the passage declined. Sebastian created a flashlight for his Uncle and him.

"My, it is dark in here, Sebastian. Do you think that dragons' eyes glow in the dark for a warning?"

"Uncle, would you stop that! Please be serious." Sebastian countered. "All we must worry about is the lava and the sulfuric fumes that can race over one hundred miles an hour. That is bad enough!"

"Oh, that makes me feel better, one hundred miles an hour. Oh my God! Mon Dieu!

"You are sounding like Arian. Is everyone speaking French?"

"It is catchy," Uncle Horatio replied.

"How do we know if we are going in the right direction, Sebastian?"

"Since this is the only passage, I can't see how we could go wrong. Uncle, relax!"

The passage opened up with five different directions to choose from.

"Oh, Oh!" Uncle Horatio complained.

Sebastian reviewed the poem. "Which one witch's rod and crystal ball?"

Lucien called. "Mommy, Daddy is lost."

Arian rushed to the crystal ball. Arian contacted Sebastian. "Are you all right?"

Sebastian focused upon his crystal ball. "Arian, I was just asking which way. The witch's rod and crystal ball suggest the third left passage. So, I must time it with the witch's rod for intervals of five minutes."

Arian seemed a little more relaxed. "Be careful."

"I will." Sebastian smiled.

The witch's rod turned the color of green to indicate to start as both Sebastian and Uncle Horatio ran. The heat was tremendous as a huge gas explosion echoed towards them.

"This is it!" Uncle Horatio cried.

Sebastian grabbed his Uncle as he dragged him through. When they reached the passage or branch. Sebastian pushed his Uncle and himself against the wall. Sebastian pulled them farther away. The fumes spouted out in every direction. They were fifty feet from the ledge. The gas still blasted as the heat from the gas expanded as it seared the stone wall touching the adjacent rock. One could still get burned; however, it cooled as the ratio of distance increased.

"My," was all Uncle Horatio could say.

Sebastian leaned upon a huge glass orb, larger than twenty feet in diameter. Sebastian wondered what he was leaning against so he turned around to see. A large crystal orb covering an abyss like portal descended straight down which one could view into its depths. Sebastian stared at it as Hexe rebounded against the glass to attack him as her arms reached out for him.

Hexe screamed. "Sebastian come to me! I will haunt and kill you for this!"

Sebastian, shocked, pushed back against the glass towards the wall in horror.

Hexe disappeared into a piece of dust and then reverted back to a ghost, floating in the medium of the pit or abyss. Hexe screamed and banged against the glass from the inside trying to get out. "Come to me! You will join me for Mort will kill you! I shall make you mine!"

"Mommy!" Selena cried.

Arian ran to Selena as she gasped. "Sebastian!"

"I am all right, you don't think that Hexe can come out? I hope not." Sebastian tried to reassure Arian."

Lucien held onto his Mother, as did Selena.

Hexe appeared again, as did Hagatha and Brujia. "Murderers!" They screamed. "We will see you here soon." They vortexed away to dust appearing and disappearing.

Arian cried." Mon Dieu! Sebastian!"

Sebastian asked the witch's rod and crystal ball. "What is this?"

"This is the Pit of Tartarus. Only the condemned can pass into there, you are safe."

Hexe shouted. "Witch's rod, kill them if you know who I am!"

Sebastian held the witch's rod. "You belong to me, ignore them."

"Yes, my master. " The witch's rod and crystal ball responded.

"Witch's rod, you traitor! You like Sebastian. Death, to you." Hexe wailed.

"Let's get out of here, Sebastian. "Uncle Horatio urged.

"With pleasure." Sebastian spoke with concern. "The next stanza that pertains is to avoid the ooze of molten lava. Step only on the stones of magic. Here it is." Sebastian pointed. "Witch's rod, how far is it to our goal?"

The crystal ball displayed one half mile. Sebastian and Uncle Horatio left the Pit of Tartarus.

Three witches yelled. "Death to all!"

"We can't even fly, there is no room and if we miss a stepping stone, we burn up, so touching." Uncle Horatio complained.

"Uncle, let's try our best. It's only a half a mile." Sebastian tried to be optimistic.

At that moment, the path opened up, as ooze hissed up rising almost over the stepping stones and then fell back. They were crossing the cliff's edge as the stepping stones descended towards the caldera. Deep down, where they were heading against the walls of the volcano, a myriad of tremendous waterfalls of lava converged as the rivers merged. In the center, the lava rose and fell caused by pressure, but off to the side one could see a peak.

Sebastian awe struck by the scene countered. "We seem to be heading deeper into the caldera basin." An earthquake suddenly shook the volcano. Both Sebastian and Uncle Horatio almost fell off the edge. Both tried to keep their balance knowing what would happen to them if they didn't. Sebastian held on, trying to control his footing for he almost fell. They were passing a fumoral, a volcano's hole of gas. Bursts of gas were heading towards them as Sebastian pulled his Uncle further down the path.

"Mommy, Mommy! Daddy is in hell!" Lucien called out.

"What!" Arian cried. She again rushed to see the crystal ball." Oh, Mon Dieu! Sebastian, Are you all right? Is it safe to talk to us?"

Sebastian heard his Arian. "We are still here. We will be entering a tunnel again instead of this ledge of the caldera."

Arian whispered. "There is a pedestal in the center of the caldera's peak, on the other side. It is in the lowest section in the caldera. I asked the witch's rod and crystal ball. The moment one takes the crystal and the neodymium dopa glasses, the volcano will erupt. The temperature can reach as high as 2460°F or 1,350°C. You must conjure up a plug to prevent the eruption. Do you know that the lakes of lava below you are at least 50 feet deep? Lucien is right, you are in hell. Oh, Sebastian, how I love you."

"We will make it. Don't worry. I won't fail you."

"Sebastian, you are such an optimist. I think I melted or wilted down here. I am certainly bedraggled." Uncle Horatio confessed.

"Would you want some water. I could transfer it down there." Arian suggested.

Sebastian replied. "No, thank you. We want this over with." They disappeared into the tunnel. According to the poem, keep to the left side, Uncle."

The tunnel opened up to the bottom of the caldera's center. "Witch's rod, make me a plug that fits in securely. For these items, Uncle, when I steal the crystal and doped glass, you will take the witch's rod and tell it to plug the crater. Keep your distance. Let the rod do the work. Are you ready, Uncle?"

"Yes, Sebastian."

"Good."

"Mommy, Mommy, Daddy is going to take the items now." Lucien reported.

Arian immediately stopped what she was doing as they all watched. Arian held her breath. She clutched both children. "Mon Dieu!"

Sebastian, on a flying run, picked up both items in one sweep as he created a satchel, placing the items securely inside and strapped it around his shoulder. He flew faster than ever to escape and contact his Uncle. Uncle Horatio ordered the witch's rod to seal the hole with the plug of granite. Sebastian reached his Uncle.

"Sebastian, where should we fly to? The whole mountain is shaking; even the walls are cracking." Uncle Horatio announced in horror.

Sebastian pointed. "Over there seems safe. Witch's rod where is the fastest route out of here?"

The crystal ball revealed. "Try the left East face."

"Witch's rod and crystal ball, can you bore a hole for us to go through?"

"Yes." The crystal ball displayed as a hole emerged. Both Sebastian and Uncle Horatio flew threw it.

Arian called. "Sebastian, the entire caldera is filling with lava. The plug has exploded out. Is the tunnel you are flying through going up at an angle because if it is not, the lava will reach it, and it will travel towards you."

Sebastian had his crystal ball out. "I understand, Arian. I will ask the witch's rod to make this tunnel at a steeper angle and larger."

"Please hurry, Sebastian The lava has filled the basin and it is erupting with geysers of up to five hundred feet high."

"We are doing our best, Arian."

"I am sorry, I am so worried about you."

Both Sebastian and Uncle Horatio could now fly together due to the width of the tunnel. However, another passage intersected it, filling with lava, as it approached them.

"Look! "Uncle Horatio cried. "It is blocking our path completely!"

"I see it, Uncle. Witch's rod, make another passage through here around this obstacle to override this so we can return to the original path."

The witch's rod complied. There was no choice as Sebastian and Uncle Horatio flew through.

Arian screamed. "No, Sebastian!" But it was too late.

Sebastian activated the crystal ball to respond to Arian when all of a sudden, Hexe, from the Pit of Tartarus, attacked him. (Sebastian and his Uncle were now in the Pit of Tartarus to divert them from the lava). Hexe grabbed Sebastian's head and kissed him fully on his lips as she entwined herself around him.

Sheer disgust and horror possessed Sebastian. Sebastian took his free hand to strike Hexe but he lost the crystal ball and the witch's rod. So he tried to pull Hexe off but she was too strong. Uncle Horatio flew close to help Sebastian, but Hagatha accosted him in the same manor, being kissed as Uncle Horatio fought to get her off.

Arian screamed in horror. "My Sebastian, what can I do?"

If Sebastian or Uncle Horatio lose their brooms, they will be condemned forever with the witches for eons of time because they couldn't escape. The crystal ball indicated.

Now, Brujia attacked. "Having fun, Sebastian. You deserve this."

Brujia grabbed Sebastian's free arm pulling it towards his back, holding it. She then tried pulling Sebastian's broom bending his back to lie against the broom for Hexe. Hexe had him at a better angle but not quite. Hexe, with one free hand, tried to extract Sebastian's grip on his broom.

Arian harnessed the witch's rod. "Bring me the expulsion spell from the cellar." It appeared. Arian created another witch's rod. "Here Lucien! Take this rod and tell it to locate your Father's crystal ball and witch's rod. Make sure the witches can't take it or they will escape the pit."

Brujia was still trying to take Sebastian's broom away while Hexe finally got Sebastian's thumb pulling it away from the broom. Sebastian lost his grip .One could see anger and fear in his eyes. Three bodies fell from the broom like a sandwich hurtling in space downward. Hexe was tearing as Sebastian's clothes as Brujia held both arms of Sebastian behind his back. Hexe was still kissing him.

Arian used her emerald ring to send a lightning bolt towards Hexe's head. Hexe could feel the electrical wave hit her, yet, she was in no pain being dead, but a ghost. Hexe stopped to see what it was.

Sebastian screamed in horror. "Don't touch me! Stop It! How dare you! How I hate you!"

"My Sebastian, I will make you mine right now the moment I take your clothes off. Now, hush, I will never leave you alone. Your body will die in time but I will have your soul. But wait, Brujia did you see where that witch's rod went? We will resurrect ourselves with the other souls in this pit. But don't let him go yet. Sebastian will be mine now and for all."

Arian shouted. "Let go of my husband!" The expulsion spell dispensed via the witch's rod onto Brujia and Hexe as Arian's voice could be heard." Begone, begone."

Both witches' souls were torn from Sebastian, blown far away screaming at the top of their lungs. "No!" The voices echoed from within the depths of the pit.

Sebastian had tears in his eyes. "Arian, I am so upset and in shock. Where is my broom?"

Sebastian's broom appeared directed by Lucien's witch's rod, along with the crystal ball and Sebastian's witch's' rod.

"Arian, I must help Uncle Horatio." Sebastian flew to his Uncle's aid. Sebastian tried to pull Hagatha off his Uncle.

Hagatha wailed. "Stay away Sebastian, Horatio is mine!"

"Never!" Sebastian took his fist and struck her hard. Hagatha was buffeted off the broom due to Sebastian's pent up anger, hate and fury.

Arian's voice could be heard. "Begone, begone!"

Hagatha was blown off down the pit screaming. "Curse you!"

Uncle Horatio also had tears in his eyes. "This is one of my worst nightmares come true. Sebastian, I feel awful and violated. Thank you, Sebastian and Arian. I am shaking so badly; I can't even fly straight. Take me home, Sebastian. I can't take this, I would have rather had the lava."

The mountain rumbled again, as if the whole top would explode off.

"I feel terrible as well." Sebastian exhibited complete revulsion. "I want to be in your arms, Arian. Witch's rod, guide us home fast."

The witch's' rod complied as they just escaped. Half the mountain blew off blasting away the rocks and lava in every direction.

226

Arian and the children awaited them at the door. Both Sebastian and Uncle Horatio got off their brooms as Sebastian ran to Arian, who kissed him so softly and gently. She held him so tenderly to soothe his soul. Uncle Horatio wanted to he held as well. The children hugged him and their Father.

Arian held both of them. "Please." She still held onto them. "Let's sit down on the sofa. I love you both so much."

Sebastian held Arian again as she could still feel his anguish. Arian noticed that Uncle Horatio needed another hug so she positioned Sebastian closer to do so. Arian pulled both of them into the house and onto the sofa.

"Please sit down." Arian suggested.

Sebastian squeezed his wife again holding her so close. The children also came up to them to be held, as did Uncle Horatio. Arian kissed Sebastian so tenderly. Sebastian finally relaxed in Arian's arms.

"Shh." Arian soothed him "I love you. I would never let that witch ever have you. I vowed that long ago. Come let the children hold you." The children held their Father and Uncle Horatio. "I am sorry this even had to happen." Arian spoke to them so softly." Are both of you all right? Let me bring you a brandy. Witch's rod, please bring my cavaliers brandy and some tea for the rest of us. It is 4:30. Maybe, we should have an early dinner? Quest III must begin or I will have to wait six months more."

Sebastian, on Arian's left side held one arm of Arian. The children sat on each half of Arian's lap, while Uncle Horatio held Arian's right side of her arm.

Sebastian upon hearing the time stared at his watch. "Oh God, the time is flying away from us." His eyes only focused on Arian.

Arian started to sing after dinner. They were a few spirited and gay songs from the 17th century to cheer up her gentlemen and her children. "Music always soothes the soul. This should cheer you up. These pieces, reminds me of my grandmother on my Father's side. She sang these same songs whenever I fell down or when I lost a game in chess. Should I hug you again, my Sebastian? I always love to hug you, besides having these two that are upon my lap. I would hug you, Uncle Horatio, as well. Unfortunately, time is flying. Let's prepare. The third quest will be in the Realm of Reality starting with the magical stone that shuts the witch's cave." Arian read the poem:

THE THIRD QUEST

Unbeknownst and profound, through chasms of forgotten past
Once acceded through a magical stone, the unforeseen might last
When twilight commences, the angle will be shown
By this angle, locate the tombstone with a Gaelic cross name unknown
Unearth it to seek the orb of essence
With this orb, it will reveal a presence
Abstruse deep inside this grave
Guarded by an untimely knave
A duel to the death must ensue

For one must die or rue
If one lives, only then can you attain your goal?
You must be remorseful, for your very soul
MORT.

"This sounds as awful as the other two. Mort means death in French. It is also the name of the knight. May I come with you part of the way, like I did the last time, Sebastian, with the children?"

Sebastian smiled. "Yes, you may."

"I will have to materialize within you again." Arian winked.

"I know." Sebastian conceded.

"Do you think we should ask the witch's rod to make you a suit of armor? Mort probably has one."

"A suit of armor is quite heavy. I have never fought in one, but returning to another matter, I left a hole in the pit of Tartarus."

"Don't worry Sebastian, I plugged that hole. Hexe will never escape from there. I made sure. 5:30PM will be twilight, which means we only have less than an hour together. Please, maybe you should eat more for your strength. Let me give all of us another refreshing spell. I hope I deciphered this accurately. Witch's rod please clear the dishes and clean them, thank you."

Sebastian looked depressed. "So soon."

"We should rest. I want you in my arms for an eternity and even that is too short." Arian lamented.

Sebastian asked the witch's rod. "Take us to our room." Sebastian stayed on the chair as Selena and Lucien were on his lap and Arian held them by placing her arms around everyone, except Uncle Horatio, who was resting on the sofa.

"Daddy, I keep falling through your legs. It is also very hard to sit on." Selena complained.

Arian said. "Selena, all laps of father's are like that. My Father's was that way. My I haven't thought of that in ages." Arian kissed Sebastian's forehead so carefully as she slid passed his nose and unto his mouth. He kissed her back. She then kissed Lucien and Selena. "If I could hold a moment of pleasure in time, it would be right now. Where all my love ones are so close to me, which is my dream of ecstasy. I consulted the crystal ball. Mort is dressed in full armor. What do you suggest? I would die if anything happen to you. I know I would have to go on for the children's sake. But, I haven't felt so bad since. Never mind."

Sebastian finished the sentence. "Since Alain De La Vega, correct?"

"Yes, Sebastian, I love you but we must leave now. Would you like to drink something before we go?"

"No." Sebastian murmured. "So, Lucien and Selena, I must move. My legs are asleep." They all rose. Sebastian held Arian so close to kiss her. His eyes said it all. If anyone would see Arian and Sebastian stare at each other, one would see the magnetism as the electricity between them pulled them so close oblivious of anything else. "I guess I must wake my Uncle as usual."

"Will he be all right and you? It always takes time to heal." Arian whispered.

"Uncle Horatio, let's go, we must face Quest III."

"Oh, do we have to, Sebastian. I am quite done up today."

The witch's rod had everything ready. The children sat on their Father's broom. Sebastian was at the back as he held Selena while Lucien sat at the helm. Giselle positioned herself in her birdcage tied to Lucien's waist. Uncle Horatio mounted his own broom. Arian as usual recited the spell waving the witch's rod.

Arian waved saying. "In a very short time, I will be with you." Arian focused on the crystal ball, seeing that all of them were at Uncle Horatio's house.

Sebastian called. "We all await you, my lady."

At that moment, Arian materialized into Sebastian, as Sebastian had his arms ready to embrace her. He kissed her neck as Arian leaned into him. They flew to the magical stone. They all dismounted. Arian held Lucien and Selena's hands. Sebastian held the poem.

"This is when twilight commences, the angle will be shown. "Sebastian reiterated.

At that moment, a golden beam sprang forth. Sebastian seeing it had the family back on their brooms.

Uncle Horatio followed suit. "Don't worry Sebastian, I won't get lost, again."

Arian leaned even more against Sebastian, as she wanted to stay glued to him. Sebastian's arm caressed Arian to comfort her. Arian tried to hold onto Sebastian more. The golden beams aimed for a tombstone with a Gaelic cross. There was no name.

"There it is!" Sebastian pointed. He slowed down as everyone dismounted.

Uncle Horatio just came by. "Here I am Sebastian. This is it? A tombstone, with no name, is this symbolic?"

"I have no idea, Uncle. We must unearth it to seek the orb of essence."

"Must we? I hate opening graves. I have been spooked enough for one day."

"Yes, we must! Witch's rod find the orb of essence!"

The earth fell into a pile. The crystal orb displayed its pearlescence in the inside, which was augmented by crystalline facets on the outside, as it twinkled. Sebastian bent to pick it up as the children and Arian ran to see it.

"It is so beautiful, Sebastian." Arian expressed. Each of them touched it while Sebastian held it in his hands." How does it feel? Does the stone give a feeling or presence?"

Sebastian replied." It feels alive as it pulses. It is warm and full of life. It gives a presence of peace."

"Maybe, it will protect you, Sebastian?" Arian whispered hopefully. "For I love you more than this world has given me, besides these two. Holding these two precious ones I have my children from the past, here with me at last. And now you must go."

Sebastian had tears in his eyes touched by what Arian had said as he kissed her and Lucien and Selena. Arian kissed Uncle Horatio, as did the children.

"Wish me luck." Sebastian called out. Arian ran back to Sebastian and kissed him again.

"I know you always sacrificed for me. You would have done so three hundred years ago, but I just didn't let you. I couldn't see you suffer so with that. So now, I must wait for you. Be careful, my loved ones. Oh, Uncle Horatio let me kiss you as well. Good luck."

Selena and Lucien kissed their Father and Uncle again. All of them had tears in their eyes.

The earth shook as steps revealed themselves going downward. Sebastian stared at his family as he headed down the stairs towards the passageway.

Uncle Horatio followed saying. "Good bye again. Well Sebastian, at least the place lights up as we pass. How does the orb tell you where to go?"

"It pulses more violently, if we are going in the right direction." Sebastian answered.

"My, what lies ahead? Why don't we ask the witch's rod and the crystal ball?"

"I don't think the results will cheer you up, but if you insist. Witch's rod and crystal ball, what lies ahead?"

Inside the crystal ball one word emerged, "Maze or knot in stone."

"We are going to figure out a maze?"

"There, in front of them, a force field of electricity exuded.

"I think we found it." Sebastian came close to it, even from that distance, it swallowed him up.

"Sebastian! "Uncle Horatio cried.

Arian transferred the children and herself home. She saw the results on their crystal ball. "Sebastian, are you all right?"

"Yes, it is just dark in here. That is why you can't see me." Sebastian created a flashlight. "Uncle, I am all right. Can't you join me?"

"Oh, yes, of course, Here I am, Sebastian. Why don't I see you?"

"Because, Uncle." Sebastian responded. "You aren't with me. Did you create a flashlight?"

"Yes, Sebastian, so where are you?"

"It must be two different mazes, Arian."

"Yes." Arian confirmed. "Each of you are in a separate maze, exactly the same type. However, I see you as if you were opponents from above. Sebastian, you are closer to the center. My, Sebastian you are fast. You are already through it."

"Well, I got stuck once, but it wasn't too bad. Come on Uncle."

"I seem to be in a quandary or to put it into blunt terms. I am stuck!" Uncle Horatio complained.

Sebastian, being at the other end, tried to find the exit for Uncle Horatio's maze to extract him from the other side. To find the exit, Sebastian worked backwards.

Arian called out. "Uncle Horatio, try turning left. Yes, that is correct."

A voice from within this realm, a man's voice, spoke. "There will be no interference! Madame, you must be only a spectator!"

"Forgive me, Monsieur. Had I known, I would not presume. Forgive me again, and my apologies. "Arian spoke clearly and apologetically as she held her children closer.

"Your apologies, Madame, have been noted!"

Sebastian stared into his crystal ball at Arian who was staring right back at him in disbelief.

"Are we in trouble, Sebastian?" Uncle Horatio whispered.

"I don't know, Uncle." Sebastian located his Uncle.

"Oh, thank God." Uncle Horatio spoke gratefully. "Where to or am I cheating? Did you see the man or being, who spoke to us? It must be Mort."

"No Uncle." Sebastian reiterated." Shall we go?"

"What choice do I have? I will follow."

Sebastian extracted him out of the maze. He pulled the orb of essence from his pocket as it pulsed in the left direction. It took them to an atrium garden with fountains, which were spouting its crystal water drops in sprays.

"My, this is beautiful. Nothing scary here." Uncle Horatio speculated.

"Never trust appearances, Uncle." Sebastian fathomed.

"It looks like a Roman or Italian garden." Uncle Horatio proceeded.

"How do we escape from this? It must be by that doorway." Sebastian and his Uncle approached. Sebastian hesitated. "Wait, Uncle." Sebastian placed his hand through, but quickly withdrew it.

A hissing sound of extreme pressurized steam spouted out from the top of the door entrance and also, the bottom did the same thing.

"How do we pass that, Sebastian?" Uncle Horatio spoke perspicaciously.

"We must time it at certain intervals." Sebastian calculated as he used his watch. "Every three minutes." He timed it again.

"Shall we proceed. Sebastian?"

"No, Uncle. Let's inspect it further. Here, there is a fruit tree over here. Let's take this orange and roll it through for I can't find anything larger." Sebastian timed three minutes for the steam and then rolled the orange through. From a side panel the orange was skewed horizontally by row of fine lances.

"Oh, God, that could have been me." Uncle Horatio panted.

Sebastian then decided to use a branch from the nearby tree and broke it off. As the last lance horizontally receded, Sebastian, then thrusted the branch through the entrance. Another set of lances from the top crashed down spearing what was left of the orange. "We have three minutes for the steam, 1 minute for the horizontal panel and thirty seconds for the top panel "

"There must be a diagonal one, Sebastian. Don't you think so?"

"Not by this lay out, Uncle, so let us time it again."

"We could stay here."

"For how long, Uncle?" Sebastian seemed agitated.

"All right."

Sebastian rolled the orange; the grid went by horizontally. Sebastian then thrusted the branch again as the top lance fell Sebastian grabbed his Uncle as he dragged them through .The steam then issued forth.

"Oh God, Sebastian. What is around the corner?"

"Patience," Sebastian murmured. "I would ask the witch's rod or crystal ball but will it ruin my chances. I better not."

They entered another room. The orb stilled pulsed.

"I don't think we have to worry. This room looks like a dead end. There is nothing in this room." Uncle Horatio contended.

"There must be a panel." Sebastian scrutinized the walls. "Here it is."

"You, being an architect of course, would find it." Uncle Horatio countered.

"I will go first, Uncle." Sebastian pressed the button as the wall reverted by itself taking Sebastian and twirling him to the other side. Sebastian clung to the wall for if he had taken another step; the precipice cliff could have been his end. Sebastian was inside of a mountain ledge with only two feet to walk on. Spanning the view downwards, there was a thousand foot drop to ones death, as it sprawled before him." Uncle, be careful as one exits, it is very dangerous."

Arian gasped as the children held onto her. "Sebastian!"

Sebastian still clung onto the edge making his way towards a path.

Uncle Horatio tried but as he emerged he slipped holding onto the edge. "Sebastian!"

Sebastian rushed to pull him up as he caught his free hand.

"That was too close! Thank you. It seems I will die a thousand deaths with this ledge."

Sebastian stayed close to the edge as the orb proceeded with its pulses. "There is a door in front of us, Uncle."

"Oh, is that so. All I do is look where my feet should go or should I look down? Which is too scary?"

"Don't look down," Sebastian affirmed. "What lies past the door?" Sebastian focused on the crystal ball to see Arian staring right back at him, giving him reassurance with her loving eyes. Sebastian proceeded. Sebastian reached the door and opened it carefully. The room had a high ceiling and seemed very functional. There was an altar on the other side of the wall, with the yttrium target placed under glass on the top of it. Sebastian entered the room with Uncle Horatio. The orb pulsed changing its color to ruby red.

"This is it, Sebastian. Where is Mort?" Uncle Horatio commented.

"I am here!" Mort entered. He had the same voice as the being that stated not to interfere. "Your Uncle is no match." Mort with the slightest movement from his hand levitated him to the corner of the room. A force field of electric impulses surrounded him." This fight is between us, Sebastian."

"What will become of my Uncle at the end?"

"He will be released." Mort assured him. "I regret to do this to you. I seem to like you. I see you are fighting for your Lady. This Arian has favored you. She is an honorable prize. You have married her many times before. She is special even in my eyes."

"I know she is." Sebastian conceded.

"I leave the choice of the weapon up to you. I will supply you with armor. There will be no advantage taken here."

"Are you always so gallant to your opponents?"

"You are an opponent. If you were an enemy, you would be all ready dead. I pity this fair Lady, for if I had known of her predicament I would have rescued her. But, if you should die Sebastian, in which you will, I promise, I will release, Madame Arian Simons, from her purgatory by constructing this laser. But, what the Pillars of Hercules does to her is up to the Fates, not I. But, if I had met you before my commitment, Arian, here, your life would be completely changed. I really regret this, Virtuous Lady. Shall we commence, Sebastian? I envy you with all my heart."

"She is my mother!" Lucien interrupted.

"Yes, Lucien. That she is, only of the past." Mort enumerated. "Choose your weapons from the assortment on the table beside you."

"If you are so versatile to be able to fight with any of these weapons, I would rather choose something that I am accustomed to which is a rapier and I would prefer no armor since I never fought with any." Sebastian answered.

"So be it." Mort removed his helmet revealing his face. He was handsome with dark black hair, white skin and black eyes that could unravel one's soul with sensitive features. His stature matched Sebastian's. "If you would excuse me, I must remove my armor. I will return shortly to deal with you. You can be assured."

"I would never assume to doubt you." Sebastian countered." Arian, maybe the children shouldn't watch. Not that I am ashamed if I lose, this man is a professional. I can sense that. It is that I don't want to traumatize the children more."

"Please don't say that. This is traumatic no matter if it is viewed or listened to." Arian pleaded.

Lucien added. "I want to see you until the last Father, please."

Selena cried. "I want to see you too, Daddy."

Sebastian conceded. "I don't know how to make it easier for anyone."

Uncle Horatio replied, "How about me? I don't want to see you hurt either. But, I can't do much for you over here. I feel so useless."

"Uncle, I sympathize but it is only fair that one fights one on one. He already had given me the honor to fight using the weapons that I am used to. I already like him. I don not relish the thought of vanquishing him, which is a lofty term meaning to kill. But I believe he will not give me any other option."

"You are correct, Sebastian. There is no option but death." Mort coldly stated. His attire was of the seventeenth century.

Sebastian removed his coat and picked up the rapier, as did Mort.

"En garde." Sebastian challenged him.

They commenced. Sebastian hit hard testing the skill of his opponent who seemed nonchalant as he matched blow for blow with the same strength. They equally counteracted each other. Sebastian cornered him making every blow count. He knew his counter part would wait until the last moment to pour forth his strength being immortal compared to Sebastian. So he tempered his actions taking Mort's lead, so he could last as long as Mort.

"You are quick. You time your moves well." Mort smiled with gleaming white teeth.

Sebastian thought to himself. "Either Mort is daring one to do something foolish or he wants to appear more dashing to my wife since he already said he would have changed his life had he met her sooner. Is he trying to make me jealous? He is conniving. So I must keep a cold calculating mind to dispose of him. I know he is trying to impress Arian for why is he wearing seventeen century clothing?"

Sebastian now backed to Mort's advances. So Sebastian flipped away to leave more space, but Mort flipped closer.

"Two can play this game, Sebastian." Mort smiled again.

Sebastian lunged towards home but Mort hit Sebastian's rapier out of his hand. Sebastian quickly remembered what Arian had done and used his foot flipping the rapier up, caught it and continued to fight.

"Interesting move." Mort commented.

"I learned it from my wife. She trained me." Sebastian remarked.

"She seems more fascinating as a women than I have had dreamed."

"Excuse me, you are talking about my wife!" Sebastian exclaimed.

"Yes, I know!"

"I don't like that tenor, but I will temper myself to the task at hand."

"Well done, despite how I love her from afar." Mort's eyes flashed at Arian seizing the moment.

"How much more can I endure." Sebastian lunged again but Mort stepped out of the way quickly nicking Sebastian's forearm, which bled.

"Hasty aren't you." Mort tilted his head at Sebastian for effect.

"An inevitability on my part." Sebastian conceded as he rammed the hilt of his rapier against Mort as the two clashed by only strength.

Sebastian attempted to angle Mort into the corner passing the table that held the candelabra and lighted candles. Sebastian thrust hard breaking them apart then he slashed at the candles while kicking them at the same time into his opponent so the candles would burn him. Mort brandished most of them away except one, which landed on his chest igniting Mort's lace shirt. Sebastian lunged again engaging Mort. Mort fought back not even flinching as he took his left hand to quench the small flames with a roguish grin on his face.

"You didn't quiet get me, Sebastian, but I will be more on guard the next time. You certainly can't be trusted." He thrust Sebastian back.

Sebastian regained his balance as now Mort, who appeared more concentrated, approached him. Sebastian flipped over the table to separate them while he breathed hard from the effort. Mort smiled with his eyes fixed on Sebastian as his face intensified with what had to be done and how.

"Having a small breather. You will need it. You are tiring. I can't say your not entertaining." Mort moved to get Sebastian as Sebastian using the table so he could catch his breath kept Mort out of reach.

They commenced again.

"You don't seem to tire." Sebastian noted.

"You forget, I am immortal like your wife. I still regret that I didn't save her earlier. We could have been together instead of you." Mort's eyes flashed at the prospect.

"You forget," Sebastian inferred. "She is totally faithful and devoted to me. She is entirely virtuous and she loves me beyond anything."

"Ah, you are referring to your love letter. Beautifully written. I had to do something to pass the time." Mort beamed with the insinuation as he quoted." For your eyes alone."

"This is intolerable!" Sebastian seethed with fury attacking again with forcible blows inciting and provoking Mort to more action. Sebastian could see Mort grinning profoundly while calculating at the same time.

"We need more room." Mort suggested waving his hand towards Uncle Horatio." Return to the Realm of Twilight. You are in the way."

Uncle Horatio commented. "Well, excuse me." He wanted to say more but he just disappeared.

Sebastian spoke to the crystal ball and Arian. "Is my Uncle with you?"

Arian answered. "Yes, your Uncle has just arrived but he doesn't seem to be able to speak."

Mort laughed. "That is because I didn't want to hear any more banal or droll comments. He will be able to speak afterwards." Mort focused his eyes on Sebastian and emphasized, "Upon your death to be more blunt."

Lucien spoke out. "Why must you kill my Father who only wants to help my mother. If you say you love her, why don't you help all of us."

Arian held Lucien closely saying, "Lucien, please don't interfere. This man has sworn to defend the Pillars' of Hercules. You are too young to understand all this now."

Mort lamented. "To hear the dulcet tones of an angel as you soothe your son."

At that moment Sebastian struck Mort with the hilt of his rapier hard knocking him off his feet while Sebastian positioned his rapier along Mort's neck saying. "If you would only allow me to use it to change Arian back to reality, that is all we ask. For I cannot kill you, you are too honorable a soul for me to condone that."

"I cannot. So, therefore, you must kill me." Mort responded.

Sebastian relaxing a bit on his hold said "Why? Why are you so stubborn?"

Now Mort thrust Sebastian back and rose with his rapier in hand. "Because that is the way it is. I have sworn. So I shall do my duty. But I am touched by your empathy." Mort admitted striking Sebastian as Sebastian defended himself again. "Forgive me for not keeping my concentration on you. Arian is very distracting." He smiled at her." You were foolish not to kill me."

"Why is it so important to kill me when you promised you would set it up for Arian. It is too ludicrous to contemplate!" Sebastian said exasperated.

Sebastian flipped and kicked Mort's rapier out of his hand. Mort ran to pick it up while Sebastian pursued him.

"You are devious, aren't you." Mort sighed while trying to pick up his rapier.

Sebastian kicked at Mort's side so Mort would fall and not get his rapier. Sebastian tried hitting Mort with the hilt of his rapier to knock him out but not kill him. However, Mort then kicked Sebastian in his stomach to get him out of the way so he could retrieve his rapier to finish him off. Sebastian doubled up but suddenly straightened holding his rapier as Mort returned. What choice did he have?

Arian called to Sebastian. "Sebastian, he is coming back."

Lucien said. "Father!"

Selena holding onto Arian cried. "Daddy, Daddy, Please don't die!"

Mort commanded. "No more interference from you, Madame or your children or I will silence you as well. You have distracted me from my duty to even be manipulated by your husband. You have been warned." Mort glared defiantly while he struck blows at Sebastian.

"You can't talk to my Lady in such a manner. What she says would be natural in a situation such as this. If you had a family, maybe then you would understand."

Mort was silent but relentless as his attacks were sheer force blows one after another with such determination for the kill.

Uncle Horatio hummed trying to say something but then he couldn't even hum as Mort pointed his left hand as Uncle Horatio saying. "Enough!"

Sebastian crossed rapiers again and again. His arm was bleeding worse leaving drops of blood on the floor but Mort kept coming, invigorated by the fight.

Both men clashed again hilt to hilt when Sebastian slipped a bit backwards on his own blood. Mort ran him through his stomach. Sebastian grabbed Mort's shirt. He was in so much pain.

Sebastian not releasing Mort's clothes requested. "Please finish me off. I am in agony."

Arian screamed. "No!"

Lucien, Selena, and Uncle Horatio screamed. "No!"

Arian took the witch's rod immediately. "Transfer me to the Realm of Reality!" She ran to Sebastian with the witch's rod and the healing spell. "Take your hands off my husband!"

Mort replied. "I only tried to put him down gently so I can retrieve my rapier." He pulled it out of Sebastian.

Sebastian screamed in utter agony.

Mort was taken by Arian's beauty. He just stared at her in silence while Arian poured the healing spell directly on Sebastian's gaping bloody wound. He screamed again wincing from the pain.

She held him to her chest saying to the witch's rod. "Please heal him quickly as soon as can be feasibly possible.

"Arian." Sebastian said." I can tell you are with me by your perfume. I am at least in your arms. Please forgive me. I couldn't kill him. I have failed you but I love you so much, please take care of our children. Where are they? I want to see them too. I don't know how long I can take the pain. Mort did promise me that he would assemble the laser. What time is it? Is the moon still shining on us? I cannot tell."

Arian soothingly whispered. "Please save your breath. Are you feeling any better? I will place another spell on you for your recovery." Arian waved the rod over her husband.

"Arian, please kiss me one more time. If I have to die, I want your kiss on my lips."

Arian kissed him ever so tenderly as tears fell from her eyes.

Mort stood there in silence.

Arian's eyes had so much compassion for Sebastian but when she glanced at Mort, they were full of fury. She concentrated her full attention on Sebastian as she loosened his shirt and belt from his pants so he wouldn't have any restrictions. She said to the witch's rod as Sebastian's breathing became more labored. "Please give me the prognosis?"

Arian stared at the crystal ball's response in writing. "Too many complications please wait."

Selena and Lucien both cried. "Mommy, Mommy we want to see Daddy."

Uncle Horatio finally said. "We can't read the crystal ball's prognosis from here, Arian." He held each child in his arms with tears falling from his face. "Can't you do something for him? He is my only nephew."

Sebastian held tightly to Arian's left hand while breathing in gasps. "I want to see my children and don't let go of me. I have to savor every second with you."

The children along with Uncle Horatio appeared as everyone ran to Sebastian in Arian's arms.

Mort stood aside watching in silence. They all gathered around him. Lucien and Selena were openly weeping as they clung to him. Uncle Horatio knelt beside Sebastian holding his hand as tears fell from his face too.

"It is always worse to see someone so young die before the old. Another of my worst fears have come into reality for me." Uncle Horatio sighed.

Sebastian's breathing was more erratic. "I think I am going to faint or die I cannot tell which one. I am very light headed." He stared at Arian and then he addressed Mort. "You promised me that you would assemble the laser. Time is running out. Why are you not fulfilling your promises or must I be dead before you can honor them." Sebastian's fury rose as he raised himself staring at Mort.

Arian literally had to restrain Sebastian from rising any further. "Please, try to conserve your strength." Arian kissed his cheek and rubbed her cheek against his. He glanced at Arian.

"You are so beautiful, please help me down so I can be next to you. Lucien, Selena, I love you. Don't worry, I think I am feeling better. I don't feel spasms of pain when I speak. I just need to rest more."

Arian kissed Sebastian repeatedly out of joy. "The witch's rod is working!"

Lucien and Selena kissed their Father too.

"With your permission, Mort interjected." I will extract the yttrium target. "He established eye contact with Arian. "You see I was supposed to have killed him. I knew the witch's rod would heal him in time but I have strict instructions not to interfere. I envy your husband, Madame."

Sebastian asked Mort. "What sort of radiation will beam across to the Realm of Twilight? Surely you must know all aspects of what you have dedicated your life to protect. What should we do to save my wife? I must know."

"It is classified information which I am not at liberty to divulge to anyone." Mort stipulated.

Sebastian rose again still in immense pain. How does one get through to you? If you set it up and we eventually see it's consequences, why can you not tell me in advance? If you can see my past undoubtedly you can see my future."

"The future is not set in stone. I can't tell the future or I would have foreseen your moves in the fight. You were entertaining." Mort remarked.

Arian's eyes flashed again with anger.

Sebastian held Arian's hand. "Calm yourself. Don't let your Spanish temper amuse him. He is infatuated with you or he wouldn't have stayed by your side for this long." Arian resumed her position making Sebastian lie down while the witch's rod worked on correcting the damage inflicted by Mort.

Mort pressed buttons on a panel as the yttrium target rose from it's hiding place with not a speck of dust. "Come we must go to the crystal blue temple. Where is the xenon flash tube and the crystal like potassium dihydrogen phosphate with the neodymium-doped glasses and crystals?"

Uncle Horatio intervened. "I don't want to seem droll, but I have them."

Mort waved his hand and the items flew into his possession. "You certainly have made havoc with the protection of these devices. I will have a lot to fix."

"More than you know." Sebastian stated." We made tunnels through the Pit of Tartarus where you will find three witches spirits full of hate ready to attack anything that enters for eternity. I wouldn't want you to suffer that or anyone."

"I thank you for that information. So Arian saved you again. She is honorable no matter what she thinks of me or for that matter of what your children and Uncle think of me. I had to do my duty. Forgive me Sebastian."

"It could have been avoided, but I don't understand all your obligations either. I forgive you." Sebastian held out his hand.

Mort held Sebastian's hand with a steel grip.

Sebastian shook his hand afterwards trying to get some blood back into it. Arian kissed it so Sebastian would feel better. "Arian, how are you? Are you tiring from the strain of reality? Have I taxed you too much? I am so exhausted and in pain myself I have forgotten. Arian." Sebastian caressed her check." Witch's rod, please give Arian a refreshing spell immediately. We must assemble the laser. Time is running out." Sebastian tried to get up but couldn't. Arian tried to help Sebastian but fainted. Sebastian reached out for her so she would faint towards him as she rested on his chest. Sebastian kissed her cheek full of concern.

Mort came immediately to her aid as Mort held Arian's frail form gently taking her off Sebastian's chest. He relished every second, from her beauty to the scent of her perfume to the softness of her skin as he held her shoulders raising her from the floor with her head on his chest. Her silken gown draped over his arm as he now supported her legs. He walked with Arian in his arms.

"Uncle, Arian had fainted, please see to her." Sebastian cried. "Oh, just help me up Uncle! Lucien follow them!"

Lucien promptly obeyed his Father wanting to protect his Mother. He found Mort placing Arian on a flat surface that jutted out by pressing a panel on the wall with his foot. Mort gently held her until she was supported. Her gown flowed over the edge revealing her small feet and ankles. He lowered her back with her hair cascading over his arm in ringlets of curls. Her perfume lingered as he watched her breathing softly. Mort noticed that his cuff link on his sleeve was caught in Arian's hair. He had to lean over her closely to untangle it but it became more complicated as he leaned over her face and her lips. Her perfume reeled his senses.

"How is my mother?" Lucien's eyes had piercing gleams solely directed at Mort, holding his Mother.

Mort gave a quick rejoinder. "I am having her rest here instead of the floor. That wouldn't do."

Lucien ran to his Mother holding her closely. Mommy, Mommy, are you all right?" But he noticed that Mort's cuff link was tangled in his mother's hair. "Let me help you." Lucien offered.

"How like your Father you are?" Mort responded with a regretful sigh while Lucien's nimble fingers unraveled Arian's hair. Mort could hear Uncle Horatio helping Sebastian to move to where Arian was taken.

Selena ran to find Lucien and Mommy as her golden curls bounced rhythmically as she located them. "How is Mommy? Daddy is better." She addressed Mort. "Could you help me up, Monsieur, so I can kiss Mommy?" She held her arms up so that Mort could help.

Mort struck by Selena's charm, innocence and helplessness acknowledged. "Of course I will." He picked her up like she was a feather and placed her beside Arian's head, who was still unconscious."

Arian surrounded by both Lucien, who placed his head on Arian's chest and Selena, who kissed her cheek and held her head, looked up to see Mort staring down at her. Arian asked. "Where is your Father?" She feebly whispered.

Sebastian heard Arian ask for him. "I am coming." He called out still being supported by his Uncle.

Arian murmured. "I will dissipate soon. I can't stay any longer. I am sorry Lucien and Selena. Could you help carry Selena down, Monsieur Mort, for I have not the strength."

Mort complied taking Selena from Arian's arms. "Will you be all right?" His voice had concern in it as he was held captivated to Arian's beautiful eyes. He held Selena with one arm and held Arian's hand and kissed it with the other.

Lucien, who still clung to Mommy glared up in surprise and re-kissed his Mother's hand.

Arian said. "Adieu." She reached out for Lucien and then disappeared.

Sebastian just came to Mort's chamber to see that Arian had already disappeared and that Mort was still holding Selena. Lucien had waved to his Mother.

Sebastian removed the crystal ball from his satchel in order to check on Arian. "Arian, how are you?"

Arian transferred to her bedroom. She lay on her bed holding the crystal ball. "I am a bit better. I am sorry I missed you. How do you feel? I see your are still being supported by your Uncle. Giselle has given me a refresher spell so I am in good hands. Please kiss the children for me. You look so pale."

Sebastian nodded. "You seem to be the same, pale. We will transfer the parts of the laser to the blue crystal temple of the Fates so we can assemble it. I will transfer back to you with the family so we can be together, followed by returning to the laser to recompense the Pillars' of Hercules and actually find out our fate. So please rest as much as you can for my sake. I love you. Take all the precautions possible when you feel up to it. Shall we transfer, Mort?" Sebastian asked while still viewing Arian." I assume you know the coordinates to the blue crystal temple of the Fates?"

Mort enunciated. "Of course."

"I know this sounds a bit skeptical but when was the last time the Pillars' of Hercules were in use? It may not work, if the machine was not in use for long periods of time." Sebastian queried.

"Mortal, you test my patience." Mort voiced. "I am in charge of the device. It works, be assured."

"What did you test it on?" Sebastian continued.

"I would not divulge such information to you." Mort waved his hand and all of them were in front of the blue crystal temple of the Fates.

The temple seemed to hover over the waves of the lake reflecting the silver moon, which appeared more luminous than at any of the previous two days.

Sebastian was still assisted by Uncle Horatio. Lucien held Selena's hand as all of them entered the temple. Mort held the devices and waved his hand at the crystal doors, which opened to let them pass. He hastened down an unknown corridor. Sebastian had to harness all his strength and that of his Uncle to keep up while the children had to run. Mort pressed another panel, which revealed what seemed to be electrical components, made of crystal, rising from the floor. Mort assembled the laser in its' proper alignment as if he knew it by heart.

Sebastian commented. "I do thank you. I wouldn't know precisely how to assemble this. I am in your debt. Perhaps, if all goes well, you could visit us. Arian serves wonderful dinners. You can give your preference in advance. It would break up your usual routine. You could even make conversation. You are very quiet."

Mort seemed oblivious of Sebastian as he worked. Lucien's curiosity got the better of him as he observed Mort closely. Mort could feel his presence.

Lucien exclaimed. "What wonderful tools. May I examine one?"

Mort chose one for Lucien to examine.

"Thank you." Lucien said joyfully as he held it in his hand.

Mort shook his head as he resumed his task.

Sebastian had Uncle Horatio help him to see what Lucien held, for he was just as curious but he didn't want to disturb Mort. Selena fell fast asleep in Sebastian's arms. Sebastian checked the crystal ball on Arian. She was in the chapel singing religious hymns of Charpentier while lighting candles. She was dressed in a lace gown of white holding a rosary and wearing a necklace with a cross containing an emerald in the center. Giselle was on her shoulder.

Mort, upon hearing Arian singing, stopped his work and walked to Sebastian to gaze at the crystal ball for himself. "I have never heard singing that beautiful. It touches the soul."

Sebastian added. "I heard her singing before I met her. But she has a multitude of talents. She plays an assortment of musical instruments and she is excellent in deciphering Old Greek, Latin, German, English, Italian and French. I am fortunate that she deciphered the Old Greek this well or I would never had the pleasure, if one can call it that, of meeting you, who keeps all his promises. Thank you, again. If I may be so bold, do you happen to have a black body that absorbs radiation? If that laser fires at that level, it would be nice to be prepared or do I ask too much?"

Mort stared at Sebastian. "I was going to offer it but I still have no idea if it will work?"

"That doesn't sound very comforting." Sebastian confessed. "But I will try anything to protect my wife." He noticed Arian was playing the violin, she was too upset to sing any more. Lucien came and held onto his Father as he noticed the time. "Arian," Sebastian called to her." I will transfer the children so they will have you. They are exhausted. Uncle Horatio will accompany them for safety and to cheer you up from being so lonely. I will watch how Mort will handle the laser just in case there are any problems, which he assures me, won't happen. But after all we have been through, I just feel better if I know when and where it will occur. I am waving the witch's rod now."

Uncle Horatio carried Selena, who was still asleep while Lucien held onto his Uncle's hand. Sebastian transferred them as all of them dissipated.

"Arian, Do you see them?" Sebastian asked.

"Yes they are here, Sebastian."

He witnessed Arian being kissed by the children and even Uncle Horatio. He wished he could kiss her too. "Arian, please rest as much as you can. Take the children along with yourself to bed. Have Uncle Horatio rest on the couch. I wish I could be with you," Sebastian lamented. "Please take care. I love you."

Arian nodded. "You heard your Father. Let's rest, you look so tired. Come Uncle Horatio". She glanced at Sebastian." Please come back to me." She ushered her children up through the grand staircase.

Mort watched, catching every detail. He heard Arian singing to cheer the children up through the gallery of the chateau with the numerous oil portraits of Arian's past. She held the candelabra as the candles with their flickering light revealed shadows of luxurious woven carpets and tapestries. The hue of the candlelight upon Arian's face etched every nuance like Rembrandt's works of art using light and dark accented with color.

Sebastian still breathless from Arian's beauty noted Mort was in the same condition, speechless, as the images were impressed upon them both. Sebastian wanting Mort to continue his work stated. "Does this laser use ultra fast x ray pulses altering the atomic lattice yielding to disorder to counteract immortality to reality?"

Mort, now brought back to reality by Sebastian's question instead of musing about Arian, glanced at Sebastian for shattering his thoughts from her, promptly answered. "How did you know?"

"I just assumed. Is it in femtoseconds, which is equal to a quadrillenth of a second? How can the xenon flash tube activate and then energize the Pillars' of Hercules from such a distance?"

"This information is classified. You have asked enough." Mort warned.

"Please, excuse me for my curiosity. But I must know how much time Arian has before she has to endure it's effects. Can you give me an estimation?"

Mort became pensive. "I would say ten more minutes. Then there will be enough energy to recompense the Pillars' of Hercules in the area of Gibraltar."

"Ten minutes! I better transfer to Arian. Where should she be positioned?"

Mort stated. "By the centerpiece of bronze by the ancient elm tree."

Sebastian took the witch's rod and the crystal ball." If you would excuse me, I must return to my family." He preset his watch for the appointed time. "I will return momentarily." Sebastian faded from view. He materialized into the master bedroom. There, Arian with the children, one on each side of her, slept so blissfully he really didn't want to wake them. He whispered. "Arian, time is upon us again." He leaned over to kiss her forehead gently. Arian immediately opened her eyes. He smiled down upon her.

Arian asked. "How much time?"

"A little less than ten minutes. Come my lady, let me hold you in the moments we have. I think we have to dislodge you from the children. So I can be with you."

Sebastian used the witch's rod. Both Lucien and Selena rose about a foot from the bed while Arian slipped out. He lowered them gently. They embraced trying to console each other.

"Arian, I love you so much. You mean everything to me. How can I express it more?" He kissed her. "Everything is always a question with the words of if except for our love. Everything stands before us or can be taken away. If we are parted forever, I will promise you I will not marry. You are the only love of a lifetime and I will always be faithful to you. But if we don't try to attain our happiness, we will let our opportunities pass us. We must think of our future with our children or our future ones. So we must have courage for our destiny. I shall be with you until the last second. If I could take the laser for you, I would. I wouldn't hesitate." He brushed away Arian's tears." The children will be difficult. They love you so much. Lucien listens. Selena tends not to let go. I even have to constrain myself from holding you to eternity. We better wake the children. They need you just as much as I." He kissed her so tenderly as Arian's tears now streamed down her face never letting him go. Sebastian spoke. "Lucien and Selena. It is time. Kiss your mother."

Lucien rushed, as did Selena to hold their mother as tears were shed by all except Sebastian who just held all of them. Giselle flew to Arian's shoulder placing her head on Arian's cheek.

"Uncle," Sebastian stated. "It is time. We must go to the ancient elm tree at the bronze centerpiece."

Uncle Horatio immediately roused himself from the fear of what would happen to Arian. "My God, here we go again." He rushed to Arian." Here, let me hold you too. I am getting too old for all this."

Sebastian, still holding his family, commanded the witch's rod to transport them to the bronze centerpiece by the ancient elm tree. "We have two minutes."

Sebastian picked up his children as he let them kiss Arian who held Sebastian 's waist surrounded by Giselle and Uncle Horatio who completed the circle around her.

Sebastian whispered into Arian's ear, "In my pocket is the orb of essences. Take it with you. I have a feeling it will protect you. It gives off the feeling of peace. The assembled pieces at the crystal temple will start an energizing activation to recompense the Pillars' of Hercules which in turn will cause a photon stimulated emission. I conjecture, it will arc through the emerald solid phase laser to the gold pillar aiming at the yttrium target that will enter the Realm of Twilight at ultra fast pulses to distort the lattice of unreality to reality. Don't stand on the bronze centerpiece. The orb of essence may shield you. I am not sure but my instincts say it will. Hold it above your head as an offering, my beautiful sacrificed one. We all await you. Adieu, my only true love." He kissed her for who knew if it would be the last time.

Mort projected his voice to the Realm of Twilight. "It is time."

They all transported back to the reality with the exception of Arian who knelt holding the orb of essence above her head as tears ran down her face. "If you can hear me, my loved ones, I love you for eternity. My spirit will be always with you as now I commend my spirit to the Fates who know all. Adieu, maybe I shall see my Father and Mother who are long gone. Adieu." She gave herself the last rites, singing prayers.

"You certainly took your time." Mort reprimanded, but stopped speaking upon seeing them. The children were in a state of shock being separated from their Mother.

Sebastian held the crystal ball constantly viewing his wife who sang French prayers for comfort.

Electrical noises emanated from the equipment, as a build up was imminent. The sounds knocked everyone to the reality of what was yet to come. The large crystal revealed Gibraltar and the African coast as beams seared across space and time. The pillars burst forth being raised from where they lay hidden from the past. It was awesome as they projected higher and higher. Superimposed on that image, the three fates reappeared as they held Arian's thread of life pulsating in their hands.

Mort only concentrated on Sebastian's crystal ball, as he watched intently. Arian sang with her arms raised, holding the orb of essence, when he realized that Sebastian had given Arian the orb. "That orb should have stayed here. Why did you give it to Arian?"

Sebastian turned to Mort being questioned in such a manner. "I thought it could protect her. Witch's rod," Sebastian ordered. "Please protect my wife with a black body. Do all you can for her."

Mort continued. "She will be destroyed as you now condemn her for your wishes."

Sebastian's eyes flashed. "Arian wanted me to save her from the purgatory of the Realm of Twilight, whatever the outcome. After three hundred years, her soul could not endure it any longer. So don't talk to me about death. It could work so that we can have a future, to your dismay for not finding her sooner for your own wishes. You seem to dismiss that she loves me entirely as she does our children."

A coil tube with a lamp flash now covered the emerald pillar. Atropos who held the sheers cut Arian's thread. Arian's fate has been designated as the thread fell. Both Selena and Lucien started to cry as Sebastian, Mort and Uncle Horatio held their breath. Distorted ionization's now build up from the pillars' aimed at the yttrium target as they exploded in flashes rupturing the Realm of Twilight.

Sebastian stared at Arian as the beams entered the Realm of Twilight. Arian screamed in shear agony as sheet lightning obliterated the view. "Refocus the crystal ball." Sebastian demanded.

After a few minutes the crystal ball complied. The orb of essence was completely shattered into splintered bits but not a trace of Arian could be seen.

"Where did she go?" Sebastian cried.

Mort relented. "Isn't it obvious. She is dust. You annihilated her or can't you accept the truth. I should have never helped you!"

Sebastian released the children. "Uncle, please take the children. I will look for Arian."

Mort raved. "You fool. What can you look for when she is dust?"

Sebastian countered. "She may have returned to reality at the same place she departed from, in Sussex. Crystal ball can you locate her?"

The crystal ball wrote. There is too much interference for any type of location.

"I will have to materialize into her by the emerald ring."

Uncle Horatio declared. "If she is dust, you will be materializing into nothing."

"I have to take that chance. Lucien, Selena, I will try to find Mommy. I will return. Uncle, I will make a copy of another witch's rod and crystal ball. Time my departure for three minutes so if I am nothing that I can return to a functional body in three. If I am as you see me now, I will signal for a longer duration. Don't think I would forget my responsibilities to my children. He kissed both Lucien and Selena who promptly didn't want to let go. Uncle."

"Yes, yes I am coming." Uncle Horatio checked his watch and then grabbed the two children.

"Three minutes as in right now." Sebastian indicated on his watch.

Mort shook his head. "You are crazy. She is dead, absolutely dead!"

"Yes, I heard you." Sebastian concentrated on his emerald ring and dissipated.

"How can he do that? It defies science." Mort stared unbelieving.

The Pillar's of Hercules now receded back to their hiding place in the crypts of time. The crystal ball was transparent and clear. The devices subsided from making noise as absolute silence enveloped them.

Sebastian, in immense pain, tried to rise but exhaustion prevented him. He called out. "Arian!" All he could see was darkness. "Witch's rod give me a flashlight." It materialized in his hand. He pressed the switch scanning his surroundings. He held the crystal ball and spoke to his Uncle. "I am in one piece but I seem to be in a dark chamber. I will update you later. I love both of you Lucien and Selena. Take care. Thank you Uncle, Adieu." He stared underneath him. He could detect scorch marks made from lightning bolts from long ago. This must be where Arian was hit by Hexe's lightning bolt originally in the bedroom in 1699, but where is she? It must be a ruin by the look of the aged wood and that would explain why it is so dark. It is boarded up. He kept scanning. Two inches from his hand was Arian's hand, she lay, not moving. "Arian, you are here. Can you talk to me?" He immediately went to her focusing the flashlight on her. She was in shock with very shallow breathing. He attempted to touch her so he could hold her to his chest while saying to the witch's rod, "heal her and dispense the healing spell." Upon contact with Arian he received an electrical shock that repelled him. "Witch's rod, discharge the electricity so she can function." She stopped breathing. He gave her mouth to mouth resuscitation and massaged her heart to calm her down. He thought to himself, the faster she gets to the crystal temple where Mort may have more facilities the better. He kissed her tenderly and she resumed breathing." Witch's rod, take us back to the crystal temple of the

Fates where my children and my Uncle are." The witch's rod transported them back. Sebastian held Arian in his arms as they materialized.

Lucien cried. "Mommy!"

Selena wriggled to escape her Uncle's grip saying. "Mommy, Mommy!" She wanted to run to her parents.

Mort stupefied and amazed. "She is here?" How can that be? My instruments didn't detect anything!"

Sebastian asked. "Where do you have medical facilities. She is comatosed and with the electricity and the radiation, I fear she will have a heart attack. Don't just stand there, tell me!" Sebastian demanded.

"Follow me." Mort hastened as he pressed another panel and a chamber opened with a table so Arian could lie down." Here, let me help you." Mort held the other side of Arian. He secretly rejoiced holding Arian again in his arms though her condition was doubtful.

"You could be exposed to the radiation too. Do you want to risk it?" Sebastian warned.

"I know what to do." Mort responded.

"Uncle hold the children. It is not safe yet." Sebastian stated.

Sebastian and Mort gently put Arian on the table. Mort opened a drawer from below and removed a material and placed it over Arian who seemed motionless except for shallow breathing. She still held her rosary clutched in her hand while being struck by the beams.

"Witch's rod, please make a prognosis of Arian and heal her at the same time by decontaminating all of us from the radiation." Sebastian asked. He hovered over Arian while kissing her hand gently checking for any response of improvement. Arian breathed more regularly.

Sebastian asked the witch's rod for the read out of her prognosis in the crystal ball. The crystal ball wrote. "A multitude of complications to solve which is being processed to heal. Be more patient. A heart attack is immanent "

Sebastian said. "Please, do all you can for her witch's rod." He held Arian and whispered into her ear. "Arian, you made it back to reality. We are all here safe." He asked the witch's rod. "What is her radiation level?"

The witch's rod wrote:" She has been, as all of you are, decontaminated."

"Uncle, you can let the children and yourself see Arian. Maybe with the children's presence and all her loved ones she will improve."

Mort reiterated. "You are no longer logical, but mad as well."

Sebastian irritated at this callous statement spoke. "Love is an inexplicable force that compels others to exceed rather than fail."

The children once released by Uncle Horatio ran to their parents.

Lucien called. "Mommy, Mommy, you are here with us."

Selena cried. "Mommy! Daddy, please hold me up so I can kiss her."

Sebastian carried her up and guided her gently to Arian's face. Selena kissed her cheek with her arms gently around her. "Mommy!" Selena's tears fell from her eyes. Lucien was tall enough to reach Mommy's face and kissed Mommy's nose.

Lucien whispered into Mommy's ear. "Please, Mommy, wake up. We love you."

Sebastian gently kissed Arian on the lips still holding onto Selena. All of them waited patiently for any response. One eye peeked out as Sebastian had seen before followed by the other eye. Lucien detected it while staring at his mother at eye level.

"Mommy is waking up." Lucien gently kissed her eye.

Both Sebastian and Mort stared down at her while Uncle Horatio's view was blocked.

"Arian, how do you feel?" Sebastian and Selena kissed her cheek. Seeing that, Lucien kissed her too. Giselle chirped loudly.

Being kissed by three loved ones, Arian couldn't say very much except sigh.

Sebastian gave Arian some breathing room by holding Selena and himself away but Lucien persisted holding Mommy's head and kissing her cheek repeatedly.

Sebastian put Selena down speaking to the children. "Hold my upper arms as we all will carry Mommy." Both Lucien and Selena held onto Daddy's upper arms as Sebastian now carried Arian in his lower arms and swung all of them in a circle and placed her back on the table. Uncle Horatio finally got the chance to kiss her as Giselle nuzzled her head to Arian's cheek.

Mort stood there unable to comprehend all this exuberance of emotion.

Sebastian kissed Arian again on her forehead saying, "I love you. Are you feeling better? Perhaps, I should have waited until you have rested. But I had to do something. You are mine at last, all mine!"

Arian's eyes were tearing from the joy and love that she could have with Sebastian and the children not being banished in the Realm of Twilight and non-existence. The children surrounded her, as did Uncle Horatio who was having tears as well.

While Sebastian held her again in his arms, he suspended her in the air, being too elated for words. "I believe it is your bed time, Madame. You need to rest, as do all of us. Let me check if the Realm of Twilight still exists." He put Arian back on the table and carried two children up onto the table so they could hold her more while Sebastian asked the crystal ball to focus on the Realm of Twilight"

Arian hugged the children as all of them gazed at the crystal ball. The chateau and the grounds surrounding it remained intact.

"It seems all is well." Sebastian added. "I want to thank you, Mort, for all your help. My offer still stands, if you want company, please call on us. We will be leaving you shortly." Sebastian gave his hand to Mort.

Mort not being accustomed to all of this gave his hand to Sebastian. "It was nothing."

"I feel bad that we left you with quite a mess from the extraction of the xenon flash tube and the potassium dihydrogen phosphate crystal, etc. I could leave one witch's rod with you to mend the damage. If that is all right with you."

"You are most generous." Mort stated still gazing at Arian who had both children in her arms as they clung to her full of joy.

Sebastian handed one witch's rod to Mort. "Adieu." He turned to his wife, children, Giselle and his Uncle. "May your life be as happy as mine." Sebastian waved the witch's rod as all of them dissipated back to the Realm of Twilight.

Sebastian carried Arian to the master bedroom with two children clinging to their Father. Uncle Horatio with Giselle followed. Arian was light as a feather to Sebastian seeing everyone radiating with jubilance. All of them were safe from their fears with a future, which included a mother.

Sebastian placed Arian on the bed and then lifted both children up along with her. "This calls for a celebration. We shall drink champagne and retire. Perhaps, a little alcohol will make us sleep better after today." He kissed Arian joyfully. "Uncle, you will stay for one glass, won't you?"

"Of course." Uncle Horatio echoed, smiling." We deserve it after a day like this one."

The witch's rod produced a bottle of champagne with the glasses on a tray, which was placed on the table. Sebastian opened it and poured. He offered the first glass to Arian, next was Uncle Horatio, followed by Lucien and Selena. He then raised his own glass as everyone did. "To a successful, loved, happy and healthy future. A votre sante which means in French to your health."

Selena didn't know what to make of it. "I like the bubbles hitting my nose but it tastes very strange."

They all laughed.

Sebastian soothed her. "You don't have to finish it if you do not want to." He winked at her. "Now I know of two children whose bedtime has gone past. So let's change for bed. We all will be together to calm this trauma. Hopefully, you won't have any nightmares. So please go to opposite bathrooms so we can all go to bed. Uncle, I will take you to your chamber or do you want to be with us and sleep on the couch. You are welcome."

Uncle Horatio smiled. "I think I will go. I am exhausted. I need some rest. Thank you. Good night to all of you."

Sebastian walked his Uncle to the door. "Good night Uncle and thank you again for taking care of me and the children. I wouldn't know what to do without you."

Uncle Horatio hugged his nephew. "Good night."

Sebastian closed the door seeing two children dash for their nightclothes to their respective bathrooms while Arian smiled still lying on the bed. Sebastian took out Arian's and his nightclothes. "If I remember, I was the one who tightened your corset, so since I don't have the patience, why don't we use the witch's rod to undo it?"

Arian only smiled too happy for words.

Sebastian kissed her. Both children were ready at the same time and watched their parents. Lucien helped Selena up onto the bed while he jumped up. They all hugged Mommy.

Arian grabbed for both of them.

"We better hurry, we all need our rest." Arian smiled.

Sebastian carried Arian along with the witch's rod.

Lucien asked. "What magic do you need to change Father?"

"It is your mother's corset." Sebastian added.

Both children laughed while Arian blushed. They returned shortly as Sebastian carried her to bed. He placed her in and tucked in the children kissing both of them. He kissed Arian. "Good night all my loved ones. Sleep well. Don't hesitate to wake us if you have any bad dreams, we understand." Sebastian whispered. He blew out the candles and snuggled into Arian for a long needed rest.

CHAPTER 14

ANCILLARY

Arian awoke in Sebastian's arms as the sunshine streamed into the room. The rainbow pattern from the chandelier reflected on the white wood paneling. Arian could hear her family breathing quietly in deep, deep sleep as Arian admired her Sebastian. She felt so secure in his arms. All she wanted to do is kiss him, but she thought she had better let him sleep. Arian couldn't resist; she so tenderly and softly kissed Sebastian's cheek trying not to wake him up. However, at that moment, Sebastian's eyes flashed at her, kissing her back so gently.

"I am so sorry I woke you up." Arian whispered." Please, I will be quiet if you still want to sleep. I am so happy, I can't sleep. I love watching you, being so close to me. I am still upset that you were stabbed. Do you feel all right? I will kiss it for you."

"Good morning, Madame. Let me hold you." He held Arian so tight and close as she melted in his arms.

The sunlight changed it's pattern as Arian wanted to see Sebastian's wound. "Sebastian, what is on the table near the sofa?"

Sebastian sighed. "Must I let you go." He turned around at the bed's edge to see the table.

There on the table, stood a vase of red roses and a letter written in calligraphy.

To Arian Simons:

> To my dearest love from afar.
> I regret with all my heart, that I have missed out on your love.

I write this letter to return your rosary that you had
left behind. I really wanted to keep it, but that would not
be the act of a gentlemen. I see that you are in love with this,
Sebastian. However, if you could forgive me for being so
blind and calculating, not knowing love for so long, not fully
understanding it, I condemn myself for not going after you when
my instruments told me that you did not exist. Wishing myself,
not to be so proud thinking that mortals were beneath me. How
can I ask for your forgiveness and a myriad of thousands of pardons?
If you ever reconsider, to marry me, not forgetting your children, of
which, I would take care of. I would be honored to take you for my
own. I even found out the herb to make your life span longer, for I never
want to be parted from you. Please say yes,

Love, Mort

PS. I don't know how I can now live without you!

Sebastian read the letter out loud. "I should have killed him. How dare he! Giselle, was Mort in this room or was the vase, flowers and letter just transported here?"

Giselle chirped.

Arian responded. He came in person to bring his letter and he picked our flowers from our garden with the use of our vase. He also stared at us sleeping."

"I'll kill him!" Sebastian repeated.

"No, Sebastian. He will kill you. I only love you. Ignore him, I beg you, please. We are so happy together. If he is a gentleman, for whom he prides himself on, he will have to get over it. For, I will never give you up. Please, let's go somewhere, so we don't wake the children. Please Sebastian."

Sebastian took Mort's letter and threw it into the fire. Yet, it didn't burn. "I should have guessed, fire retardant paper. The nerve of that man, I should have killed him. I even told him to be happy in his life, but not with my wife."

Arian walked towards Sebastian, kissing him repetitively. "Lets go, Giselle will alert us if the children wake. Please, Sebastian. Please, ignore Mort. We have all our lives." Arian kissed Sebastian again, as she gently pulled him to leave the room. When they returned, the children were still asleep. Arian blushed as Sebastian held her in his arms. He relaxed being so happy.

"We are free at last." Arian smiled at her Sebastian. "What do you want to do today? Do you want a picnic or a long walk, or we could row down the river with all of us. I never travel far. I am too happy for words."

Sebastian was so content, having his Arian in his arms. "Let's take a boat ride down the river. That would be fun."

Lucien, on hearing his Father's voice, peeked an eye at him and then the other. Arian went to kiss him.

"Good morning, my Lucien, did you sleep well? "Arian smiled over him.

Lucien smiled as he kissed his mother." Good morning, I slept well, knowing we are all together."

Selena finally started to stir. " Mommy." Selena's arms rose up. "Daddy."

248

Sebastian and Arian kissed her together.

"Let's take a boat ride down the river." Sebastian suggested.

"Let's get ready." Arian announced.

Sebastian asked the witch's rod to send Mort's letter back, writing an ancillary. "Sorry, the lady loves me and please, never contact us again. Thank you, for returning the rosary. Sebastian."

Arian read Sebastian's return note, as she smiled at him. "I love you Sebastian."

"I hope this will deter Mort for more than a life time." Sebastian abated.

"I hope so too." Arian gave him such a loving gaze. Sebastian melted.

"Let's get ready." Sebastian held her.

Everyone was ready even Uncle Horatio and Giselle. Arian had asked previously the witch's rod to pack breakfast as Sebastian rowed the boat. They stopped for breakfast at a lovely spot as they enjoyed the view.

"Sebastian," Uncle Horatio quoted." What fiction will we make up so that you could meet Arian at this time frame? Obviously, you will tell your sister the truth, but even that is doubtful that she will believe you."

"The only way my sister will believe us is to transport her here. Besides, I have to get the adoption papers ready." Sebastian responded.

Arian' eyes fill with tears of joy. "Oh, Sebastian, I love you." She hugged Lucien and Selena.

"How are we going to get Arian into the computer?" Uncle Horatio continued.

"By the witch's rod," Sebastian declared. "Lets see, I know you were born in Rome's French embassy in 1676. We will make it easy. The year will be 1976. You are 23 years old. What was your mother's maiden name?"

Arian smiled. "Francesca De La Vega, it was an arranged marriage. She married my Father at the age of seventeen. They had me when my mother was twenty-one. My Father chose her. My mother died of pneumonia at the age of twenty-four years when I was three years old. I remember running into their room to say good morning, to find her as cold as ice, dead with my Father crying, facing the window. My French grandmother took care of me. Her name was Gabrielle Jovan. I had a myriad of nannies, tutors and governess. We moved to many embassies. We stayed for varying periods of no more than two years at any one place. I never had many friends with the exception my family and my cousins. With all my academics, which included my Father 's fencing lessons as he tutored me, he became my best friend. Before I was born my mother's family decided to marry me off to Alain De La Vega, but my Father had his doubts. I think he would have said no to him, but since Alain De La Vega did not show up in June of 1694, my Father was no longer obligated, which delighted him. He didn't even think of marrying me off. A year later, I met you, Alexus/Sebastian. My Father coincidentally received his commission to England before we met. My Father liked you the moment he saw you. So knowing that I would be living in England, with his commission in London, he wouldn't be so far away from me as it would be if I were in Mexico, so he agreed. We were married in Versailles. We waited a month to obtain the papers but during that month, his parents engaged Alexus/Sebastian to his cousin, Jane Simons. Alexus/ Sebastian brought me home to his parents who had just received his letter, telling them of his marriage and we just received his parent's letter telling Alexus /Sebastian that Alexus was engaged to marry Jane. We read this letter on the coach taking us to his home in Sussex.

What an awkward situation for all concerned, since Alexus/Sebastian was introducing me as his wife with his Uncle Cecil. Jane Simons broke out in tears. His Father, Thomas, who was very polite, wanted to talk to Alexus alone, especially for not being included in his future daughter-in-law's marriage. Alexus was shocked that his letter had just arrived since he sent it so long ago. Alexus/ Sebastian tried to clarify the situation to Jane to soften the impact. (Alexus only saw his cousin Jane once a year in the summer.). He remembered, whenever he did correspond to his cousin, which was also once a year, Jane would always talk of the man she liked, Richard Darney. Therefore, Alexus didn't perceive the short engagement arranged by his parents, would be so bad of a hardship on his cousin, if he broke it off. Alexus had no knowledge that Richard Darney was married off to his cousin Agnes, severing Richard's proposal to Jane. So Sir Thomas Simons, liking Jane, then made the announcement for his son, Alexus and Jane's betrothal. This caused Jane to have two set backs. Richard Darney, in my opinion, wasn't handsome, his interests were only hunting and fishing. He seemed mindless when I met him. My Alexus/ Sebastian on the other hand was so handsome. I thought Jane crazy to even compare them. However, I found out much later that Jane always did have a crush on Alexus. It was just Alexus who never cared or knew that Jane loved him. Harboring two indiscretions: the first being Jane's predicament and the second being that his parents were not notified, left the conversation inundated with apologies.

Sebastian/Alexus 's father, Thomas, saw me and immediately understood why Alexus/ Sebastian had chosen me. He invited me into his family with open arms. His mother, Elaine, was on Jane's side. Alexus's mother was quite upset that she was not invited to her eldest son's wedding. Alexus and I were at Versailles waiting for the papers for our marriage license to come through for a whole month, chaperoned by Louise, my father, and Uncle Cecil/Horatio who accompanied his nephew. We then departed for our wedding trip followed by our journey to see his parents. Alexus wrote his parents the first day he met me that he would be marrying me. He also wrote a letter to Jane to inform all the rest of the family, but it seemed the ferry that brought the mail to England sank and only Alexus's letter, to his parents, managed to be retrieved. My Father had business in London and would come the following day to see Alexus's parents. We did travel together until London. Alexus/Sebastian's sister, Helen, favored me immediately with his baby brother of twelve, Christopher. The moment Helen and Christopher met me, we cherished each other's company and Helen became my best friend. She married Martin Jovan, my second cousin. I introduced them for he was working with my Father at the embassy. Helen was two years younger than I. We grown quite close, but Alexus's mother, Elaine showed only politeness. She didn't like foreigners and that I introduced my cousin to Helen at our own home, annoyed her. My Alexus/Sebastian designed our house of course."

"Jane departed for home with her chaperon that very evening that we arrived. She never contacted Alexus/Sebastian again. I felt sorry for her, but what could be done. Since Thomas Simons approved, everything finally quieted down. When I was with Dorian and had my beautiful son in my arms, Elaine Simons finally became so nice to me, and even admired me. She never left us alone since. Every day or every other, she would visit us. She loved Dorian so much she could never be parted from him for long. So I knew when I disappeared, that my baby would be taken care of, as was my Alexus. As for my Selena, she was taken from me. I finally have my children, and you. It is like a beautiful dream come true. This couldn't have happen if it wasn't for all of you rescuing me. Arian's eyes also included Giselle. I am sorry I digressed. I love you so much."

"I enjoyed it," Uncle Horatio smiled. "So you met at a fountain in Versailles. Why don't you meet here by the lake? You could then sing and write a letter to your friend and Sebastian can retrieve it as the wind blew the sheets into the lake. He could then read the pages that state you love him from afar, just like at Versailles. We could say that you are a music student trying to get into the symphony here in London."

Sebastian wanted to hold Arian, but she was too far away from his reach. "Shall we walk a bit? Where does this river go?"

"I really never traveled this far, Sebastian. I know twenty miles in the other direction for I walked that to find Quintessence. We are ten miles in the opposite direction. You rowed quite well, Sebastian. I should have been more adventurous, but not knowing this realm, I was afraid of meeting the inhabitants, of which have never bothered me for 300 years."

Sebastian offered his arm as Arian linked hers as they walked together watching the children.

"How should we meet, Sebastian? I know it will be love at first sight. That is the feeling I have whenever I see you. I felt so awkward when I first materialized into Selena, at your Uncle Horatio's house. I worried what your reaction would be like? Of course, it was a shock for Selena. All I wanted was for my misery to end. But seeing you in reality, not from a crystal ball, being finally close to you after so long of a solitude. I loved you even more. I couldn't sleep at all after writing that sonnet, hoping you could save me or at least, release my soul or that maybe, you could be able to fall in love with me again." Arian was quiet.

Sebastian kissed Arian and held her so close saying. "Shh!" Sebastian agreed. "My Uncle is right, we will meet here by the lake, at my Uncle's. You will be a music student who traveled with your Father to the embassies. In doing so, you could never attend a famous music school. Your Father unfortunately died in a car accident, so you had nowhere to go. So you put your furniture in storage and tried to get an audition in Paris but they could only give you an audition later this month. So now your hopes are in London .You go, but when you try for your audition they lose your transcripts along with your recommendations. They won't let you audition, so your opportunities are dashed until they find them. Therefore, upon returning to your hotel you are so dejected and upset that you take the wrong bus and end up here, where my Uncle lives. If you would return to your hotel, there will be a delay of 4 hours to catch another bus. You thought you might as well see some of the sights since you are stranded. Therefore, you walk to the lake crying on the way for twenty minutes. Seeing the lake makes you think that it is useless to cry, so you play your violin, while you sing a French song to cheer yourself up. When you see my children and I, you noticed we were listening to you. You decide to write to your friend so that writing out your troubles would ease your mind. You write as you still watch us. The more you watch me, the more you fall in love with me. You write all your misfortunes down explaining that the more you see this man, the more in love you are with him which only makes this day even worse since it is obvious, if this man has two children there must be a wife. This day, which didn't include the death of your Father, has been the most trying, what else could go wrong! At that moment, a breeze blows your letter into the lake as you sigh. I realize it and I retrieve it, but as I am bringing the pages back, I read that you are in love with me along with reading about all your misfortunes. So now this stranger returns your letter. I know everything divulged in your letter as I introduce myself with my children and tell you that I have returned your pages. You are so embarrassed. All you can say is thank you Monsieur and that you have me at a disadvantage. I will tell you the reason why I lingered by the lake is because I am falling in love with your singing voice, your violin playing and your beauty. That my wife died in a car accident five years ago and that I would love to assist you by asking if you would stay here. Please, for my sake, you could even stay at my Uncle's or I would pay for your room if you would permit me. I am visiting from Montreal and I couldn't bear to lose you, because I want to marry you. You will demurely say yes. You consent to marry me and we will be very happy together. My Uncle will and has married us, because if you weren't in the Realm of Twilight, I know I would have asked you that same day, crazy as it sounds. Just touching your hand or hearing your voice, I couldn't resist." Sebastian kissed Arian's hand ever so tenderly. "Now, I will have to think of all the paper work. You obviously stayed at my Uncles' for dinner. The children loved you, the moment they saw you. I know that much. My, what time is it?" Sebastian glanced at his watch. "It is twelve noon. Where does the time go? We need a birth certificate, college transcripts, marriage license, Canada's citizen papers, passport, nationality papers, and driver's license. I will fix your wedding band from Alexus to announce that you are all mine! I will have the witch's rod create one for myself.

Arian kissed Sebastian again. "My favorite part is being with all of you. Shall I ask the witchs'rod to make lunch? I better check on the children, Lucien just got out of site."

Sebastian twirled Arian around." I love you, My Lady and you are mine." Arian laughed out of sheer joy just being in his arms.

"We better check on our little ones." Arian confirmed.

Sebastian put her down gently.

Uncle Horatio called out. "We are over here, Sebastian. Don't worry, I am watching them."

Both Sebastian and Arian walked towards them. The witch's rod had the picnic table-cloth ready with their lunch. The witch's rod even prevented them from being bothered by the ants and the wasps that buzz around the wineglasses.

"Can we stay?" Lucien urged, "Here at Quintessence. It is so lovely here."

Selena tried to anticipate her Father's reply eagerly.

"I am sorry, but my job takes us back to Montreal. We will visit as often as we can. Besides, we have at least two weeks of vacation left. I have tickets for Italy, Vienna and Paris, as we will go back to London and fly to Montreal. Uncle, do you want to come with us? You are such a part of the family, I would miss you."

"I would be happy to." Uncle Horatio expressed joy.

Arian eyes showed excitement. "Italy, Vienna and Paris, Oh Sebastian! How wonderful!" She bent to kiss Sebastian. "This is like a wedding, trip. What is a vacation?"

"A vacation is a period of rest and freedom of work or from study and time for recreation." Sebastian quoted.

"Oh, Sebastian, you spoil me." Arian rejoiced.

"Maybe, we should use the witch's rod to return home? We can't miss out on these tickets, they are nonrefundable." Sebastian appealed to the witch's rod saying. "Take us home by the lake. "Come let's race to see who will reach the boat at the landing first." Sebastian grinned. They complied. Of course Sebastian, Arian and Uncle Horatio let the children win (Lucian) as the witch's rod transported them back as they disembarked and walked to the house.

Sebastian suggested. "Let's get the computer here so I can try to create the paperwork. I will need your help Uncle. I will make two computers with magical simulation for electricity. I will create, one for each of us, so that you can find the correct forms for me to place in the data.

The witch's rod will get us onto the Internet, therefore, if we are traced, it will have a fake code being in the Realm of Twilight. Hopefully, they can't arrest us." He smiled.

"Sebastian, you really think this will work?" Arian's eyes elated being so hopeful. "I don't want you to be arrested."

"We shall try, my Lady. It can even buy the extra tickets, we hope. Why don't you find your birth certificate, marriage license and nationality papers (both of them) and your transcripts for the College or University that you attended. I will make you a French citizen since that goes with the story we came up with. Even though, you have been in England since 1695."

Arian asked." Where do you want to set up the computers, in the library, Sebastian? There is a spare room which opens up to the main library."

"Wherever it is convenient." Sebastian confirmed.

"When do you want to talk to your sister, Cassandra? Sebastian?" Arian continued.

"Oh, my God. I keep forgetting her, but I am so worried about the paper work. Let's solve at least that problem. I want you forever with me." Sebastian seemed anxious.

"The children are reading the children's book that I owned so long ago. I will only be a moment to retrieve the paper work." Arian kissed Sebastian's neck." I hope there is enough space. This room was empty because here is where all the mail and packages would be placed. This room was used basically for acquiring and sorting new books for the library." The computer appeared with the wave of Sebastian's witch's rod. Arian examined it closely. "The monitor feels soft why?"

"The reason for that is, it is a liquid crystalline. There is no need for a screen saver. " Sebastian responded.

"Does that mean it is like the crystal ball which seems to have a crystalline liquid as well to project its images?"

"You maybe be correct but it is obviously more advanced." Sebastian pondered.

Sebastian and Uncle Horatio started typing.

Arian turned to go upstairs to retrieve the papers as she kissed her children. "I shouldn't be long. Then I will read to you."

"All right," Lucien seemed excited. "Hurry back!"

"I will." Arian smiled. She lingered by Selena while she played with her curls. "I want to devote all my time on my family."

Arian walked entering her bedroom.

"You certainly keep me waiting, Madame!" Mort revealed himself emerging from the balcony of Arian's boudoir for he was gazing from the opened door-window.

"Oh my God! Why are you here? Please leave, you have no right to be in my boudoir, Monsieur."

"I waited in the garden for you but you were at a picnic, I imagine."

"Please Monsieur, You must leave. My husband has stated everything clearly. There is nothing more to be said, bonsoir."

Indeed, Madame! There is plenty that needs to be said. If, you would only give me a moment of your time, I beg you. Please."

"A moment of my time, Monsieur? I will retrieve my papers that my Sebastian needs. If you are not gone, I will scream for help. For this is not proper." Arian went to her bureau to find her papers. She pulled out her diary, where she kept her marriage license.

Mort walked closer to Arian. "Please, forgive me." His eyes went to Arian's face and then to her diary. "Did you draw these pictures?"

"Yes, Monsieur. Please I do not like this clandestiness. I have only a few more papers to find. I want you to leave. I don't want to see my husband fighting with you. You have hurt my husband enough. It was very hard this morning to prevent his way of dealing with you." Arian clarified showing distress.

"Yes, I saw how you dealt with him. I would be more satisfying."

"How dare you, Monsieur! Is there no privacy! "Arian blushed with anger and embarrassment. "How could you intrude so! So you watched us? You are beyond contempt, Monsieur! I love only him beyond anything in this world."

"That's because you don't know what you are missing. You are too naïve, Madame! That is something you could change, if only you would reason!" Mort advised.

"My Sebastian saved me. He loves me so much, that he sacrificed everything imaginable to rescue me. Even when your instruments could not find me, my Sebastian wouldn't give me up and he saved me again. Please leave me. All you do is upset me. I feel sorry that you have chosen a life that gives only a quest. However, you alone chose your fate. Maybe, you believed that because you were an idealist. If you have other options, go find your own immortal ones. We mortals are too beneath you, according to your standards. Please go! I now found my birth certificate. The only reason I am even speaking to you is to prevent my husband's wrath!"

"Arian, please don't be angry with me. I love you more than my own life. If I could prove it to you, I would. How can I express myself for what I feel? I am wrong about some mortals. You sing like an angel. You read. You speak many languages and you play many instruments with such passion and beauty. You love astronomy and architecture. You draw exhibiting such life and exactness. You have such a sympathetic, understanding and forgiving nature. How else could you forgive this man you say you love. All these virtues prove to me, beyond a doubt that you are perfect for me alone. You are very intelligent and adaptable. Please, stay with me. You say you are in love with Sebastian. But you don't even know me to compare. I could defeat Sebastian in every round in any activity including love. Please give me a chance. I have found the herb that Giselle ate to make her immortal, for us to be together. I will even give it to the children. Please, I beg you. I know you love them even though they are really Marisa's, not yours."

"Monsieur, you have stabbed me in the heart. They are my children, I will repeat the words and my children are mine, not Marisa's. I know their very souls; these souls were once mine to take care of three hundred years ago. My Lucien even looks like me. He gets this from my Sebastian."

"I should not have brought this up. It has angered you. I am sorry, but you can't say that about Selena. Selena resembles Marisa exactly." Mort added." You should face the facts and be honest to yourself."

Arian's tears fell from her face. "Why do I talk to you at all. You infuriate me and hurt me beyond measure. I can't say this more bluntly than this. I do not love you. If you care, you would respect me and leave my family and me alone. I love my Selena. She has her soul that I once had the privilege to own for such a short time and she is very beautiful. Nevertheless, I have her now and she loves me as her own mother." Arian burst into tears.

"You are crying because you know that Sebastian loved other women especially, Jacqueline." Mort continued.

"You are not a gentleman to read my diary. Did you spend the whole day reading here when we were away down the river?" Arian's tears flowed more. She kept searching for her citizenship papers.

"Sebastian did love Jacqueline even more than you, Arian. " Mort attested.

"How would you know! All you want is to hurt my Sebastian in my eyes for your own ends. Are you blemishless, I suppose, with no past? I can't believe that either. You never, throughout time, ever loved a woman. I can't endure you any longer. I have found my papers. Leave me and if you pride yourself, being a gentleman, never return!"

"Arian, you aren't properly married. What judge is Uncle Horatio in the law's eyes?"

"And who is your judge to marry?" Arian contradicted with anger. "The door is that way. Leave me and never return!"

Giselle flew to Sebastian using her wing to brush Sebastian's cheek repeatedly.

"What is bothering you, Giselle?" Sebastian queried.

Giselle flew to the crystal ball. She concentrated. Arian appeared in her boudoir, which revealed that she was not alone, Mort was there. Sebastian heard the conversation. "Leave me and never return." The children and Uncle Horatio ran to the crystal ball.

"Sebastian seethed in anger." Oh my God!" He ran to help Arian followed by Lucien. Uncle Horatio picked up Selena and ran too.

Sebastian focused upon the crystal ball to see what was happening as he jumped four steps at a time.

"Please," Arian warned. "Do not advance, I do not want a confrontation."

"Please Arian. I am sorry I hurt your feelings. Let me make it up to you. I need you so badly."

"No, stay where you are. If you leave now, I won't scream."

"You won't scream. I won't hurt you." Mort advanced.

Arian screamed. "Sebastian! Help me, Sebastian!"

"Good, I will finally end this with Sebastian. I long for another challenge." Mort confessed.

Arian rushed to Dorian's rapier on the wall but Mort ran faster grabbing her arm. Arian didn't anticipate that.

"Let go of my arm!" Arian pleaded. "Leave me alone. Please, I beg you, Please. I don't love you. Please, understand! I don't want to kiss you, ever. Leave me alone, please." Arian's tears fell freely from her face. "You are a blackguard! This is abuse! You are hurting me!"

"All I want to do is kiss you so you can compare!"

"No, please." Arian slapped Mort's face." No! "She pushed him away with her free hand.

"How dare you hit me! " Mort grabbed the other arm and pulled her towards him. "I love you."

"This is one sided or abuse. I want my Sebastian. I have a choice, not you!" Arian was terrified.

"Let me kiss you."

"Never, I will be worse if you don't stop." Arian cried.

Mort waved his hand. Arian was immobilized standing against the wall. Arian's tears fell even more.

Sebastian upon witnessing this became fully enraged. He concentrated his thoughts as he materialized into Arian. Mort closed his eyes to kiss Arian. He got Sebastian's fist into his

S. and S. Antonson

face, with such vented anger that only waited to explode. Sebastian couldn't stop hitting him. Mort finally realized that this wasn't Arian but Sebastian, but how?

Arian was so relieved feeling Sebastian materialize into her as he rescued her again.

"Where did you come from?" Mort struck back hard.

"I am appalled to even talk to you. How dare you use my wife in such a manner!" Sebastian relentlessly kept hitting him because, if Sebastian stopped, Mort might immobilize him as he did to Arian.

Uncle Horatio and Lucien arrived into the room. Lucien didn't stop as he ran to hit Mort from behind at Mort's kidneys.

"Like Father, like son." Mort attested.

Sebastian punched Mort to the ground.

Mort rose quickly. "Lucien, if you don't stop, I will hurt you and I don't want to do that because that would hurt Arian."

Uncle Horatio maneuvered between Sebastian, Lucien and Mort to help Arian as he still held Selena.

"Arian, can you move? I guess not. I was like that. I know how you feel. Let's see." He moved next to her. "Selena, stop clinging and holding Mommy, I must try to release her." Uncle Horatio tried pulling her from the wall but Arian didn't budge.

Giselle flew with her witch's rod to Arian. Sebastian hit Mort again.

Uncle Horatio coached." Hit him again, Sebastian!"

Giselle aided with the witch's rod mobilized Arian as she fell to the floor. Uncle Horatio picked Arian up.

Selena cried. "Mommy!" Selena clasped Mommy.

Mort turned from buffeting Sebastian back while grappling with Lucien and threw him into the bed. Lucien gasped falling into the canopy's curtains, tearing them down as he fell.

Arian screamed. "Lucien!" She kissed Selena and ran to her son. Uncle Horatio then picked Selena up again. Arian held Lucien tightly.

Lucien tried to escape his mother's grip "I want to hit him again, Mommy!"

"Oh, no you don't. I won't let you get hurt." Arian responded.

"But, what about Daddy?"

Mort punched Sebastian simultaneously changing his angle to kick him in the stomach repeatedly if he could.

Sebastian, being so angry, just hammered Mort back viciously what ever he could get a hold of, not really reacting to the last blows. "You aren't playing fair," Sebastian noted." I am too enraged to care."

"I will win, Sebastian. I will take Arian with me. That, I promise you." Mort assured.

"Never, this gives me license to kill you." Sebastian vowed.

"Just try! I am waiting for you. You already have two children. It is time she had mine." Mort contested.

Sebastian first smashed Mort's nose. Sebastian rushed at Mort grabbing his neck as he throttled him.

Mort's arms were trying to get the upper hand, as Arian held Lucien running to Giselle to obtain the witch's rod. "Take this creature, Mort, out of the Realm of Twilight, to where he belongs, never to return to Quintessence or where my family or I will ever reside. Witch's rod, also fetch me the filigree key. I am now placing a lock on the spell so that Mort will never be able to break out. Do it now!"

Mort, shocked at Arian's words, disappeared out of Sebastian's grasp.

Uncle Horatio cried. "You didn't wait so I could say. Kill him!"

Arian ran to Sebastian still holding Lucien. "Sebastian, how do you feel? He kicked you in the stomach. Oh, God! How are you?"

Sebastian held his stomach. "Now, that I am relaxing from the fight, I am feeling the pain. If you didn't send him away, my anger would have killed him. I am still infuriated at what he could and would have done to you, but, I am glad I didn't kill him."

"I would have helped, Daddy." Lucien assured.

"Yes, I know Lucien, thank you. You are my brave son. I am very proud of you."

"Sebastian, please hold still while I use the witch's rod." Arian pleaded. Sebastian's head was in Arian's lap "This reminds me of last night." Arian eyes filled with tears.

Sebastian attempted to calm Arian using his hand to comfort and wipe Arian's tears away from her face.

"Witch's rod, heal my Sebastian, Please." Arian poured the healing potion on Sebastian. "I am so proud of you for saving me, Sebastian, Lucien, Uncle Horatio, Selena and Giselle. I was so helpless. When he immobilized me, I was so afraid. I am not as strong like a man to protect myself. If you didn't come!" She burst into tears holding her Sebastian and Lucien.

Uncle Horatio went to Sebastian with Selena still in his arms. "You fought wonderfully. I am proud of you! I commend you. I would have helped had he had the upper hand, but you handled it perfectly. So did you, Lucien until he threw you into the air."

"Daddy, Daddy are you all right?" Selena implored. "I am so upset."

"I'll be all right Selena, don't worry. Mommy is working on it."

"Sebastian, are you feeling better?" Arian cried.

"Yes, Arian." Sebastian kissed her cheek so tenderly." I really understand how you feel. I felt that way with Hexe. However, she did kiss me, which still gives me shivers and disgust. I will cheer you up. I love you so much."

"I am emotionally exhausted. You don't know what he said. How he insulted you for his own ends. He made me cry even before you came in." Arian cried again.

"Tell me later, when we are alone and when you feel better." Sebastian tried to soothe her.

"He didn't respect me." Arian contested." I should have materialized into you, instead. I tried to talk some sense into him. He is past being contemptible. He watched us ever since we read the letter this morning."

"How I hate that man." Sebastian reiterated.

Arian soothed him. "I love you Sebastian and my Lucien is so brave just like his Father. I am so fortunate I have you two and Uncle Horatio with my precious Selena. Oh, my Giselle! How can I ever repay you. You protect me like a mother. Let me kiss you." Arian held Giselle and kissed her." I know Giselle, sometimes I over kiss you."

"What does that mean?" Lucien returned.

"See, when you put Giselle down on the table. Giselle walks crooked. Her equilibrium is all off. She dislikes it when she doesn't walk correctly. But, I can't express my love to her any other way so when I become emotional, she endures it. Poor thing!"

The children smiled in glee watching Giselle try to walk correctly but still off balance going sideways instead, even Sebastian smiled.

Sebastian stated. "Mort still has a witch's rod. Come back, witches' rod to the Realm of Twilight, where you belong. I don't want him to use it on you, my Lady!"

"Sebastian, How clever you are." Arian kissed him with relief.

"I guess I should release my anger and continue with the problem at hand, your paper work, Madame. I want you more than a lifetime with me." Sebastian's eyes flashed at Arian.

"Witch's rod, please fix all the broken items in the room." Arian supplicated. "Including the canopy curtains. Thank you."

Everything returned to what it was as Arian helped Sebastian up to his feet. They all returned to the library.

Sebastian typed relentlessly to recreate Arian's records. Arian sat next to him, as she held two precious bundles, her children, one on each side of her lap. Arian told them a pirate story.

"What was your grandmother's maiden name?" Sebastian pondered.

My grandmother's maiden name from my mother's side, was Aragon. Her first name was Theresa but on my Father's side it was Gabrielle D` Orleans. My, we are really delving deep. Maybe, I should start dinner. It is getting late. Witch's rod, please serve dinner. We will have lemon chicken with green beans, mushrooms, mashed potatoes and a salad. Maybe we should have croissants and for desert a fruit gaze of strawberries. Please, choose an appropriate wine. Thank you."

A bell rang announcing dinner.

"My, this witch's rod certainly spoils us," stated Sebastian. "At least, I have your citizenship papers. It is being processed now. I have to take a photo of you, Arian, for this and your driver's license."

"But, Sebastian, I can't drive." Arian quietly affirmed.

"Don't worry, I will teach you. I will even give you a written test and a driving test."

"But, the license was issued today and also the citizen papers. At least the marriage license has the correct date. It is 4 days that we are married Sebastian. It seems like a moment ago. Yet, so many things have happened."

"My, times flies, Madame, everything is constantly happening. It seems longer. Too much has occurred." Sebastian abated.

"We still have to talk to your sister, Sebastian. She must be worried to death and I must thank her."

"Thank her for what, Arian?"

"For helping you raise these precious children. I couldn't have instilled so much in them if I raised them myself, except for teaching them languages and music. They are so good and well behaved. I must tell her how grateful I am. If there were anything that I could do for her, I wouldn't hesitate. I owe her five years of very hard work, of which, if she has a need for me to do the same. I would gladly volunteer. She is exceptional and so are you, my Sebastian, for you trained them too." Arian expressed.

"I was fortunate to have a sister who cared. You are right. I should notify her. But the only way for her to believe that any of this had happened is to bring her here so she has irrefutable proof. Otherwise, she will think that I have gone mad, being happily married to a lady who is three hundred and twenty three years old."

Arian nodded her head.

"We also have to have the children memorize the fictitious way we met according to our new fabricated papers which include the adoption papers. They cannot mention what really happened or they will be as mad as I am."

When Arian heard adoption papers she immediately hugged Sebastian not letting go. The children would be hers as well. She had tears in her eyes as they embraced. She held the papers carefully and kissed them.

"By the way, I am going to have the witch's rod give you all the immunizations so that you, Arian, will be healthy when you contact the outside world. The bacteria, viruses and the like have gotten more resistant since the use of antibiotics. I would never forgive myself should you die after all we went through because of a cold or worse. I will need your signature on all of these." Sebastian handed more documents to Arian.

Arian was too enraptured about the adoption papers as she held them next to her heart and smiled. "It is just too wonderful. I love you so much."

Sebastian smiled. " At least that is done. I hope there are no glitches so that we don't have to explain any of them. I will make the witch's rod check it thoroughly just in case. I even altered our flight tickets to include you and bill me by credit card. If we are traveling, you will need a new wardrobe. So I have to download some fashion magazines that may be appropriate. You might be a bit shocked but the times have changed dramatically. Some catalogues have virtual images to ascertain the look and fit. However, it is imperfect. Maybe with the witch's rod, you can have them materialize to see how you would look and if you like them you may keep them."

Arian smiled. "Please choose them. I don't know anything about today's fashion. What ever you like, I will wear because I trust your judgment."

"It will be fun." Selena commented. "And you have to have makeup too just like Aunt Cassandra."

Sebastian wondered what Arian would think about that.

Selena continued. "Mommy will be my live doll."

Lucien marveled. "Really, we could see Mommy in modern dress."

Uncle Horatio perked up. "When can we start?"

"Uncle, you will make Arian blush again. " Sebastian reminded them.

Arian blushed just hearing the topic.

"You see," Sebastian smiled. "Come my Lady, modernization awaits you. Selena will be just too happy to help you as will the rest of us. What dresses or garments do you prefer?"

"I can't relate to any of them at all. Please, you choose." Arian remained undecided. "I would prefer it if you would."

Sebastian hugged her. "If that is what you prefer. We all now have a live doll."

Everyone peered at the monitor of downloaded clothes, which included an assortment of dresses, skirts, blouses, pants and suits. They scrutinized Arian as she stared in utter amazement. Sebastian asked the witch's rod for Arian's size privately printing it on a sheet of paper.

"I think it would be easier on your mother when I choose undergarments that Uncle Horatio and you, Lucien and Selena, should go for some exercise." Sebastian hinted.

Arian blushed constantly holding her hands to her red cheeks.

Sebastian asked the witch's rod to duplicate the chosen apparel, which appeared in minutes. " Well, I think you will have to try them on. Upstairs my lady."

The children came back with Uncle Horatio.

"How does Mommy look?" Selena, unable to control her curiosity, asked.

Lucien noticed. "Daddy, Mommy has makeup on!"

"Yes, Lucien. What do you think of Mommy?" Sebastian kept watching for their reaction.

"She is beautiful." Both Lucien and Selena concluded.

Uncle Horatio stated. "She certainly is. How do you like it Arian?"

"I don't know myself, but the clothes are so light and non-constricting. I am still amazed. The color assortment is astonishing and there are so many different fabrics." Arian expressed with enthusiasm.

Sebastian smiled with approval. "You are exquisite for any age." He smiled as he made her pirouette for a complete inspection." I think now is as good a time to explain all of this to Cassandra so she can see you as you are in modern dress as we materialize her at Uncle Horatio's and then take her to the Realm of Twilight. Uncle! Has the witch's rod transferred all your furniture and items while fixing the duct taped windows, boarded up fireplace and not to forget painting what needs to be done while fixing your closet wall in the basement into a doorway?"

"I believe so. Thank you witch's rod, that would have taken another two weeks at least if I had to have it all done." Uncle Horatio sighed with relief.

"Let's transfer to your house to meet her, Uncle." He checked his watch for the time it would be in Montreal. "Without any further delay I will contact her with the witch's rod and the crystal ball." Sebastian concentrated on the telephone number while waving the witch's rod to connect through the lines to Montreal. A familiar voice answered.

"Hello?" Cassandra responded.

"Cassandra, how are you? I apologize for not contacting you earlier, but up to now things were quite precarious. Forgive me for being so mysterious but I fear that you will be skeptical or utterly in denial if I explain what has happened without some tangible evidence that you cannot refute. So bear with me. From what I see, you are appropriately dressed. I will transfer you here in England in a matter of seconds. You will be slightly dizzy but don't worry. That is a normal reaction."

Cassandra only asserted. "Sebastian?"

Cassandra still spinning from the transfer finally focused on Sebastian, Uncle Horatio, Lucien, Selena and Arian, who had Giselle on her shoulder? Holding out her arms for balance and bearing, Sebastian caught her before she fainted.

"Welcome. Thank you for not calling earlier and getting involved, which would have only complicated matters. You look reasonable well. I would like you to meet Arian, my wife. If you were here when we married, I could not have guaranteed any of our lives. We did not know any of our futures. So I could not risk your life as well."

Cassandra showed astonishment.

"This may be trying for you. Here, please sit down while I elucidate."

"Wife?" Cassandra repeated. "How did you get me here?" She surveyed her surroundings and concluded she no longer was in Montreal.

"With magic, a witch's rod and a crystal ball, I informed you earlier that you wouldn't believe me. But how can you be here if it was not for magic?" Sebastian reaffirmed.

"I must be dreaming. This can't be happening. You are not here but in my imagination. I must be going mad."

Lucien and Selena ran up to Aunt Cassandra.

"You will be all right. We will hold you so that you will feel better." Lucien stated.

"You are really here, Lucien and Selena, Uncle and Sebastian. And if I am dreaming, why is that bird waving at me with her wing on this beautiful lady's shoulder. Please explain. I am all ears, if believable or not. Thank God you are all well." Cassandra continued.

"To fully understand, Giselle, that is the bird who waves at you, purposefully dropped nails on the roadway so that I would have a flat tire at the site of the abandoned grave site when we drove up to Uncle Horatio's. She then instigated to have Lucien and Selena follow her while I fixed the tire so they would locate this emerald ring, a filigree box and key which belongs to the three witches that have tormented us in the present and in the past in the year of 1699. I was, through reincarnation, Alexus Simons who married Arian Jovan. We had our first born, Dorian, who is Lucien in the present. Arian, who was with our second child, Selena, sacrificed her life to save me from Hexe, Brujia and Hagatha, who would have transferred me to another dimension, the Realm of Twilight, to a facsimile of our chateau so that I would be immortal as her lover through eternity. Because she took my place to save me from a fate worse than death, she lost our Selena and was doomed to view any of my future lives of love, knowing we would be parted forever. Arian has resided in the Realm of Twilight for three hundred years. By taking the emerald ring from the filigree box with the key two weeks ago, the witches resurrected by the rousing spell from an accidental death to find me again in the present. Luckily for us we had Giselle, a magical bird(a blue tit) who showed us the Anthology of Magical Spells to discover a spell to literally kill the witches. They threatened to torture Arian and then kill her, have myself, Uncle Horatio and Lucien as lovers and have Selena put into suspension to be used as body parts for any more of their spells. We didn't have much of an option. Even to solve the spells were a feat in themselves with an uncertain outcome."

Cassandra blinked unbelieving.

"I knew you wouldn't believe it and I haven't given many details either. So to prove it to you, we will transfer to the Realm of Twilight so you can judge for yourself."

Cassandra still dazed murmured. "She doesn't look three hundred years old."

"Actually, she is three hundred and twenty-three years old but for our papers which we contrived with the computer and the witchs'rod to enter her into the files she will be only stating that she is twenty-three years old." Sebastian smiled but Cassandra was too overwhelmed. Sebastian waved the witch's rod while reciting the transfer spell over everyone as all of them transferred to the library of Quintessence. The beauty of the room with twenty-foot ceilings decorated in wood paneling accenting the antique furniture with volumes upon volumes of beautiful leather bound books impressed her. The chandeliers were lit with candles. A globe stood in the corner with the representations of what the world's countries were at the 1650's.

Cassandra, shaken by the experience cried. "My God! It must be true, for I can't reason any other explanation of how we traveled and my senses are jarred by the past representation after seeing this globe of the 17th century."

Sebastian opened the library door exposing the foyer, which revealed the portrait of Alexus Simons and his son, Dorian, in 17th century clothes. The comparison of the two standing side by side one in modern attire with the 17th century counterpart made Cassandra dizzy. Uncle Horatio held her steady guiding Cassandra to a chair.

"Would you like a refreshment? "Arian asked concerned. "A brandy or cognac perhaps?"

Lucien and Selena held Aunt Cassandra's hands as Uncle Horatio patted her shoulders.

Sebastian smiled. "Will you be all right or do you wish to retire? I will carry you to your room if you are too overwhelmed by it all. Please say something. I am distraught that you are unwell. Cassandra! Hello? Very well if you do not answer." He carried her up from the chair and proceeded to walk up the grand staircase past the galleries to her room. He lay her in her chamber upon a large canopy bed. "I will sit with you, as all of us will, until you can make some sense." He covered her with a silken quilt. He held his sister's hand quietly waiting for Cassandra to say something.

Cassandra responded. "Sebastian. I am sorry. I am a bit light headed. Please tell me every detail. I am happy for you to be married. She is lovely and the children seem to love her. But I want to understand."

Sebastian pulled up a love seat for Arian and the children while he placed another chair close to his sister's bed. He held Arian's hand. Both children sat and nuzzled into Arian. He related the entire episode while Uncle Horatio and Giselle settled into an adjacent chair on the other side of the bed. When Sebastian spoke about Mort and ended up with all the paperwork needed for Arian's identity, Cassandra shook her head in disbelief.

"You are correct. If you told me this at home, I would believe you are mad, but by being here and seeing images in the crystal ball of your past misfortunes, I am thankful I even have all of you. My God what a nightmare."

"I keep thinking. What is in Uncle's house that caused the previous owners to sell it for such a reasonable low cost? Maybe we should ask the witch's rod what is really there? We didn't seem to be affected in the short duration that we were forced to leave by the witches smoking us out." Sebastian speculated. "Witch's rod, what caused the previous owners to sell so rapidly and what caused the previous house to burn down?"

The witch's rod responded in writing. "The suspended bodies, souls, and parts must expend their pent-up energy by vibrating at witches' holidays to insure their longevity, which can last up to one thousand years. That is why the house was burned down to consume the bodies previously. However, in the suspension mode they cannot be destroyed."

"Oh my God!" Sebastian expounded. "How many are there?"

Everyone, including Cassandra waited patiently to read the result in the crystal ball while Selena buried her head and peeked and buried her head back into Mommy not letting go.

The witch's rod wrote. "Full suspension not including parts or including parts? Please be more specific."

Uncle Horatio stood up aghast. "This is in my house! Oh my God. It is all mine! I paid the full amount. I should have known, nothing could be priced that low without a catch."

Both Lucien and Selena clung to their mother, one on each side. Sebastian still held Arian's hand.

Arian said soothingly. "I think I will put them to bed. It is well past their bed time."

Selena sobbed. "I don't want to be alone Mommy. I want to sleep with you and Daddy and Lucien like we always do."

Sebastian reaffirmed. "Don't worry. We are always here for you." He stared at Arian with wary eyes. "I will check the Anthology of Magical Spells on all the witches' holidays and also for an anti-suspension spell if we can handle the outcome. For if we cannot, we will have to leave them in suspension."

"You cannot do that. I have to live somewhere. All my money is tied up on this house." Uncle Horatio emphasized.

"Uncle, calm yourself. You are upsetting the children." Sebastian hinted.

Cassandra asked. "Sebastian, may I sleep in your room with Arian and the children? Even I don't want to be alone."

Sebastian surprised in his sister's request stated. ""Why not, if it makes you feel better. How about you Uncle, the sofa is still available. We might as well be all together. It will be easier to protect everyone just in case. I will have the witch's rod bring the Anthology of Magical Spells to the master bedroom."

"Very well. I will join you in the master bedroom." Uncle Horatio responded. "It will be like old times."

They all walked to the master bedroom as Sebastian opened the double door entry.

"Ladies and children first," Sebastian announced. Arian with two clinging children passed.

Arian murmured. "I have never seen any activity in the Realm of Twilight so I think we will be fine, don't you?"

Sebastian whispered. "Before you never had the witches' paraphernalia in the Realm of Twilight either so until we can confirm with the Anthology or the witch's rod, I am not taking any chances. We didn't think we would have any trouble with Mort and that turned to be a mistake, which if Giselle had not warned me, I would have lost you. I don't want to lose you ever."

Arian's anxiety grew as she stared at Sebastian still holding onto the children.

Cassandra overheard and clung to Arian as well. She passed followed by Uncle Horatio with Giselle on his shoulder.

Sebastian closed the double doors. Magically, the witch's rod summoned and delivered the crystal ball and the Anthology of Magical Spells. They suddenly appeared by the table. Sebastian immediately hastened to his task. It was past midnight for it took about four hours for Sebastian to summarize the past events to his sister.

"Arian, please put the children to bed. This may take longer than expected."

Arian smiled at Sebastian. "Come, you heard your Father." She brought the children with their night attire to one of the bathrooms. "Cassandra, the other bathroom is right past the armoire on your left. Please, take your suitcase. Sebastian had the witch's rod transfer it for your trip from Montreal, so you can change. Sorry Uncle Horatio, ladies first." Arian, with both children dressed for bed and robed, lay on the chaise closest to Sebastian. She held two sleepy children who nuzzled into her too exhausted to stay awake. Cassandra in her robe and night attire sat on the couch, which would be Uncle Horatio's bed, next to her Uncle and Giselle.

Sebastian consulted the witch's rod and the crystal ball. "To be specific." He enunciated, "How many suspended bodies and parts are there? What do they do on the witches' holidays? Do they pose a threat to any of us and to conclude once they are no longer in suspension, what can be done about them?"

The witch's rod complied with the questions presented by having the crystal ball print it on sheets of paper. "The total amount of full-suspended beings is equal to one and thirteen souls. As for the suspended body parts involving organs, limbs, brains, etc., there are approximately four hundred components. After being in suspension for long periods of time, built up energy of muscular movements as well as vocal involvement must be expended through the whole day to keep them in a state of optimal use. As dictated by the Book of shadows, they will contort so that all the muscles can be mobilized. As prisoners of their confinement, violent hatred of captivity is exhibited as is ranting and raving like in an insane asylum in babbling and loquacious chatter for their mentalities are warped. Anything that is in their way would be destroyed. They are controlled by the emanations of the filigree key, which keeps the bodies in the proper flux." The witch's rod listed the witches' holidays (eight of them). "The closest would be August 2, Lammas. If the victims are only anti-suspended by the warm water due to their long duration, they will be uncontrollable. But, if the victims are anti-suspended first by the unlock-spell while reciting the anti suspension spell, (refer to the Anthology), their minds will be unlocked to communications and perhaps through a restoration spell may become manageable."

Sebastian scanned the index in the Anthology and read the spells out loud.

THE ANTI -LOCK / AND ANTI-SUSPENSION SPELL
To enliven that, what is not
From continuance of the non-living to phantoms that alter the plot
Repressed to breathe after so long an abeyance
The cessation of movement, to writhe with conveyance
Recessed from time, from any apparent stimulation
With a power like zombies to resume one's own circulation
Lulled through ages past, as halted by retardation
Excised from silence, to excessive animation.

THE RESTORATION SPELL
Embalmed in suspension as frozen instilled
Grieved from the poison and rancor from thy unexpressed will
To resuscitate from embitterment to somehow revive
To reawaken the good from thy spirit to be alive
Heal thyself so that one will survive
With an elixir of life to cure, so one can rectify

The witch's rod continued with its analysis as the printout lengthened. "Since the filigree key is now at the Realm of Twilight, the proximity is too distant to the witches' cave so the suspension will lapse causing them and the components to transverse towards the filigree key here within the next five hours."

Sebastian replied. "Five hours!" He glanced at his watch, which showed three A.M. "At eight A.M. we will be beseeched by them. Witch's rod if you sent the filigree key back to the witches' cave, will the situation be abated?"

The witch's rod wrote through the crystal ball. "It would only delay it ten hours since the key has been in the Realm of Twilight since you came."

Sebastian confirmed. "Do it, and put a protection spell around the key. Without it, we cannot use the Anthology or keep Mort from visiting of which I absolutely insist upon." The key disappeared.

Arian flashed Sebastian a worried stare as his eyes met hers. Cassandra clung in the meantime to Uncle Horatio who exhibited an unbelieving glare.

Sebastian supplicated. "If the souls (thirteen of them) were anti-suspended wouldn't they be able to go where all souls go as if one dies? So why were they suspended?"

The witch's rod steadily had the crystal ball print out. "The suspended souls could be manipulated into live bodies ousting the bodies' own souls to be replaced by the suspended ones to do the witch's' bidding for gain."

"What had happened to the suspended souls' bodies?" Sebastian reluctantly asked.

"Processed into witches' spells," was what the witch's rod responded.

"How appalling!" Uncle Horatio voiced.

Sebastian pursued his questioning. "Are the suspended entities confined to the witches' cave where the filigree key was or now since there is a doorway to my Uncle's house would they venture everywhere?"

The witch's rod promptly wrote." They would venture everywhere."

Sebastian commanded. "Seal the doorway. We just had my Uncle's house fixed and unpacked. Can we circumvent this demonstration by releasing the souls with a restoration spell to free them as normal?"

The witch's' rod expounded. "It depends on the duration of captivity."

"Witch's rod, I have been avoiding this, but who is the suspended full being?" Sebastian languished.

"She is a child of seven years originally who wandered to the witches' cave fostered by curiosity in the year of 1799. Genevieve was a foundling being brought up by the church. Upon hearing the musical notes emanating from the filigree key, she entered the witches cave. Hagatha placed her in suspension because in Genevieve's haste Genevieve spilled Hagatha's potion, therefore, she was doomed to purgatory." The crystal ball revealed Genevieve's image

Arian gasped and tears fell from her eyes as she empathized with the poor child.

Sebastian stared in disbelief and horror as he rose to hold Arian's hand. "We must try to save her. Witch's rod, is there a psychic healing spell in the Anthology of Magical spells?"

The witch's rod wrote." Please check the Anthology. It does list one."

Sebastian quickly got up and thumbed through the Anthology as he read out loud.

PYSCHE SPELL
To reconcile to a harmonious life
Amend thy spirit to quench your strife
Soothe thy hallucinations to one of calm
Pacify from reckless insanity to balm
Tranquilize with serenity so one can mend
Clearing delusions racked in one's head to fend.

Upon finishing the refrain Sebastian asked the witch's rod. "Can we see this room with the crystal ball?"

The crystal ball flickered with light as it focused into the witches' cave. The door opened slowly as electrical sparks in flux radiated with bursts of brilliance in sine waving lines of force as it pulsed through hundreds of body parts. The view altered to one central figure. Lighted souls as phantoms of transparent iridescence white, calmly slept. One frail girl, thin from two hundred years of captivity, slept in endless repose still being in suspension. She was clothed in a white night gown, which bore holes. She had black jet hair neatly braided with pale white skin and long fringed eyelashes as she gently breathed shallowly. Fluxes of light distorted the beams causing occasional flinches in the bodies, souls and parts.

Cassandra buried her head into Uncle Horatio's shoulder. "I can't look anymore."

Sebastian quietly stated. "Thank you crystal ball, please stop the transmission. I believe that after about five hours of sleep we shall attempt to rescue this unfortunate child. I can't let this girl suffer any longer. We will release the spirits after attempting to rectify their psyches so they will go to where they are supposed to go. As for the body parts, we shall give them a decent burial. But the child, we must try to save. Imagine a life of two hundred years of suspension. Witch's' rod, what are the chances of making her normal?"

The witch's rod wrote nothing in the crystal ball for an extended period of time. Finally it printed. "I am unable to fully analyze it. Suicidal tendencies are very high with an absolute fear that consumes her."

Sebastian concluded. "It is not unlikely considering. Let's retire. Since the suspended entities won't enter the Realm of Twilight, Cassandra and Uncle can retire in their own rooms respectively."

Cassandra reflected. "I don't want to be alone. I will have nightmares."

Sebastian answered calmly. "It will be all right. You can take a sleeping tablet. If you stayed here, you would be sleeping on the chaise or sofa, so it won't make that much difference, especially with one door apart. Will it? I haven't slept since five A.M yesterday, which included within a day, fighting with Mort, typing furiously in the computer, transferring you here from Montreal, explaining what had occurred here in the past two weeks, and now attempting to save a two hundred year old suspended girl. I am beyond the point of reason. I need to rest."

Cassandra could see that Sebastian was exhausted and nodded as she walked to her room accompanied by her Uncle.

Uncle Horatio profoundly offered. "Come I shall escort you back to your room in perfect safety. Good night! Sebastian, Arian, Lucien, Selena and Giselle! Come Cassandra don't linger. You will be fine. I have excellent hearing. You will be protected."

Arian smiled with some reassurance. "Good night Cassandra."

Sebastian held the door. Good night! Cassandra and Uncle! I will knock at your doors approximately five hours from now." He smiled at his sister to comfort her. "Don't look at me so. It won't work. Good night." He closed the doors and stared at Arian.

"My God! What person could normally come out of being in suspension for two hundred years seeing body parts of others and thirteen souls being dismembered so that all that is left are souls which still can be manipulated. Does this treachery ever end? The more we find out about these witches, the more appalling it becomes. I am thoroughly repulsed and shocked. We can't bring the children. I utterly refuse to have them see this. I am afraid for my children's sanity. Here, let me help you my Lady." Sebastian picked up two sleepy bundles and put them to bed. "Arian, are you numb again?"

Arian shyly smiled answering. "Yes."

"How are you? Are you still traumatized by Mort's insults and now I saw you in tears for Genevieve. What cruelty! We were supposed to have left tomorrow for our trip to Italy." Sebastian stared at his watch. "It is three thirty in the morning." He set the alarm for five hours and frowned. " I must sleep." He pulled Arian from the chaise gently holding her very close. Arian could feel Sebastian's tension just by holding his arm muscles. She massaged him.

"Don't stop, that soothes me." Sebastian whispered so that the children wouldn't wake. "Let's go to bed. This time my Lady, you will undress even faster because you don't have a corset on. Though I have seen you pull your hem repeatedly because the length of your dress is too short according to your standards."

Arian blushed still in Sebastian's arms as he kissed her forehead.

"Five hours will be too soon for our sleep and too long for one kept in suspension. Her frail form is still indelibly printed in my mind's eye that I see her now."

Arian whispered into Sebastian's ear soothingly to help him focus on something else. "Come to bed my handsome cavalier and my protector. I feel foreboding. Genevieve had such a loveless life of sheer fear, loneliness, and abject cruelty. How can one rectify all that suffering." She pulled Sebastian to the bathroom. "I have gathered our night clothes already. Would you undo my zipper? I am afraid to. It might not work since it is in the back not like yours." She blushed crimson.

Sebastian finished her sentence. "Like my trousers?"

They both laughed.

"I love you." Sebastian grinned broadly.

Arian smiled while Sebastian helped her with her zipper. They changed so they could finally rest. Sebastian snuggled into Arian with his arm holding her waist. He fell asleep. Arian watched her family sleep. Giselle was on her perch. Arian fell asleep for about ten minutes when a knock was heard at the door.

Sebastian asked. "Who is it?"

Cassandra sobbed. "I can't sleep and I took a sleeping pill too. Now what should I do?"

Sebastian rose and opened the door. Cassandra didn't wait in the hall but just came in. Sebastian didn't even have a robe on because he intended to stay behind the door.

Sebastian astonished hinted. "And where do you think you are going?"

Cassandra firmly stated. "I will sleep in-between the children and Arian, please, please, please."

Sebastian exasperated said. "I am past being reasonable. I am too tired. We have only four hours left. And if you wake the children I will be upset and so will Arian. She is a fierce protector. You just don't know her yet, as I do."

Cassandra made her way to the large bed. Arian got up so Cassandra could get in. She settled herself by Selena and Arian while Sebastian shut the door quietly and nuzzled back into Arian.

"No one say anything, understand!" Sebastian's voice trailed off.

Arian caressed Sebastian's cheek to soothe him. It worked. He put his arm around Arian's waist again and fell asleep. Arian thought to herself that she wished she could fall asleep as quickly as Sebastian could. Cassandra couldn't sleep either as both Arian and Cassandra stared at one another in the dark smiling. Cassandra felt she had imposed so she turned around towards Selena and tried to sleep.

Selena woke. "You are not Mommy. I want my Mommy."

Arian whispered. "Come to me."

Cassandra carried Selena to Arian and now was next to Lucien.

Lucien's eyes widened. "How did you get here?"

Cassandra's face portrayed guilt. "I couldn't sleep so I came to your room. I will sleep on the outside so you can have your sister and mother."

Lucien rose standing to get closer to his sister and his mother.

"Have we all finished with musical beds so we can sleep!" Sebastian stated.

"I agree," Uncle Horatio affirmed. "I can't get sleep from the musical beds either. By the way, Cassandra hasn't changed since she was small.

Cassandra drew the blankets over her head, obviously embarrassed.

"I am sorry Uncle. Let's all sleep please." Sebastian reiterated, as he placed his arm back around Arian's waist.

Selena murmured. "May I be in-between you and Mommy, Daddy?"

"Very well." Sebastian carried Selena over Arian so that Selena could have both parents. Lucien snuggled into his Mommy.

The witch's' rod tapped upon Sebastian's shoulder as the clock chimed eight thirty in the morning. Sebastian, who stayed at the edge of the bed all night so not to crush Selena, nodded to the rod that he, was awake. He rose quickly as the rest of his family and his sister slept. He leaned as far as he could to kiss Arian's forehead so not to disturb anyone else. She opened her eyes seeing Sebastian's face.

Sebastian whispered. "It is time my Lady to rise. I tried to be careful not to scratch your face with this being unshaved."

Arian held her arms up to him so Sebastian could lift her from in-between the children. With that accomplished, she quickly gathered her and Sebastian's clothes while following Sebastian to the bathroom.

"Good morning." Arian whispered. "Did you sleep well?"

Both of them smiled knowing how careful they had been with the children so close.

Sebastian shook his head and kissed Arian carefully so not to inconvenience Arian's face. She held him closely. "We had better hurry. We have a lot to do before we leave for Italy if this problem doesn't override all our plans."

Arian turned her head away still thinking of Genevieve. Sebastian held her chin gently.

"I know. I have no idea about the outcome either. I will have the witch's rod make us some hot water." Sebastian hurried thinking about what was yet to come. Once ready, he opened the bathroom door and went to wake the children. Arian was fixing her hair. Sebastian touched Lucien's shoulder.

"Lucien, it is time to rise." Sebastian whispered. "Selena, come it is time."

Lucien woke and smiled at his Father. "You won't be taking us this time with you, Father."

Sebastian nodded. "It has to deal with various anatomical parts and one unfortunate suspended girl of seven years of age, just like yourself, suspended for two hundred years. The chances are she will be quite insane and I don't know if the spells will combat all those years of abject fear and torture. I don't relish the idea but I must save her from that fate. It will be dangerous and I can't, as a parent, expose you to it. Can you understand?" Sebastian touched Lucien's head with his own and hugged him. Lucien hugged his Father back. "Selena." Sebastian whispered again. "It is time to rise."

Selena opened her beautiful long eyelashes to reveal her eyes. She held up her arms to kiss Daddy.

Sebastian kissed her forehead. "We must get up."

Lucien commented. "Aunt Cassandra is still sound asleep."

Sebastian whispered. "Let her sleep for a while."

Arian came to the bed whispering. "There you are. Did you sleep well?"

Selena got up to hold Mommy, as did Lucien. Arian kissed and hugged both of them.

"Come, off to the bath with you. The water is just perfect now. If you will excuse us, Monsieur, I must take care of my children."

Sebastian acknowledged silently with a nod, while Giselle chirped that breakfast was in the making.

"Thank you Giselle," Arian smiled.

Sebastian noticed Arian was dressed in her 17th century attire probably for Genevieve's benefit.

Arian gazed at Cassandra. "Should we wake her?"

Sebastian whispered back to Arian smiling. "Ever since I know her, she is a late riser. So let us give her ten minutes. I will wake Uncle Horatio. Isn't that what you were going to say?"

Arian nodded while both Lucien and Selena grinned.

Sebastian left the master bedroom to knock at his Uncle's bedroom door. "Uncle, it is time. Are you awake?"

Uncle Horatio opened his door. "Yes I am ready. I couldn't sleep well thinking of what our itinerary will consist of today. I take it Cassandra is still sound asleep."

"Correct again. You know her well, Uncle." Sebastian smiled.

Arian whispered from the master bedroom. "We are all ready with the exception of your sister."

"I will have to wake her." Sebastian admitted. He returned from the hall. "Cassandra?" Sebastian walked up to her quietly. "Cassandra, please wake. It is time. I have to wake you now for we will be late. Cassandra." He could hear her steady breathing. He touched her shoulder, no response. He took her hand and held it up and let it fall. "She took a sleeping tablet. She is out like a light. Witch's rod, what is Cassandra's diagnosis?"

All of them including Uncle Horatio stared at the crystal ball. "The sleeping tablet has taken its' effect."

"Can you wake her and negate the effect of the sleeping tablet?" Sebastian stated.

The witch's rod complied.

Cassandra woke seeing everyone staring at her. "What is the matter?" She noticed they all were dressed while she still lay in bed. "Did I over sleep again?"

Uncle Horatio smiled. "As usual, my dear."

"Oh, all right. I am up." She covered her face with the blanket.

Sebastian whispered. "We shall let you get ready. We will be in the dining room waiting for you so we can have breakfast. The witch's rod will show you the way and provide for your needs."

Everyone left the room so Cassandra could get ready.

Arian played the harpsichord while they waited for her.

Cassandra ran down the stairs following the witch's rod. She could hear the music playing throughout the chateau in its harmonic symphonies attempting to calm the inhabitants from the unknowns. Sebastian copied the needed spells as Arian played with two children sitting next to her. Uncle Horatio looked over Sebastian's shoulder as Giselle waved to Cassandra while perched on Uncle Horatio's shoulder.

Lucien and Selena noticed Cassandra's appearance.

"Hello, Aunt Cassandra." Lucien announced.

Selena turned, "Good morning, Mademoiselle." She rose from the harpsichord bench and curtsied while Lucien bowed followed by Arian.

"Good morning," Arian curtsied. "Did you sleep well?"

Cassandra astonished by her reception cast a bewildered glance at her brother and Uncle.

"Good morning," Sebastian acquiesced. "Come, let us have breakfast. Shall we all go to the dining room?" He gave his arm to Arian and his daughter and Arian taking Sebastian's arm and Lucien's arm walked to the dining room. Uncle Horatio took Cassandra's arm and followed them, with Giselle on his shoulder.

Uncle Horatio added. "Good morning, Cassandra. Has a cat got your tongue?"

Cassandra murmured. "This is so formal. I feel out of place."

Uncle Horatio reaffirmed. "Nonsense. It just takes a little getting used to."

The dining room with its elevated molded ceilings and fine furniture accented breakfast. It highlighted a gleaming table of fresh fruit, scrambled eggs, bacon, and toast with a deceptively simple embroidered white tablecloth. Fresh brewed tea and coffee in silver sets enhanced the crystal candelabras, which were lit beckoning them as the aroma of hot French bread made its presence known.

Cassandra overwhelmed by the elegance of her surroundings expressed. "Everyone seems to be so somber this morning. I want to apologize for the inconvenience last night. I don't know how you deal with all this stress."

Sebastian stated. "It is not a matter of choosing, you are thrust upon the situation and you make the according decisions or perish. You, Cassandra and Uncle Horatio will stay with the children while Arian and myself will transfer to a nearby chamber close enough to the suspended bodies, parts and souls. Through the witch's rod we will dispense the anti-suspension spell, the restoration spell and the psyche spell. Watching the crystal ball's view, we will see if the spells will counteract some of the damage, which we will have to improvise, because I can't predict the outcome. Arian and I will view the crystal ball kept behind a screen so the only view I am allowing the rest of you to see is our reaction not the actuality of what is occurring. If we go in, I want Uncle to stop the transmission and only ask your witch's rod, for I will carry one for ourselves, to acknowledge our safety in which Uncle will ask how to help."

Uncle Horatio stunned lamented. "You aren't taking me with? I am shocked."

"Uncle," Sebastian said soothingly. "The reason for that is, I believe a woman's empathy is more calming than my presence. I am going for Arian's protection. Arian always calms the children and me down instinctively. She has that quality about her." He stared at Arian lovingly.

Arian rose to hold Sebastian's hand and then hugged him.

Sebastian continued. "Let's not delay any longer. The rest of you please finish your breakfast. I can't let Genevieve stay in suspension." He alighted from the table. "Witch's rod, I will need another witch's rod and two crystal balls. Thank you."

The items instantly appeared.

"It is goodbye for a little while, Lucien and Selena. We will take care. I would not wish to endanger any of us but this treachery has to be dealt with. Adieu." Sebastian kissed both children. "Uncle, be ready. I need you as a back up to protect the children and Cassandra. You will help us as the liaison in-between. Cassandra, please try to calm your nerves so that the children will be calm. Arian, soothe the children and then, let's go."

Arian quickly kissed both children and then returned to Sebastian as they both transferred to the witches' labyrinth. They disappeared from sight.

Uncle Horatio ordered his crystal ball with his witch's rod to view their reappearance in the adjacent room. The children huddled over the ball catching the view of their parents. Cassandra, still amazed at their disappearance stared in awe.

Sebastian commanded the witch's rod to view the suspended beings and reiterated each of the three spells with the elixir of life being sent to them. The noise that emanated was akin to a large crowd with sounds of fury rising to a crescendo as electric and magnetic flux sparked intermittently obliterating the view as all the component parts writhed. Sebastian had the crystal ball focus on Genevieve as her eyes flashed opening and closing in spasms coughing as air actually entered her lungs. Fear absorbed her face as she contorted with jerks in her legs and arms with excruciating pain from the movement. She screamed out in agony as tears fell from her eyes. Sebastian had the witch's rod make a visible portal so that Genevieve could see Arian and himself. He also had the witch's rod partition Genevieve away from the body parts and souls so that they could help her in isolation, away from the noise.

Sebastian asked the witch's rod. "Can Genevieve see and hear us? And if so, what is she thinking?"

The witch's rod, through the crystal, printed out. "Yes, she can see you. She is terrified of what you will do to her."

"Can she understand what we are saying, witch's rod?" Sebastian urged.

The witch's rod was silent and then wrote." She hears the words but it has been so long that she can't associate it with all the meanings."

Arian spoke softly. "Genevieve, do you understand? We will not harm you, Genevieve." Arian held out her hands. "We want to save you. The witches are dead. They cannot harm you any longer."

Sebastian hinted. "Arian, sing a lullaby so that it will soothe her. Music effects the soul better than words. But sing one in English."

Arian sang a lullaby that she sung to Dorian when he was small.

Sebastian pursued the witch's rod. "What is Genevieve thinking? She is not moving." Sebastian waited impatiently for the witch's rod to respond.

The witch's rod wrote. "She is in shock. She cannot make out all the words but she likes the lullaby."

Genevieve went into convulsions for a moment but then calmed again listening to Arian and attempted to get up to walk. She seemed transfixed on Arian extending her arms out to her. She fell, not used to the manipulation of her legs or any of her muscles. She then crawled. She spoke. "Are you the angel to save me?"

Arian calmly whispered. "I was a prisoner like you were by the witches. I am three hundred and twenty three years old and you are two hundred and seven years old. We are now both set free for the witches are dead. Come, let me help you."

Sebastian queried the witch's rod. "How is she mentally right now? Does she comprehend?" He waited diligently for the printout.

The witch's rod complied. "She seems to have a grasp of things."

Sebastian reaffirmed. "Reapply the psyche spell and the restorative spell before you open this door."

The witch's rod carried out its orders.

Genevieve with eyes as big as saucers walked upright towards Arian's extended arms while still extending hers.

Sebastian asked again. "Witch's rod give me an update on her mental condition." He watched for the printout.

"Her brain emanations and functions as well as her mental state are normal." The witch's rod continued printing.

Sebastian, while still holding the witch's rod, had the portal open allowing Genevieve to walk to Arian. As both of them touched their fingers, both cried releasing their torment of captivity as now they embraced. Arian held Genevieve swaying her to and fro to calm both of them.

Sebastian asked the witch's rod. "Can Genevieve have a relapse in mentality?'

The witch's rod wrote." Unknown!"

The two were inseparable as the scene of flowing tears effected Sebastian as well.

Arian murmured. "It will be all right. No one will hurt you again. Cry it out. It will relieve your soul."

Sebastian came closer to help soothe both of them. Genevieve relapsed back into spasms as Arian tried to hold her.

"Witch's rod," Sebastian ordered. "Help Genevieve, she seems to have heart problems."

The witch's rod printed out." The stress is too much for her. I will attempt to rectify her aneurysm in her heart."

Sebastian asked. "Can you fix it?"

The witch's rod wrote. "Please wait for further analysis."

Genevieve calmed down and held Arian tightly. Arian glanced at Sebastian giving him the reassurance that the child was better.

Sebastian spoke. "Genevieve, we are here to help you. How do you feel?"

Genevieve turned her head towards Sebastian staring. "What will happen to me?"

Sebastian affirmed. "We, Arian is my wife and I am called Sebastian, will take care of you, if that is all right with you. This is two hundred years into your future. The year is 1999."

Genevieve screamed. "No! Everyone I know is dead!" She convulsed again.

"Cut the transmission Uncle! Witch's rod help her while giving me an update of her condition," Sebastian insisted. He tried to help hold Genevieve with Arian but she died in both Sebastian's and Arian's arms. Arian burst into tears uncontrollably upon the frail body. For her it was the re-enactment of the death of Selena and three hundred years of captivity.

The witch's rod wrote. "Too much stress. She had a heart defect. The device we added by reading your thoughts, Monsieur Sebastian, was overridden by her fear, causing an overload. She wouldn't have lasted in stasis either."

Sebastian held his wife and Genevieve. "God be with you. You have suffered far too much as it is. We will bring her into the Realm of Twilight. Witch's rod, also bury the four hundred body parts separately in the abandoned gravesite. As for the thirteen souls reapply the restoration spell and let them go to where they would be if they had died a normal death."

Sebastian picked up Arian who still had Genevieve in her arms, carrying them both. He transferred back to the Realm of Twilight away from the house to an open field where the gravesites of Quintessence were located.

"Witch's rod," Sebastian commanded. "Please dig a grave for Genevieve. Arian, I am so sorry. I know it effects you more than anyone considering your trauma. But I cannot change her fate now. May she rest in peace, at last, after such a long suspension. At least she knew that you cared. She was overwhelmed by your sympathy. For her to have survived she would have to face the facts. She didn't want to. Her constant anxiety of captivity to something new, a fear that I believe, consumed her in addition to her heart defect. She will always be remembered by all of us who will mourn her now and for as long as we live. Sebastian took Genevieve gently from Arian, who sang prayers while crying, and placed her into a ready-made coffin by the witch's rod. He lowered it himself and started to shovel the dirt in carefully saying. "Dust to dust and ashes to ashes. I commend thy spirit. May you finally know happiness and love and forget this nightmare. Please, be at peace at last. I regret I couldn't save you." He finished the grave and placed roses on it. He also had the witch's rod make a head stone with her name. "Genevieve, may you find love and happiness."

Arian held Sebastian tightly. "Thank God I have you. I would be worse without you."

Sebastian held her. "Let's walk in the garden and look at nature. Witch's rod, please have our children, Uncle Horatio and Cassandra please join us in the secret gazebo. That should cheer my Lady a bit. Loved ones always soften reality."

"Oh Sebastian," Arian whispered. "Let me hold you. I know you are very upset. I know how strong you are. I must stop crying. We are alone. I need you, but I want to comfort you as well. It has stunned all of us. I wonder how my little ones are?"

Sebastian held Arian so close as she could feel some of his tensions being released by holding her in his arms. Arian stared into Sebastian's eyes. She could see his eyes were moist as he kissed her. They held each other as they slowly walked to the secret garden. As they approached, two sad crying children ran up to them.

"Where is Genevieve?" Lucien called. "The transmission went dead."

Selena finally caught up to Lucien.

Arian choking said. "Genevieve is in heaven. She died of heart failure and shock. The witch's rod couldn't save her."

Selena burst into tears as Sebastian picked her up hushing her as he cradled Selena back and forth. Arian picked up Lucien.

Lucien proclaimed. "How could the witch's rod fail?"

Sebastian continued. "Genevieve's heart problem must have been congenital. She had a pacemaker added, by the witch's rod but, the witch's rod couldn't handle the excessive electrical impulses…" Sebastian's voice trailed off.

Lucien's eyes were moist as he held his Mommy. Arian's eyes established contact with Sebastian's for sympathy. " Is it possible to have a heart transplant?"

"Yes." Sebastian confirmed.

Uncle Horatio finally rushed to them with Cassandra. "Sebastian, Where is Genevieve? Unless, Oh God, did she die?" Uncle Horatio hinted as he turned to Arian. "Please, tell me Arian."

"She didn't make it. My Sebastian and I, but basically Sebastian buried her. I held her until she was placed into the ground. She died of heart failure."

Sebastian still rocked Selena, for she didn't stop crying. Lucien was quiet in Arian 's arms as he buried his face into Mommy whenever he felt like crying.

Cassandra turned white. "She died? But I thought the witch's rod could do everything."

" The witch's rod could have alleviated the problem, but she died of sheer shock. I had the witch's rod scan her body. Genevieve had all the electrical components but her trepidation of the present over rode it." Sebastian became silent.

"Oh my God." Tears came forth from Cassandra' eyes. "That poor child, where is she?" Cassandra lamented.

"At Quintessence's grave yard, " Arian whispered still rocking Lucien. Lucien clutched at her like a new baby. "Let's walk, all right Lucien. I will carry you as I walk."

Sebastian walked with Arian ,still holding Selena who seemed to be crying a little less. Cassandra's tears just flowed as Uncle Horatio held her having moist eyes as well. They all walked in silence as the breeze blew quietly past them while the birds sang. Giselle was with them, on Arian's shoulder rubbing her head against Arian's neck trying to cheer up Lucien. She used her wing and tickled Lucien's nose with no response. The sun became brighter as the time flew past. Sebastian looked at his watch. It was eleven o'clock. They have walked over a mile and a half. His arms were getting tired. He listened to Arian singing a lullaby to Lucien as she still held him. The two seemed inseparable. Arian was so upset she didn't even exhibit tiredness, nor did she notice Lucien's weight.

Sebastian stopped her saying softly. "Would you like a rest? It is quite hot and you must be thirsty, for I am."

"Oh, I haven't noticed. I am sorry. It seems Lucien is asleep. Even with Giselle' tickling his nose, it just doesn't wake him up. Turn around please, so I can see Selena." Sebastian complied. "She is asleep too. What shall we do Sebastian?"

"Well, we missed the flight to Italy. It should be landing in a half- hour at Rome's airport but we could take the witch's rod and go there. So we could have an early lunch. A trip would help all of us, for we are coming back to bring Uncle Horatio home from Italy before we leave Quintessence for Montreal. The witch's rod will be taking care of Quintessence for us. We can always visit it whenever we wish."

"I will ask the witch's rod to make lunch. If anyone, eats that is another question." Arian pondered.

Uncle Horatio reached Sebastian and Arian with Cassandra. "Shall we rest? I need something to drink. The sun is getting to me."

"Of course," Sebastian agreed. "Shall we, Madame?"

Arian walked to Sebastian as she gently touched his cheek with her cheek. She was still silent as they all walked into the chateau. The witch's rod patiently waited for them signaling them that a message was printed for Sebastian from Uncle Horatio 's telephone. It simulated the message.

First message from Italia airlines is for Sebastian:" Sorry the flight will be delayed until tomorrow morning. The flight leaves at seven thirty A. M. The delay is due to engine trouble."

Second message is for Uncle Horatio. Your daughter, Ophelia, called saying she will call later tonight and that she has the perfect match for her cousin Sebastian. Marguerite Bryant is a lovely girl of twenty-nine and she is a librarian. Marguerite cannot wait to meet Sebastian for I know he needs a wife.

"Oh my God." Sebastian read the messages from the crystal ball's printout. "Uncle, you must tell her about Arian and that we will be leaving for Italy tomorrow."

"What is it?" Arian wondered. " Oh," As she read the message. "Well, it is kind of her to care." She smiled at Sebastian. "Can you help me with this bundle. I should put Lucien down but my hands are so cramped, I can't seem to let go of him. Not that I would really want too ever let him go. I love our children so much."

Sebastian placed a sleepy Selena on the foyer's sofa as he lifted Lucien out of Arian's arms slowly. Arian held her hands trying to shake them out to relieve the cramp. Arian walked towards the children and hugged them. Lucien opened his eyes, as did Selena.

Lucien grabbed for Mommy as he held his hands on her face. Arian reassured him again and Selena. "Do you think that you could eat something or can you drink something for Mommy?" Arian beamed a hopeful smile.

"Oh, yes." Lucien responded. "I am very thirsty."

"How like your Father you are. Shall I bring it to you or shall we go to the dinning room? We have a meat salad, French bread, fruits and lemonade. For desert we have ice cream. Which is something special for me." Seeing the children's reaction Arian stated. "I guess we shall go to the dinning room."

Sebastian was behind Arian. "How are you two? Our trip is postponed until tomorrow. So we will at least be with Aunt Cassandra one more night. Which is nice."

Selena pleaded. "Can't we take Aunt Cassandra with us like Uncle Horatio?"

"I think she must work." Sebastian countered. "Besides, we must learn dancing. I am going to teach Mommy all the new and old dances so we will have a lot of fun."

"Really." Arian eyed Sebastian. "What about the music?"

"Don't worry. Since Uncle Horatio's CD player works, I will have the witch's rod transfer the music here."

Arian caressed Sebastian's cheek, but Sebastian twisted her waist to change the angle and kissed her mouth. After lunch Arian played for Cassandra the harpsichord and sang. But then the music changed to Uncle Horatio's CD and Sebastian took Arian for his partner as Lucien and Selena were paired as was Uncle Horatio and Cassandra. They were learning the Tango. They then switched partners as Selena went to Sebastian, Arian to Uncle Horatio and Cassandra to Lucien. They danced in the chateau's ballroom. The dance changed to a Waltz as the partners changed again until Arian came back to Sebastian. Arian was very happy.

"I am enjoying this so much. I love being in your arms. When did you learn how to dance? At school?" Arian hinted.

"No." Sebastian responded. "Marisa insisted."

"Oh." Arian quietly whispered.

"I love you. " Sebastian repeated. "More than anything. I hope you will like the house. It is not like this. And I couldn't stay in the house that Marisa lived in. Too many memories, it was a townhouse with no yard. Our new home is a French manor house with three stories and a large yard for the children. But you don't know the design. I want you to make it our own. Since I bought it, there are still rooms with no furniture in it. Arian." Sebastian drew her closer.

Arian stopped dancing too absorbed in Sebastian's gaze. She knew she was melting just by looking at him. Uncle Horatio just crashed into them.

"Oh, I am terribly sorry." Uncle Horatio professed.

Sebastian didn't even notice but Arian hastily spoke. "Oh, we didn't mind. We are too absorbed within ourselves. I must think of dinner. Time is flying."

"Cassandra, it is time we switched partners but I don't think Sebastian is willing at this moment." Uncle Horatio suggested.

Sebastian flushed. "Sorry, I want to stay with Arian. We have a lot to attend."

"Well, excuse us." Uncle Horatio danced Cassandra away.

"Your look, " Arian expressed. "Is so intense. I know. But we have guests. I really am excited for our trip. We will have time alone with the children in the other room."

Sebastian still stared at her. "I must be more of a host, but I cannot get you out of my mind. I am a bit worried for your transition. Times are more liberal."

"When will Lucien go back to school? And does Selena have to go to kindergarten? I really am selfish. I want them with me."

"Lucien starts in September and we will see if Selena could skip kindergarten for I take it you want to teach them. Selena would probably learn more, I dare say. Don't worry. Let's just enjoy ourselves. This is our vacation."

After dinner they danced to nine P.M.

"We must get some rest for tomorrow. The children should have been in bed earlier." Sebastian declared.

"Sebastian," Cassandra reiterated." I would love to come with you, but my work prevents me, unfortunately. I will miss you for the next two weeks, but, I expect phone calls regularly."

"Can't Aunt Cassandra come." Selena protested. "Uncle Horatio is coming."

"Selena," Sebastian put in. "Cassandra's working schedule is preventing her, besides Paul's."

"Oh, my, Paul, I forgot all about him. Oops! I love this house too much. Are you really going to drive to the airport and go to a flight when you have the witch's rod?"

Sebastian eyes flashed. "Yes, I must return the jaguar which has sat for approximately two weeks, never moving."

"Oh yes, How could I forget." Cassandra teased him. "Oh how I regret this! Aren't you seeing Vienna and Paris as well."

"Yes, Cassandra, but you knew that before I left for the trip."

Arian reflected. "Excuse me, I must put the children to bed. It has been a long day. Good night Cassandra sleep well, and you Uncle Horatio."

The children ran to Aunt Cassandra and Uncle Horatio to say good night as Arian hurried them up the stairs holding onto the candelabra.

"When will we visit Quintessence again, Sebastian?" Cassandra pleaded. "Soon?"

"Maybe, on some weekends but I have my own house." Sebastian clarified.

"Well, this is your house too." Cassandra interjected. "Sebastian?"

Sebastian replied." Good night to both of you, sleep well." Sebastian took the candelabra and escorted his sister and his Uncle to their rooms.

"I am going to miss this house." Uncle Horatio replied regretfully. "We are old friends."

"So am I." Cassandra grieved. "I can't wait until you come home. I guess now I will work full time. Then Paul and I can buy more furniture for his apartment, which is so small compared to your houses, Sebastian. Is Arian going to take anything with her?"

Sebastian smiled. "I want that painting, in our bed room, of her. Arian probably can paint a copy for this house. But I know she definitely wants to take her instruments via the witch's rod. We have three spare rooms now. I know one will be the music room. Anthony Phillips, my best friend, will fall for her, I know. Anthony plays professionally the violin for the Montreal Symphony by night and is an astrophysicist by day." Sebastian continued staring at Uncle Horatio. "I used to play the trumpet, but I haven't told Arian since I haven't practiced it for years."

Arian past them in the hall, "Lucien and Selena are thirsty, I will be right back. Do you want me to bring any of you anything since I am going downstairs?"

Uncle Horatio stated. "A cognac would be nice. I shall miss this."

Arian continued. "And you, Sebastian?"

"Nothing, thank you, "Sebastian smiled.

"And you, Cassandra?" Arian turned to her.

"No, thank you." Cassandra replied.

"All right, I'll just go down." Arian turned in the direction of the stairs.

"Mommy," Selena called. "Could we have some juice instead?"

"Of course." Arian answered. "If you would excuse me." Arian descended the stairs.

"I better say good night. Sebastian, please wake me. I want to have breakfast with you. "Sebastian?" Seeing that Arian was out of sight. "I am so happy for you. The children love her as their own mother just as Arian loves them so much as her very own. You are so lucky. She is thoroughly in love with you, one can see that by the way she gazes upon you. I have never seen you so truly happy. I was so worried for you when I would go away with Paul."

Sebastian smiled. "I am so delighted that you like her. I can tell."

Cassandra whispered, "I feel I have known her before. She is like a sister I have always wanted. She just fits in." Cassandra stepped into her bedroom.

"Well," Sebastian countered." Since you were my sister, Helen, three hundred years ago, you were also very close to Arian then."

Cassandra shocked choked out. "Would you repeat that, please."

Sebastian had a twinkle in his eye. "I think I should say good night." Sebastian closed Cassandra's bedroom door.

"So," Arian whispered. "I heard you play the trumpet."

Sebastian eyed her. "Is your hearing as good as my Uncle's?"

"Perhaps." Arian smiled. She offered Uncle Horatio his cognac.

"Thank you, Arian. Good night again." Uncle Horatio calmly stated. "See you tomorrow."

Sebastian and Arian walked towards their bedroom. Sebastian got ready for bed as Lucien and Selena were in bed waiting for Mommy. Sebastian could hear Arian speaking.

"Here you are." She offered the drinks to the children. "I will be changing for bed." She knocked at the bathroom door. "Sebastian?"

"Please enter Madame. Let me help you. So we can retire quickly."

Arian blushed. "Please do."

Arian undressed fast so they could go to bed.

Sebastian stared longingly at her. "Until tomorrow, then I will have you at last, alone." He tightened his arm around Arian's waist.

Arian said. "Good night Sebastian, Lucien, and Selena."

Sebastian quickly fell asleep but in the middle of the night he felt for Arian but reached Selena instead. "Where could she be?" He turned in his bed and looked for Arian at the bureau but she wasn't there either. "If she would be writing in her diary, she would have the candle lit." He gazed at the window as the moonlight entered the room. There was Arian whispering quietly to the soul of Genevieve. Genevieve's soul floated and hovered around her. Arian embraced her as Genevieve's soul disappeared.

Arian walked back to bed. "Sebastian, did I wake you? I am sorry. Did you see Genevieve? She came to both of us but you were so sound asleep. She visited to say thank you and that she wished one day that she could repay our kindness." Arian had tears in her eyes as she climbed over Sebastian and hugged him. "I thought you wanted to know." She snuggled into him. "I love you."

"Do souls come here often?" Sebastian softly asked.

"No Sebastian. Only once did yours and now Genevieve's come, but I do recognize souls when I meet or see them in the crystal ball, which is quiet strange. They talk to me. Maybe, I am bewitched. How soon do we have to rise?

"We have another two hours. It is two thirty in the morning. Sleep my lady. I am very touched that Genevieve's soul will be all right. Thank heaven."

Sebastian awoke by the witch's rod. He turned to wake Arian who was still asleep. He hated to wake her but they must rise. "Arian," he whispered.

One eye opened followed by the other. She smiled at him. "All ready."

"You sound like Selena. I hope we have packed everything. I will ask the witch's rod if we have forgotten anything. I do not want one toy to be displaced. We will also use the witch's rod to transport Giselle for I couldn't see her in transit on the plane."

"Oh my, I must choose traveling clothes for Lucien and Selena. What were they wearing when they came from Montreal?"

Sebastian reiterated. "I will ask the witch's rod to retrieve it. I also thought that this dress would be nice for you."

"This will be provocative." Arian smiled.

Sebastian went to get ready as Arian straightened up. The witch's rod had chosen the clothes.

"Sebastian?" Arian called gently. "I need your night things to wash and pack them." A hand emerged out from the bathroom. Arian went to collect the clothes but they dropped and Sebastian grabbed Arian inside to kiss her.

Sebastian then whispered. "Your bath is ready, Madame"

Arian answered. "I am coming." She blushed. "Selena, Lucien! It's time to wake up. Your baths are ready. Selena, I am taking you with me." Arian hugged them and hurried them off as she whispered. "Lucien, this is my first trip out. I will need yours and your Father's support. I am afraid of airplanes."

"Don't worry." Lucien affirmed. "I will hold you." He ran to the bathroom.

Sebastian emerged fully dressed. "I will wake Cassandra. We will be leaving at 6:00 AM to get to the airport by 7:00 AM plus I have to return the car, check in the luggage, etc. Where are the tickets and the passports?"

"They are on the bureau, Sebastian. Please check on Lucien?"

"I will." Sebastian knocked and opened the door. He saw Lucien dressing as he rubbed his son's head. "Good morning, Lucien! I must see to your Aunt." Sebastian hurried to his sister's room knocking on her door. "Cassandra?" He knocked again.

Uncle Horatio poked out his head from his door. "You would need a gong to wake her up."

"Good morning, Uncle." Sebastian smiled." Cassandra?" He opened the door a crack calling. "Cassandra!"

"Ok, I am awake. Good morning, Sebastian."

"Good morning Cassandra." Sebastian returned to his room while Arian was dressing Selena. Arian buttoned Selena's dress and added a beautiful silk bow to her hair. "She is so pretty just like you are, Madame."

Arian blushed. "I believe we are ready."

Giselle flew up to say chirping: "Breakfast is ready."

Arian held her saying. "We will transport you later. All you would do is wait all day, if you would stay with us until we arrive at the hotel." Arian kissed her.

"Cassandra?" Sebastian called. "Are you ready?"

"No!"

"Don't worry, I will take the witch's rod and you will be ready in no time." Sebastian suggested.

"You wouldn't dare!" Cassandra indignation rose.

"Try me!" Sebastian rejoined.

"I am ready." Cassandra resigned." No make up, but I am ready."

"Well, if you want to ask for make up, you can."

"This is intriguing, I think I will. Oh, witch's rod, make me up. My face is on!" Cassandra opened the door.

"Mommy has make up on too." Selena echoed.

"My, that is shocking." Uncle Horatio alleged.

They dined on breakfast prepared by Giselle's witch's rod. Arian appeared more and more apprehensive. Arian visited the gardens one more time before they left. Everyone promenaded. Sebastian held Arian's hand comprehending that for three hundred years, Arian had never left Quintessence.

"We will visit it soon." Sebastian reassured her. "We will first transport to Uncle Horatio's house and then say goodbye to Cassandra, and finally we will leave for the airport. Giselle will then be transported to our hotel when we arrive there. Shall we? Ladies and gentlemen?"

Cassandra had tears in her eyes. "I will miss everyone of you." She kissed everybody." It is 6:00AM here but in Montreal it is 10:00 PM. I guess I will go back to bed. Why did I put make up on? Oh well. Good bye, remember, call me."

Sebastian kissed her again, as did Lucien, Selena, Uncle Horatio, and Arian, who also gave her flowers for her trip home. They all said goodbye again. Cassandra was touched.

"It is a custom to give flowers in my time when one leaves for a trip. I shall miss you." Arian waved.

Selena and Lucien with everyone else waved. "Good bye and take care."

Sebastian recited the spell as she disappeared. "Now, we will drive to London, my Lady."

Sebastian and Uncle Horatio put the luggage in the boot. Lucien showed Arian how to buckle up her seat belt.

"Do you want to sit in front with your Father?" Arian commented.

"Daddy said with the air bags it is too dangerous for children, so we have to stay back here. "Lucien explained.

"Oh," sighed Arian.

Sebastian went in on the driver's side as Uncle Horatio sat with the children in the back. Arian held Sebastian's knee as Sebastian backed the jaguar out of the driveway. Arian enjoyed the drive except for the traffic, which made her nervous. Sebastian handled it in stride as he returned the car with hardly any mileage on it. Arian held onto Lucien's and Selena's hands and a small suitcase as Sebastian and Uncle Horatio took care of the rest. Sebastian found a transport cart as they made their way through the crowds. Sebastian could see Arian's nervousness for she never let go of the children. She stayed by Sebastian's side. The lines were long.

"This is like a stadium or an exhibition, too many people." Arian mused, glued to Sebastian's side. Arian pulled Selena and Lucien closer to her. "I have been on ships but this is too crowded."

Their luggage was checked in while their passports were being examined. Arian looked worried. Sebastian held her left hand with her fixed wedding ring and emerald ring. He played with it. He smiled at her to change her mood.

The man checking the passports replied." I could have sworn I saw you two weeks ago approximately. For I remember your daughter. She is so sweet but I don't remember your wife. Being that she is so pretty I would have remembered her."

Sebastian astonished scrutinized him. "This is my wife. You just don't remember. Maybe you mixed us up with somebody else. Isn't the paper work correct? Her passport is stamped like mine. How can you explain it?"

"I can't. But I never forget a beautiful face. I even remember that you are an architect, Mr. Simons."

Arian smiled. "I am their mother. Lucien, my son, looks just like me. Do you remember my Lucien?"

"Well, I think so."

"Well, then how can you explain it, if I look like my son. It means we must have gone through here."

"We are in a hurry." Sebastian pleaded. "Our flight was canceled yesterday and we are a bit late. We have tickets if you care to see them."

"Yes, I would."

Uncle Horatio complained." This is absurd."

"I don't remember you either, Mr. Horatio Simons."

"That is because I wasn't here two weeks ago. I did not arrive like my nephew. I am British. My nephew came to visit me and now I am traveling to Italy with them."

"We are going to miss our flight." Sebastian seemed impatient.

"Let me get my supervisor." The man went on.

"For what? "Sebastian asserted. "The paper work matches and we are late.

"Oh, all right! Go through!"

Arian smiled saying. "Thank you ever so much!" Sebastian gathered his family and left.

"You know." Sebastian enumerated. "If he had checked your age. You would have had Lucien at the age of 16."

"It is still possible." Arian whispered.

Sebastian had reserved the seats by the window but now with the addition of Arian and Uncle Horatio their seats were in the middle of the plane. Arian pulled out the pamphlet which explains if the plane losses altitude or pressure, the oxygen masks drop. Arian stared at Sebastian as he reassured her.

"It will be fine. Let's check the seatbelts." Sebastian reached over to Selena and Lucien.

Lucien had his seat belt already on as Sebastian checked Selena's and Arian's. Lucien was pointing out toward the window while the plane lurched forward toward the runway. Arian held Sebastian's hand so tightly and looked over at the children. She stared at Sebastian for dear life. Sebastian reassured her but Arian didn't let go until they were in flight. Sebastian smiled at her constantly. There was a French couple in front of them.

Arian turned to Sebastian "That voice of the gentleman sounds exactly the way my Father's voice did."

Sebastian seemed surprised. "What a coincidence. Have you seen him?"

"No," Arian murmured

The man stood up. "Excuse me (in English). Have you seen my wife's ring? It just has fallen off her finger and it might have rolled in your direction."

Arian stared in shock for his voice and his looks matched her Father's.

"Forgive me, for staring." Arian gasped. "We will all look for it. I didn't catch you name, Monsieur. "

"Do you speak French?"

"Yes, let me introduce us. This is my husband Sebastian, our son Lucien, our daughter Selena, my Uncle Horatio, and I am Arian Simons."

"Enchanted, Madame. My name is Nicholas Boyer and this is my wife, Nadine."

"Let us see if we can find it. Monsieur."

"We would be grateful if you do, Madame."

Arian took off her seat belt and bent, as did Sebastian but Sebastian's voice triumphantly stated. "Here it is."

"Thank you again, Monsieur. Merci beaucoup! My wife has laryngitis; otherwise, she would also say thank you. Forgive me, but do I know you from somewhere, Madame Simons? I feel that I should know you."

"Maybe, Monsieur from the past. May I ask if you work in an embassy for France?"

"You are quite right, Madame. I am the ambassador for France and Canada; I will be stationed in Montreal after my vacation in Italy for two weeks. How did you know?"

"A woman's intuition."

"I feel like you could be my daughter. The way you look at me. I am so sorry to embarrass you. I can't explain it. It is a pleasure to meet you and your family. I even feel that I have met you before, Monsieur. Your daughter is so beautiful just like your son is handsome. I have a son the same age, as you are, Monsieur. His name is Raoul. Forgive the intrusion. I hope I will see more of you. Thank you again. " He sat back in his seat.

Sebastian held Arian's hand for she had tears in her eyes.

"That 's him. I feel it. He was once my Father and his wife, Nadine, was my father's second wife. I want to hug him but I dare not, poor man."

"I feel the same way. "Sebastian rejoined. "But we can enjoy their company for two weeks, since they will be on the same tour. "Would you like to see a movie, Madame?"

"A movie? What is that?"

"You will see. Be patient. I just hope it is a good one."

Arian was fascinated by the movie. They gathered their belongings after they were informed that they were landing. Nicholas Boyer and his wife even had the same hotel just one room away.

"This hotel is beautiful Sebastian," Uncle Horatio added. "Well, I will see you in the morning. I can't wait to see the Coliseum! Good night to all."

"Good night, Uncle." Sebastian called trying not to disturb Lucien in his arms as Arian carried Selena. The porter carried the luggage. Sebastian and Arian placed the children in the adjoining bedroom.

Arian smiled. "I better get them ready for bed. This room is so beautiful, Sebastian. I love it."

Sebastian smiled. "Anything for my Lady." Sebastian tipped the porter.

Arian was helping the children get ready for bed when there was a knock at the door.

Sebastian affirmed to Arian. "I will see who it is." Sebastian rose for the door.

"Excuse me. My name is Alain Vega De La Certa. I have been trying to get a hold of you, Mr. Simons, for the past two weeks. I have tracked you down here by your office in Montreal. I am sorry that I am bothering you on your holiday with your two children, Lucien and Selena and yourself. But I had to find you. I have heard about you professionally and I want to commission a chateau from you. Money is no object."

Sebastian recognized him immediately. He was Alain De La Vega, the man who wanted his wife three hundred years ago. Sebastian walked quietly to shut the children's door, so that Arian wouldn't be seen. Sebastian slowly said. "I am on holiday, Mr. Vega De La Certa. Couldn't this wait until I go back to Montreal?"

"I know I am rather impetuous, Mr. Simons. For two weeks I couldn't get a hold of you in England. You didn't stay with your itinerary. But, since I was in Sussex, I have bought this painting which needs to be restored. It was partly burned in a fire in 1899. This fire also burnt the chateau that the painting was housed in. I want you to build me that chateau exactly the same way except with modern conveniences. This, is the photo of the painting that I have purchased. The woman in the painting is extraordinary. Her name is Arian Simons. Her maiden name was Arian Jovan, who married an Alexus Simons in 1695. Actually, you look quiet like him. Oh well, she was quiet an accomplished person being an ambassador's daughter. She knew many languages. She spoke Spanish, Italian, German, English and of course her own language, French, in addition to old Greek and Latin. She played many instruments and she sang like an angel. She also painted extremely well and by her picture she was very beautiful. She had a wonderful disposition. I saw her painting, I know this sounds crazy, and fell in love with it."

At that moment Arian started to sing a lullaby to the children while she played the lute.

"Who is singing? She sounds like an angel." Alain expounded. "She sings French and Spanish lullabies?"

"That is my wife." Sebastian elucidated. "She speaks quiet a few languages."

"But your wife died in a car accident five years ago, and her name was Marisa."

"How in the devil did you know that!"

"When I want somebody to work for me, I find out everything."

"This is my second wife. I just got married in England about a week ago."

"So that is why I couldn't get a hold of you. Congratulations! However, this marriage couldn't not have been planned?"

"It wasn't foreseen. Yet, thank you, but," Sebastian continued.

Alain interrupted. "Your wife really impresses me with her voice and I am enjoying her performance. However, back to business. I only have a few pictures or drawings of that chateau. I would need you to research it in more detail. Forgive me, is this your ticket from your flight?" Sebastian nodded a yes. "Who drew this sketch of the Spanish Steps? Was it you, being an architect?"

"No, that was drawn by my wife." Sebastian affirmed.

"It is so exact, I must confess it is sheer art." Alain marveled. "Your wife is still singing. My mother sang this song to me in French. I am touched. I am sorry for the interruption. Let me continue. They say that Arian Simons did have one son named Dorian and was with child with her second who was to be a daughter named Selena, but a lightning bolt struck, killing her and crippling her husband Alexus. He couldn't walk for five years. Alexus and his son were very close. They lived together even when Dorian got married to Nicole Dubois, in the same house Alexus built for Arian. Dorian kept his father's passion for architecture and also became one working with his father. Alexus Simons commissioned buildings that are still noted today, Alexus died in 1745. Dorian's children inherited it as his line still continues today. Your name is Simons. Are you a long lost relative? You would be the 12th or 13th generation. Never mind, exactly two hundred years later, the chateau was hit by lightning again which burnt the chateau to a shell. It was never refurbished. I visited the site. I have also seen the scorched floor. There was also a secret garden that Alexus made for Arian, which had a beautiful gazebo. You know Alexus never remarried saying that nothing could compare to his Arian. She must have been something. He even had to fight a duel for her with one of Arian's Spanish relatives from Mexico. This man was supposed to have married Arian but due to a shipwreck in the Caribbean Sea, he was prevented. Some say that Arian's cousin, Antoine De La Vega, being a pirate, made sure that this fiancé couldn't marry Arian by paying the captain off in gold to flounder the ship safely. The act proved fruitless because Antoine didn't cross the sea fast enough for Arian fell in love with Alexus. I wonder if Arian ever knew how much her cousin, Antoine, who used to tease her like mad when she was small, really loved her. This fiancé, who Alexus had the fight with, was smitten by his first sight of Arian's portrait over the mantel piece in Nicolas Jovan's study when she was the age of sixteen, while visiting her father's home in France. By observing a copy of another painting of Arian's, the one I have here in this photograph in a lavender gown, he asked for her hand immediately demanding that they are still betrothed. Upon hearing the state of affairs of Arian's marriage from Nicolas Jovan, he desperately traveled to England to dissuade Alexus to give Arian up. I can understand his feelings when I saw the portrait of Arian as well. Even I, seeing that painting, would have done the same. I guess I should have found out this man's name."

"To be precise." Sebastian remarked. "The man Alexus had the fight with was named Alain De La Vega."

"Really! How extraordinary to have my first name!"

"Perhaps!" Sebastian argued.

"Nevertheless, since I am so taken with Arian Simons' painting. You must research it completely. So, you have been married for a week. Did you spend your time with her family for I couldn't trace you? How did you get the paper work done?"

"My Uncle has a few connections. "Sebastian reverberated.

"I can't believe I missed you. I was so close. What did your wife do before she married you?"

"I fail to see the importance but she was trying to join the London orchestra."

"Did she succeed?" Alain asserted.

"Her paper work and transcripts were lost, but that 's how I discovered her. Is there anything else you want to discuss? I am on holiday and this is my wedding trip as well."

"I wanted to talk to you about the gardens."

Arian just left the children's room closing the children's door as she turned towards Sebastian. She recognized Alain De La Vega. "Mon Dieu!" Arian curtsied upon seeing the gentleman.

Alain Vega De La Certa stared in disbelief. Love struck as if a lightning bolt had struck him or a cupid's arrow.

Arian rising from her curtsey spoke. "Pardon, Monsieur. I am sorry I interrupted. Pardon, Pardon."

Selena opened her bedroom door and ran to Mommy. "Mommy, my stuffed bunny, Flumpy, fell in between the bed and the wall. I can't retrieve it. Neither can Lucien." Lucien poked his head out of the room as well.

"Oh, I will help you," Arian took Selena's hand and Lucien's. "Pardon, Monsieur. Excusez-moi." She curtsied again and went to the children's bedroom closing the door.

"This is your wife, your son, and your daughter?" Alain finally found his voice.

"That is obvious!" Sebastian returned.

"But your wife looks like? What is your wife's name?"

"Arian is my wife's name, Monsieur."

"She must be Arian Simons from 1695 for your son looks like Dorian and Selena was the name of the lost child. You even look like Alexus!"

"Are you insinuating that my wife is three hundred and twenty three years old?" Sebastian rebutted.

"She must be! She looks exactly like the painting. What is her maiden name?"

"I am going to bed and you are leaving. I am very tired. If you want this chateau I will discuss this in my office in Montreal."

"She must be three hundred and twenty three years old. I should tell you there was a rumor that three witches wanted Alexus for their lover, but Arian sacrificed herself to save her husband. She was placed in some parallel dimension of which Alexus could never extract her from. He searched for any magician or occultist to try to save his wife. He failed! I know this is hard to believe but that is the rumor. How did you extract her? She is really here. I must talk to her." Alain was determined.

"I think that this is absurd. "Sebastian announced.

"Then she is not telling the whole truth and that she found a way to escape that dimension. She is the original Arian Simons. She even curtsied like they did in the 17th century. I must see her."

"Let me remind you that she is my, and I will repeat this, my wife. I have married her with her consent and you will now leave this room. Good night."

Alain doesn't budge as he stared after Arian who had retreated into the children's room.

"Let me show you to the door. If I may be so blunt." Sebastian opened the door. "I will not say this again or be polite. Good night!"

Alain Vega De La Certa walked out turning to face Sebastian. "Why don't you tell me the truth! She is Arian Simons! I missed out on her by just two weeks. Where was she, by your Uncle Horatio's house? There are rumors about that house being haunted or possessed. I went there and the house was empty for all the time I was there in search of you. Though your rented jaguar remained there untouched. I even checked the mileage for it never changed. Obviously, you were with her, but where? Nevertheless, maybe Arian consented to you, for what else could she do in her situation? I must speak to her!"

"Monsieur, She is married to me. So where does that leave you? I will never give her up and I know she loves me thoroughly. She has proved this to me. So, you must forget her. Recreating a home that only accentuates her memory will only cause you pain. You are romanticizing. So before this goes any further, get over her! Good night again!"

Alain stayed at the door facing Sebastian. He was about to say something but stopped to think of a good response.

"Sebastian?" Arian gently appealed. "Did he leave?"

Sebastian still stared at Alain as he slammed the door in front of his face. "Yes, he has just left, my Lady."

Arian emerged out of the children's room. "They are finally asleep. Giselle is with them. Why did we have to find him again?"

Sebastian smiled. "It is fate! But he will never have you. I vow! You are mine and I have you at last alone, Madame! And you are in my world!" Sebastian held Arian by the waist as he swung her around in a circle. He brought her close to him. "How I love you."

Arian beholds Sebastian with such a loving gaze. They kissed.

Uncle Horatio heard that someone was out in the hall. He opened his door and encountered Alain De La Vega. They both stared at one another.

"You are Alexus Simons' Uncle Cecil Simons aren't you!" Alain points at Uncle Horatio in disbelief. "We seem to be all here again, together. But this Sebastian will not win, I promise you."

"Well, we shall see. By the way, my name is Horatio Simons." Uncle Horatio shut his door and locked it. He then ran to the phone and dialed Sebastian's phone number. The connection finally came through. "Sebastian? Did you know that Alain De La Vega is right outside your door? Oh, am I disturbing you?"

The Petit Anthology

Of

Magical Spells

I. *AFFAIRE DE COEUR*

Caressed by a whisper, as fleeting as the breeze
Impassioned by expressions inferred by ease
More than complaisant, touched by blush
Frail by beauty, softened by a hush
Flamed as sensuality with petals of a flower
Perfumed in intervals of hallucinating powder
With the elixir of illusion, concealed as a disguise
Transfixed as one beholds, to fool ones eyes.

II. *AFFAIRE DE COUER ANTIDOTE*

To keep your lover always at bay
Use musk from a skunk and run away

III. *THE CLOAK OF INVISIBILITY*

Auspicious signs that must be quenched.
No trace, no imprint left but drenched.
From head to foot anoint thee must
With a bit of toad spit yee must thrust
Once upon thee, a cloak of dark.
Will cover thee effervescently with a spark
Clandestine now so don't delay
It's time for thee, to get away.

IV. *ANTI CLOAK OF INVISIBILITY*

To undo or expose the unforeseen
Into tangible shapes discerned from what has been
Sprinkle spectral dust to divulge or unveil
It always attaches to silhouetting one for betrayal
Unmasked, they know not of their being exhumed
Believing themselves cloaked, still assumed.

V. *RE-ESTABLISHING COMMUNICATIONS: THE SILENT UNRAVELING*

Spanning through time for me to behold
Sacrificed endeavors to trade thy soul
So one can live, and the other go, entombed alive forever.
From now to eternity, I vow, I see
A purgatory of mind, never to be free
Don't be fooled by what seems not
For if you do, illusions alter a lot
Discover the key to unlock the spell
For in the Realm of Twilight I must dwell
Shrouded for three hundred years and past
Until you came to me at last
With a whisper of hope, the ring prevails

As a liaison between the ion's trails
Where the witches curse will now be veiled
Find them in their gravely plot
Possess their book, for they are not
To release their spells you will need a key
Buried in a box of filigree

VI. TO ACTIVATE THE CRYSTAL BALL

An amorphous orb that one conjectures through
Delphic in nature, which procures omens too.
Where illusions or images profess and beguile
Foreshadowing events including denial.
A wave of my rod will now instill
The power prophesied, shall be thy will.

VII. DEBITUM NATURAE/ANNIHILATION

Cerberus, the dog, cries at the gates of hell
Mutilates the intended from where they must dwell
Massacred in devastation with mutable disarray
Mottled, misshapen, flailed, and betrayed
Desecrated bones added to the acrimonious brew
Created by sulfuric acid to improve the stew
Titrated with potassium hydroxide for the crux
Defaming sounds waves added with a thrust
Add some ferric ions to make a magnetic flux
Consecrated curses, contused is a must
Now add some fresh hemlock aged with time.
Electrophoresised to separate distinguishable brine
Placed into a Infernal Abyss that animates the dust
Shriveled rapaciously becoming musk
Governed by the alter of Twelve.

VIII. ENCIRCLED ACQUISITION

To constrain the unforseen's accessibility
Repressed or cloistered from availability
Deliminate your global portal
From all intruders including mortals
Exculpate your exclusive rights
By avowing your assertion through ones sights
Retinal variations will ensure
Ones biased inclinations shall now endure.

IX. EXODUS FROM THE REALM OF TWILIGHT

Upon a blue moon where moonbeams derive
Will transverse through the stone, becoming alive

Once the center of the stone's vibrations accelerates
An ionizing vapor exudes and disseminates
A corresponding wave will sinuate through the past
But hurry, follow it expediently, for it will not last
Through the ethereal and to the beyond
Vessels across the threshold of an eau of a pond
Vacillated through a medium to dispense
The pedestals of time will recompense

X. _EXPULSION_ OF SPIRITS

(Cross-reference: besides spirits, it is applicable to any form of
life temporarily up to a radius of fifty miles)
Into a flask one must combine
Successions of ingredients, in specified time.
A liter of water, which has been blessed
With the use of Black Tara that has been possessed
Petals from one red rose, with a fragrance
Which helps the spell, show some vagrance
One final ingredient comes from the sun
Golden drops counted one by one
Use a candle through the crystal ball
And golden sun drops will silently fall
Into the elixir one should mix very well
To insure the readiness, of the spell
Upon your intended splash with a throng
Repeating the words Begone, Begone

XI. _HEALING_ SPELL

Brew rosemary and thyme to bind they wounds
Use chamomile tea internally so that it will soothe
Make a poultice salve about thy chest
To extract the sickness from thy breast
Amend thy spirit with positive vibes
Recuperative in nature so to survive
Add electrolytes to insure the cure
Mix very well so you can endure.

XII. THE _ILLUSION_ SPELL

Altered visions to demonstrate what is not
Misconceptions, to deceive one from the untimely plot
Tossed in fallacies, delusions, or dreams
Misapprehensions, to hallucinate from what seems
A mockery or sham to fleece one's ghost
Betrayed to divert it from the real host.

XIII. *IMPUISSANCE*

Degressed from nervelessness becoming decadent
Crippled, hampered as waning to beckon it
Dwindled by diminishment in size
Unbeknownst, like a surprise
Inundating within a stifling force
Gravitating all the power in it' course
Quailing to retrogress
Especially when under duress

XIV. *PROCTECTION FROM LIGHTNING BOLTS*

A burst of brilliance between two clouds
A flash expelled as lightning goes through the shrouds
Effusing flex may strike the ground
Conducting the accumulation or deficit in electrons found
Use iron filings suspended, diverted down
So if discharged at its' potential, it bounces around
Like a liaison ousting, which is quite profound.

XV. *ODE TO LOVE*

To my precious love, Sebastian. (For your eyes alone)
Embraced by your tenderness, charmed with rapture,
Impassioned with delight for me to capture,
The ecstasy of your love, endearing and enticed,
Sumptuous in depth, esteemed and blessed more than twice,
Fondled with pleasure, embellished as a treasure,
Devoted with such sentiments as sacrifices your leisure,
Redeemed and adored as cherished in forever,
Transcended through time, captivated by being together,
Sensuousness revered with symphonies of variation
Beautiful and graceful, exquisite in all it's adulation.
PS The only thing I desire in life is to be with you.
Love

XVI. *MEMORYLOSS SPELL*

To simulate a bump on the head
Where facts are lax, from what you've read
The attention span of the intended will fall
Very oblivious of it all
An hallucinating power with a libation
Will be the only inspiration
In a mixing bowl combine
Some brandy and a lot of wine
A quantum of lightning to disrupt
So your spinal cord will be cut

291

S. and S. Antonson

In a powdered form of dust
One inhales it with a gust
Resulting in an ignominious oaf

XVII. ANTIDOTE TO THE MEMORY- LOSS SPELL

To heighten one's knowledge in one's head
To stimulate retention before it goes dead
Supplement with oxygen to magnify recall
Enhancing perception what increases it all
Peppermint sprigs leaves one reminiscent
Inhaled perspicaciously, bubbled like effervescent
To improve one's wit, to preserve reason
Amplifies enlightenment in every season.

XVIII. PUISSANCE SPELL

Swayed from impugned uncertainty
Perniciously recoiled to instill its ability
Osmosed efficacy from tottering dominions
Unrepressed by squelched nisus as a resilient minion
Nimiety capacity assimilated
Nigh tangency, thoroughly infiltrated
Redeemed and amended from being taunted
Totally expressed, omnipotence undaunted

XIX. PYSCHE SPELL

To reconcile to a harmonious life
Amend thy spirit to quench your strife
Soothe thy hallucinations to one of calm
Pacify from reckless insanity to balm
Tranquilize with serenity so one can mend
Clearing delusions racked in one's head to fend

XX. TO RECOMPENSE THE PILLARS QUEST I

From the ethereal now imprisoned, where time and reality cease
Energy from within, will exude in bursts, will then be released
Harassed from beyond, bathed in waves, so not to correspond
Hidden clandestinely, unless recklessness is depended upon
With the zenith of the sun, make a 90° angle left of the ancient elm tree
This will be where the quest for what one construes as a starting for thee
64 paces due east, look for a centerpiece of bronze
From hence, 86 paces to the west, towards the lake and ponds
Sail across, if one can not step, until the count is correct
From the center of the lake, plunge and pull the latch direct
As it opens it reveals, a subterranean portal
Traverse it, if you dare, merely being mortal

292

For this is the portal of disremembrance
Giving one a sense of disembodied semblance
Pursue to undermine its' infinity
Which only can end its' own morbidity
With a spark of hope, you may achieve
Your goal at last which can upheave
Resulting in a hydrogenous aftermath.

XXI. TO RECOMPENSE THE PILLARS QUEST 11

Up through the mist of a mountain with time
Hidden caverns with diverging paths will align
Start with the bronze centerpiece from the first rhyme
Focus upon the line of cypress and pine
Go north 100 paces to the mountain's base
Turn clockwise at the hour of three on the sundial's face
An entrance will open if one presses the crystalline stone to the right.
Enter quickly for the entrance seals itself by night
Beware of the sulfurous fumes which attacks with a blast
Like Pompeii's mount Vesuvius from the past
Run quickly for it is timed in five minute intervals or less
That will suffocate and glue your esophagus at best
To avoid the ooze of molten lava step only on the stones of magic which controls
Keep to the left narrow tunnel as it inclines towards your goals
Your goal is within reach in the caldera delicately placed.
So as to disturb it, will be dangerous, so do make haste.

XXII. TO RECOMPENSE THE PILLARS QUEST III

Unbeknownst and profound through chasms of forgotten past
Once acceded through a magical stone, the unforeseen might last
When twilight commences, the angle will be shown
By this angle, locate the tombstone with a Gaelic cross name unknown
Unearth it to seek the orb of essence
With this orb, it will reveal a presence
Abstruse deep inside this grave
Guarded by an untimely knave
A duel to the death must ensue
For one must die or rue
If one lives, only then can you attain your goal?
You must be remorseful, for your very soul
MORT.

XXIII. THE RESTORATION SPELL

Embalmed in suspension as frozen instilled
Grieved from the poison and rancor from thy unexpressed will
To resuscitate from embitterment to somehow revive

To reawaken the good from thy spirit to be alive
Heal thyself so that one will survive
With an elixir of life to cure, so one can rectify

XXIV. *THE <u>RESURRECTION</u> SPELL*

Squashed from sod six feet and under
Hackneyed and decomposed in slumber
Languid from sleep in years gone by
Lachrymations, in acrimonious cries
To resurrect, one has to die
Then trade thy soul, for the other to lie.
Interchanged and disconnected
Excised first, and reconnected
Writhing, squirming, before affected
Emboldened upward, towards the sky
Passing each other, being awry
Now you stir, while the others putrefy

XXV. *THE <u>ROUSING</u> SPELL*

Roused from my sleep by a piercing cry
Languishing echoes by a watch-full eye
Stabbed by disbelief, yet, she dares to defy
Purloined ring will transpose through the sky
Mired in my moldy decay
Emerge to vengeance, needs no delay
Embodied with evil and pitted respite
Rising upwards and upwards and on through the night
To finally reach that box with a key
Displaced by that bird, how shall I barb thee?
Closer and closer until I feel a chill
Vortexed as the wind upon the hill
Then will I leave to change my fate?
I shall be waiting forever, don't be late.

XXVI. *<u>SANCTUARY</u> SPELL*

Into the circle of the one to defend
A mixture of Holy water one needs to depend
A protective shield without an end
Rimmed with strength that shall not bend
A lightening spark will once inspire
A circle of indistinguishable fire
Add molten lead into the cauldron's pot
Watching the patterns that will begot
Add salt for the crystals will devour
The ionization of Satan's power.

XXVII. SLEEPING SPELL OR POTION

To summon unconsciousness as if dead.
Like comatosis in the head
A hypnotic spell to induce some rest
As if in hibernation, sluggish at best
To drowse and slumber in repose
Somnolent of one's intimate woes

XXVIII. SPELL LOCK

To secure any spell from being tampered
Conjuration interlaced instilled and hampered
Clasping the spell with the filigree key
Pretend to turn it while reciting enchantments to thee
Evocation pronounced seals the decipher
Unable to be charmed by any further magical cipher.

XXIX. THE SOOTHESAYERS' PROPHESY

Who will tempt fate and have their fortune read.
We can make a believer out of you, for we call upon the dead.
Spirits rise and encircle us,
Whisper truths, unbeknownst and feared.
Love potions, spells and amulets we give out.
To protect you and entice you, and throughout.
Despondent cries pierce the night.
Goblins, ghollies scream in fright.
Demons, witches, and apparitions enthrall
For Strega, the gypsies will now tell all.
Be patient as we consult our crystal ball
It's fogging up!
Please place your hands on Sir Andrew's skull.
For he is our liaison from the world above.
Now, shuffle the cards, for your vibrations ensure,
The card of your future shall then endure.
Place the card face up and await, for we, the Stregas, will tell your fate!
Keep your eyes shut, and make no moves,
So to concentrate our thoughts, for we can amuse.

XXX. AWAKEN THE SPIRITS

Strangled through the inside out
Muffled cries, attempt to shout
Awakened from untimely sleep
Scathed by burdens, that must weep
Stirred up jealously and doubt
Now from a stupor, will all come out.

XXXI. <u>SUSPENSION</u> SPELL (Use in conjunction with the collection of at least 100 exotic spiders' venom preferably administered by a blow dart gun)

Once circulating through thy veins
Cessation of feeling quenches thy pains
Heartbeats diminish to an indistinguishable hush
While hindering your life force in a rush
Intermittence is shunted, retarding delay
Siphoning the will, lulled away
Remission results, keeping one semi-permanently at bay.

XXXII. THE ANTI -LOCK / AND ANTI-<u>SUSPENSION</u> SPELL

To enliven that, what is not
From continuance of the non-living to phantoms that alter the plot
Repressed to breathe after so long an abeyance
The cessation of movement, to writhe with conveyance
Recessed from time, from any apparent stimulation
With a power like zombies to resume one's own circulation
Lulled through ages past, as halted by retardation
Excised from silence, to excessive animation.
Remission results, keeping one semi-permanently at bay.

XXXIII. <u>TRANSFERRING</u> SPELL

Vanquishing from time and space
Where gravity and magnetism are displaced.
Where purgatory dwells, no time can escape.
Trapped between the ether.
Vibrations compound the ion's trails.
As the Pillars of Hercules communicate quails
Energetic bursts like x-rays wails
Vacuuming through an endless void
Transformed as a vapor being employed
This is the Realm of Twilight.

An alternate form of the transfer spell or ancillary

XXXI. (<u>TRANSFER</u> SPELL) TO RID THEE SPELL

To rid thee of an untimely lout
This is where one can spout
Get thee gone by sending them out.

XXXV. ANTI-<u>TRANSFER</u> SPELL

Unable to convey
So that nothing will ever stray
Impeded so one can't depart
Not consigned away like art
Un-transportable to remain
Unceded so to stay the same.

XXXVI. *TRANSFORMING SPELL*

To alchemize from one configuration
Barter thyself an altered fabrication
Metamorphosed and rearranged
Until what is left, is utterly changed.

XXXVII. ANTI-*TRANSFORMATION* SPELL

Reduced back into ones absolute soul
Condensed to be changeless despite your goal
Undeceiving from what portentous fallacies profess
Add denaturation powder, steamed and possessed
Immutable, as it holds firm and fast
Making the pretender static and constant to the last.

XXXVIII. *UN-MANIPULATION*

To divert from ones original with outside help
Influenced by altering means, uncontrollable to thyself
To utilize an objective opinion
Instead of being governed by exploiting dominions
To no longer be bridled by subjugation
Curbed by it's confrontation
Wield thee self with the absolute truth
Abated by honesty or soothe.

Use with the witch's rod.

XXXIX. *TO ACTIVATE THE WITCH'S BROOM*

Blithe in spirits, so one transcends
To flit and flee to no ends
Soaring like wind in levitation
Rising upward with anticipation
In a whirl, one alights
Hovering, gliding, in delights
On thy broom one tends to sweep
Until lifted, from thy feet
Absconded through, one darts and weaves
Bursts of energy, like fluttering in the breeze.